MW01618063

ONE MILLION DEAD

· Volume One ·

CLUNY CLASSICS

RICCARDO BACCHELLI
The Mill on the Po: God Save You (BOOK ONE)
The Mill on the Po: Misery (BOOK TWO)
The Mill on the Po: Nothing New Under the Sun (BOOK THREE)

ROBERT HUGH BENSON
Come Rack, Come Rope
Dawn of All
The Light Invisible
None Other Gods

GEORGES BERNANOS
A Bad Dream
A Crime
Joy
Under the Sun of Satan

ORESTES BROWNSON
Like a Roaring Lion

MALACHY G. CARROLL
The Stranger

G. K. CHESTERTON
Wanderings over the World

MYLES CONNOLLY
The Bump on Brannigan's Head
Dan England and the Noonday Devil
Mr. Blue
The Reason for Ann & Other Stories
Three Who Ventured

ALICE CURTAYNE
House of Cards

GERTRUD VON LE FORT
The Pope from the Ghetto
The Veil of Veronica

JOSÉ MARÍA GIRONELLA
The Cypresses Believe in God (TWO VOLUMES)
One Million Dead (TWO VOLUMES)

RUMER GODDEN
A Breath of Air
Five for Sorrow, Ten for Joy
In This House of Brede

CAROLINE GORDON
The Life and Passion of Aleck Maury
The Malefactors

NATHANIEL HAWTHORNE
The Shattered Fountain: Selected Tales

ELISABETH LANGGÄSSER
The Quest

FRANÇOIS MAURIAC
The Dark Angels
The Desert of Love
Genetrix
A Kiss for the Leper
The Lamb
The River of Fire
The Unknown Sea
Vipers' Tangle
What Was Lost

DOROTHY L. SAYERS
Whose Body?

IGNAZIO SILONE
Fontamara
Bread and Wine
The Seed Beneath the Snow

SIGRID UNDSET
The Burning Bush
The Wild Orchid
Four Stories
Images in a Mirror
Madame Dorthea

LEO L. WARD
Men in the Field: Eighteen Short Stories

One Million Dead

· Volume One ·

José María Gironella

Translated from the Spanish
UN MILLÓN DE MUERTOS
by Joan MacLean

CLUNY
Providence, Rhode Island

Cluny Media edition, 2021

This Cluny edition is a republication of
One Million Dead (Foreword, Part I, Part II, and Glossary),
originally published by Doubleday & Company, Inc., in 1963.

With the exception of actual historical personages, the characters are entirely the product of the author's imagination and have no relation to any persons in real life.

For more information regarding this title,
please write to info@clunymedia.com, or to
Cluny Media, P.O. Box 1664, Providence, RI 02901

• • • • •

VISIT US ONLINE AT WWW.CLUNYMEDIA.COM

This edition is published under license of Preservation Books,
a non-profit corporation dedicated to promoting
the fair use, appreciation, and preservation of great works.

Cluny Media edition copyright © 2021 Cluny Media LLC

ISBN: 978-1952826955

Cover design by Clarke & Clarke
Cover image: Santiago Rusiñol, *Entrance to the Sóller Cemetery at Night*, 1896, oil on canvas
Courtesy of Wikimedia Commons

CONTENTS

One Million Dead

VOLUME ONE

TO ALL THOSE WHO DIED
IN THE SPANISH WAR, 1936-1939

And Cain said to Abel his brother: Let us go forth abroad. And when they were in the field, Cain rose up against his brother Abel, and slew him.

GENESIS 4:8

EXPLANATORY FOREWORD

THE first volume of my announced trilogy, entitled *The Cypresses Believe in God,* embraces the period immediately preceding the Civil War in Spain, that is, the epoch of the Republic, which began in April 1931 and ended in July 1936. The present volume, entitled *One Million Dead,* is a sequel to that, and covers the entire period of the war, which lasted from the 18th of July, 1936, to the 1st of April, 1939. The third volume covering the period of the present, of the postwar years, is needed, then, to close the ring. The outlines of that volume already have been traced, but it presents extraordinary difficulties, owing to the interposition of the Second World War, from 1939 to 1945, to the dynamic Odyssey of the exiles, and the labor, still actively in progress, of restoring in our country a system of laws and mental attitudes.

One Million Dead is an immediate continuation of *The Cypresses Believe in God.* The Alvear family remains the psychological nucleus of the *dramatis personae,* whose members or components are changed permanently by the war. The city of Gerona remains its geographic center, but to the rhythm of the episodes of the war the stage broadens, until it has reached out to the four corners of Spain.

The story opens in Gerona, with Ignacio's visit to the cemetery in search of the body of his brother César, and ends with the shudder that ripples across the entire land at the announcement of the end of the war.

My plan has been to give a panoramic view of what our struggle was and what it meant; to try to strike a balance by canceling out one happening with another, and to synchronize the situations on the two sides, the side called "Nationalist" and the side called "Red." Such an aim posed extremely difficult problems of construction for me from the beginning, given the diversity of the two theaters of action and the spasmodic quality of events. May God grant that I have resolved them, that the undertaking has not proved beyond my abilities.

I have written the book three times from start to finish over the past five years. The first version was a chronological arrangement of the facts. It consisted largely of drawing up a sort of catalogue of honors. The second version eliminated the purely anecdotal and, through the employment of logical situations, succumbed to the grandeur and the poetry that can doubtless be found wherever man dwells. The third, the definitive, and the most laborious version, consisted of endowing my book with the character of verisimilitude, an indispensable ingredient. Indeed, the events of our Civil War were so crowded and of such a character that any mere relation, any unilateral judgment, turns immediately into caricature; it falsifies the truth; it falls a thousand leagues short of the detached story of humanity.

How was I to strike a balance between my own preconceived attitude, my own opinion, and impartiality, the necessary and sought-after impartiality? Only by seeking the perspective given by time and space, by painfully facing the facts, and by charity. A large portion of this book was written hundreds of miles from Spain. I began it fifteen years after the guns had fallen silent. I poured into it my personal experience, always a basic ingredient. I had the good fortune to have lived in both zones of the war, and I spared no effort to learn all that I needed to know by interrogating many Spanish and foreign eyewitnesses, by reviewing the periodicals, the photographic archives, and the pamphlets of the time. I read nearly a thousand books and monographs published after the war, and so on. Finally, as in *The Cypresses Believe in God,* I tried to love each of my characters without unjust distinctions, to sprinkle them all with loving kindness, were they murderers or angels, were their political anthems this, that, or the other.

The task of informing myself, to which I already have referred, became plagued with difficulties as prickly as sea urchins. Frequently my personal experience has proved to be so much dunnage, for memory is a mirror that gives me back distorted and spectral images once the facts are isolated from the complex that produced them, the complex that created them. Something more or less similar occurred with respect to the testimony of other people. Each person I questioned showed a tendency to exaggerate or to draw such important conclusions from the mere fact of being alive that the immediate effect was to embarrass me and cause me to lose sight of the whole. As for the books, aside from those of a technical nature and the diaries of the modest fighters on both sides, which were useful to me in every way, most of the books suffered from an unbalanced fanaticism. Reality became atrophied; the merits of the enemy were belittled; all the authors' own errors were omitted with downright willfulness. In the end, my strongest staffs were the newspapers and photographs, the unquestionable authority of the daily news, accompanied by its appropriate graphic documentation!

I see that I must repeat the warning given in the first volume of my trilogy: what I have aimed to write is a novel, not a historical or sociological study. Accordingly, in *One Million Dead,* as in *The Cypresses Believe in God,* "I have reserved the right at all times to have recourse to imagination," conjoining incidents that were not conjoined in the war, placing in such and such a city or warfront incidents that occurred elsewhere. That is, I have aimed to make my shot by a carom, as in billiards. What has always been important to me, all my life, is primarily the psychological rigor, the circumambient atmosphere!

One Million Dead attempts to make an orderly, methodical reply to several works written outside Spain which have had a decisive influence on the concepts their readers in Europe and America have formed of our civil war: such works as *Man's Hope* by Malraux, *For Whom the Bell Tolls* by Hemingway, *A Spanish Testament* by Koestler, *Les Grands Cimitières sous la Lune* by Bernanos, and Arturo Barea's trilogy, *La Forja*, *La Ruta*, and *La Llama.* Apart from their literary value, those works cannot stand careful analysis. They set forth the drama of our country to suit themselves; they abound in folklore, and whenever they resolutely face up to the subject, in all its magnitude, they are obliged to turn tail. They often sin through unfairness, through arbitrariness, and they arouse a remarkable feeling of discomfort in the informed reader.

My work also sets out to present a chronicle of the Spaniards themselves, so poorly endowed for dispassionately embracing the sum of the facts. As a rule, not even the actors in the struggle had any clear idea of what actually occurred. Each one remembers his own saga, and more or less dogmatizes about the area in which he operated, but completely omits any reference to what was happening farther north or farther south, to say nothing of making any sound appraisal of the opposite zone, the enemy zone. Such ignorance is a source of amazement. Those who lived in Nationalist Spain throughout the war have only the haziest notion of what Red Spain was like; and those who lived in the Red zone are completely ignorant of what the terms *discipline, conviction relying on Providence, the intoxication of victory* all meant in the other zone. As for the young people, the Spaniards under twenty-five years of age, they manipulate the theme with typical frivolity and incompetence.

It is urgent, I think, to take an inventory.... For the war that our *patria* underwent was an important one. It was so important that the whole world spent three years pinning little flags on the map of Spain. At that time, to be sure, the whole world had not yet been shaken to the foundations of its homes, as it is being shaken now, and the sight of a few southern men, with dark skin, fighting hand to hand was a fascinating one. But there was more to it than that. Even then the suspicion was growing that the hand of cards being played behind the scenes of the spectacle on our soil was to have broad historical repercussions. Soon several civil wars in which Communists intervened broke out in the wake of our Civil War. How could it be otherwise? Added to that, at the beginning of the year 1937, there were Germans fighting in both zones. And Italians. And Frenchmen, and Englishmen, and Americans, and Belgians. Plus lone individuals from the most remote communities on the planet. Spain had become a staging area. The river of blood was Spanish, how Spanish! But a thousand little foreign rills were flowing into it.

The card game was important, and, as a concomitant, very complicated. Its long duration brought forth a political evolution. Weak, secondary principles were succumbing as the months and the men died. And from their ashes, the basic, visceral ideas for which the combatants of both camps were fighting sprang up with increasing and autonomous strength. The phenomenon of absorption. At the beginning of the war, both adversaries had hoisted a number of flags. During the last months, each adversary was virtually following a single banner.

I have written this book in sadness. The body of my Spain was lying stretched out on the table, and there was I with my scalpel-pen. For each verification, a grimace. For each statistic, a deep incision. Three years of fratricidal war. Days and nights of total immersion in a war that seemed to have no end. The combatants were my brothers—not *en masse,* but each in himself. And so were the killers. And the victims. Was there a killer for every victim? Perhaps there was.

I have written this book in fear, an almost superstitious fear. Has any man the right to accuse others, to set himself up as a judge of his own people? Have I actually set myself up as a judge? Is it true that each of our words constitutes an aggression, that we may wound our neighbor even by saying goodbye?

The title of the book, *One Million Dead,* might be called misleading. For the truth is that the victims, the actual dead, the cadavers at the fronts and on the home front, added up to approximately five hundred thousand. I have used the figure of a million because I am including the murdered among the dead—all those who died at the hands of men who, in the grip of hatred, killed their own capacity for pity, their own souls.

I need only recall what I indicated in the first paragraph of this prologue—that this book will, in its turn, be followed by a sequel that will permit me, God willing, to describe in retrospect a number of incidents in our war which I have touched on only lightly in this volume and which some readers might miss.

A novelistic triptych has its own peculiar exigencies of form, and, of course, it forces the emotional rhythm to be followed so minutely that oftentimes the author has no choice but to postpone and even to sacrifice many outstanding details.

JOSÉ MARÍA GIRONELLA
Areyns de Mar
Summer of 1960

PART ONE

July 30, 1936 to September 1, 1936

ONE

AN hour later, all the militiamen who had taken part in the big roundup had gone home and most of them were asleep. Professor Morales was sleeping, too, suddenly overtaken by immense weariness. Shortly after opening the bedroom door on tiptoe in his bare feet so as not to awaken the child, Cosme Vila too had sunk into sleep. His wife had spoken out of the darkness, asking, "What time is it?" and Cosme Vila had replied as he was undressing, "Four-thirty."

The exodus of the bereft began at five. As long as there were still stars in the sky and trucks filled with militiamen roaming the streets of the city, no relative of any detained man, not even of those dragged from their homes that very night, would dare to go out. News of what had been about to happen had spread rapidly, but to be afraid was no valid excuse for confronting the patrols. Accordingly, throughout the night, the soul fainted at every slither of tires and the eyes remained riveted on the slats of the Venetian blinds. Only now and again hope would rise. "Perhaps our name is not on the list." Maybe it's true that they're going to shift them to the Cárcel Modelo in Barcelona..."

Just at five, the dawn began to break. A great silence settled over the city, seeming to solidify at ground-floor level. The last star had vanished. Perhaps none of the militia would be out now. The light was strangely white, and it seemed to move, fingering things one by one.

By that time uncertainty in the minds of some families, few in comparison with the many still keeping vigil, had become unbearable. Relatives stared at one another in the hope that a voice might be raised, crying "Enough!" Ah, yes, enough of uncertainty. It was better to know! It was better to find out and to know, once and for all, whether the husband, the son, the brother had been spared or had died.

Someone would have to make the trip to the cemetery... In every case, the boldest, the one on whom the choice fell, rose with a mingling of fear and decision. "God go with you!" In every case, this daring kinsman timidly opened the outside door and went down the stairs without turning on a light. The street door would creak and the knocker strike unbidden. Outside lay the street—a street blanched in that strange whiteness as of a newly created world.

One silhouette, two, five, a dozen... A dozen, or perhaps a score of shadows emerged from all the corners of Gerona and moved forward, hugging the walls like those who had gone forth bearing arms on the day of the uprising. But now they were simply on their way to make certain whether the husband, the son, or the brother had been spared or had died.

Some women, among them the wife of Professor Civil, were carrying a basket of bread in one hand, or a couple of bottles of milk, on the pretense of running an urgent errand. Some of the men chose to look as though they were setting out on a trip and accordingly carried a package or bundle under one arm. At that hour certain forms stood out in unaccustomed relief, forms like those of the confessionals set up at the Stone Bridge with the inscription "Red Relief" concealing the name of the confessor; like the outline of a small truck, Future's, wrecked on the very spot where Teo had burst into tears; like those of the flags...

The group was headed by a very old woman, the mother of the boy who used to work crossword puzzles in the Café Neutral. When she came to the awe-inspiring wall of the cemetery, she began to moan to herself: "Let me in, let me in!" Some fifty paces behind her, a man dressed in black also was moving forward with a resolute air. He snatched off his cap.

The gravedigger and his wife had thrown themselves on the bed, fully dressed, but they were not asleep. Wide-eyed in the darkness, they were listening to every sound from outside, for they had been given strict orders to leave the gate open. There was no guarantee that another truck might not arrive.

The muttering of the old woman startled them and they sprang up and stationed themselves at the gate just as she reached the threshold of the grille, still moaning, "Let me in."

The custodians, man and wife, exchanged a glance of understanding, they could hear the ring of footsteps on the other side of the wall; the steps of the man with the cap nearing his destination.

The gravedigger went out to the street and saw the man; and, some distance behind him, recognized Don Pedro Oriol's widow turning the corner.

The gravedigger decided not to drive away the arrivals. He let them pass, standing in the doorway of his dwelling, beside his wife. How many would be coming to keep faith with the dead? They had no way of knowing. Soon they observed that everyone reacted in the same way to the sight of the open gate. They would set down their bulky packages, or the baskets holding the milk bottles, and enter the cemetery quickly as though sucked in by an invisible force inside.

What would they do once they were inside? The old woman and Don Pedro Oriol's wife reacted in a like manner. They covered their heads and split the dawn with a scream. For the bodies were there…not yet buried. They lay on the ground, scattered along the broad central avenue and the two narrow lateral paths.

Each person began his search along the right lateral avenue, where the bodies had been laid out one by one, thus making identification easier. How strange the simultaneous desire to find and not to find the beloved body! The peregrination was slow. Each corpse not that of the beloved, each strange body, implied a hope. "Thank God! This isn't he; this isn't he…" The visitors covered their mouths with their handkerchiefs. The baskets and bottles at the gate seemed to be provisions brought to feed the dead.

The pile of bodies along the broad central avenue was so shapeless that there was no way to search it without touching the corpses and separating them. The first visitor who nerved himself to do this was the brother of Juan Ferrer, the first man called out of the prison. With cautious revulsion, even using his foot, he stirred the heap while the man with the cap and three or four newly arrived women, the wives of Civil Guards, approached him as if awaiting the results of his efforts.

"Oh my God! Here he is!" As a rule identification was based on such a minor detail as a sock or a necktie. But no one was convinced until he had seen the face. When the body was turned over, the face looked like an image in a church, set in a final grimace at the moment of the volley. The torsos were rigid.

The bodies of well-known persons—the rector of the cathedral; the owner of the music store, attacked on the first day—were successively identified by everyone; others were left to one side, discarded, as if resigned to going unrecognized.

The first person to identify a kinsman was the son of the man who used to visit the retable of Saint Stephen's martyrdom in the Diocesan Museum. He was a boy of twenty. At the sight of his father, he raised his right hand to his head and held it there, his eyes rolled back until they seemed to narrow his forehead. Then he raised his other hand to his mouth and bit the index finger with unbelievable force. Finally his whole body began to tremble, and, babbling something in a quavering voice, he turned and stumbled away.

The second was the old woman who had moaned, "Let me in!" Her son, the boy who had worked the crossword puzzles, was stretched out, but intact. It would have been hard to guess how death had come to him. The woman flung herself down on him, snatching movements like kisses from his dry lips.

The sister of one of the priests had to pull down the shirt covering his face to make certain it was he. A soldier's wife stole away, sighing with relief, after she had examined a hundred bodies. Señor Corbera's wife recognized her husband from afar, and approaching him with an odd naturalness, she knelt beside him and covered his face with her kerchief.

Don Pedro Oriol's widow, in mourning despite the ban against it, awakened a special kind of pity, as did the widow of the assistant manager of the Arús Bank, and the father of Captain Roberto, a Civil Guard, because their dead, fallen on the first night, already were buried. Therefore they could only stand mute before the mound of fresh earth pointed out by the gravedigger.

Once identification had been made, hands began to search the bodies with loving insolence, seeking a remembrance: the pen, the wallet, the watch, the packet of cigarette papers! One woman managed to find some writing of her husband's in a small cigarette package: "We shall see each other in heaven."

Ignacio was one of those sorrowing people. It had taken all the boy's powers of persuasion to obtain permission to leave the house. When Don Emilio Santos himself had noticed that day had dawned, he kept saying to the boy repeatedly, after innumerable trips to the balcony facing on the Rambla: "Yes, it's true that everyone seems to have retired. But don't go out." Ignacio could not stand the uncertainty, however, and at exactly five-fifteen he went to his father, Matías Alvear, and to his mother, Carmen Elgazu, and said to them: "Forgive me, everyone. Forgive me. But it's got to be done."

With those words, he flew down the stairs. As he went out into the street and closed the door, he heard the clap of the large knocker above his head. Once on his way, he no longer tried to conceal from himself that he still cherished a shred of hope... Why shouldn't he? He remembered very well the words of Agustín, the militiaman: "We got there too late." But Agustín and Dimas had not gone to the cemetery. They had not seen César's body with their own eyes... Agustin had admitted that. "Cosme Vila told us..."

On his way to the cemetery, Ignacio saw the sign on Warning Voice's balcony. It was torn so that only "Dent—" could be read. Along the riverbank, he saw the barracks with the names of Marx and Lenin on them. A little farther along, he descried in the distance the school building where Marta had gone into hiding.

By the time he reached the gate, his legs were trembling. Please God! Light was streaming down on the rectangles of the niches; the green of the cypresses was dark and dense. He recognized no one, for he was staring at the ground. Not knowing why, he began his search along the path to his right.

In the first cadaver he came to, he recognized the Treasury Delegate who had made frequent trips to the bank. Ignacio stood as though riveted to the spot. Then he gazed all around him, and it seemed to him that César was there. Weaving catlike through a group of women, he moved several yards ahead. The sand whispered loudly beneath his feet and he felt himself surrounded by sobs that at times seemed to have escaped from his own lips.

César was not there. Ignacio turned and, seeing no one, nothing but the tombs and the crosses, he moved toward the left-hand avenue, where he discovered instantly that Cosme Vila and Agustín had not spoken vainly and that his parents and Don Emilio Santos were right. Very near him lay César, flat on the ground, his back to him, his legs apart, and terribly motionless.

Ignacio stifled a cry and his feet dug into the earth. César's head was thrown back so that all Ignacio could see of it was a single ear, terribly yellowed. Some icy creature—a cold pencil—had written César's name on a sheet of paper, and someone actually had shot him. Ignacio wanted to kneel, but could not. Something, something stirring deep within him, clouded his eyes, clouded even his grief. For a moment he experienced a hatred so keen that he clenched his fists in rebellion. He was rebelling against the cold pencil writing on the sheet of paper, but against that individual, too, who directed the destinies of human beings from some indeterminate height, decreeing their beginning and their end. Look! All around him, dozens of crosses stood out against the gray sky of dawn. Ignacio stared at that cropped head thrown back, and did not move. A flash of memory reminded him that he had often patted that head. "Hi, Holy Joe!" And suddenly he noticed that in spite of the clay and the blood, César's body lay in a posture of perfect repose. His face could not be seen.

Then he was able to move forward with the certainty that César's face would express the same sweet tranquility... But what a revelation! After a bare glance, Ignacio raised his hand to his face and looked away. César's face was disfigured; no longer a face, but a mask of dried blood. Nothing of him was left. Ignacio dared not look again. Why had it all had to happen? His first impulse was to run away.

But he did not flee; he stayed there, forcing the other searchers to circle him. So it was possible that a face molded by a fine life could be blasted by a shot between the eyes which would make a monstrosity of it. A Psalm he had once learned in the Seminary came back to him, he did not know why: "They laid out the bodies of their servants to feed the birds of the air, with no one to give them burial."

Because one must go on living, he finally turned, looked at his brother again, then knelt by his side. He even found the strength, not knowing whence it came, to search César's remains for a remembrance. But he found that César had carried on him nothing whatever... Neither watch nor key nor pencil, much less a ring or a package of cigarettes! César had needed nothing either for living or for dying. Next Ignacio opened his shirt to find the medal that had been the gift of Mosén Alberto. The moment he touched it, the little chain came loose in his hand, surrendering itself to him.

This was enough for Ignacio. He kissed César and rose. He understood that there was nothing more to be done, though it had not occurred to him to say a prayer. He crossed himself, turned, and began to walk toward the exit, avoiding two impassive men who had an air of simple curiosity. One of them was wearing a red necktie.

At the gate the custodian surprised Ignacio by approaching and asking whether the family owned a niche. Ignacio was disconcerted. He felt completely stunned to hear a voice speak without tears of something mundane. He could not reply.

The custodian was insistent. He had often seen Ignacio with "that boy from the Seminary" whom he remembered now because "for a whole summer he would come every day to the cemetery, so you were bound to notice him." Ignacio could not speak; he knew nothing about a niche. The custodian finally told him that he would await instructions until the following day.

Ignacio nodded and left the cemetery. Outside the gates, he noticed with particular attention the numberless the tracks left by the trucks in the asphalt. He looked toward the river and to his left saw Montilivi Hill, which he had climbed so often in the past and from the crest of which he had been able to make out the entire rectangle of the cemetery. At that time it had looked rachitic, and, above all, alien; but from now on it would be one more room in his house. He stared at the school. Marta would never be able to suspect that he was so near her at that moment, lacking the strength to go to see her, with scarcely the strength to put one foot ahead of the other.

He started toward home along the riverbank. The croaking of the frogs began to enliven the morning, and aloft the first rays of sunlight, like a shower of gold, rebounded from the façades of the buildings. The walls were covered with notices; a revolution was going on. The Artillery barracks, drab and gray, looked cowed. Dogs began to snuffle in the rubbish and a family of gypsies went slowly past, huddled together in a covered wagon.

The thought of climbing the stairway of his house filled Ignacio with anguish. Suddenly he thought: What about Mateo? He had escaped... And Mosén Alberto? He had escaped. The one who had not escaped was César, the boy who had never talked about conquering empires or about courage.

He went into the Rambla, which looked immense without the festive tables in front of the cafés. He came abreast of his house and went into the hallway. Immediately he heard the door to the apartment opening above him. He climbed the stairs one at a time as though his feet were sinking into them. Agustín was no longer standing in the vestibule; another militiaman had relieved him. No one was waiting for him in the hallway. All of them were sitting in the same spot as before, in the dining room. A large empty milk bowl stood on the table in front of Pilar.

Ignacio knew that they had been watching him from the balcony and that one look at his face had told them what had happened. He went into the dining room, and soundlessly, wordlessly, with an inner aridity that dismayed him, placed on the table César's little chain and medallion. At the sight of its glitter, everyone rose as though a spring had been released. But Carmen Elgazu anticipated the others and succeeded in taking possession of the relic. Ignacio went straight to his mother, to stand behind her and put his arms around her, kissing her hair over and over again.

TWO

VARIOUS people among those in the city who had remained loyal to the Republican Government felt overwhelmed and filled with deep misgivings. Chief among them were the three professional soldiers: the General, Colonel Muñoz, and Major Campos. After forbidding his daughters to leave the house, the General did not even have the heart to shout: "To jail with all that rabble, to jail with them..." Had he not been repelled sincerely by what the uprising signified, he might have thrown up his hands and gone off to take a rest on his own land, in the province of Alicante, or in Barcelona. For their part, Colonel Muñoz and Major Campos were ready to admit that they could never have imagined human hatred reaching such extremes. They kept reminding Julio García with bitter irony of the advice he had given them repeatedly: "There's no way out of it but to arm the people!" Julio García replied that he had advised them to arm the populace *before* the military uprising, *before* the fighting had begun. "If that had been done, everything would be different now."

In addition, what most irritated the three military men was the "angelic unawareness," as they called it, of the Committee, the people, and even the government-controlled press and radio. Indeed, they could not understand how people could be preoccupied with anything but the exclusive, the very elemental problem of channeling their efforts toward smothering the military uprising definitively. To be devoting themselves to murder and pillage was suicidal madness at the very time when the rebels were fortifying themselves in the capitals of the twenty-three provinces initially seized. They, too, were on the march, advancing toward certain points without encountering any organized resistance. On the one occasion when the General had deigned to speak to Cosme Vila, he had made a categorical statement over the telephone: "Instead of drawing up lists for the firing wall, you ought to be turning the regular soldiers over to me and letting me know the number of volunteers with military training you could place under my command..."

Obviously the three professional soldiers were seeing events from a particular point of view: the point of view of the map of Spain. They even pinned little flags on this map. And they had reached the conclusion that the enemy command was being organized with discipline, in accordance with the unvarying laws of the art of warfare, although the territories seized were the poorest and most backward in the nation—food for thought in itself. The area added up to less than half the total number of square miles and a third of the total population. As professional soldiers, they gave cardinal importance to the enemy's procedure. The General thought the most urgent task was to halt the constant reinforcements from the Moroccan bases, from Africa, and he could not understand why the Government had not deployed its entire flying squadron through Málaga and along the adjacent coast and assigned its auxiliary air force units to guarding the Straits of Gibraltar around the clock, instead of planning to infiltrate secondary objectives. The General had sent five dispatches containing those suggestions to Madrid, but had had no reply.

Julio García asked him: "Where did you send your dispatches?"

"To the Ministry of War."

Julio lighted a cigarette. "I doubt there's anyone there who knows how to write."

The three military men realized that the principal object of the rebels, the only thing that could save them, was to consolidate a continuous front along the Portuguese border. Queipo de Llano, whom Colonel Muñoz had met long ago and considered to be a braggart, kept saying night after night that on the day when his Southern Column, heading toward both Badajoz and Huelva, should succeed in making contact with the troops descending from the north under Mola, everything would take a turn for the better. That was true. And what a shock that would be to those poor militiamen in Gerona who thought themselves masters of the world because they were cutting short so many helpless lives every night. What had started as an adventure would become a war, a ruthless war. Then they would have to learn again to salute like soldiers; they would have to forget The "*¡Salud!*" and go back to the "Yes, sir" which had fallen into such disuse. From that moment on, the outcome of the struggle would be unpredictable, and in the final analysis everything would depend upon whether the Government of the Republic lay in the hands of madmen or in those of men capable of imposing its authority. Its resources were abundant. Indeed, the Government could buy arms with its gold, and it seemed assured of receiving aid from several of the great powers—or, more accurately, from their Popular Fronts—as well as from the Soviet Union. Well handled, this should suffice, provided that the land, sea, and air commands were reorganized. But it should also be borne in mind that Major Martínez de Soria, the rebel commandant of the garrison, had made a trip to Rome before the elections. That meant that the rebels, for their part, would undoubtedly obtain, indeed they might already be obtaining at that very moment, the protection of Hitler, of Mussolini, and—much more important from the strategic point of view—of the Fascist government in Portugal.

Julio García was another of those who were deeply disturbed. He was going through some of the worst hours of his life. Julio García knew full well that, aside from the military considerations stated with overwhelming logic by his officer friends, the Government, from the psychological point of view, was squandering the loyalty of important masses of the country. Out of respect for lives and property alone, the nation should have repudiated the rebel soldiers unanimously and thus forced them to abandon their cause! … Now the Government was making countless enemies by an offensive tax that was the outgrowth of desperation. Doña Amparo Campo had done her part to crush the policeman. Julio's own wife was so elated by what was happening that she kept mouthing the jargon of the rebel radio and declaring that merely to go out on her balcony made her feel nauseated. She had always aspired to climb a little higher in the social scale, to be able to invite to her table people in Dr. Relken's class, the architects Ribas and Massana, and Colonel Muñoz. Now her latest guest was Murillo with his walrus mustache, and she was expecting to roast a chicken for El Cojo at any moment! … "This is all a shame, and if you were what you pretend to be…you'd admit you've been wrong and we'd emigrate."

At home the policeman would pet Berta and watch the snow falling in the paperweights in his office. He was forced to admit that for once his wife's words contained a measure of truth. He didn't like to go out on the balcony, either. He was a man little given to sentiment, and the absence of certain people pained him less than that of others. Why not admit it? But gratuitous cruelty upset him, and to have failed in his intention to restrain minor officials from their madness humiliated him. Perhaps Canela had hit the mark when she had said: "Don't you think the other side would suit you better? Don't be a fool. Shout 'Long live the Inquisition!'"

Yet how could a man fight his own nature? His nature was his very self, his *persona.* He had only to set eyes on Warning Voice to feel his mouth go dry. The sight of Blasco, on the other hand, made him want to stick out his foot and say: "Go on, shine my shoes!" And it gave him a rare pleasure, plus certain ideas, to picture that little devil of a Santi asleep in the library of the Club, his head resting on three pillows. No, no, it was far from easy to know when you were on target or when you missed, even less easy to know to what extent you were responsible. And, being squeamish, he could not find out. His place was here, and he must wait until he could see the definitive path of the little flags on the map that belonged to his three military friends. When their course became clear in either direction, he would make up his mind. In the meantime, what more did his wife want of him? He was doing all he could to help. Wasn't he sheltering Mosén Alberto's maid under his own roof? He had given the warning that had enabled the architects Massana and Ribas to save the Episcopal Palace. Thanks to another warning from him, Major Martínez de Soria and his nineteen men were still alive. "You see, Amparito...I'm turning into a secret agent in spite of myself."

Aside from all that, it had become quite clear that for the "white glove" people matters were not improving, judging by the news from the zone occupied by the rebels. His wife was seeing only the surface, and was accordingly applying one standard to Lieutenant Martín, another to the pot-bellied Gorki. But it was nonetheless true that the Falangists, the Requetés, not to mention the Moors, were committing the same atrocities in Castile, in Navarre, in the South, at the same time and with the same blind rage as their adversaries in Gerona. And no wonder, for they were all the same race of people, as Dr. Relken had conclusively proved by measuring assorted crania. The only difference was that instead of Don Pedro Oriol, who had fallen riddled with bullets in the rebel zone, some republican manager or worker carrying an old Syndicate card was being shot. Perhaps the firing squad in Valladolid knew how to handle a gun with more elegance. So much the worse for them... Their standard—Mateo's standard—might be more refined. So much the heavier their responsibility! Oh, to be sure the pickets in Pamplona used to fall in line calling upon Christ the King! But if Major Martínez de Soria had not surrendered, the fate of his own policeman's skin would hardly bear thinking about. The Ovid Lodge! Suffice it to say that Doña Amparo Campo would have learned the meaning of loneliness thenceforth and forever.

David and Olga, similarly disoriented, rode that unleashed hurricane with equally complex feelings. Their visit of condolence to the Alvears had taken a disagreeable turn at the end. Ignacio, polite in the beginning, soon rose and left the house, slamming the door behind him. Several of their old alumni, perhaps those who used to read *Claridad,* had written on the school wall in huge letters: Heretics of the World, Unite. All day the teachers' eyes would keep wandering, zealously seeking some sort of coherence in all that had happened. And often they had to confess themselves defeated. At night it was still worse. The fusillades from the cemetery could be heard with painful clarity in the room they were occupying in the school—but not in the kitchen, where Marta slept.

They must have echoed off the niches and rebounded thence to the panes in the teachers' room.

David and Olga could not accustom themselves to the idea that people of a single place, breathing the same air and witnessing the migrations of the same birds, could harbor such irreconcilable ideas. As they sat on the rim of the fountain in the garden, they stared at each other as they always had, and each sought in the other justification for the bloodshed. They had not exchanged impressions with Julio, but they had with Antonio Casal, who assured them that at the outset of any revolution, the first sights of death made it hard to assess the benefits the upheaval would bring to the future. "A thesis," the local chief of the UGT said emphatically, "that the Christians doubtless embraced in their famous Crusades. Let's go forward, I say!"

David and Olga bit their lips and agreed. Casal, who was demanding more and more help from them, more and more friendship, was right. Why raise up new specters? The three professional soldiers were managing to keep their balance, their capacity for synthesis whenever they meditated on their one enemy, "the Fascist uprising." Yes, this was the site of the tumor, the abscess, this was where the struggle was taking place, however the cards might fall, and Olga had never forgotten that back in October 1934, Major Martínez de Soria had kept her standing on her feet for four hours while he interrogated her.

On the other hand, was there any appreciable difference between Warning Voice and the militiamen in Vich who had played football with the skull of Bishop Tones y Bages? Wouldn't he be capable of playing football with the skulls of Galán and García Hernández, the people's martyrs, whom the rebels had disinterred in order to shoot them again, or so it was said? Beware of mirages... Beware of excessive qualms. If they restrained themselves too much, they might some day see a Navarese youth come through the school door with fixed bayonet or, perhaps, a servant of Allah with his poniard between his teeth.

Of course it was painful and disillusioning to see how many soldiers had begun immediately to ape the bourgeoisie in everything. They settled into their apartments—El Responsable in Don Jorge's, Blasco in Don Santiago Estrada's—and began to eat and drink as those men had, to use the same perfumes! And—even more disillusioning—messengers of death were in the skies instead of the comets they always had longed to see. But who had lighted the match? And when all was said and done, how long could a cyclone last? The law of satiety was always operative, imperious as the law of gravity. In the end even Gorki himself would come to realize that he looked ridiculous in the mayor's chair. And after the storm had blown over, wouldn't the conquered receive some compensation for their property? They must keep in mind their duty to be objective and to remember what the French Revolution had accomplished. How many prejudices, how many clerical garments, how much class privilege, how many phantoms it had eliminated forever! Now it was a question of putting an end to the eternal threat to the nation signified by the crozier and the sword.

Yet they had noticed one thing: no bank had been attacked... How unpredictable the masses were! Banks were the very symbols of the power that the people who had nothing were rebelling against. How could Cosme Vila, who scarcely could forget his former employment, possibly respect the banks?

And the fact remained that the post reserved for David on the Anti-Fascist Committee still was waiting... The teacher would soon have to make up his mind. Antonio Casal, who now had the Citroën that had been the property of Señor Corbera to drive to the school in, was trusting in the revolutionary instinct of the pair of teachers, vestigial though it was in them as in many other children of suicides, and he believed that the balance would finally tip in the Committee's favor. Accordingly, he talked to David as though the teacher's consent were a foregone conclusion.

For this reason, he was keeping the couple abreast of the results of the Committee's deliberations, the agreements it had made, and the difficulties it had overcome, assuredly not few, thanks to the moral ascendancy won by the Anarchists in a fair fight, conferring an authority that had transformed El Responsable into an authentic and capricious star performer.

Antonio Casal had discussed this point with his characteristic truthfulness: "We must not deceive ourselves," he said. "The Anarchists are so many madmen, and they have been guilty of countless follies; but wherever they have fought they have given their all, in the proportion of four to one over any other organization. The number of dead from the CNT-FAI in Barcelona, Madrid, and Asturias is appalling; and they're still ready to offer their naked chests wherever necessary."

David and Olga fully understood this. How could they not? In any case, it would be stupid and disloyal to judge the entire anarchist organization by the deeds of El Responsable and his acolytes in Gerona. The CNT-FAI could be evaluated only on the basis of their total action, their capacity for heroism throughout the territory. And it was only fair to judge individual members by the same standard. True, Ideal greased his boots and Sam Browne belt with butter, and El Cojo chose to adopt as passwords such phrases as "The Pope is an old goat," and "Darling, I'm dying for you," but this did not mean that either of them would not be ready to risk his skin a hundred times a day if he had to.

"Of course," David admitted, "we owe it to the Anarchists that we're drinking coffee right this minute."

Olga agreed. But she added that, in her opinion, a more subtle and uncontrollable attrition than that signified by the FAI and its nonsense was boiling up in the heart of the revolution—attrition from the neutral, indifferent masses, the people who meandered hither and thither guided only by unhealthy curiosity and at no risk to themselves, people as flabby as gelatin or a brain on the operating table.

Olga considered such people more dangerous and hateful than the fanatics, for fanaticism can be cured by time, but indifference cannot. Such people were capable of collecting stamps or telling jokes even while the city was in a state of eruption. According to Olga, they were of no importance; it did not matter whether they killed or were killed, and it was undoubtedly their fault that three men had been parading through the streets since the preceding night with signs announcing the arrival in Gerona of "Miss Nadia" and "Mister Adrien"! Yes, two automobile acrobats, accompanied by a fakir named Campoy, who was to be buried alive for several hours the next afternoon in front of the Post Office.

David smiled with a faintly bitter irony. Casal noticed it. Antonio Casal was experienced in reading David's face. When David flexed his jaw as if a muzzle were galling him, he was thinking of Fascism. When he stared around, frowning, as though seeking something, he was thinking of God. When he smiled ironically, he was admiring some apposite remark of Olga's.

Casal addressed them both with affection. "You've changed a great deal since I first met you," he said. "You've changed as much as Gerona."

The teachers admitted that it was true. One matured, and as wrinkles were traced on one's face, doubts were engraved on one's soul.

"In the old days you wouldn't have put your money on the fanatics. You'd have bet on the neutrals, those indifferent people. You'd have said: We must respect their privacy,' or, 'Perhaps indifference is a way of protecting the human ego.' Ah, yes. Olga was not so beautiful then as she is now. Remember, Olga? You used to wear a badge on your sweater... It was a challenge."

"Bah!" Olga laughed. "That was an Alpinist badge for mountain climbing."

"All right, all right. Who knows? But the fact is that you were given some sharp kicks by the people who used to talk about redeeming the world. You'd still prefer those who can spend a whole afternoon applauding motor acrobats and 'Miss Nadia' and 'Mister Adrien' to the ones I've been talking about."

David smiled in agreement with his friend. "You're right," he admitted. "But we've found out now that there are many things more important than public spectacles. There's a trick in every show."

"Trick?" Antonio Casal asked, pulling the cotton out of his ear.

"Yes. Look at that fakir, Campoy. He gets himself buried, but only for a few hours. He dies…but he rises again, on schedule."

THREE

JULIO had spoken truly. Had it not been for the energetic intervention of himself and Colonel Muñoz, Major Martínez de Soria—Marta's father—and the nineteen officers who had made common cause with him all would have lain among the victims in the avenues of the cemetery at dawn that day. The People's Committees and many militiamen's wives who felt an ingrown distaste for uniforms kept asking tirelessly: "What are you waiting for?" El Responsable, in particular, kept asking that question. Much better informed than Antonio Casal and the teachers about the tribute of blood paid by the Anarchists all over Spain, he had come to consider as jokes in bad taste the ideas he once had embraced. One of these was the idea of forming a People's Tribunal to judge according to the rules of a court-martial. "What better tribunal could you find," he said, "and what more effective law than a whiff of grapeshot?" Accordingly, with Future at his side in Mateo's apartment, and with the special collaboration of Murillo, he had planned as assault on the Infantry dungeons. Murillo had reasoned, "It's not right to make the civilians pay before the soldiers do, for the civilians were nothing but their accomplices, after all."

The plan failed. Julio and Colonel Muñoz had sent a platoon of Assault Guards to the compound, armed with the machine gun that Ignacio and Pilar had been examining on the day of the uprising. Cosme Vila followed sternly the orders he must have received: "The forms must be observed in dealing with the military."

Pending some other notice, then, Major Martínez de Soria and his subordinates would have to stay there. Among his officers, Arias and Sandoval were conspicuous for their high morale, and Lieutenant Martín and Second Lieutenant Romá for their inconsolable distress.

The dejection of the prisoners arose primarily from the consciousness that they themselves had provoked the catastrophe—as David had said, "Who lighted the match?"—and secondarily from the stupidity of their defeat. Indeed, they had withdrawn to their quarters and laid down their arms without a sign of a struggle while they were absolute masters of the city, and only because General Goded had surrendered in Barcelona. It had all happened with stunning simplicity, without their even questioning whether another alternative lay open to them. Major Martínez de Soria had given the order, and all of them had obeyed it without a murmur. But as the hours went by, the crushing weight of their responsibility bowed their heads ever lower. To add to that, news kept coming in, telling them what had happened in garrisons more isolated than Gerona's—for example, in Oviedo, at the Alcázar in Toledo, at the Sanctuary of Our Lady de la Cabeza, and at other points of less strategic importance than Gerona, which bordered on France. And yet the officers and commandants of those other garrisons had chosen to resist...

Their situation was serious. Now they were lying in a dungeon, deprived of their uniforms by Colonel Muñoz's orders, awaiting, from one moment to the next, the clatter of feet on the stairway, the creaking of the hinges on the doors, and the abrupt chatter of machine-gun bullets.

The officers sat in their shirt-sleeves or lay on the tickling straw, suffocated by the heat. They kept going over in their minds all the "might have beens" and thinking with impotent irony what an arbitrary force geography could be. For if the uprising had occurred first in Seville, Salamanca, or Burgos, they might now be feeling proud of their efficiency and be at the head of their troops, carrying swagger sticks and binoculars.

The most humiliated of them all, the most anguished, was Major Martínez de Soria. Each straw was a thorn to him. The major felt that he alone was responsible for the disaster and that he had been directly to blame for the burning of the city. A heavy weight to lie on a single head! ... He had led the uprising by virtue of his rank, and the determination to surrender had been his own personal decision. His only consultant had been a glass of cognac. True, he had not extemporized, and his reasons for issuing the order had seemed valid. Barcelona could move eighty thousand troops against them, their stores of provisions and munitions were scanty; the city had lain at the mercy of the bomber planes from the Prat airfield, in enemy hands. Their surrender would offer many endangered persons the opportunity to escape... And naturally he had acted on the basis of the strictly military fact that the nearest triumphant garrison was in Zaragoza, so that for the time being there had been no hope whatever of receiving reinforcements in time.

Yet there was no escaping the fact that now everyone who went abroad armed was hunted without fear or favor, and that resistance would have diverted many enemy forces and would have made it impossible for the time being for them to receive international aid from France. Ah, an uprising was certainly not the same as theorizing in the Armory! "Let every man know how to die with honor!" "I believe I have served Spain." "I'd do the same thing a thousand times over!" These phrases, undeniably his own, now echoed with bitter irony.

The major was occupying a corner of the jail situated beneath the window. During those three days he had raised his left shoulder countless times. He had found four mothballs in the pockets of the summer trousers his wife had sent him. They smelled like the devil but he caressed them with enjoyment, for they symbolized the gentle world that was lost to him forever. His wife! His daughter, little Marta! ... Were they still alive? How he longed to be able to concentrate undisturbed on his memory of them during that last morsel of time now left to him! But that was not permitted him. A distant shout, the sentries' jokes, the shootings in the cemetery, and especially the silence of the officers were like spikes driven into his forehead with a pain like nothing the major could recall. He knew those men, he could read their minds. Only Lieutenant Delgado and a couple of second lieutenants still approved of his decision; the others were pronouncing him guilty.

The major was suffering. He kept recalling his campaign in Africa, his decorations... With the coming of night, insomnia impelled him to stare at his surroundings. And to see his subordinates stretched out, defenseless, increased his conflict. Let them all know how to die honorably! Honor? This word kept hammering at him ever more insistently. He recalled numerous examples of defeated commanders who, to justify themselves, had fired bullets into their brains. The major rubbed his temples, and if some officer looked at him, he pretended to be caressing his head or coughing a little.

It would have been a great help to him to be able to consult his own people, his family. His wife, of course, and also his son, José Luis, who was most certainly fighting in the Sierra; but he would have liked more than anything to hear the verdict, as between father and son, of his other boy, Fernando, who had preceded him in the sacrifice, shot down on a street corner in Valladolid while shouting the slogans of the Falange.

The major suddenly awoke with a start, imagining that those four persons of his own flesh and blood were seated in front of him, staring at him with the imperturbability of a tribunal. He himself had taught to be just, to be implacable! From time to time it would seem to him that all of them, like the officers beside him, were condemning him, he did not know why. All but one... All but Marta, who came to him and said fondly: "Why don't you take me to the Dehesa to ride horseback? Do you hear what I'm saying, Papa? Why don't you take me?"

SOON it had become clear that despite the Anti-Fascist Committee's will to rule, it could not undertake everything. The instinct of the persecuted for self-preservation succeeded in opening innumerable breaches. Caravans of "mutineers" who made use of every kind of stratagem managed to make a mockery of any guard and to go into hiding or flee. Cosme Vila was forced to recognize this fact, and Future, sucking in his lower lip between his teeth, gave a long whistle when he read the first list of fugitives submitted to headquarters by the French authorities in Perpignan.

France was the goal sought by the fugitives because she was handling the problem amicably. They would approach the easiest mountains by car, by carriage, or on foot, and then attack the heights by guess and by God or with the help of a guide. The guides were the smugglers of the region, and they charged according to the risk they took. The frontier guards from the People's Committees were on watch in the passes and hills, together with the carabineers, but the Pyrenees were so vast! ... A man could filter through them with incredible ease. And the smugglers knew the way; some of them even knew the sea routes along which the rowboats moved cautiously in the depths of the night.

Word flew from mouth to mouth that another way to escape was to obtain the asylum of some foreign consulate, especially in Barcelona, in whose harbor ships of all countries anchored daily to repatriate their citizens. Some consulates—the Italian was one of them—functioned with great efficiency. The question was to get a passport and then to be daring and lucky during the minutes just before the raising of the gangplank. Sometimes a passport could be had by suborning a militiaman. Sometimes luck would smile upon a clever, ingenious disguise. A professor from the Gerona Instituto, hotly pursued by Morales, appeared at the harbor in Barcelona dressed as a horse-breaker with a high-crowned hat and gold-headed cane, greeting everyone in faultless Hungarian! By the time the sentry from the FAI began to react, the professor was safely aboard ship. The false passport had been the means used by Warning Voice. In fact, the dentist had barely arrived with Laura in the village of their maid, Dolores, before he realized that he was in great danger owing to the "flying patrols" scouring the region. Beside himself, he begged his wife: "Go to your brothers! Tell them to get me out of here!" The Costas did not dare to accompany their brother-in-law to the frontier, but they did go with him as far as Barcelona in a small truck belonging to the foundry. In Barcelona they succeeded in persuading the Provincial Government to have the doors of the Chilean Consulate opened for a modest price, but only and exclusively for Warning Voice. Laura had to remain behind. It couldn't be helped! Believe it or not, as soon as Warning Voice was safely aboard, listening to the shrill wail of the sirens, he faced in the direction of the militiamen on the pier and babbled: "So long, red pigs!"

Octavio and Miguel Rosselló, the Falangists who had left the Alvears' apartment for the Pyrenees and France, ran into some major difficulties. They got lost in the convolutions of the cordillera and did not dare to ask their way either in the cottages or of the farmers. Octavio was not carrying anything with him, and Miguel Rosselló had nothing but his pistol and the hundred pesetas that Matías Alvear had given him. They were harassed by hunger and fatigue and by the barking of the dogs. A hundred times the boys wandered away from the track and found themselves back in the same spot, surrounded by mountains. They slept in the open, and the next day, pistols in hand, entered the hut of a shepherd, an old man who knew nothing of what was going on. "What is the matter?" he asked. "What do you want of me?" "Take us to France," Miguel Rosselló ordered, feigning assurance. The man looked them over slowly. He did not understand that, young as they were, they had been forced to flee, and that they had no packs of provisions. He could not possibly accompany them; he was exceedingly lame, but he could give them real encouragement; they were only ten minutes from the frontier. "Behind that cliff is France." "Thank God!" Miguel and Octavio embraced the old man, gave him all the tobacco they had with them, and blessed him with all the fervor of their volatile youth. They reached the cliff, the border, running and, once there, turned around to say goodbye to the shepherd. But he had disappeared. They then said goodbye to Spain, the land where they had known happiness and suffering. Octavio proved cautious, but Miguel Rosselló, he of the abiding affection for automobiles, with the Studebaker emblem on his lapel, could have sung "Face to the Sun" from sheer joy. He managed to make Octavio bow his head in the direction of Gerona and say a *Salve Regina* with him.

Twenty-four hours later the notary Noguer and his wife reached France in the company of Mosén Alberto by crossing a hill half an hour away from the route taken by the two Falangists. Following the directions of the guide who left them at the boundary line, they reached the first French village, Morellás, without wasting any time. The presence of the three fugitives awakened the curiosity of the neighborhood, and a pair of gendarmes took them to the little guardhouse and began immediately to interrogate them in a hostile manner. But the notary, who knew the letter of the law, said to the gendarmes: "Please, gentlemen... We beg asylum under the existing laws of France. We are surrendering to you in our status of political refugees." Although they hesitated, the gendarmes were acquainted with the law and promised them that they would be allowed to leave for Perpignan on the first truck to come through. "Inside of an hour, more or less."

Mosén Alberto asked permission to visit the village church. "You may go." Excited, they went out into the street and saw the rustic belfry above their heads. Oddly enough, Mosén Alberto seemed more compliant in secular garb. They knelt before the Cross. They prayed for Spain and for the success of their own venture. As they were leaving, the notary's wife commented: "How beautiful it is to find crosses everywhere."

On the following day, near that same hill, a group of eight men and their guide was taken by surprise. It happened that one of the travelers had sprained a foot and the others had been taking turns carrying him. Luckily, the border guards were not militiamen, but carabineers. If they had been militiamen, it would have meant instant death. The carabineers led the fugitives to Gerona, to the Seminary Prison, where Professor Civil identified one of the prisoners and rose with evident feeling to embrace him. The man had been one of his schoolmates. He stood mute, but his face spoke for him, and besides he played the piano a thousand times better than Professor Civil. "My dear Manuel!" The "veterans" among the detainees began to instruct the newcomers with regard to the customs of the prison, which they called "the waiting room." For the moment the professor spared them his discourse upon the Jews and the Mediterranean Sea. On the other hand, he let them know that they all said the Rosary every day. And that there was a cross in every cell! His friend Manuel blinked. "Yes, man, there is, look." And the professor showed him a cross scratched very lightly on the wall with a fingernail.

Farther to the right, in the Pyrenees, along the pass called Perthus, Mateo and Jorge had crossed the frontier. It had taken them three days and three nights, warm July nights, for Jorge wanted at all costs to avoid entering upon land owned by his family. His last sight of Gerona had been of the columns of smoke rising high into the sky, growing more numerous as the boys climbed higher. They could practically look down on the whole of the Ampurdán plain dotted with pillars of smoke, and the sight upset them.

What had happened in Gerona? What was happening all over Spain? They had not met anyone or read a newspaper.

Once in France, the boys threw their pistols into a ravine and headed straight toward the nearest village, Banyuls-sur-Mer, among lovingly tended vineyards. At the moment when they set foot on the railroad tracks, two gendarmes who had been watching them through field glasses ever since they had appeared around the bend of the Fuente, intercepted them. "Your papers, gentlemen, if you please."

The policemen conducted them to the little guardhouse and proved much more amiable than their colleagues at Morellás, informing them at once that they could take advantage of the existing law of asylum in France and could change their money there. They apologized for having to search them carefully. "Then we'll take you to the prefecture in Perpignan."

The chief of police in Banyuls-sur-Mer asked them to strip off their clothes. Nothing in particular, except for the map of Spain sewn inside Mateo's blue shirt. "*Curieux,*" the gendarme muttered, shoving back his kepi.

Mateo set his face in the expression of a Falangist and said, addressing them all: "We wish for you that you may never be placed in this position, that you may never feel forced to hide the map of France."

The chief stared searchingly into his eyes and made a skeptical grimace. "Thank you," he replied.

A gendarme came in with two glasses filled with a thick black liquid. "Coffee?" he asked them.

"Oh, yes, thank you!"

An hour later they found themselves on the train going to Perpignan. The younger of the two gendarmes was accompanying them. The countryside was triumphal, filled with birds. The train ran through vineyards, and to the right the sea played hide-and-seek, coquetting.

How beautiful that all was. Why, then, did Mateo feel such discomfort? Ever since their arrival at Banyuls-sur-Mer, he had been conscious that the country was alien to him. Perhaps this was an aftertaste from anti-French propaganda. Nothing pleased him: neither the shrill reds of the stores, nor how well they were stocked, nor the slogan "*Liberté, Egalité, Fraternité,*" nor the superb trucks and tractors—if only Spain had them! Nor, of course, the gendarmes' kepis.

"Jorge, what do you think of those kepis? Do you think anyone could take them seriously?"

Jorge said yes. Everything French pleased Jorge, and from the moment they had stepped over the boundary line he had been wide-eyed as a doll. Mateo deplored Jorge's point of view, and slowly lighting a cigarette, he held his tongue. "Of course, of course," he thought. "To each his own." Then he thought of how strange it was that the mere crossing of a line, a frontier, could effect such a radical change in the world. "On this side," he said to himself, "there are no machine guns or declarations of war. Only vineyards and peace. On this side, Spain's troubles make no sense and no one ever heard of El Responsable, nor Cosme Vila, nor Giral."

"There's Perpignan, gentlemen!"

Mateo came out of his submersion in self, and Jorge, clapping him on the shoulder, said: "All right, come down to earth."

They alighted and went out to the street, toward the Prefecture. The street was not wide. A butcher shop was displaying a row of hanging little pigs wearing gilded skullcaps on their heads. Mateo thought of Azaña, for some reason and the idea filled him with enthusiasm. "France!" Like Rosselló, he wanted to whistle "Face to the Sun." He saw women whose bearing was free and forward, and found traces of Voltaire in them. The boys passed men carrying long loaves of bread under their arms. "Look, Jorge." "Sure," said Jorge. "That's as it should be. In Spain we men would be ashamed even to carry our children in our arms." Mateo said nothing. In the atmosphere there was something denoting that this was a country with water.

Everything went quickly at the prefecture, for the gendarme who had accompanied them had a written report to present. The prefect read this report, then the gendarme said goodbye to them and shook their hands. "So long, gentlemen." Only two precautionary measures were prescribed: vaccination against something or other and fingerprinting.

They were vaccinated in a dirty room by a woman wearing a leather hunting jacket. Jorge said as a joke: "She's a Yugoslav." This was the usual joke from Jorge, the orphan who did not yet know he was one. Each time something amused or shocked him he would say "He's a Yugoslav." Mateo stood the vaccination well, but the inexpressible facility of the French police in fingerprinting bothered him. "It's humiliating," he stammered. "The hell with democracies!"

At last they were free. A strange sensation! Now the streets seemed broader. They were the owners of a paper that signified their right to stay in the city' until further notice and to choose a domicile. Their only obligation was to report daily and not to provoke any incident or speak in public about politics.

"Bah!" remarked Mateo. "As if they'd understand."

They began to walk aimlessly toward the center of Perpignan. As they had left the station, they had seen groups of their compatriots chatting and also showing traces of flight. Perhaps they would find Padilla, Haro, Rosselló among them... Perpignan was the meeting place. Unfortunately it did not turn out that way. All the boys were from Figueras or villages near the frontier. No one was from Gerona. Nevertheless, it was useful to talk with them. They said "the province was a volcano" and that all the news from Spain with reference to the situation there was adverse. No French newspaper was admitting the possibility of a triumph for the "military uprising." All of them were reporting extraordinary feats by the Spanish people, the "defenders of liberty, whose heroism has aroused the admiration of the entire world..." In Asturias, in Toledo, in Huesca, the surrender of the regular troops was expected momentarily. The Loyalist reconnaissance planes were reporting that the Requetés had raised the flag of monarchy, thus "arousing the greatest indignation among the people." Sanjurjo, the general who was to have commanded the rebels, had died in an airplane accident flying from Portugal to Spain!

Mateo wiped his forehead with his blue handkerchief. And even though he said to Jorge: "You must remember that those papers speak for the Popular Front," he felt intense discouragement spreading through him, a discouragement that the painful excitement and fear still staring from the eyes of the other refugees could only augment. Who was that boy, pale as death, approaching them? One among many. His personal Odyssey had begun with three knocks on the door of his house at midnight and had been climaxed by the sight of six heads of Civil Guards impaled on the six points of an iron gate as he was leaving the town. "I don't believe in anything anymore. Not in anything!" Having said this, he went on, almost staggering, with one of the women soliciting in the village.

Greatly downcast, Mateo and Jorge went along in search of a hotel. Their feet were dragging, and their souls too. The bootblacks, seeing their rope-soled sandals, followed their progress indifferently. They were assailed by sad presentiments as they thought of the people they had left behind in Gerona. Mateo was thinking of Pilar especially. "The province is a volcano." He lighted another cigarette. A man came up to them muttering: "I buy wrist-watches, I buy…" Of course, everything could be bought! And everything sold. Everything, except this terrible weariness and fear.

They came to a hotel with a sign that said Cosmos.

"Hey, let's go in here." Jorge was joking.

Cosmos… It must be a very big hotel.

Not all the persecuted in the "Red" zone had the opportunity to escape. Countless people had no recourse but to hide. They were at their wits' end to find the safest spot. Chance would play an important part, for it frequently happened that the poorest of the hideouts would pass unnoticed by the militia, and on the other hand, that places chosen with the utmost care—the interior of the water tank, for example, with a lid that almost touched the ceiling—were discovered in the first search.

When the militiamen entered a house looking for some suspect, they would initiate what Professor Morales called "the dance of the eyes." As they stood quietly in the dining room or the hallway, the militiamen would let their eyes roam slowly in every direction as they spread their nostrils to sniff. At the same time, the family of the person in hiding would try not to betray him, avoiding alike the involuntary glance at the hiding place and the determined stare toward the opposite corner.

The great scattering, the swift flight of the "Fascists" was taking place. In Gerona and throughout the territory. In the large cities, it was easier to use camouflage, and moreover the foreign diplomatic establishments were there. The embassies in Madrid—called islands—had opened their doors to a great number of the pursued. The relatives of such persons used to say: "Manuel has gone to Turkey." "Juan went to see a Canadian film." In Madrid, Santiago, the brother of Matías and father of José Alvear, used to make it a point to visit the diplomatic mansions each time he came down from the mountains after a skirmish with the Falangists, just to see what he could pick up. One day he collared a man with a fear-stricken face, who was holding something in his mouth as he was making for the Brazilian Embassy. Santiago went up to him and dealt him a violent blow on the back that forced him to spit out the object, a Lilliputian Portuguese dictionary. The man had been afraid he would be searched along the way, and that incredible piece of stupidity had occurred to him.

It happened that not everyone was willing to lay his life on the line. The trauma was extreme. Santiago, José Alvear's father, was in his element. But there was only one Santiago Alvear in the entire country, an excellent combination of sentimental anarchist and police dog. In a letter to Matías he wrote: "You know I enjoy the game."

A cousin of the owner of the Crocodile had hidden out at a farm, in the pigpen where the pigs came to accept his company. Ana María's mother—Ana María, Ignacio's idol with a roll of hair at each side of her head—spent fifteen days in an elevator stopped between the third and fourth floors. When danger was near, the porter would halt the elevator there as if it had broken down and then would raise or lower into place when calm was restored. The vacant tombs in some cemeteries were much sought after, and to carry food to the people hidden there, a fake funeral would be staged with the compliance of the custodian. The coffin held food and supplies instead of a corpse. By day the occupants of such tombs had to eat and live supine in their shelter, and they dared to venture out only on occasional nights, to roam about for a short time among the dead, the stars, and fear. Jaime, Matías's friend in the telegraph office, always used to say that for his part if he had to hide, he'd choose the woods after hollowing out the trunk of a tree in advance.

Many of the pursued in Gerona demonstrated ingenuity and imagination in concealing themselves, and this brought real despair to Cosme Vila. He would have liked to install himself on the roof of the Cathedral campanile, along with the angel decapitated by a French shell during the War of Independence. From there he would have liked to spot and point to the Bishop, Marta, Don Emilio Santos, and all the other enemies of the people. And especially, those who had taken up arms. To single them out as Queipo de Llano reputedly pointed out the workers in Seville who had opposed the rebellion, and whom, according to El Responsable, he had marked on the forehead with the initials UHP, for the Syndicate to which they belonged, before lining them up against the firing wall.

Well, even the Anti-Fascist Committee could not accomplish everything. Marta was being well taken care of; the Bishop might have been swallowed up by the earth—"He's lying down with some slut," El Cojo opined—Don Emilio Santos was safe in the Alvear house, sleeping in César's bed. Through some instinct for solidarity, strangers, never knowing why, were offering shelter to imperiled people, particularly to nuns, nuns not wearing their habits, some of them with wigs. Delegate Axelrod, Vasiliev's substitute in Barcelona, a very tall man with a good-natured air, who wore a black patch over his right eye like a pirate and who was always accompanied by a beautiful dog, had said to Cosme Vila on his first visit of inspection to Gerona: "Never mind, don't be impatient! We'll soon have the necessary means to put an end to all this."

La Andaluza was one of the most hospitable. The owner of some flourishing bordellos in the city, she opened her doors to the most diverse types without giving up her business, and she kept Canela, now a militiawoman, from finding out about it. The latest of her "pupils," as she called them, were Alfonso and Sebastián Estrada, the sons of Don Santiago Estrada, head of the CEDA, who was shot on the first night. The first people she hid were a professor from Tarragona who swore he could speak Arabic correctly and a cattle dealer from the province of Lérida whose panic was so great that he had had a notice of his death published in several newspapers in the hope that no one would bother to look for him because of it.

The Estrada brothers delighted La Andaluza, and she was grateful that through a mutual friend they had accepted her hospitality. She liked Alfonso, the older, because he was educated and knowledgeable about the cocktails with which she tranquilized the young girls, nervous over the war. She liked Sebastián, the younger of the brothers, because he had a talent for inventing fables and always gave an original interpretation to facts. La Andaluza used to remark admiringly: "If I'd thought about that for ten years, it would never have occurred to me."

The professor from Tarragona and the cattle dealer from Lérida finally had escaped to France. La Andaluza bade them goodbye, saying: "Ah, if only I could go with you! I'd make a pile of money there." The Estrada brothers wanted to leave, and La Andaluza, concerned about them, said: "Patience, patience. What's your hurry? Don't I treat you well?"

"That's not the point, Andaluza. The point is that they've murdered our parents, and so the sooner the better."

Perhaps the most complex man among those hidden in the city was Mosén Francisco, whom the Campistol sisters, Pilar's dressmakers, had taken in. These ladies had put at his disposal a clothes closet with a false back which could have hidden a corpse. The vicar would wander about the apartment like a lost soul, muttering: "Look how I live here surrounded by mirrors!" He took his meals in his room, and he and the dressmakers had a system of signs or mutterings like those in the confessional so that a masculine voice might not be heard from the stairway.

Mosén Francisco was embarrassed. He was wearing a false mustache that he often longed to snatch off, a blue smock, and rope-soled sandals. He kept constantly playing with one tooth, as if it ached, and thinking that everything was a great nuisance. From his room he could see a stretch of blue sky, shabby roofs, and, there in the background, the mountains. He read the newspapers—one of them had published a caricature of the Bishop standing on one foot and saying: "Fly away, butterfly"—and he listened to the radio. This was his connection with the outside world, as it was Marta's. A small radio was buried beneath a cover on the little night table. Mosén Francisco spent hours listening, prey to all sorts of surprises, such as that given him by an itinerant priest—he could not remember his name—who had a fine voice and who claimed to be speaking from Madrid through the microphones of the Ministry of War. A priest who had come out against the military uprising and whose message, expounded with fascinating precision, was that Christ, a carpenter by trade, had risen from the people and that the people's state of mind had its justification in the selfishness of the rich and their marriage in perpetuity to the Catholic Church. As usual, he gave statistics of the treasures stored in the churches and he made a strenuous effort to emphasize the spiritual neglect to which the humble had been relegated. Indeed, he spoke with conviction and passion. His final sentence was: "We priests would be playing our proper role only if we wore ragged soutanes and used chalices of lead."

As Mosén Francisco turned off the radio, he looked at himself in one of the mirrors. He was recalling his gold chalice, seeming to see it in the mirror confused with the false mustache he was wearing. He remembered the Bishop entering Gerona to take possession of the diocese. He had been standing in a black automobile with the top down, scattering blessings to right and left. A huge multitude was acclaiming him. What had happened?

Mosén Francisco turned his back on the mirror and went to sit down on the edge of the bed, blowing smoke at the ceiling. He would have liked to know the whereabouts of his bishop, to rush to his aid, to risk his life for him. The Campistol sisters had said to him: "He's hidden in a railroad man's house. Don't worry." Well, how was he to know whether the two women were telling him pious lies or the truth?

Hidden—that was the axial word that ran unceasingly from his mind to his sandals. The body feared death and hid wheresoever it might, in railroad men's houses, in dressmakers' houses. Mosén Francisco blew unnecessarily on the tip of his cigarette to watch it turn red, and instantly recalled some mysterious words of the Gospel: "He who would save his life must lose it." How clear that was! His bishop, he, hundreds of priests and monks wanted to save their lives, and they would lose them. The sparks of the cigarette brought to memory, however, other very different words, also from the Gospel, also enunciated by Jesus, words that the priest who had spoken over the radio from Madrid had forgotten to mention: "Wheresoever they reject ye and wish not to hear ye, withdraw ye from thence, shaking the dust from your feet, in testimony against them."

And yet again, Jesus had said: "Meanwhile when they persecute ye in one city, flee ye to another."

Mosén Francisco went on smoking, smoking ceaselessly and tapping the tooth. Was it right that he should save himself? "A ragged soutane..." He was wearing a blue smock. The Campistol sisters had whispered: "It's your duty; you have a duty to try to save yourself!" Nevertheless, other priests infinitely better than he already had fallen. He was afraid of the sin of desertion, of scandal. And he was ashamed of being afraid. The Campistol sisters brought him frequent cups of coffee to keep up his spirits. Meanwhile, his hands again picked up a filthy deck of cards that he had found in a box and dealt out a game of solitaire and then another, spreading the cards out on the white sheet.

Mosén Francisco was perhaps the most complex of the men hidden in the city. Thousands of thoughts were hidden... And many hearts. Indeed, there was no way of knowing whether what men were doing, what they were giving of themselves, arose from their innermost selves or from borrowed ones.

FOUR

THE dramatic, sweet shadow of César escorted the Alvears wherever they went. To the Telegraph Office, to the Arús Bank, to market, in the kitchen, in the warm intimacy of the bed. Sometimes this shadow grouped the whole family in the dining room, sometimes it scattered them, each member seeking solitude. They were inconsolable, so overwhelmed by the amputation that they scarcely looked at one another. Matías and Carmen Elgazu, yes. To learn that each one's sorrow was unchanging, he to observe two deeply engraved dark circles under Carmen's eyes, she to sense the unprecedented fatigue that weighed down Matías Alvear's shoulders.

Matías in the Telegraph Office—how strange it seemed to him to have to go back to work!—talked over everything with his son. His gray dressing gown reminded him of that other yellow one that César used to wear in the Collell. When he looked at the calendar, his eyes were immediately drawn as if by a magnet to the date of the 21st. If, while he was counting the words in a telegram, their number coincided with César's age, Matías's hand would pause in the air a moment. He wondered why the telegraph paper was not black. During the first days, Matías would turn his head every time the machine started to click, and he would go to the tape expectantly as though to receive news of his son.

Among his fellow workers, Jaime was the one who helped him most effectively, consoling him with tact and frequency. Jaime's family owned a niche, and he succeeded in persuading them to grant César burial there. The inscription read: The Casellas Family. This of course embarrassed Matías when he went to the cemetery to visit his son. Jaime appeared at Matías's house with an old but powerful radio to substitute for the one with the earphones. Matías did not want to accept it, but Jaime insisted. "We don't need it anymore! A good radio will be lots of company for you."

They wanted to keep some of César's things in a safe place, such things as the medallion, some drawings he had sent them from the Collell, his first communion certificate. Jaime suggested an unusual hiding place for them—an empty footstool. "The wood is insulated and it will keep them well."

Matías did not know how to thank his colleague for all he was doing. "You're a good man, Jaime. You once invited Ignacio to spend his vacation in Cerdaña."

Those days were a great trial to Matías. He could not understand why such a mortal blow had fallen upon his peaceful home. And this time he could not count on the strength of his wife, Carmen Elgazu. She was undone. Seated always motionless in her chair near the balcony that faced the river, she would squeeze her handkerchief in her right hand. Sometimes she would close her eyes and there was no knowing whether she was asleep or on the point of slipping to one side in a faint. Repeatedly Matías had run for the bottle of eau de cologne and patted her lovingly on the cheeks. "Forgive me, Matías, it's stronger than I am. Forgive me..." Matías begged her to be brave for César's sake, and he was always telling his wife that if there were really angels in heaven, their son would be one of them, one of the most resplendent. "I know, Matías, I know... Forgive me..."

Neither could Matías understand why something as sacred as the feeling of paternity might result, as it had, in a mirage, an illusion of the mind. He thought of that whenever he recalled the assurance he suddenly had felt, at once strong and warm, that Dimas would save César. With what faith he had gone in search of the head of the Committee de Salt! And all in vain... "Well," he kept saying to himself now, "then it would seem that it is useless to love. Hatred can be anticipated and your son can be taken from you as easily as the wind can carry off a hat."

Sometimes as he walked through the streets, he would come up to a group of militiamen and would feel a particular kind of shiver. He would stare at them one by one, as though seeking to find out which of them had shot César. Other times he would come home half-inclined to call Ignacio aside and ask him all manner of details about his son's death—where he fell, the posture in which he lay, the color of his face and hands. But he never dared to, and soon he was reproaching himself for failing to curb his son's mysticism in time, as well as for having thrown into the river the hair shirt that César had worn on a certain occasion.

Carmen Elgazu was living through a different kind of sorrow. Pilar wanted to relieve her of almost all her tasks, but she would not hear of it. She would not have been able to go down the stairs and out into the street; on the other hand, with Don Emilio Santos as a guest, she considered it her duty to cook. She never thought, of course, that there were details surrounding César's death. She felt within her that immense bereavement, nothing more. And she never supposed that anything but a sweet serenity could emanate from César dead. How could it? God had been visible in the depths of César's eyes, and even his fingernails had always grown rounded and crescent-shaped—peaceful fingernails.

In the end, Carmen Elgazu was confronted by her own vulnerability. She was the one whose duty it was to set an example, and she was not doing it. Her heart cried out, demanding explanations. What a great gap there was between offering and giving! Like Matías, she could see César everywhere. César burgeoned from the apartment, as though the walls remembered him. Sometimes when she set a cup down on the table, she seemed to feel again the touch, the hand of César on it. When she went to the balcony to look at the river, she instinctively left beside her a vacant place for César. When Don Emilio Santos retired to his room to sleep in César's bed, she felt as though Mateo's father were profaning it.

And yet, who had inculcated in her son the desire to go to God? She, she above anyone, from his infancy on. A thousand times she had said to him: "This earth is nothing." Her son had believed that, and he had gone. And now she realized that this earth meant a great deal. It meant so much that often when Pilar came to her and put her head on her shoulder, Carmen Elgazu would caress it crying out within herself: "Ah, no! They won't take this other child from me!"

Another cause of Carmen Elgazu's suffering was that she could not bring herself to forgive. Only to evoke the memory of hard faces or to hear the revolutionary anthems over the radio would arouse in her an irrepressible surge of anger. Her nephew José, from Madrid! With hammer-blow insistence she kept recalling something the boy once had said to Ignacio on the balcony, something she had overheard when she had opened the door noiselessly. "We'll have to stamp the vipers into the earth and the mothers who bore them!" She could not bring herself to forgive him. Nor Cosme Vila either. Nor Julio, nor the teachers, nor… Ah, God, so many people!

For the first time in her life, Carmen Elgazu even had lost the desire to go to confession. She was suffering much more keenly now than over the death of her father in Bilbao. At that time she had seen her father in his coffin, and death had seemed a natural mystery. Now, even though she should have been able to confess freely, she would not, and this feeling increased her unease.

For his part, Ignacio was going through the most complicated moment of his life. On the day when Matías had to report again to the Telegraph Office, he had to return to the bank. Father and son were in a similar state of confusion and disorientation. The two men went down the stairway together, and as they separated on the sidewalk, it seemed as if their shoulders had grown together and must now be cut apart. Ah, the times that Ignacio had stood looking at his father and had asked him with a shake of the finger, "Have you got a cold?" and Matías Alvear had answered, taking off his hat: "Michelin tires!"—the ritual of a family joke going back to childhood.

The bank director, seeing Ignacio, called him into his office and then was at a loss for something to say. The man seemed to have aged, and it was evident that it surprised him to keep busy over monetary matters under the circumstances. Tower of Babel. Doubtless remembering the violence with which he had refused to hide the assistant manager in his house, he now said to the boy: "They're a mob, a mob. I can't understand how anyone can be capable of such a thing!" Ignacio's appearance made an impression on all his fellows. The death of the assistant manager, whose desk was being occupied by Padrosa, had created a still more abnormal atmosphere.

At the bank, however, the routines remained always the same. The employees changed the direction of their thoughts as they changed their penpoints. Each time the doorman brought in the Barcelona papers at midmorning, everyone's attention turned to the news. This was the high point of the day. How much news there was! "In Catalonia, Durruti, the legendary Anarchist leader, is organizing a column of volunteers prepared to leave at once for an assault on Zaragoza." "The athletes congregated in Barcelona to compete in the abortive People's Olympiad have come out for the Government of the Republic." "The Loyalist air force has bombed rebel concentrations in Huesca, Cordova, and Teruel." No one commented on these items, but everyone displayed a vague satisfaction. And they would laugh, as usual, at anything that might betoken radical subversion. "Did you see the sign Raimundo hung out? It says, 'Members of the militia who so desire will be shaved gratis!'" "Grocery Street is called 'Potemkin Street' now!" "The patrols who are picking up the Fascists, or saying they do, are called 'Domestic servants!'"

Ignacio had only one faithful companion in the bank, the counterpart of Jaime in the Telegraph Office. This was the cashier, who treated him more kindly than ever. "If you need anything, let me know." He was constantly trying to find news items that might please the boy. He would frequently call to him from the cashier's cage and toss him a cigarette. As he went by, he would pat the boy on the shoulder, and if Ignacio seemed especially preoccupied, he would stack the silver coins on the marble counter with the least possible noise.

Ignacio was soon in a much greater state of rebellion than his parents. Why did it have to happen? What had God gained by César's death for His sake? Wasn't He a Pure Essence, sufficient unto Himself?

His hatred was even more bitter than his mother's… And, in addition, he considered that he himself had failed. At the very beginning he had tried to save this one and that one, the assistant manager, and the whole world… and he had succeeded in saving only Marta—though that was much—and Mosén Alberto's servant girl. No one else. And what now? Ah, the harmony that Mosén Francisco had talked to him about! The colors, the forms, the sounds! The cactus plant that fell off a balcony and was caught between the branches of a tree! The limpid skies over Gerona, swept by the transmontane wind! And now here was Durruti, ready to go forth with thousands of volunteers to attack Zaragoza… Here was El Responsable, who had jokingly called the blind people Fascists "because they asked to pass by on the other side." Here was Raimundo, giving away shaves, and here were the newspaper kiosks filled with pamphlets such as: *Sexual Reform in Russia* and *Ten Ways to Induce an Abortion.* If the occasion arose, he, too, would be capable of squeezing a trigger… Anger was increasingly enchaining hearts! And the sun was not to blame for that, nor the dried-up river, but only man, men like himself, human beings with brains like his.

Marta was his great consolation… In the very depths of his being; he took refuge in that love, which had prevailed against events. More than ever he drew nourishment from it. He had never loved her more than on that day when they had gazed at each other in that small round mirror and then thrown it into the river, most of all when they had put their ears to a telegraph pole and Ignacio had cried: "Come here, Marta! You can hear my father's voice!"

And yet he could not visit the girl. David's refusal had been firm. And though Pilar went to the school almost every day on his behalf and kept Marta informed about everything, her absence weighed on Ignacio's heart. It seemed to him unfair, for in his opinion love was made for every moment and most particularly for when the heart was broken. Pilar did not conceal from Ignacio that Marta would not be able to stand that hostile retreat much longer. Oddly enough, since she had learned of César's death, she had languished in the kitchen, frightened by cockroaches and the knocking of the water pipes at night. Besides, David finally had accepted the vacant post on the Committee!

Ignacio pondered, pondered…and sometimes it wore him out. Luckily, he could count on Pilar. Once before, when Ignacio had contracted a venereal disease, Pilar had showed herself mistress of the situation; now she was revealing her courage anew. In spite of the girl's suffering over her double bereavement, first through César's death and later through Mateo's absence, she could be said to have been transformed by the war. She had heard nothing about Mateo since he had left for the frontier. To make matters worse, Don Emilio Santos, the boy's father, was constantly questioning her with his eyes and waiting for her to come back from outside with some news.

In reality, Pilar was as anxious as the others. How could she fail to experience moments of weakness? In her room she sometimes exhausted herself with weeping. After supper she would sit dozing with her elbows on the table. But she was alert to the slightest wish of her family. She would fetch the sugar bowl at the right moment; she would polish the shoes and the metals, scrub the floor, and, uttering minor blasphemies, would keep the flies from coming into the apartment during the heat of the day. Blessed Pilar! She was the pure young presence in that world of ghosts. The only one whose eyes, now that César's were closed, seemed still able to look at the world with innocence.

As for Don Emilio Santos, he felt that his friends' sorrow was his. He would have preferred to avail himself of another hiding place so as to leave them to themselves, but he did not dare even to hint at that. They never forgot that he must close himself in his room without a sound the moment the doorbell rang. With what speed Don Emilio Santos used to comply. Actually he spent long hours in the room debating whether he ought to go out from time to time and try to help with some small tasks. He would have liked to wash his own shirt, his handkerchiefs! Pilar used to scold him while she energetically polished the mirror: "But what nonsense is this you're talking, Don Emilio! Don't I do it to suit you? Aren't you one of the family?"

EVERY time Matías and Ignacio went out, the two women and Don Emilio Santos felt sure they would bring back some comforting news from the street. For their part, father and son kept hoping day after day that good news would await them when they returned home. They were all mistaken. Things were happening in Gerona, all over the world, but nothing could restore to the Alvear family what was missing from it.

There came a time when they lived through the whole day in feverish anticipation of the evening hour of ten. That was the moment when General Queipo de Llano would say "Ahem, Ahem!" as he stood before the microphone in Seville. Then he would add immediately: "Good evening, ladies and gentlemen." This was the ritualistic formula marking the beginning of his nightly talks.

General Queipo de Llano's broadcast had become enormously popular among the "Fascists" in the "Red" zone, among the afflicted families and the wholehearted adherents of the military uprising. Such families would wait all day to hear the whisky voice of the general as if they were expecting manna or great promises. For his talk was their only link "with the other side," their only source of news. In the Alvears' apartment Don Emilio got set to listen long before the customary hour, seated beside the radio that Jaime had given them. Like Mosén Francisco's radio, it was hidden beneath a cover so as to mute the sound, for the ban against listening to "Fascist" broadcasts was strict. If there was interference or if the general was late, Don Emilio Santos began to gnaw his fingernails and press his right cheek tightly against the loudspeaker. "Here, let me," Pilar would beg. At last the general would keep his appointment and a circle would form. Not even Queipo de Llano could restore to the Alvears what they lacked, but it seemed miraculous to hear that "all was not lost," that "the troops were advancing toward Huelva," or that "in the cathedral in Seville a *Te Deum* had been sung."

Unfortunately, this escape did not last long. For the general, as though wishing to justify Colonel Muñoz's opinion of him, often turned unbelievably gross and gave the impression that he was drunk. Matías could not understand why the man found it necessary to fool around as he did, why he could not show a little more respect for the sorrow of his listeners; but so it was. Frequently his level descended to the garbled insult or to the sexual. "Is Mr. Eden certain that his wife, Mrs. Eden, *Lady* Eden, is not two-timing him? And what about *Monsieur* Blum? Isn't someone putting a pair of the large-size horns on *Monsieur* Blum, the kind so frequently worn by the French *messieurs*? Oh, forgive me, young lady radio listeners!" Carmen Elgazu was horrified. Never knowing whether he might not finally come out with something more specific or would go back to talking about the Cathedral in Seville, she would turn off the radio. As for Ignacio, he considered it an evil augury that the general, actually the mouthpiece of Marta's New Spain, should give such massive proof of amorality.

Beginning with the 1st of August, the timetable of the Alvear household was changed. Matías was assigned the night shift in the Telegraph Office until further notice. Under the circumstances, this was a hard blow to everyone, particularly to Carmen Elgazu. He had to leave the house at ten fifteen every night, just as the Seville radio was emitting General Queipo de Llano's "Ahem, Ahem!"

As if that was not enough, it was dangerous to pass through the streets at that hour. Julio García himself advised Matías: "Have someone go with you." Immediately Ignacio settled the question: "I'll go with you." He would not agree to let anyone else do it. And as Matías was to return every morning at six, another dangerous hour—it was then that a patrol pompously calling itself "the Dawn Patrol" was out—Ignacio was to go and meet his father for the return trip.

That was agreed upon, and the new rhythm was established. Every night on the way to the Post Office, Matías Alvear felt at once happy and unfortunate. Happy because few things in life could give him as much pleasure as walking through the streets with Ignacio; unfortunate because a man like him had to be escorted to and from work.

The nights were warm. Father and son scanned the darkness with the thousand eyes lent by fear. The trip was short, but to them it seemed endless, for any shadow might cease to be what it appeared to be and become an enemy. The vapor arising from the asphalt and the stones was still hot, for all day the sun had scorched the earth. The passersby, in shirt-sleeves or undervests, were dragging their feet. On the balconies men could be seen smoking. Falling stars were a frequent sight. It was not unusual to meet a couple of militiamen escorting some captive toward the Seminary. One night they thought they recognized El Rubio among the prisoners. It might be he, simply because the man was smiling. When they came to the Plaza San Agustín, now called Plaza Odessa, they would glance at the neglected stairways to motion picture theaters that had not reopened their doors. Militiamen were constantly running down the stairs to the public urinals, not caring whether they said MEN or WOMEN. At the Post Office, Matías and Ignacio would go in through the side door, used in times past by Julio García, on which it said: "*Do not enter.*" Once inside, they spoke to Jaime. Whether or not there was a guard in the building, Ignacio never left until he had seen his father settled at his desk wearing the gray jacket and with the headpiece to his ear.

The trip at dawn was different. The revolution was asleep in the streets of Gerona, wide awake in the outskirts. There the dead bodies were visible in turn to the truck drivers, the gypsies, and the workmen going past in cars or on bicycles. Dawn was the time of silence and slight chills along the spinal cord. Matías invariably appeared at three minutes past six, and his expression was always one of joy and almost of gratitude because Ignacio was there waiting for him, playing at avoiding the cracks in the pavement or staring absently at the copper lion into which the people of Gerona had dropped their letters from time immemorial.

"Hello, son!"

"Hello, father!"

They seldom talked much. Sometimes a car would speed by with rifles pointing at the lower floors of the houses or the militia would stop them on the bridge: "Your papers!" Matías would bite his lips and show his credentials. Ignacio would show his. From some building a revolutionary anthem suddenly would burst forth. The songs had become a nightmare to Matías; Ignacio, on the other hand, would parody them. He hated them all except "To the Barricades." For some reason this song moved him as if touching something deep within him. He struggled against it and refused to admit it to anyone, but there it was.

On the night of the 4th of August, something unexpected happened. They were searched as they went out, and the atmosphere smelled of gunpowder. People were saying that some "Fascist" airplanes had bombed the city, aiming for the powder magazine and the railway bridge. No one knew whether or not to lock himself in his home; everyone was a neophyte in warfare. Ignacio kept close beside his father on their way to the Post Office, and as they said goodbye, his father warned him: "Be careful!"

As he turned to leave, Ignacio recognized the Balilla that had once belonged to Don Santiago Estrada and now belonged to David and Olga. The car was parked at the corner. He saw the schoolmistress perfectly, and she made a gesture inviting him to get in. Ignacio ostentatiously took the opposite direction. The car started after him, came abreast of him, and Olga's voice echoed clearly: "Ignacio, we have to talk to you." Ignacio kept going and turned onto the parterre of the Plaza Odessa, where wheeled traffic was forbidden.

He increased his pace and made a wide circle with the object of throwing the teachers off his trail. In the headquarters of the Communist Party there were more lights, more flags than usual, and the cats were staring uneasily in every direction and making sudden sallies.

Ignacio finally headed toward the Fishermen's Bridge and paused there awhile, looking at the reflections in the water. He was in no hurry now. He felt the need to light a cigarette and stroll, as if saying goodbye to things he had loved. He was thinking of David and Olga. How could they have grown so remote from him in such a final manner? They had been friends, all three of them, intimate friends. They had spent hours and days together, questioning the world with subtlety and loving one another. David and Olga had exerted a powerful influence over him, over his development. He owed to them his ability to think and act simultaneously and the evidence that man lives surrounded by secrets. But, suddenly, strange songs had flown around the city. Hymns of challenge, honoring contrary words. Then everything was turned upside down and Ignacio had seen and heard Olga at the top of the Rambla, screaming "Pigs!" at some nuns because they were going to vote, and he had heard from David's own lips: "Half the men will die that the other half may live." A vertiginous and pitiless contagion had been contracted. "Olga, in my mind, you're my wife sometimes." One day Ignacio had spoken to Olga in this fashion while he was still studying for his high school diploma. He had been falling in love with the teacher unawares. His hand would move toward Olga's head to caress her smooth, shining black hair. And with her eyes she had let him love her. Now it had all gone up in smoke and not an ember was left, not even a reflection in the river water. Now the proximity of the teachers aroused repugnance in him, as if they belonged to another species. What did David and Olga hope to gain? Why did they cross the city a hundred times a day? What kind of purification would be suitable at the other end of that sea of blood? Why had David consented to become a member of the Committee? Ignacio felt warm. From the bridge he could see the balcony of his house facing the river. He could see light inside it, because everyone was forbidden to close the Venetian blinds or the French windows as a precaution against "sharpshooters." In that apartment, César had loved him, and in that apartment, he still loved César, his parents, and Pilar. Why were the teachers showing off those hunting jackets and why was Olga wearing a red kerchief around her neck?

He went down the steps from the bridge and out into the Rambla, fifty yards from his house.

"Get in, Ignacio… We have to talk to you."

There was David and Olga's Balilla. They had stopped to wait for him. He went on, refusing to notice them.

"It's on account of Marta. Please."

Ignacio stopped. Olga had opened the car door. She was smoking. Since when had she smoked? Above the windshield a straw figurine, a clown, dangled on the windshield. Ignacio threw away his stub and Olga hers.

"Come on, don't be stubborn."

Ignacio looked toward the balcony of his house. Pilar was there, waiting for him… "They're expecting me."

"It won't take long."

Ignacio got into the back seat, and the car started. David's hands looked strange gripping a steering wheel. Olga's profile still had authority.

David said: "Before we start to talk about Marta… Is there any chance at all that you could go on thinking of us as friends?"

"Not the slightest."

David paused a moment. "All right. Agreed."

Olga corrected him: "No, it's not all right. It's all wrong." Then she added, "Worse than wrong."

Ignacio made a grimace as if he were cleaning his teeth, and then said: "Couldn't we cut this short?"

David nodded. He noticed that he had taken the road to the cemetery and made an abrupt swerve.

"What's the matter, David?"

"Nothing."

Driving perfectly, he entered the Calle de Albareda and stopped in front of the City Hall.

"We won't be disturbed here."

Indeed, no one was about and the colonnades lent the plaza a particular intimacy. The car was parked about twenty yards away from what had been the Diocesan Museum, and in a few seconds the clown on the windshield had stopped swinging.

"Marta says for you to get her out of there. She can't take any more..." David was looking at Ignacio in the rearview mirror.

"You may be sure she did ask it," Olga said, taking another cigarette. "It's up to you."

Ignacio frowned. For a moment he felt discouraged. Every minute a new decision! He tried to speak and his voice failed him. He cleared his throat and said: "I'll have to talk to her."

"Impossible. We've already told you that you couldn't. We don't want you to be seen in the school."

"Then you'll just have to overlook it."

Olga turned part way around. Seeing Ignacio's face, she thought: "Ignacio is suffering." It brought a catch to the teacher's voice: "Why won't you help us a little, Ignacio? This is all very sad, terrible. We know it as well as you do. Why won't you help us?"

Olga's voice came to Ignacio enveloped in the smoke from her cigarette. A strong, black, unfamiliar smoke.

"What kind of tobacco is that?" Ignacio asked, coughing.

The schoolteachers were silent for an instant.

"I'm sorry, Ignacio," Olga replied. "It's Russian tobacco."

She turned toward the boy, making an effort to be natural. "With a tip, you see, so it can be smoked with a glove on."

Ignacio realized that he must conquer his nervousness, that he had to do it for Marta's sake.

"Tell Marta that Pilar will come and see her tomorrow." He loosened his tie. "I'll think about what I ought to do."

Some militiamen approached them, and seeing the UGT flag on the radiator, went on their way with a clenched-fist salute.

Ignacio cleared his throat again.

"That business about the bombing tonight is one of Cosme Vila's inventions," David told him. "You can rest easy about that."

Ignacio lied: "I'm already resting easy."

Olga turned her head to face Ignacio directly. The teacher's eyes scanned the boy's face. Ignacio felt them as a troth can be sensed.

"Ignacio...can't we be friends? We need you..." Ignacio stared at the door handle. "We're in great doubt, do you know that? Honestly...we're not sure of anything."

"With your permission, I'll go," Ignacio said. He tightened the knot of his tie.

"You'll go anyway, with or without my permission," Olga chided.

Ignacio's expression changed as he felt a flash of anger: "Do you mind telling me what it is you want?" He struck with his fist the back of the seat against which David and Olga were leaning. "What do you want of me? What do you stand for? What does David stand for as a fiery member of the Anti-Fascist Committee in this immortal city?"

Ignacio's face was momentarily distorted. And Olga's too. David, on the other hand, remained calm.

"If I remember correctly," the schoolmaster said, "it was not any member of the Committee who proclaimed a state of war."

Ignacio stared insolently at the back of David's neck. "I know that," he replied. "I know my history. That's what *El Demócrata* says, and what foreign correspondents are reporting. But I'm right here, and I've lived through all of this, minute by minute."

"We know your version from A to Z, too, the version of the armed forces' radio," Olga said. "They revolted as a preventive measure, because the Communists were going to rise up in November."

Ignacio agreed. "It so happens that this version is the truth."

David, calm as ever, turned his profile to them. "And how are you going to prove that? Has some leader told you so? Has Stalin said so? And was it going to be precisely in November?"

Another mouthful of smoke assailed Ignacio, and the boy waved it away with his hand as he would brush aside a fly. "Throw that cigarette away, please, Olga! Throw it away..."

Olga complied. Then she turned toward Ignacio. Her face was composed. In an insolently sweet tone she said: "That's the first time you've called me Olga..."

When Ignacio heard this, he wanted to stay there. He did not know what had happened. A kind of voluptuous curiosity came over him. This was not the first time that Olga's nearness had suddenly brought about a change of mind in him. One afternoon shortly before he had completed his high school work,

Ignacio had been able to do nothing but laugh in school. Olga had come to stand in front of him, saying, "Be honest, Ignacio. Which would you rather do, laugh or cry?" The boy had been embarrassed and felt ready to suffer all the pain of the world himself.

This time, however, David's admirable control influenced him. Ignacio was too disturbed to countenance David's emotionless talk of Stalin, the Committee, the nightly inventions of Cosme Vila. A throng of words uttered by the three of them in the days of their friendship, a parade of thoughts forged through their common effort, came into the boy's mind. Ignacio forgot his haste, even forgot that Pilar was waiting for him on the balcony.

"What hurts me most," he began, as though the syllables were being dragged out of him, "is knowing that when you talk about your affection, you're sincere."

"Heavens!" Olga cried.

"Yes, that's the trouble. I'd rather that you were a couple of fakers."

David touched the car key briefly. "That's a fine compliment."

Ignacio added: "It hurts me because your very sincerity shows just how blind you are. You've chosen your road"—his words were dragging again—"and to follow it you'd wipe out the past... You'd even wipe out each other if need be."

Involuntarily Olga made a frivolous comment: "It's you who are wiping out our friendship."

That made Ignacio angry. "Please, Olga. It's you, spending the day with your clenched fist in the air, who's wiping out my friendship for you. Making check marks on a list of 'rebels' means wiping out my friendship until the end of time."

David intervened. "Be quiet, Ignacio. We haven't made any check marks on any list," he swore. "Keep cool..."

Ignacio smiled and put another cigarette in his mouth, lighting it with a trembling hand. He took the first draw, and immediately Olga took his hand away and removed it neatly from his mouth to smoke it herself. Ignacio stared at her, controlled himself, and spoke to David.

"You can check a list by compliance," Ignacio said in a firm tone. "Of course you haven't checked one with your own hand, and you'll probably never squeeze the trigger of a gun, but you're accomplices all the same." He paused. "You're partners in the bloodshed that's spattering us all."

David's hands were motionless on the wheel.

"Ignacio, take it easy!" David was about to add something more, but the same thing happened to him as to Olga; he saw the sad, angry eyes of the boy in the rearview mirror and thought: "Ignacio is suffering."

David declared: "We're not partners in anything. We're the same as we always were."

"I know that!" Ignacio exclaimed. "Inseparable, perfect… The integrated couple."

"What's wrong with that?"

At this point Ignacio was transformed as he had been once before in the apartment on the Rambla on the occasion of Mosén Alberto's visit. He felt ready to rid his heart of all he was carrying in it, and he did so, to the sad perplexity of David and Olga.

"Being integrated may be a bad thing, David," he began. "You've spent years laying down the rules in the district and almost throughout the city. Your attitudes are the law to many; they were to me in the past. So that if Olga strikes a nun in the Rambla, then poor Santi, and with him all the poor Santis in Gerona—and they are legion—automatically discovers not only that nuns can be slapped, but that it must be healthy to do it, a sign of security. And so the chain begins…a chain that in a country like ours leads to the lethal gun at the end of it. Anything I could tell you about how much I loved you would fall short of the mark. I adored you, as I now adore my parents and Pilar. I went running, leaping, to see you every night at the school, and every night I went back home thinking I had learned something fundamental. Only in the UGT did I begin to suspect that beneath your Socialism and your theories lay a deep resentment. The February elections confirmed my fears, and now, you see… You're here, there, and everywhere with a red kerchief around your neck and driving a stolen car. Oh, yes, a great many things have happened since you inculcated in the students the idea that the scent of wax is detestable, there in San Feliu de Guixols, among the pines! You've come a long way… You spent your lives crying out against the fanatics—watch out for Mateo, watch out for Warning Voice—and now you yourselves are more fanatical than anyone. Adoring freedom, but you don't permit your enemies to be buried in a coffin and you harass them so they don't even dare to go to work without an escort. And all for what? I don't know. What do you expect to find on the tips of those flags? A better world? Will Cosme Vila be a better man some day? Will El Responsable? Well, answer me! Here you've got a flesh-and-blood boy behind you and he's shaking. This is not a question for the blackboard or a manual on pedagogy; it's a question of a man who's ready to listen to you. But you can't answer me. I can guess it from your attitude. Yes, I can see it because there are nights like this, days like today, clear nights when people go through the streets in their undershirts. Why bawl me out, in any case? You've made your bed, as I've made mine, as César made his! The individual no longer counts with you—only the masses. The first law counts less with you than the favorable news vomited out by the radio. This is the avalanche that sweeps everything along with it. None of your pals, none of your revolutionary comrades will wear a hat, and the architects Massana and Ribas even try to hide the fact that they're well educated. What's happening? Tell me. Will everything rise to a higher level some day? If there is no God, how can a miracle like that be possible? Heretics of the world, unite! All those who work in the mines, in the fields, on the sea, unite! All who suffer, all who feel downtrodden or injured, unite! It's unthinkable that you're not aware that everyone has to suffer in his turn and that what is an injury to me may not be an injury to Padrosa or to Tower of Babel. Oh, no, don't be impatient! And, please, Olga, leave that puppet alone… I'm almost through. But first I want to tell you one thing, to explain to you the reason that has moved me to accuse you this sultry night. It's not a matter of an idea, but of a fact, a fact I lived through at daybreak in the cemetery, beneath a gray sky where I saw a hundred dead bodies lined up, and one of them was César's… No, no, I won't dwell on a particular one! I just want to remind you of the number: a hundred. Naturally I'm young yet, and as you can see, I'm too sad to put my mind to prophesying. I'll avail myself, however, of what César, my brother, said to me one day: 'Ignacio, what makes me happiest is to feel that I love,' and I'll venture to anticipate that if you keep on the road you're following, God knows why, for it's dyed red, most likely you'll consider yourselves defeated at the end of it. I'm not referring now to the struggle, to the war, for that's the unforeseeable; I mean that you'll have lost your happiness."

Ignacio finished speaking, and a sudden calm came over him. How hot it was! People were wiping off sweat as they went by. It would be easier to breathe under the arches. The tension inside the parked car was so great that it seemed as if Ignacio was still talking or the motor running. Olga raised her window not knowing why.

It was David who answered Ignacio. As soon as the schoolmaster was sure that Ignacio was not going to add anything, he struck the steering wheel two leisurely blows as if to indicate that his turn had come. He began to speak immediately. He would have spoken very sternly, for he knew that Ignacio had exceeded all limits, had he not been reminding himself again and again: "He's suffering." Yes, he understood that to have demonstrated such a lack of moderation in his speech, Ignacio must also have passed the limits of suffering. Olga, noticing that David was about to speak in his turn, rested her head on his shoulder, prepared to listen.

"Ignacio…all that you've just said is pretty strong. Yes, you've been unfair. I'd venture to say too unfair; and if circumstances were otherwise, you may be sure I'd answer you differently. No, don't move! And please don't say: 'You can answer me however you like.' I'm not intending to do that. I'm taking into account that you're excited; and that this isn't just a sultry night to you, it's a bad night... I only wish you knew how unfair you've been. You've placed on our shoulders responsibilities that don't belong there, not by any means. You would have spoken otherwise if it had been Olga and I who...well, what does it matter! Now it turns out that even our integrity is diabolical; and that the murder of nuns took place because Olga insulted them during the February elections. No, Ignacio, that's not true. Two people—we're still talking about Olga and me—are hardly big enough to have unleashed this orgy. It seems logical to admit that we've all been guilty in one way or another, and that, to cite one example, the Church itself has been creating the popular hatred of the Church, little by little, from a base of errors, intolerance, and omissions, as you yourself in former days, were given to cataloguing them with extreme accuracy. As for allusion to Santi, that hurt me, believe me. For you know very well that if Santi used to strangle goldfish and is now going around with a machine gun, he did it and he does it *in spite of* and not *as a consequence of* all we've taught him. In the past you used to bear in mind, too, before passing judgment, the importance of heredity and of the education received in childhood. I think I can even remember that you used to sum this all up by saying: 'Ideas are transmitted through the blood.' So we're accomplices, are we? Ah, who can doubt it? What do you want? We're bound to one another by nature. The strange thing is that you don't remember that the one who revealed this to you was Olga, when you were both discussing the 'collective soul' in the philosophy class. Oh, well, I could go on talking, knocking down your accusations one by one; but I've already told you I won't, in view of the circumstances and because it seems to me I saw Pilar on the balcony waiting for you... I shall tell you, however, that what moved me to accept the position on the Committee was not the orgy of blood you spoke of, but the defense of some principles that we consider more lasting than militia patrols. No, I'm not going to work for the Committee to add my death crosses to the lists, Ignacio, but to erase all of them I can. And oh, how I wish I'd sat there on the first day, and Olga, too; perhaps there would be less mourning in the city, and you may accuse us because of that omission. It's clear that I've wounded you in your flesh; but we still think this is an eruption, fully as horrible as you say; but it would be worse to assent to Fascism in Spain. In fact I feel that I'm better able to make common cause some day with Future, even with Cosme Vila, than with Mateo and Warning Voice. For Future is a frivolity and Cosme Vila would shock the people of this country in the long run with his undisciplined temperament. On the other hand, Mateo and Warning Voice not only know what they want, but also have speedy means of imposing their ideas. There lies the key to the mistake. We partisans of democracy find ourselves forced at a certain moment to beg help of and even issue guns to what the Fascists call the mob and which perhaps is one; that is, to men like Teo and El Responsable. On the other hand, when it's Fascism that's making the attack, it can find its servers among well-dressed and apparently honorable people. Mosén Alberto and Don Jorge's son, for example. People 'not previously known to the police.' Seen from the ground floor, there can be little doubt as to who's right; but in the long view, everything looks different. That's all, Ignacio, that's all, for the time being… I think you must understand our position now. We're not in agreement with anything that's happening now. Number One is still operative for us, and if it lay in our hands to do so, we'd settle the whole thing with a stroke of the pen; we'd give you back César, and your father would be able to go to the Telegraph Office alone. But granting that our country is as it is and not otherwise, granting that nothing can be done peaceably here, we must adapt ourselves. We were dreamers, of course, putting so much faith in blackboards; but, I repeat that it was not the blackboards that declared a state of war, nor are they what is killing as many innocents in Valladolid and Burgos and Galicia as are being killed here. Referring back to what you said at the end, about the inevitable loss of our happiness, what can I tell you? Ignacio, we are not under any illusions. Olga and I lost our happiness a long time ago; we lost it at the moment that we inherited from our parents a brain that can think. We are not motivated by selfishness—you're wrong there; we are motivated by thought. We think, and therefore we seek difficult and sometimes unhappy paths. But what can we do about it? It can't be helped. You know very well it can't be helped, Ignacio, because the same thing is happening to you… If you could not think, you wouldn't be afraid sitting there in the back seat of this car you say has been stolen…and I repeat you shouldn't have said such unjust things. But that's the way life is, and I cherish the hope that some day we may understand one another."

Ignacio did not answer. Ignacio said nothing. He was indeed afraid, and his hands ached. He looked at the back of Olga's neck, at the arches in the plaza. He thought that a rain of shooting stars was falling at that very moment.

A great discouragement took possession of him, and he suddenly decided to go. He took hold of the door handle. "All right, let's call it a day," he said abruptly. And he opened the door and bent over to get out. "Goodbye until another time." He paused a moment then turned and looked at the two teachers. Olga returned his stare.

"Until some other time, Ignacio."

"Goodbye."

The boy stepped down, and for a moment his legs felt weak. Then he started to walk and almost staggered. He heard the grinding of the car motor as it passed alongside him, and he said to himself that when all was said and done, the one true thing that David had said came near the end—that all three of them had lost their happiness long before.

When he came to the Rambla, the shoeshine boy from the café was loudly playing "To the Barricades." The anthem moved him as it always had. There were lights in almost all the windows, for the order not to close the blinds was scrupulously obeyed. From a distance he could see the door of his house and Julio García coming through it.

Ignacio stood still a minute. He could not even begin to guess what had caused the policeman to pay them a visit. He hastened his step, ran quickly up the stairway, and found himself in the dining room of his house in an instant. For the first time since the 18th of July a wave of lightheartedness held sway.

It pertained to Pilar. Julio García had just brought them great news: on the 21st of July, Mateo had reached Perpignan without mishap, together with Jorge. Their names were on the latest list officially sent by the French authorities to the Civil Government.

Ignacio tried to control himself, to overcome the mental fatigue caused by his interview with the teachers. Pilar deserved this and more. He went to his sister and kissed her on the forehead.

"Thank you, Ignacio."

"I'm glad, *petite*."

"Thank you,"

Ignacio approached his mother and kissed her hair as usual.

"Hello, son!"

Ignacio did not move, he did not take his lips away from Carmen Elgazu's hair.

"Don't forget to congratulate Don Emilio, too," Carmen Elgazu suggested. "Go and do it right now, Ignacio."

Ignacio complied at once. Of course! How stupid of him! Mateo was Don Emilio Santos's son. Hand in hand with Pilar, he went to the room that he shared with Don Emilio. They opened the door slowly so as not to alarm him. Don Emilio was on his feet in the middle of the room, brilliant in a pair of canary yellow pajamas which had once belonged to Matías Alvear.

"Congratulations, Don Emilio! Congratulations on Mateo's account…"

Don Emilio smiled so brightly that the yellow of the pajamas gleamed. Ignacio went to meet him and opened his arms.

"Thank you, Ignacio." Don Emilio embraced him. "I felt in my heart that it would happen someday."

They held their embrace. Ignacio did not dare to break away, for he sensed that Don Emilio was weeping.

Pilar was jealous and went to them. "So you don't love me, Don Emilio?"

"What!" Don Emilio freed himself from Ignacio and moved to embrace the girl. But Pilar slipped quickly away, laughing, and went to the door.

"Ah, aha!"

Ignacio stared at Don Emilio. The expression on the face of the former director of the Tobacco Office was beatific. Ignacio again recalled César's phrase: "What gives me the greatest pleasure is to feel that I love."

FIVE

EVENTS were moving rapidly, and so great was their complexity that on the one hand they stimulated the imagination and on the other encouraged credulity. Anything was possible, anything likely. The most discreet people were surprised to find themselves forming strange cabals or making an effort to present the fantastic as real and based on logic. Few persons escaped this contagion.

Obviously those who yielded least to fantasy were the General, Colonel Muñoz, and Major Campos, still riveted to their maps and military data. The three chiefs relied additionally on firsthand reports that came to them through the meetings of the Ovid Lodge, as well as through the incessant trips made by Colonel Muñoz and Julio García to Barcelona, where they had friends in the Commissariat of Defense itself, particularly Lieutenant Colonel Díaz Sandino of the Air Force who was in command of all operations relative to his branch of the service, and Don Carlos Ayestarán, head of the Health Services.

The sum of all the reports gathered by these commandants demonstrated the truth of their prophecies. The word "war" was beginning to circulate, though many people still believed the balloon would collapse soon. Already there was talk of "the front," the "enemy line," "operations," "strategy." Mola's project—to advance toward Irún at the head of the Navarrese troops—was becoming known as "the Northern front." The advance of Queipo de Llano, already crowned by the conquest of the city of Huelva, had become "the Southern front." The "Central front" was constituted by the fighting that had broken out in Somosierra and the Guadarrama Mountains between the volunteers for "Spanish Renewal" and the Falange from Castile and the heterogeneous volunteers from Madrid. The most talked-of front, however, was the "Aragón front" owing to the column organized by Durruti in Barcelona with the object of taking Zaragoza. Zaragoza was, of course, the quid, the key point, not only because of its geographical situation, but also because, according to rumors, no fewer than thirty thousand clandestinely organized militant Anarchists were waiting inside the city, all ready to charge into the streets at a moment's warning and facilitate the entry of the column from Barcelona.

And that was not all, in the opinion of Colonel Muñoz. Brother Muñoz had brought back proof that foreign intervention on both sides of the Spanish conflict already had begun. In fact, the Government of the Republic had sent a commission to Paris to solicit from Léon Blum and the French Air Minister, Pierre Cot, the urgent dispatch of four Potez machines. The effort had been successful except for the recruiting of pilots. At the same time, some French and Belgian volunteers had crossed the border into Spain at Hendaye. They were ready to collaborate in the defense of the Basque country, threatened by Mola's Requetés coming up from Navarre. And, what was still more important, the Comintern and the Profintern in Prague, hastily called into session, agreed to organize a propaganda campaign through all of Russia immediately and to set up an extensive network in factories and democratic centers in many other countries. Some Spanish delegates, La Pasionaria and Jesús Hernández, had been present at the meeting. The members further agreed to activate a previously prepared plan for a brigade of five thousand international volunteers with whatever equipment they would need to operate independently and to displace Spain if the opportunity arose. Meanwhile, aid to the Rebels was following a similar course. Their SOS had obtained from Mussolini the expedition of some squadrons of "Savoia 81s," the exact number unknown. The aircraft were based in Africa, of necessity, and had been assigned to begin transporting troops from Morocco to the Peninsula at once. Nothing definite was known regarding help from Hitler; on the other hand, Portugal already had gone into action, offering her ports and opening her land frontiers to the passage of whatever arms and men the Rebels might be able to obtain.

The business meeting of the Ovid Lodge, in the course of which these and other facts formally were laid before the members, took place in the Calle del Pavo on August 6th, the feast of the Transfiguration of Jesus. It was the whim of Brother Julián Cervera always to call the extraordinary business sessions on days designated as feast days on the Catholic calendar. Not one of the Brothers was absent, not even Antonio Casal, who could not understand why they were still required to wear white gloves in the Lodge in the midst of such bloody events.

Colonel Muñoz, speaking in the name of the military men present at the business meeting in the Gerona Lodge, emphasized his fear that foreign participation in the struggle initiated in Spain might harm more than help the government of Madrid, in view of the lack of any guarantee whatsoever that the men defending the Republic would make good use of the matériel received, while the Rebels, professional soldiers, undoubtedly would utilize theirs to the last round of ammunition.

"The situation is as follows," Brother Muñoz announced. "The forces fighting on our side lack unity. They're guerrilla fighters who will rush impulsively hither and thither without any planned strategy whether they are in the South, in Madrid, or ready to go to Aragón. For lack of commanders, they are completely undisciplined and untrained. The only officers they can turn to are the ones called 'finger-made,' that is, men commissioned by the simple expedient of pointing them out with the index finger, 'You, Lieutenant,' 'You, Captain.'

"In Somosierra, military decisions are taken by majority vote. Almost invariably the one with the loudest voice gets his way. Any jackass dares to plan victories simply by standing in front of a map, and even in the Ministry of War there are some who will defend the thesis that a shoeshine boy may suddenly reveal himself a genius of strategy. The voluntary character of the militia permits a man to disobey or to obey, to answer back 'I don't feel like it,' or simply to throw away his gun and take off for the home front whenever it suits him.

"As for the execution of the officers in the Land, Sea, and Air arms, that was outright suicide for us. This is how it all adds up: the greater part of the naval units and all the Mediterranean and Cantabrian ports are in our possession, but we haven't a single man who knows what a rudder is. The naval officers at the Cartagena base were executed wholesale; data regarding other ports are lacking. And given the length of the coastline, the naval squadrons may constitute the decisive force! About the air arm and the artillery, the less said the better. On the Cordovan front, cases have been cited of artillerymen who have fired into our own lines, and of others who, seeing that the batteries were overshooting, had recourse to the intelligent stratagem of pulling back the guns."

Brother Muñoz took out a slip of paper and read it over to himself before going on. Evidently its contents interested him, for his tone of voice kept growing more and more solemn.

"Brother Díaz Sandino of the Northeastern Iberian Lodge in Barcelona, a lieutenant colonel in the Air Force, informs us that a Loyalist aviator named Rexach took off on August 1st from the Prat airfield and headed for Ceuta to bomb it on his own. Brother Carlos Ayestarán, from the same Northeastern Iberian Lodge, head of the Health Services in Barcelona, reports that the militia are taking their women to the front with them, and that the miners in Asturias carried out their nocturnal ambuscades by the inconceivable method of advancing on the enemy posts singing the 'Internationale' at the top of their lungs.

"I could go on and on giving examples, but that's not necessary. Each brother in the Ovid Lodge will be sent a full memo. For the moment let me add, because it affects Gerona, only that the names adopted by the battalions or the companies of a hundred men now being formed in our city and beginning to encamp in the suburbs, are more eloquent than any notes of mine. 'Germ Company,' captained by Future. 'The Jackals of Progress,' captained by Gorki. 'The Anti-Fascist Hyenas,' whose command is being disputed by Murillo and El Cojo, and so on and so on."

Brother Muñoz put away his notes, took off his glasses, and concluded, staring at the audience: "Personally, nothing that has been specifically reported strikes me funny. Quite the contrary, and I don't mind wishing that Brother Julio García could share my standards and save his ironical expression for other less serious circumstances."

A long silence ensued. Colonel Muñoz stepped down from the platform and went to take a seat near the Jakim column. Brother Julián Cervera, who was presiding over the business meeting, thereupon rose and went forward to voice some suggestions made advisable by the facts Brother Muñoz had just given them and those previously reported to him.

The first suggestion: To send off a new message to the Government of the Republic in Madrid and the provincial government at Barcelona, pledging the loyalty of the Ovid Lodge.

The second suggestion: To send the main lodges in France, England, and the United States a detailed report on the situation in the region, playing down the unfavorable portents.

Third suggestion: To report to the said lodges the aid Portugal was lending to the Rebel troops, as well as the outright support given during the first nights of the Revolution by the lighthouses on the Rock of Gibraltar to the Fascist convoys from Morocco that had crossed the Straits carrying regular troops and abundant equipment.

Fourth suggestion: To veto the admission of women to the battlefronts, to the front lines, and consign them to the auxiliary services.

Fifth suggestion: To accept the offer of two ambulances and a train of medical supplies offered by the lodges of Paris, and to delegate Brother Julio García to report on them to Brother Carlos Ayestarán, head of the Health Services in Barcelona.

Sixth suggestion: To request Major Campos, the eminent artillery officer and Dr. Rosselló, the illustrious surgeon, to join up with the militia of Gerona and make ready at once to leave for the Aragón front as members of the Durruti column.

At the conclusion of the reading, Brother Julián Cervera sat down without comment, and debate and the round of questions began immediately.

Julio García was the first to speak. Going up to Colonel Muñoz, he begged his pardon for his earlier grimaces, fruit of an incorrigible mania for seeking the satirical side of everything. "Forgive me," Julio repeated, bowing. Brother Muñoz bowed in turn and the incident was closed.

Major Campos spoke next. He had hardly risen before everyone noted that the suggestion urging him to hasten to the front had been a shock to his nerves, perhaps owing to his advanced years. He declared himself ready to comply. "Just give the word," he said. His voice was strong, even though at the moment when Brother Julián Cervera named him he had felt that he would die in the venture. For some reason he had instantly pictured himself at the bottom of one of the reddish Aragón ravines, near Durruti's command post, bleeding to death beside the battery assigned to him.

Brother Rosselló talked at length. He, too, accepted the suggestion made for him. He was not a courageous man, he never had been. His personal life, however, was in such a period of chaos that he thought the decision might possibly restore some sense to it. The escape of his son Miguel in a Falangist shirt and the indifference with which his two daughters had treated him since the outbreak of the Revolution had made him feel diminished. When he had heard Brother Julián Cervera's suggestion, he had said to himself that perhaps he might find healing for himself through dedication to his own work, surgery. Not only could a surgeon do good at the front, but he also could practice his profession there as nowhere else. He fell in love with the idea! He looked at Major Campos and, joining his hands, sent him a fraternal salute from where he was sitting.

The remaining business had to do with procedure. The architects Massana and Ribas asked the Ovid Lodge to go on record publicly against the murders committed by the Gerona and Provincial Committees. They were told that such crimes were lamentable, but the Brothers did not proceed to phrase the protest officially and collectively. Antonio Casal then asked whether his work in the bosom of the Committee was to remain the same. "The same," he was told. "Try to reconcile the criteria, to achieve unity."

Then the business meeting adjourned. The brothers of the Ovid Lodge left in pairs. Julio invited Antonio Casal to have coffee with him in the football players' café where Ignacio used to go to play billiards.

Antonio Casal smiled. "Don't you like bullets, Julio?"

"For myself, yes," exclaimed the policeman. "I'm crazy about them! I'm thinking only of my wife, see?"

Antonio Casal smiled again. Looking at him, Julio García raised his coffee cup and said: "Your health, my dear Socialist."

In accord with the opinion of the professional officers, it was palpable that the unexpected, shocking news that in Gerona and the province the recruiting of volunteers for the Aragón front still was open—and the no less amazingly favorable response—had run through the "neutral masses" mentioned by David and Olga and shaken the revolutionary forces like a train of powder. The entire city realized that this fact had lent a new significance to events. Each volunteer respected himself more. Each patrol and night watch understood that what had been done and still was being done in the name of the people was justified. The expected "satiety" had not set in. Many who had not volunteered exclaimed: "Naturally. After all someone's got to go." Canela said to her employer, La Andaluza: "I'll say goodbye, little grandmother. I'm off to the Aragón front with Murillo."

In view of all that, it was clear that the General had been guilty of the sin of superficiality when he had stigmatized the militia as mere "murderers of helpless people." Indeed many of them were ready to give their very lives for the cause they were defending, as many of their comrades already had done elsewhere. Yes, there they were, lined up in the Dehesa—El Cojo, Ideal, Teo, and Murillo, and many and many another! ... And it was unseemly to say ironically, as many of Ignacio's colleagues said, that most of them "were going to the front like novices jumping into the bull ring." Of course there came a moment of unthinking and contagious gaiety; but each man knew in his heart that even in the sunlight the butt end of a rifle can be strangely cold, and Future himself, for all his playacting on top of a truck, wearing a breechclout and issuing orders with a microphone in his hand, knew perfectly well, after his fighting in Barcelona, what fear is and how the world resounds, especially the inner world, when a man is confronted by someone who fires a gun at him.

El Responsable was one of those most convinced of the glorious rightness of it all. Beyond a doubt, El Responsable was enjoying his moment of stardom. He felt no remorse. Why should he? One image buries another. When he received Durruti's order, "Set this up for me," he began to confuse his cap with his brain. He wanted to be the first to enlist, but then there were so many who loved him, beginning with his daughters, and who tried to dissuade him and succeeded. It made no sense to leave the city in Cosme Vila's hands. His closest collaborators, the heads of the people's committees, et al., could all go to the front. Ah, yes, what a triumph for the organization! Being an Anarchist was a wonderful thing. El Responsable kept recalling his childhood, and the pomades he used to sell. Now he was ordering his men to the firing line while he would remain on the home front, always pushing the revolution a little farther ahead.

Perhaps the moment when he most relished his delicious triumph was during the last hour of the night as he was going home through the empty streets with Future beside him. His goal was the centrally located house of Don Jorge, where he had installed himself for the time being. On every corner, through every foot of the city, he could see indications of the work the CNT-FAI was carrying on.

"And to think," El Responsable would say, "that you hesitated to come to Gerona!"

"It was a toss-up all right," Future admitted. "How wrong I was."

"Well, now you see... A lot of work has been done."

"Cosme Vila is burned up."

"Let him keep on burning up."

They were silent a moment gazing at the stars.

"It's a hot summer..."

"What's the difference! We'd be just as warm if it was winter."

They walked on.

"And thirty thousand comrades are waiting in Zaragoza."

"They won't have to wait long."

They stopped to rub the soles of their sandals against the edge of the sidewalk and to snap their cigarette stubs against the wall. Sometimes El Responsable would turn his head and see Future doing setting-up exercises: "One, two, one, two."

"Don't be a fool."

"Well, that's the way I was born."

"Shall we take a leak?"

"Okay..."

"No! Not there. Maybe there's some nuns in those sewers."

If a militia patrol appeared, they stopped it to learn the new countersign.

"The Pope is an old goat."

"Up with Carlos Gardel."

"*¡Salud!*"

"*¡Salud!*"

Don Jorge's apartment appealed to El Responsable. It led him to conclude that the bourgeoisie knew how to live. Each night as he was getting ready for bed, he would say the same thing: "Don Jorge knew what I like when it comes right down to it." He liked his little joke. The pistols shone against the red damask where Future had arranged them in the vestibule, hanging from a cord with the muzzles up, so that they seemed to be giving the clenched-fist salute.

In front of the house, they stared up at the balconies and yawned.

"I don't want to go to bed. I'd like to stay here."

"Come on, there's work to be done tomorrow." As El Responsable said this, he was sitting down on the sidewalk and stretching his legs.

"I'll be damned if I understand you," Future complained, bending his knees to sit down too.

The stars looked down.

COSME Vila was going through a time of confusion… He was still the last member of the Committee to go to bed. Every night his wife would ask him when she heard him enter: "What time is it?" and Cosme Vila would answer as he was taking off his wide belt and glancing in at the little boy: "Three o'clock… three-thirty…or four o'clock."

Cosme Vila would have liked the column for Aragón to be organized by the Communist Party, but Durruti had forestalled him. And that meant great prestige for El Responsable, why deny it? Now the militant Party members who had enlisted, as well as the Socialists and the few men from the Republican Left and Estât Català would all have to ride in Anarchist trucks. He would have liked to strike back, to set an example by being the first to enlist, but the instructions of his immediate chief, Axelrod, were definite: "There's no hurry."

"No hurry." The usual slogan, reminding Cosme Vila of Julio García's tortoise. Vasiliev once had said to him: "There's so much impatience in Spain that the watchword of controlling your nerves and doing things calmly will finally win the day." But what if the FAI should conquer Zaragoza? … Cosme Vila thought that would be a catastrophe, especially if the moral authority should pass into the hands of the Anarchists after all his efforts, and if the CNT flag should become the banner of heroism.

Axelrod, a man of fifty, born in Tiflis, had laughed at such quibbling. Axelrod had a saying of Lenin to answer each of Cosme Vila's doubts. During his latest trip to Gerona he had noticed that the local leader was becoming obsessed with the desire to conquer, and he went straight to the point. "Victory?" he said harshly. "What does victory matter? We're realistic and practical men. No leader ought to believe we're necessarily going to win. The essential thing is to draw the masses closer and closer to us." This text of Lenin's completely disconcerted Cosme Vila, as he had been disconcerted by learning from Axelrod that the father of the Russian Revolution often quoted Christ in his speeches and writings. "Simple slogans for the masses, dear Cosme. But the leaders have to be useful, believe me…"

Cosme Vila applied himself to the best of his ability. But Axelrod made him uneasy. Vasiliev was a hundred times more transparent, which might be attributable to the fact that he spoke Spanish better. Axelrod was a symbol of contradiction. Round-faced and rosy-cheeked like a bourgeois, with a black patch over one eye like a pirate, a hat like a Chicago gangster's, an impeccable woolen suit. Axelrod was the first Russian Cosme Vila had seen dressed in Western style. His voice was somewhat weak, but everything that voice uttered was like a hammer stroke. "Flatter Morales's vanity, and you'll be able to play with him like a doll." "Send Gorki to the front, he'll make trouble here." "Try to keep Teo and La Valenciana fighting and loving as they've been doing." "You need furious energy, more and more furious." "Lenin detested people who would spend half a year talking about bombs but never made a single bomb." Axelrod did not seem happy. A rictus of sadness hovered about his mouth. Morales used to say all Russians were sad because they never knew whether they were Asiatics or Europeans, nor whether such an immense land mass as theirs was a blessing or a curse. Axelrod gave the impression that he followed the rules like an automaton whether or not he privately approved of them. "Will you be capable of understanding this?" he asked Cosme Vila on the August day when the Ovid Lodge held its meeting, that is, on the day of the Transfiguration of Jesus. "My dog obeys me, even though he may have ideas other than mine. Now it's up to us to be dogs! The second stage will come later." Axelrod's lieutenant, Goriev by name, was a chain-smoker of the same cigarettes as Olga's, Russian cigarettes with a long mouthpiece, suitable for smoking while wearing gloves.

Cosme Vila resembled El Responsable in one thing: neither of them felt any remorse. Their memories were prodigious. They consistently believed that tears are only water and that the enemy must be exterminated. For all that, an odd thing was happening to Cosme Vila: he was less sure of himself than everyone in the city supposed, a detail that had not escaped Axelrod. Such a short span of time had elapsed since he used to read Marx on the sly in the bank, that he soon began to doubt that his personal preparation was consonant with the sweep of the work he had set in motion. The least mistake—particularly if it was a psychological mistake—would have to be paid for so dearly! Lenin had said: "Let's look for youth!" But the truth was that some people could grow old in a single day.

Cosme Vila was as much afraid of the multitude as of society, whether in the street or in his office. In the street the constant saluting of the militia intimidated him—"*¡Salud!*" "*¡Salud!*"—and he could not reconcile himself to the idea of having a car. In the office of the Party the new ID cards that he had to sign every morning intimidated him. Certainly the photographs on the ID cards that went across his desk upset him. Those narrow foreheads, those eyes, and those jaws, and those ears all indicated century-old maladies, "shrieked of hunger" as Antonio Casal had said on one occasion. The file drawer that held them was deeper than Julio García's file of suicides, and the mummification of those faces negated any hope of raising their level in one generation.

Loneliness... Cosme Vila was suffering, basically, from an unutterable loneliness, and that might also have surprised his collaborators, with the exception of Morales, the ironical and nearsighted Professor Morales, who could read Cosme Vila as easily as the snow that falls can be read on the earth. He was Cosme Vila's confidant, the only man with whom the latter really could enjoy chatting as El Responsable chatted with Future. The time of day they liked best was late afternoon, and the place the Party car that Crespo, the former taxi driver, guided skillfully toward the outskirts of Gerona, along the road to Figueras.

The same thing happened every time. They would start to talk about trifles to rest their minds, but as soon as they saw that they were surrounded by trees, by open space, the small talk would begin to dwindle away and they would wrestle with assorted subjects and always end with the same one: the revolution, attention to detail, the need for discipline, and at what point of blind evolution nature had arrived.

"What bothers me most," Morales used to say, "is that you have no sense of humor. Axelrod is serious, but he can see a joke. When do you ever laugh? Shall I tell you a joke?"

Cosme Vila would shake his head and regret that he had never taken up smoking. "That doesn't bother me. I've got other things to worry about." They would pause while the car rolled ahead. "This living in the present and forever thinking of the future. Do you know what I mean, Morales? I never move a finger without a plan."

"I understand," the professor would say. "You'd like to do something just because..."

"Exactly."

"Those who start off doing things for no particular reason usually end up by wanting to do them according to a plan..."

"All right! But isn't there a happy medium?"

Morales would rub his hands as if he were enjoying himself. "I don't think so."

When they came to a certain spot on the road that led to Figueras, Cosme Vila would tap on the glass between the seats with a pencil, and Crespo, the driver, would turn around.

"We're going to have to send Gorki to the front."

"That's good."

"Why?"

Morales laughed. "Can't I feel glad just because?"

All along the way they could see revolutionary placards spotting the countryside.

"All this is wonderful, no matter what... You'll see!"

"I am highly amused by it," Morales remarked.

"Amused is hardly the right word."

"Come, come! You can't teach me the dictionary."

ANTONIO Casal, the Socialist member of the Committee, was experiencing a period of perplexity and anxiety. He was obsessed by the pessimism he had glimpsed in the three military officers in the Lodge. He did not care who was to organize the column to go to Zaragoza, but he did care about the possibility that it might fail. As Julio García was saying goodbye to Antonio Casal after their talk in the football players' café, he decided that the Socialist leader was not made for an active part in an armed struggle. "It's on account of the three children," the policeman said to himself.

Casal was still a fanatic on statistics and the economy. He translated everything into numbers as the transmontane wind brings a change that clears the sky. The testimony at the Lodge regarding foreign intervention on both sides made him dizzy. He was convinced that nobody gives away anything and that both the Italian Savoia planes and the French Potez would be collected for by their respective governments in one way or another. How much was a single day of war costing Spain? He could not figure it out. He had asked Major Campos the cost of a single round of ammunition and the reply had given him gooseflesh. "That's simple enough," the artillery officer had answered, counting on his fingers. "Let's see. Every man your friends shoot...costs about six pesetas." The major added, "Mercy shots aside."

But Antonio Casal's greatest worry, even greater than such waste, was over the question of his courage... Boldness, valor... The valor that such vast numbers of men were displaying all over the length and breadth of the land. He, too, would have liked to enlist—he had a good replacement on the UGT in David—but the mere word "enlist" terrified him. True, he was the best typographer in the city, and *El Demócrata* would not come out every day without him, but it hurt him to be a coward. Yes, Casal knew that he completely lacked the boldness to die, even to kill. When he read that a train conductor in Andalusia charged a convoy transporting Rebel soldiers singlehanded, he took the cotton out of his ear in respect. "Maybe I'm not like the others," he confessed to his wife. "But I couldn't do it! There's no use talking. I couldn't do it..."

Casal was a paradoxical man. All his acts were determined, conditioned, by the fixed belief of which Ignacio had spoken: that the single person, the individual, was doomed to disappear, that sooner or later the individual would be wiped out by the spirit of the times, which, as he saw it, was socialization. Repeatedly he had said to David and Olga: "Socialization is an irrefutable fact. Everything personal will vanish, as a stack of straw is blown away by a hurricane." Very well, he would suffer for each man individually, beginning with his youngest child and ending with those longhaired, ascetic Hindus, those ageless men, with bare ribs, whose photographs were published in *El Tradicionalista,* standing beside Western missionaries.

Antonio Casal's advantage over Cosme Vila and El Responsable was that his capacity for admiration was boundless. Ever since he had attained the age of reason, he had walked on tiptoe so often that he envied those who walked heavily. His opinion of Cosme Vila was: "He walks as if he knows where he's going," and he thought the same of David and Olga. On the other hand, he could not understand the other Masons in the Ovid Lodge. What did they stand for, after all? Were they democrats? Were Colonel Muñoz, Julio García, the architects, democrats? Why was there so much hierarchy, so much protocol? Why the white gloves? Of all the executives of the Republic, the one he admired most was the Socialist leader, Indalecio Prieto, whose actions denoted both an inborn talent for leadership and experience as a businessman from the North. Besides, Prieto had been the only man who, in a radio address, had asked mercy for the conquered.

Antonio Casal felt no remorse either... His hands were clean. And besides, the final cause was just. For years he had felt that in his heart. Since he had been a child. Ever since his parents had eaten the dove that used to perch in the window embrasure. But, despite his exalted temperament and his nervous hands, he was a theoretician; in practice, scabs, tumors, and ugly lumps never mentioned in the textbooks were breaking out. But he would carry out his obligations, and the UGT would continue on its course. *El Demócrata* would go on, too, quietly and monotonously. Yes, it would go on, struggling against "superstition, ignorance, backwardness, and the accumulation of capital in individual hands."

MURILLO had obtained a post on the Committee. In spite of the opposition of Cosme Vila, Comrade Murillo, the Trotskyite leader of Gerona, had seated himself at his desk and provided himself with a chair and a pencil. "Don't worry," he said seriously to Cosme Vila, "I'll soon be going to the front." Cosme Vila replied, "That I would like to see."

Murillo's situation was plain as daylight. Together with Andrés Nin, the Trotskyite leader in Barcelona, he had decided to organize the POUM in Gerona with all formality. Andrés Nin had made a deep impression on him and had guided the first steps of the indolent Murillo, with his limp hair and mustache and his bovine look, toward the beginning of an understanding of the labyrinthine and varied world of "old Trotsky," as Andrés Nin called him.

They had their own headquarters now: Mateo's old apartment. They had their office, once Mateo's, in which nothing remained but the desiccated bird and some books, one of which contained the selected writings of Trotsky! They lacked nothing except prestige, firmness. And Murillo was convinced that only a reasonably long stay at the front, on the firing line, could provide him with the aura needed to captivate the wills of men who had never been satisfied. "I'm going to the front. I'll come back with some decorations, then get to work."

Murillo was taking it all very seriously. Of course he lacked a formation. But until a few months ago he had not even known what a "formation" was. Fate had decreed that he would find some texts by Trotsky in Mateo's library, preceded by a splendid biography of the dissident Russian. Murillo spent twenty-four hours lying on Mateo's bed reading almost without a pause, and drinking even more coffee than Mosén Francisco. How moved he felt! What coincidences in timing he found! To begin with, Trotsky had been born on the 26th of October, 1877, that is, on the very day the first Russian Revolution broke out. Then "old Trotsky," with his powerful head and little goat's beard, had written much later some things now acquiring a disturbing reality in Spain. "The revolutionary energies of the workers and soldiers must be combined." "A weak man may transform himself into a strong man, a giant, once he finds his niche." Trotsky had been expelled from school! Trotsky had also mocked the Eucharist, apparently...

Murillo had Alfredo, the Andalusian, a "direct representative of the people," and a total of twelve party members to reckon with. When he closed the book on Trotsky, he went into the bathroom and stared at himself in the mirror. He did not know whether he would turn out to be a hero or the opposite. Perhaps he lacked the stimulus to be able to conduct a dialogue with someone ... Alfredo and Salvio were too harsh and incisive. Andrés Nin had said to him: "Always behave as if one million dead were watching you." Yes, indeed... If only Canela would want to go to the front with him! The girl had promised to, but she was so capricious...

Murillo had covered the front balcony with a huge sign: POUM. He was sleeping in Mateo's bed. Salvio was sleeping in Don Emilio Santos's bed, and both were being taken care of by the servant girl, Orencia, who informed against a couple of "Fascists" at least once a day.

The house was situated on the Plaza de la Estación. Pilar used to go there often and sit for a time in front of the building. If Murillo went out on the balcony, she would stare at him with a mixture of hatred, repugnance, and jealousy. One time when Murillo went down to the street, he passed close to Pilar. She noticed that the Trotskyite leader was wearing a pair of Mateo's shoes, and the sight of them moved her. She rose and followed him a long way, trying to step where the jaded man with the mustache had stepped.

THE differences in shading among the leaders counted for little, however. Everything was annulled by one concrete fact: some companies of militia had encamped in the Dehesa, ready to march away. They had come from the four corners of the province. The radio summons had been like the African tom-toms mentioned by Dr. Relken in his memorable meeting.

What a lot of breechclouts! ... What did it matter! Worn-out rope-soled sandals...an unimportant detail! The trucks were there, twenty-two of them, lined up in Indian file. They had been requisitioned from the garages, and now the immense trees in the Dehesa seemed to extend a protective awning over them.

Names were not listed: all that would be done in Barcelona. Everyone felt excited at the moment when they were issued their aluminum plates, cups, and canteens. Those three utensils to which they were already accustomed, suited the militiamen better than their rifles. Ah, the clatter of aluminum ware beneath the millions of green leaves! And the friendships formed in the twinkling of an eye!

"Hey, you... Shall we go together?"

"Sure, why not?"

"My name is Lucas."

Laughter rang out, and here and there some militiamen started long arguments at their own risk. These were the men who wanted to stand out, to shed their anonymity. "Anyone who doesn't want to play this game"—slapping himself on the cheek—"might as well go on home!" "I put a padlock between my wife's legs! You can believe that!" Some militiamen wandered among the groups, shaking hands with strangers. A freckled boy, slightly hunchbacked, kept asking various people: "What would happen to the world if it suddenly turned out that all the money is false?" And another was saying to those just arriving: "Now you take me, I'm not interested in anything but Hernán Cortés."

Not as many women were to be seen as the General's and Colonel Muñoz's speeches had led one to believe. A couple of dozen had come down from the villages, apple-cheeked and wearing blue smocks and very full trousers. Caps were worn at will. They suited some very well, others very badly. El Cojo was limping around them, taking pictures. "Oh, you're stupid! I've already got a man." El Cojo kept thinking: "When shall I be someone's man? When?"

The outstanding girl from Gerona was La Valenciana, clinging to Teo, while Merche, the eldest daughter of El Responsable, clung to Future. Canela, who unhesitatingly had accepted Murillo's invitation, had brought six other prostitutes with her. About ten domestic servants also had signed up. Since the disappearance of their employers, they had been jobless. The most conspicuous of these was the woman who had worked in the house of Noguer, the notary. Her name was Milagros, and though Andalusian, she was as merry as a pair of castanets. Milagros did not want to choose any man so soon, without any rhyme or reason. "When we get to where we're going, I'll see if I can find what I'm looking for."

As soon as the women were issued their rifles, they were transformed. None of them gave the impression that she was about to attack; they all seemed disposed to defend themselves.

Each member of the militia knew his own inner truth, and the nearer the moment of departure came, the more he would feel the cold chill along the skin which a new turn in life is bound to produce. Plus the thrill of the historic moment. Those remaining behind in Gerona, those not going to fight over the earth of Aragón, no longer breathed as before. They would be set apart, and would feel their alienation from their fellows. Whether anyone wished it or not, everything soon would relate to the militia at the front. If the weather turned warm, people would say: "They must be roasting in Aragón." If it turned cold, they would say: "Think of the frost in Aragón." When the moon was at the full, lending poetry to men's dreams, they would think: "Aragón must be beautiful in the moonlight."

And when *El Demócrata* and *El Proletario* would begin to issue news of the beginning of the first days of actual war... And when the first coffin would arrive in Gerona...

At the last moment the families began to feel an anxious yearning. "Ask for whatever you want, son, whatever you need. We'll send you packages." "Packages? Bah!" "Write, son, write. You know that..." "I'll write, don't worry." "And don't take any unnecessary risks, because you..." "There's always some risk, but I told you not to worry." Future, issuing orders from the top of a truck, noticed that everyone there was sharing a mood of gaiety not likely to reoccur.

Among the mass of about five hundred men were some whose situation was unusual. For example, Dimas, from Salt. Dimas had enlisted. He could not get "that business about the seminarian" out of his head. He had felt depressed, and the possibility of a change of environment was to him like a shower from heaven. In the Dehesa his great stature, his pallor, his profile like that of a "sick man" or a "criminal" lent him an air of pathos. Teo asked him: "Are you sure you can stand this?" Dimas eyed him uneasily and did not answer.

Gorki's situation was unusual too. Gorki was an Aragónese, and his little belly shook with delight whenever he thought about entering Zaragoza. He would stand as if turned to stone whenever he looked at the rifle they just had given him. Cosme Vila said to him: "In Barcelona, Axelrod will give you your instructions." The total number of enlisted Communists was not above thirty, and they were lost among the hundreds of the FAI's red neckerchiefs.

Major Campos also went to the meeting ground, true to the task imposed on him by the Ovid Lodge. He had not dared to report in uniform. Presentiments of death continued to depress him, and he tried to distract his mind by counting again and again the volunteers, the vehicles, the blond men, the dark men…

As for Dr. Rosselló, he was content on two scores: because he was leaving Gerona and because he had had a message from Barcelona that he would be given the use of a fully equipped ambulance. Some of the militiamen had recognized him and were whispering nearby: "Does he think we're tubercular, or what?"

As a farewell gesture, El Responsable had organized a march of the volunteers through the main streets of the city. It was a grand public show. A stand had been erected on the Rambla where the dance floor used to be set up for the *sardanas*. The authorities came in full force, from the General to the Labor Inspector. The parade marched past Alfredo, Casal, Julio García, Cosme Vila, and the Costa brothers, who were trying to avoid being photographed. Some of the banners were waggish: "On to Portugal!" "We're the Second Coming!" This last was carried by Ideal. A great crowd was gathered, and when the revolutionary songs were played, they raised their clenched fists and held them aloft like statues.

Half an hour later, the militiamen climbed into the trucks in the presence of an immense number of people. The first comers automatically took the roofs of the cabs and sat down with their feet dangling. The others were settling themselves and beginning to be aware that the vehicles were uncomfortable. Finally the caravan started to move. The hour had struck. "To Zaragoza! To Zaragoza!" The time was four o'clock in the afternoon, and the sun was turning the banners to fire. The rumble of the motors was so loud that the noise seemed to smother the sidewalks and the mortar in the buildings. Some balconies were filled with watchers as during the Holy Week processions; others were vacant, still others closed in hostility. The militiamen's voices were hoarse from shouting; they wanted to look everywhere at once, and when they spotted a young woman like Future's, they would display their opened shirt fronts to her. As they passed the *tabacalera,* something unexpected occurred: some girls from the FAI rained packages of cigarettes down on them from the windows. "Hurray! Hurrah!" "Come along with me, sweetie!" As they passed the San Feliu de Guixols Station, the engineer on the train saluted them with repeated blasts of the whistle, which moved them as if a ship's siren had blown. At the edge of the city, the militiamen in the home guard felt somewhat ashamed of themselves. "Slackers!" the men in the trucks shouted at them. "Did your grandmother just have a baby, or what?" Fifty yards farther and the volunteers could see nothing of Gerona when they looked back, nothing but an amorphous mass of houses and the straight spires of the bell towers of San Félix and the Cathedral. And suddenly after that nothing but the unending road and trees and fields and grass on both sides. Then they eyed one another with a furtive shudder and some began to sing songs that most of them did not know beyond the first couple of verses.

In the city the departure of the militia left a kind of mental vacuum. The buildings that had shaken to the passing of the trucks stood now as though firm forevermore, and a silence like the stillness of daybreak crept through the streets. Little by little, minds began to seek answers, to formulate questions as fraught with anxiety as the smoke columns that Mateo and Jorge had seen on the plain of the Ampurdán. Those whose hearts were following the militia asked one another whether the Italian Savoia planes that *El Demócrata* kept talking about might not leave off the transport of troops from Morocco for a few hours in order to seek out the caravan, locate it, and bomb it. Those whose hearts were with the defenders of Zaragoza asked one another whether the city could withstand the attack of the Durruti column, which to them seemed apocalyptic. Pessimism gripped La Andaluza's two newest "pupils," both of them cork manufacturers, and everyone else on their side, for it was obvious that the Gerona contingent was only one among the thousand that could be formed all over the nation. Besides, who could deny the greatness and idealism in the faces of those men?

A crucial moment for the volunteers came when the trucks suddenly revealed a view of the sea. The blue of the water seemed to envelop their chests like a decoration. They would have liked to dive in and swim to the horizon, or to tattoo the backs of the houses with their initials and the date. As they passed Arenys de Mar, they could descry the cemetery, motionless under the hill, and its cypresses seemed to be referring to something. But nothing could stop them or curb their enthusiasm. They began to sing again, keeping time to the rhythm of the vehicles. They were surprised that the roads and the streets of the villages they passed through were not bloodstained. Sometimes silhouettes appeared and they were incited to shoot.

When they reached the industrial suburbs of Barcelona, their eyes were round as rings, for some of the combatants scarcely knew the city, and her chimneys and factory buildings stank of the poverty of the workers, of exploitation. The caravan headed for the Marina causeway and the monumental bull ring beyond it, where most of the column would be quartered. Despite the enthusiastic shouts of the people of Gerona, their arrival was less brilliant than they had hoped. Their heroism was nullified in the anonymous mass. So many had come before them, so many had already spent more than twenty-four hours there! The few hurrahs and some welcoming applause hardly could be heard. Some men with yellow stars on their sleeves quickly surrounded the trucks, merely asking where their occupants had come from. "What's the matter, can't you read the signs? Don't they speak loudly enough?" Future kept repeating, "From Gerona! We're all from the province of Gerona!" Major Campos stared around him, vainly seeking a military uniform.

Seeing Durruti, the legendary leader, with his patent-leather visored cap, his wide Sam Browne belt, and his deeply lined face, they all felt an intimate respect and wanted to approach and gather around him. They alighted and began to mingle with the comrades whom chance had placed near them. Some were already talking like veterans, announcing that the column would leave at dawn.

Dr. Rosselló saw a shining ambulance on the corner of the Gran Via and went toward it. There he found Don Carlos Ayestarán, his brother in the Northeastern Iberian Lodge, and head of the Health Services! Don Carlos Ayestarán was a doctor of chemical analysis and a pharmacist. The two men shook hands cordially.

"What luck!" the Health Chief exclaimed. "I was just saying to myself, where am I going to find a real surgeon? And look where I found him! Friend Rosselló, I won't say a word, you already know how I feel. Many thanks!"

Dr. Rosselló felt more deeply moved than he might have expected. The indescribable makeup of the Durruti column, the ingenuousness and senselessness of the majority of the militia, had led him to suspect that his scalpel would have a great deal of work to do, and Don Carlos Ayestarán shared his opinion.

"They look at me askance," Dr. Rosselló said with a smile. "They're so strong they don't even need an aspirin."

Don Carlos Ayestarán stared at two militiamen drinking wine from a wineskin. He scratched an eyebrow and asked: "Friend Rosselló, aren't you perchance a specialist in venereal diseases? Ah, I see Dr. Vega over there! Come with me. I'll introduce you to him. He'll be your assistant."

The night was warm, and it was spent in sleep often broken by a start into wakeful awareness of the unknown that accompanies arrival. The militiamen of the "Germ" Battalion, of "The Jackals of Progress," "The Anti-Fascist Hyenas," "The Eaglets," "The Godless," and so on, were beginning to realize that a man had ceased to be a name, a fingerprint, or a son, and was in truth a novice ready for the spontaneous sacrifice. No one asked them their affiliation, no one gave them a numbered dog-tag; they got nothing but rations and more ammunition. They were quartered by platoons, but this change in the units was practical. A platoon could be formed merely by asking a "finger-made" officer for men.

Many of the volunteers went into the city itself to become better acquainted with it or to say goodbye to it. Some came back drunk, others with women. Of course there were some deserters and some, too, who came back with new recruits. Several of the militia had decided to become sailors when they reached the port, and had signed on a cargo ship bound for Marseille. In Chinatown, Future was like a fish in water with the stars shining on his cap, and he brought back with him some twenty members of the Spectacle Syndicate, scene-shifters, ushers, et al., half of them homosexuals who delighted in calling themselves by women's names. The enlistment of this tribe gave rise to jeers and loud laughter. La Valenciana said to Teo: "You'd better make sure you like me better than those pretty things."

With the first glimpse of dawn the Durruti column, made up of more than two thousand men, left the city and started on its adventure.

The vehicles used ran the gamut from aged motorcycles to trucks of several tons. The tracks were in the majority, the names of their owners or the transport companies to which they had belonged hidden beneath the flags. Many private automobiles lined up, too, and it seemed strange to see cars that always had followed varied itineraries now moving in Indian file, all following the same route. Some of them had been provided with armor. Durruti occupied one. The sheets of armor offered broad surfaces very convenient for writing CNT-FAI, or "We're the Second Coming!" In the line were many small automobiles and a Cadillac, apparently once the property of Romanones, but now occupied by six hotel waiters. The preferred seats still were the roofs of the cars and the running boards. The men on the roofs felt important, and the only thing that caused them a moment's worry was to see a tunnel in the distance ahead.

A multicolored rope that kept unwinding along the roads and highways. The militiamen would see a tree in fruit, some chickens, or a stream of clear water, and they would jump down lightly, saying a jocose goodbye to those who continued on their way. The rabbits were skillfully dispatched. "You today, me tomorrow," they would say as they struck them.

They feasted in the villages. They looted stores. Some volunteers requisitioned practical things, others any piece of junk they could hang from their belts or bullet pouches to serve as an amulet. As the column passed, the village jails were emptied. The militiamen would fire a shot, raise their clenched fists and shout: "To Zaragoza!" In every village some of the children were frightened; not so others, who joyfully would have gone off to war as mascots. Most greatly varied, perhaps, was what the militiamen wore on their heads. Gangsters' hats, handkerchiefs wound into turbans, wide straw sombreros, helmets, broken chamber pots! They would rob the tops of straw stacks to line the broken urinals, but they soon threw the chamber pots into the ditch so that their comrades could no longer bang on them. A hat shop was discovered near Lérida and the collection was enriched. Gorki, appointed a captain, put on a golfer's sports cap, Ideal a bird cage. El Cojo tied an *espadrille* to his head.

From time to time Durruti would look back and fly into a rage: "Brutes! Brutes, I say! Who brought you up?" He was increasingly aware that he would lose half his men before they reached Zaragoza.

Dr. Rosselló was riding in the ambulance. Beside him rode his assistant, Dr. Vega, who seemed a very respectful man. The two doctors were alarmed by the constantly growing number of women. "This is going to turn out a mess." Dr. Vega would always say: "The desideratum."

The "finger-made" officers were more exalted than the others and were a greater success in the villages than the simple militiamen. Future stood out from all the others, giving orders through a swimming instructor's megaphone. Equally conspicuous was an outlandish captain, like Gorki, soon seen wearing a silk hat and with a dog like Axelrod's.

Every heart was involuntarily racing. The militia were experiencing both love and hate. They loved among themselves, they loved one another, through the sweat, the breechclouts, and the common cause. They hated both the anonymous "Fascists" they were leaving behind and those awaiting them ahead, there on the broad plain of Zaragoza. Dimas would study his hands and those of the others. The hands revealed every feeling, each man's past, and some hands, if read correctly, would perhaps foretell a bloody future approaching. Dimas carried an empty tin at his belt for some reason. He would caress it with his fingers as if he had some definite plan for it. Dimas had never set foot on Aragónese land, and when he was told that they had entered upon it, he looked around him and saw two dry ravines and a whitewashed fig tree on the crest of a cliff.

When the column reached a certain point, near Caspe, it broke up. A strong contingent moved to the north, toward Huesca, while another continued southward in the direction of Teruel. Durruti himself went ahead along the highway to Zaragoza with the main body of his troops.

A courier arrived on a motorcycle, bearing a heartening message for Durruti; they would soon be joined by reinforcements from Madrid sent by the CNT-FAI.

The day was ending. The sun had set behind the reddish hills. Within half an hour, the world had changed, become another world. The headlights of the vehicles were switched on, though they were camouflaged and half-covered with burlap. What a man wore on his head mattered little now. The silence was deepening, and once in awhile a head would be thrown back and a pair of eyes would blink at the indifferent stars.

From within the trucks came the sound of oaths, kisses, barking, and snores. Some of the drivers looked tired and longed for sleep. They drew on their cigarettes, and suddenly the motors seemed to fall silent in order to let the buzzing of brains be heard.

SIX

MARTA had resolved to leave the school. She said so first to the teachers and then to Pilar. The girl felt that she could no longer bear to live with Olga, much less with David, who had accepted membership on the Committee. She would have liked best to escape to France, but she refused to do so as long as her father had not yet come to trial, and she pretended not to hear Ignacio's advice on the subject. "I don't want to leave my father alone here. Find me a hiding place in Barcelona."

"Pilar, tell Ignacio that I won't change my mind."

Marta was still wearing the false braids she had donned on the day of the uprising, and she had aged five years. The only vivid and outstanding feature about her was her eyes, almond-shaped, and her faith in her ideas, her faith in the principles of the Falange. When from her cellar she could hear David and Olga talking about the revolution, or when she turned on the radio to listen to Professor Morales, she affirmed again and again that what was useful in the enemy's theories—Socialism, Anarchism, Communism—was already implicit in the Falange.

A hiding place in Barcelona! Here Ignacio proved his efficiency, or else was lucky. He realized at once that the person indicated to get them out of their difficulties was Julio, and he went straight to his house to ask for help. Julio, in a red dressing gown, flicked the ash off his cigarette. "*Le grand complet!*" he exclaimed. He had rescued Major Martínez de Soria. He had seen to it that the major's wife enjoyed the guard to which she was entitled and that she could continue living in her apartment. Now he would have to round out his task by seeing Marta to safety. "*Le grand complet!*" he repeated. He was delighted at the idea that none other than Olga and David had agreed to hide in their house the only Falangist in the province. "Do you get it, Ignacio? This will have to be carried off by sheer boldness."

Julio asked Ignacio for two days to think it over. He knew so many people in Barcelona! But a great many loose ends would have to be tied up. He sought inspiration of the tortoise and the paperweight in his office, then of Doña Amparo Campo, for once. "What do you think of it?" Doña Amparo made a grimace as if angry and her concentration bore fruit when a name came forth like a projectile: "Ezequiel! Ezequiel. No two ways about it, Julio. He's your man."

She was right. Julio knew it instantly. Ezequiel was an old friend of both husband and wife; he was of pure Barcelona stock, and he ran a Photomaton fifty yards from the Police Headquarters. Julio had known the man when he used to go through the cafés drawing caricatures. His name was Vilaro, but he signed his caricatures "Ezequiel," and the pseudonym had clung to him. At that time he had been a Bohemian, wearing a broadbrimmed black hat and a black string tie and carrying a stick. Julio had given him the idea of setting up a Photomaton near the Police Headquarters. "Identification papers, passports. Do you see what I mean, Eze? You couldn't miss!" And he had not failed. The thing had made money, and Ezequiel felt grateful to Julio. "Eze can't refuse me. I say! He just won't be able to refuse me."

Doña Amparo Campo put their idea into effect. She went to Barcelona on one of the first trains put back in operation to and from the frontier, and had an interview with Ezequiel. He was very fond of Amparo and often used to say to her: "Just let me know when you're a widow."

Everything seemed to favor rescuing Marta, placing her where she wanted to be. Ezequiel was living with his wife, Rosita, a "blessing from God," and his son, Manolín, a model of good sense for a boy of fourteen. They owned their house, a very tranquil one, in San José de la Montaña. It had a back entrance, a garden, and two very handsome pine trees. Besides, Ezequiel and Rosita listened to Queipo de Llano every night! They were "Fascists," though Ezequiel often used to say that it was very hard for a caricaturist to take political leaders and other authorities very seriously. "You know how it is. We see the ridiculous side of things immediately."

Julio reported to the Alvears, and everyone accepted the proposed solution. "The house is quiet, it's on the Calle de Verdi, in the upper section of the city. It has a flat roof and a garden with two pines, a radio, gas, and electricity. As if that weren't enough, the owner's name is Ezequiel. He's nobody's fool. And he's a 'Fascist.'"

Marta was pleased at such a stroke of luck. "It sounds as if you could see all of Barcelona from the roof, even the port." "It seems that the little boy, Manolín, has learned how to make shadow figures on the wall with his fingers, and that Rosita, the wife, can make custards that melt in your mouth."

All of them, including Marta's mother, whom Ignacio visited occasionally, agreed on the fourteenth of August as the day of departure. The risks of the trip were wiped out with one stroke. Julio offered to go with Marta in the car from Police Headquarters! He had to pay the visit to Don Carlos Ayestarán suggested in the Lodge, and took advantage of the occasion to do it.

"In the Police Headquarters' car?"

"Why not, Ignacio? I told you we'd have to be bold to pull this off."

Julio inquired minutely into the matter of Marta's dress. When he learned that the girl was wearing artificial braids, he exclaimed: "She wears braids? Wonderful. So much the better." She was also to wear dark glasses. To carry no packages. And to be dressed in a bright, jaunty blouse and skirt.

Matías Alvear and Carmen Elgazu would have liked to see Marta before her departure, but that was impossible. The schoolteachers had decreed: "Only Pilar." But Ignacio disobeyed them. On the night before she was to leave, the thirteenth, he went resolutely to the school and unhesitatingly jumped over the garden wall.

Olga opened the door and stood there a moment in doubt; but she realized he was doing the natural thing and let him enter.

"Thank you, Olga."

The boy and girl, who felt that centuries had passed since their last meeting, were soon in a long embrace. Each was touched by the traces of suffering imprinted on the other. David had left the house, and Olga discreetly vanished down the hallway.

Ignacio drew his sweetheart to him and feverishly caressed her hair. "Marta, Marta love!" God knows how long they would have stayed in that embrace. The water in the aquarium beside them had turned green. They savored the beauty of being in love, the heartwarming quality of being in love, and felt that love could go far toward compensating for the anger and the flames in the belly of the world. "Everything will turn out right. You must trust in that." "Will you come to see me often?" "As often as I can." "Take care of my mother!" "Naturally, girl."

Ignacio promised Marta he would think of her every moment and would take no risks until after he had counted to a hundred. Marta, for her part, promised that she would not make a move in Barcelona without consulting him. Ignacio was afraid that once the girl's first stupor had passed, she would try to make contact with the surviving Barcelona Falangists, who, according to the radio, had gone underground to carry on their work.

The scene lacked nothing. They took the most they could from every second. Only they two existed at times. It was a scene to be engraved on their hearts.

Ignacio left, said goodbye to Olga, and returned to the city. He interviewed Julio, who confirmed the departure for the following day.

"Do you trust me?" Julio asked Ignacio.

"I don't know why, but I do trust you." Still unsatisfied, he added: "I know I'm a fool, but I trust you."

The next day Julio proved himself worthy of trust. He was exacting in taking care of all the details. At the hour agreed upon, eleven o'clock in the morning, the car from Police Headquarters stopped in front of the school. Julio was sitting in the back, an Assault Guard was driving, and the required official emblem was quivering on the radiator.

First David and Olga appeared at the door. Then they called Marta. She had been waiting for two hours with her braids hanging and her fingers busying themselves nervously with the dark glasses. She said a cold goodbye to the schoolteachers. Her feelings were mixed. And they were no less confused when she got into the car and shook hands with Julio. Marta did not believe that the doing of favors could wipe out a man's past.

The car started and everything seemed unreal to Marta. A prisoner since the 19th of July, she had not caught even a glimpse of the outside world; she had not seen a single placard, and had not been able to imagine how a militiaman would look. She was so disconcerted, and the dark glasses gave her such a strange view of the world, that when the car started, she did not know whether or not to cross herself, and she did not know whether what she was traveling toward was safety or its opposite.

The streets were deserted, the letters UHP defaced the walls, garbage pails were waiting on the sidewalks, and an occasional dog was feasting in them. Julio said to her: "All will go well."

At that very moment Marta started as if she had heard a trumpet blast. A check point, just at the exit of the city. The appearance of the men on duty horrified her, and when she noticed that the car was about to stop, she gave herself up for lost. But there was Julio, putting his head out of the window. "*¡Salud!*" "*¡Salud!*" The car accelerated again, and in a few minutes it was rolling along the road the volunteers had taken, among the same trees, the same fields, bordered on both sides by the same grass.

Marta was drinking in everything she could see ahead of the car. "UHP! Death to Fascism! Long live the FAI! Kill the bourgeoisie!" Every tree bore a white sign, and the letters read in passing formed orders. Someone had written on a road worker's hut, "*Three miles to hell,*" and three consecutive barricades said: "*Nitrate from Chile.*" Why so much nitrate in Chile?

Julio wanted to talk to the girl, but he did not dare. He was waiting for an opportunity to arise. Marta also realized that, as a well-bred girl, she ought to say something to the policeman, but she felt timid. Her father had once said to her: "The bad thing about politics is that men cease to be mere men and become legendary characters." Julio was playing with his hat brim and his cigarette-holder. Marta was toying with a tiny purse Olga had given her.

A few miles farther along, they met a line of swaying cars from the windows of which gun barrels protruded.

"The masters of the world," Julio commented.

Farther still, they passed a steam roller. Two militiamen who must have belonged to some neighboring patrol were seated on top of the roller playing cards. "*¡Salud!*" "*¡Salud!*"

An astonishing sight met Marta's eyes as the car was passing through the square of the village of Calella. Three men standing on a scaffold were striking some bells with tools, to the intense delight of a crowd below, which was applauding the men. The concert was a horrible cacophony. Julio explained that the men were trying to detach the bells so as to melt them down, and it was customary to entertain the populace with such a serenade.

Marta gripped the bag that had belonged to Olga and behind her dark glasses her eyes shone wet for a moment. As they left the town, they heard shots, and farther along enormous streamers tied to the trees hung above the road as if marking the boundary for bicyclists. One of these streamers said: Down with the Military. Marta seemed to sob, and Julio spoke calmly, scolding her: "Child...show some spirit. Come, don't make trouble."

Marta controlled herself, seemed to recover. "I'll try."

Julio felt sorry for the creature beside him. "Don't they say in the Falange that discouragement is forbidden?"

Marta smiled. "That's it, more or less. We say: 'Discouragement can't touch us.'"

"Can't touch!" cried Julio, nodding with feigned admiration. "So, that word is very difficult in the morning, isn't it? Come," he corrected himself, "I like to have my little joke."

Julio said this in such a soft and persuasive voice that Marta stared at him wonderingly.

"Yes, I know," she granted.

The remainder of the trip was uneventful. Courtesy won the day. Julio commented on some details of the countryside, and when the moment came, he gave Marta complete information concerning the family who would be her hosts. Ezequiel was something of a character. He was so tall and thin that he looked like a wire. He had two obsessions: that sea water should be used for irrigation and that the summer energy of the sun should be stored to give off heat in the winter. "He's a great joker, you'll see! His wife's name is Rosita, and she's always taking Ezequiel down a peg by telling him he's as ugly as the photographs that come out of the Photomaton." Their son's name was Manolín and he also had two obsessions: his Meccano set and a gray cat he always carried around in his arms.

Behind her dark glasses, Marta was listening to Julio wide-eyed. Why would people keep doing things that made them irreconcilable? Julio, in turn, was thinking: "This girl is a good listener." And it amused him to recall that he was keeping on his desktop at headquarters a medical kit labeled CAFÉ which Marta had carried into the street with her on the day of the uprising. He had set it next to a skull and some books belonging to Mateo.

When they came to Barcelona, Marta was dumfounded. The streetcars and some taxis had been painted red and black—the colors of the FAI—the colors of the Falange, too. A disturbing breath of sadness emanated from the passersby, especially all those somewhat advanced in years. Here and there small barricades still stood, and girls in blue smocks kept constantly approaching the car asking for donations to the Red Relief. Julio, always with some coins ready, humored the militia girls and invariably said to them: "Okay, this is to buy yourself a lipstick, which you really need."

Marta was much struck by three huge photographs on a hotel façade: Stalin, Durruti, and Azaña. "The mixture as before," Julio remarked. And the people's clothing was very poor indeed. No one wore a hat and few were decently shod. The heat might justify it all, even the undershirts. Wrecked vehicles were still lying about, and the sirens kept up their constant warnings of air raids. The traffic moved with a speed that made her dizzy.

The Headquarters car moved slowly toward the Vía Layetana, toward Ezequiel's photographic shop. It was closed, and Julio looked at his watch. "Of course," he said, "it's after one now." He told the driver to take them to number 315 Calle de Verdi, Ezequiel's house. "Go toward the Diagonal, then I'll direct you."

In a few minutes they halted at the address indicated. The car was parked directly in front of Number 315. It was a low building with a single floor, the property of Ezequiel, who always used to say that he bought it with the money he had made from a caricature commissioned by Maurice Chevalier. Julio put back in his pocket the cigarette-holder he had just taken out and, saying to Marta, "Wait a moment," got out of the car.

He went up to the house, knocked at the door, and a scant five minutes later came out again with a smiling face. "You can get out," he said to Marta. "They're expecting you."

Marta felt touched. For the first time she looked at the policeman with gratitude dominating any other feeling. "Thank you, Julio," she stammered, bending over to get out. "Many thanks."

Julio García seemed to turn shy as he almost always did when dealing with a distinguished person. Marta stepped down and offered Julio her hand. At the last moment, the girl took off her dark glasses so that the policeman could read gratitude even in her eyes.

She stepped up to the sidewalk and waited there for the Headquarters car to leave. She waved at the policeman, and when the car was out of sight, turned and went into the entryway to the house.

She did not need to knock. The door at the top of the three steps leading to the house was open and three persons stood waiting for her. Marta paused. She saw a very tall man, with an ugliness all his own, wearing a string tie around his neck. A woman much younger than he, with sparkling eyes, stood at his right, and a boy of fourteen at his left, holding an enormous, somnolent gray cat. Three people and a cat that were to make up the new family with which she would live beneath the same roof.

After a couple of seconds' scrutiny of them, a scrutiny Marta knew full well would be decisive, she stood still. "I'm Marta..."

Rosita said encouragingly, "Let's skip the formalities, child. Come in, come in..."

Marta went up and into the house. The door closed behind her and the unknown was shut inside.

Ezequiel was smoking a pipe and his face reflected a great, cheerful curiosity. "Guess our names," he challenged in the voice of one accustomed to dealing with strangers.

Marta was slowly scanning their faces, one by one. "You're Ezequiel," she pointed to the man with the pipe. "You're Rosita. You're Manolín." Then she added, "I don't know the cat's name."

"His name is Cat," Ezequiel said. "Honestly. He's the only cat by that name."

Marta smiled and Rosita said to her: "Come on, take off the braids!"

"Oh, that's right!"

Marta took them off, and without them she was changed so greatly that the three figures were touched. Ezequiel and Rosita thought: "Heavens, she needs a tonic!" Manolín was at a loss to explain to himself why anyone moving into the house should be carrying as her only luggage a tiny package and a purse.

The table was already set for lunch. "It's all right. I'll set another place." While Rosita was in the kitchen, Ezequiel undertook to show the newcomer the patio. Marta followed the caricaturist, and was soon exclaiming, "How lovely!" Indeed the patio was clean, sunny, graced with two wooden benches and a pair of tall, beautiful pine trees.

"We'll show you the rest of the house later, especially the roof. You can see all of Barcelona from it, as far as the *Uruguay*." They went back in and Ezequiel declared, "We even have a bathroom."

"What's the *Uruguay*?" Marta asked.

"The ship where the soldiers are being held."

Marta bit her lip. She went into the washroom and came back. Lunch could not have been more opportune. It provided human contact. Marta continued to study her new family, and came to the conclusion that Julio had described them accurately. Ezequiel was undoubtedly a knave, but good as gold, sentimental, and deeply in love with his wife, whom he was always teasing. He kept drawing on his pipe even between courses. His arms were long so that he could set it down on the sideboard every time. Marta was reminded that he was an artist at shadow figures. His main occupation was running the Photomaton now, but occasionally he still toured the cafés to draw caricatures. "The faces come out of the Photomaton looking much worse. Though I maintain that the Photomaton tells the truth."

Rosita was also a Barcelonan and in her time she had been Queen of the Flower Festivals in her section of the city. She listened to Ezequiel with enjoyment, although she stated repeatedly that he was a vain man whom a thousand failures had not cured of his worst fault, prophesying. "I don't have to tell you how it is now with a war on… This is going to happen, that will happen. And upon my word, he's almost never right!" Ezequiel pinched her. Rosita cried "Ouch!" Manolín, spoon in hand, was smiling at his parents, and Marta felt a peace such as she could hardly remember.

After the coffee was served, Rosita handed her a napkin ring. "We don't have one with an M. This is a P." Marta said, "It's all the same to me." But she felt a pang of regret at knowing she could not be completely Marta Martínez de Soria here either.

Ezequiel was busy with his pipe, and Marta withdrew. She heard a voice from the street calling: "*Soli… La Soli!…*" "Durruti in the suburbs of Zaragoza! *La Soli-i-i-!a…*" Marta was thoughtful. Then she heard a monotonous noise proceeding from a neighboring house. It occurred to her that someone might be stamping out counterfeit coins. Manolín spoke up: "Why are they sending up so many balloons, Papa?"

Ezequiel explained, "Reconnaissance."

The time came to clear the table. Rosita told Marta she would show her the rest of the house, particularly the room that was to be hers. "The wallpaper is very pretty. It's all birds and flowers." Ezequiel emptied his pipe, cleaned it, and told Marta he had to go back to the Photomaton: "I open again at four."

"Well," he added, approaching Marta with a quizzical expression, "you see now that we don't eat people. I hardly need to say that the only thing we require of you is that you be prudent. Prudent, and patient enough to put up with Rosita, and that's not easy. Help her a little with the cleaning, that's a mania with her, and that's all. Don't go into the patio if you can help it... The neighbors, you know. But you can go up to the roof whenever you wish; and when you do, you'll tell me right away that the panoramic view is priceless and that'll make me happy. As for Manolín, you'll see that he's a great prankster. I'd like to make you think he's very smart, but actually he's a spoiled child. You'll be in no danger here. Just mention anything you want, and you'll get it."

Marta watched Ezequiel go out and regretted that her host did not dare to wear an artist's broad-brimmed hat. She felt an admiration for him that surprised her, for she had never thought she could admire a man who in no way resembled her father or Ignacio. Obviously Ezequiel was trying to help her to forget the terrible events that had brought her there and that were to stay with her in that house on the Calle de Verdi. But such strange things were happening! Could it be true about Durruti?

After two days, however, Marta had adjusted herself to the people in the house. Ezequiel and Rosita were "her kind of people." Ezequiel would say that to know whom he had to deal with all he had to do was to see the faces of the militiamen in the Photomaton. "If you think they come out good-looking..." Truly the one thing that flattered the Reds was propaganda and the caricatures in the papers. In his opinion the caricaturists were admirable, gifted. And as an example he showed her a recent drawing of Churchill smoking a cannon as a cigar. Ezequiel! He was an ugly man, willful, and optimistic. His habit was to greet them when he came home with the title of some current film: *Kill Yourself to Music* or *The Cruiser Potemkin.* Marta noticed that Ezequiel's obsessions were not two, as Julio had claimed, but three: to distill sea water, to store the heat of the sun, and to talk about Goya. Goya had aroused in him a profound respect, and he would permit no jokes whatever about him. One day Rosita and he climbed into a bus and went to visit Goya's native village of Fuendetodos. Ezequiel alighted and approached the birthplace with a deliberate pace and such piety that he might have been said to have been crawling on his knees.

Marta was enjoying a period of quiet, and David and Olga and the school seemed to her incredibly far away. She was learning to cook a little, to knit, and to pet the cat without annoying it. Occasionally she stared at the trees in the patio and occasionally Rosita would call to her, "Marta, do you want to help me comb my hair?" Rosita's hair was beautiful. When it hung loose, it was like a waterfall. After dark Marta often used to climb up to the flat roof, and as she studied the night sky, she would be reminded of the "falling stars" the Falange had talked about. Ezequiel criticized the Falange in the same manner as Morales had Cosme Vila. "I'll be blowed if you Falangists have any sense of humor."

Marta was suffering from insomnia. Her room was cheering, but her solitude saddened her. In bed in the dark, she sensed the presence of the birds and flowers on the wallpaper, and that bothered her. If she turned on the light, the birds moved. She kept a bottle of cologne on the little night table and often bathed her forehead.

She still refused to read the newspapers. She was curious, but the thought of touching the paper repulsed her. Sometimes, while Ezequiel was reading, she would slip behind him and glance at the headlines from the corner of her eye. They were always much the same: the advances of the people's militia, the defeat and retreat of the Fascists. One day Ezequiel burst into loud laughter. A normal typographical error had appeared in the caption of a war story. It said "*Light siring by canons on the Aragón front.*"

Ezequiel grew fond of Marta, although there was something stubborn and reserved about her, something incompatible with the temperament of the caricaturist. "Someday I'll draw a caricature of you and I'll put only one eye on it, in the middle of the forehead." Rosita had been completely won over to Marta. "If anyone comes to 'liberate' you, he'll have me to contend with." And as she said this she displayed an arm shaped like Carmen Elgazu's. With Manolín, it was a different story. From the first day Marta had signified to the boy a creature who comes from who knows where to awaken our sympathy. Marta treated him as though he were already a man. She did not know how to deal with young boys. This was most stimulating to Ezequiel's son. Being fourteen, he asked Marta the meaning of many things. When he came home from the errands Rosita had given him, the questions were like an avalanche. "Marta, what does draft dodger mean?" "Marta, what does 'Long live death' mean?" "Marta, if I were older, would you marry me?"

Sometimes Manolín brought the girl a present: some small gift such as a stick of licorice or a balloon. One day he brought her a striped balloon like the pajamas Emilio Santos used to wear, and said: "If you love me more than the Falange, keep it to play with. But if you love the Falange better, let it go..."

Ignacio was writing to Marta, addressing his letters to Ezequiel at the Photomaton. Ezequiel had hit upon a movie title to announce to Marta that she had a letter. When he opened the door, he would shout: "*Mail from the Czar!*" and Marta knew what that meant and went flying to meet him.

On particularly hot nights the girl would climb up to the rooftop and stare at the port, where the steamship *Uruguay* lay, the prison ship. And she would think of her father in Gerona and that nothing would sway her from the Falange, not even the nearness of death.

As soon as Julio had left Marta in Ezequiel's care, on the Calle de Verdi, he had driven to Chinatown, where the chauffeur was dismissed until the following day so that the policeman could be freer.

He had three visits to pay before night, but first he would have lunch in Chinatown, filled with memories. During his stay of one long year in the Catalan capital, about 1931, when he had been in service at Police Headquarters, he had picked up several habits, one of which was to have lunch every Saturday in some cheap restaurant in Chinatown. This time he chose the "Restaurant of the Asparagus," so called because there was a miniature bench in the window with a curved back and wooden spindles set horizontally so that they looked like asparagus. The patroness was still there, the green bench was there, only the mirror etched with the words *Anís del Mono* had changed; now it reflected Julio's face older than it had been, more worn, as if too many thoughts had left their stamp on it since then, not to mention a couple of revolutions and a horde of little thwarted appetites.

At the conclusion of his lunch, he looked at his watch. He still had at least two hours free. He began to wander aimlessly through that doleful section of the city. One after another he recognized the establishments and the bars; the young children identical with those of yesterday, the movie houses with their façades still covered with garishly colored stills, and on every corner a woman, all tired eyes and wooden body, like a stalk of asparagus, selling some trinket or other.

The war had brought blue coveralls and belligerent patrols into the quarter. Watermelons were for sale on the street, and the samples, cut in half, looked like wounds from the earth. The shoeshine boys were twins to those in Gerona, with their berets, their cigarettes behind one ear, their speculative glances downward. In one show window a stuffed-looking black cat lay beside a sign saying: NO TOBACCO. At one house with an immense entryway, a notice read: THIS HOUSE INHABITED BY FOREIGN CITIZENS. Another doorway said: THIS HOUSE UNDER THE PROTECTION OF THE TURKISH EMBASSY. At least six times during the short period he spent in the quarter, he had to hand over a donation to the Red Relief.

At four o'clock on the dot he went to pay the first of the three visits he had planned: to the Police Headquarters, to which he had been assigned on his transfer to Catalonia. A newsboy was shouting: "Three militiamen disguised as priests have attacked the rebel airfield in Burgos with hand bombs!" The boy was holding a sherbet in his left hand and licking it appreciatively between shouts.

At the Headquarters he was in luck. Several of his old colleagues were still there, still under the command of Chief Bermúdez, perhaps the most even-tempered and upright man Julio ever had known, even though he had courted Doña Amparo Campo before Julio himself had. He was received with all the warmth that his hat and his ironical little cigarette-holder could inspire. They made him sit down at the desk where he had worked in the past and spent a long time reliving their professional adventures and reminding him how hard it had been for him to pass the target-shooting test. Sensitive as ever to the atmosphere of the clan, Julio invited Bermúdez and each of his friends to have one of the cigars he had brought, and between puffs he heard from his friends' lips how painful it was to them to have to fraternize with the foreigners on the force, to stand by while the militia took the law into their own hands, and to carry out all sorts of disagreeable duties. "There's a great deal of personal vengeance, a great deal," they told Julio. "It's unbelievable." Everyone was giving the police orders, some of them so absurd that the officers did not know whether or not to carry them out. "We suppose the same thing is happening to you in Gerona." They told him that the list of imprisoned policemen was long and that the political parties, not satisfied with the regular prisons available, had begun to equip basements and dungeons and some convents, too, plus a luxurious villa as their "private jails" called "Chekas." "There's no outside control whatever here, and they can do whatever they like with the prisoners." At that time three individuals conspicuously skilled at setting up tortures of the prisoners were a man named García Atadell in Madrid, another by the name of Aurelio Fernández in Barcelona, and a third, Vicente Apellániz in Valencia. A militiaman under the command of the last-named was given to bragging that he had killed so many Fascists "you could light a cigarette on the muzzle of his rifle." Chief Bermúdez informed Julio of the increase in the number of persons taking refuge in embassies and consulates, yet always fearing to fall into an ambush, even so. The crews of foreign ships that put into the harbor to pick up their citizens naturally found the sight of dead bodies in front of the convents a most shocking spectacle.

At the appropriate moment, Julio asked his friends what news they had had of happenings in the rebel zone with regard to executions. Two policemen summed up the opinion: "The same as here, more or less." Bermúdez shook his head. "My impression is that there's no comparison. Of course," he added, "it seems that the ones having the worst time over there are the Protestants and the Masons."

Julio spent a couple of hours with his colleagues, in the course of which they told him that they were getting together a fairly complete file of the bodies admitted daily to the Clinic Hospital morgue. "There are some startling cases; someday you'll see them." Julio agreed, and his eyes scanned everything around him. In spite of everything, he liked his work; he liked it better every day. He felt a kind of inner respect for police work. Even his colleagues inspired it. So much anonymous self-forgetfulness! All those men faced the danger of an ambush, of a malcontent's bullet at the start of every day.

"Why don't you join us in Barcelona? Ask for a transfer."

Julio shook his head. "I'm Don Julio there," he replied with a smile. "Here I'd lose the Don."

His second visit that day was to Don Carlos Ayestarán, head of the Health Services, the handsome analyst and pharmacist who had a political seat in the Provincial Government and a Masonic seat in the Regional Lodge for Northeastern Spain. Don Carlos Ayestarán had recently had a visit from Dr. Rosselló and Major Campos, too. "It seems this month is going to be the month of the friends from Gerona," he said to Julio as they shook hands.

Don Carlos Ayestarán was a cultivated man. He always smelled of eau de cologne. Tall, bald, always wearing a stiff collar. He was one of the five or six men in the city who had not given up wearing a stiff collar. "They'll take you for a Protestant minister," Julio said to him, "And if I were you, I shouldn't care to take the consequences." "A Protestant minister?" laughed Don Carlos Ayestarán. "I'd have a bad time in Salamanca." He had a mania for cleanliness, for hygiene. He used to ascribe a great measure of the catastrophes of the world to a lack of hygiene. "And I'd even attribute a large share of the prevailing ill humor to it. I'll forgive a great deal, but dirt I can't stand. One of the worst defects we Catalans have inherited from the French is the tendency to be dirty." Brother Carlos Ayestarán of the Regional Lodge for Northeastern Spain had ventured to foretell that the Civil War would be won by the side that proved the cleaner, the neater, "a prospect giving no grounds for excessive optimism from the point of view of the Republic," he added.

His enthusiasm for the Republic was contagious. He was a loyal, hardworking man. He believed that under a republican regime, a kind of biological instinct would operate to set each thing in its proper place, each man where he was needed, whereas under the dictatorships, each man's fate would be forced, wrenched into shape by an unlocalized, but very real pressure.

He said to Julio: "Under a Fascist government, who knows? Perhaps you'd end up as an impresario of flamenco dancers and they'd stick me in a laundry."

In accordance with the instructions he had been given by the Ovid Lodge, Julio informed the Health Chief that two ambulances and a shipment of medical supplies, the gift of the French brotherhood, were ready for delivery. Don Carlos Ayestarán all but clapped his hands. "Go on! This is encouraging..." Indeed this was the third donation to Health in a week. The first had come from some Jewish laboratories in the United States and the second from some pious ladies in England.

Don Carlos Ayestarán authorized Julio to bring the voluntary contributions to Spain and to Barcelona. This done, he rose and paced the room, moving his arms as though he felt the absence of the pharmacist's smock with the sleeves secured by strings.

"Don't ever let them deliver anything until it's passed through my Health Service. I'm ready to organize an efficient sanitary network in Catalonia, and I know what might happen here."

Julio replied, "Don't worry."

They chatted awhile longer. Don Carlos Ayestarán asked Julio for details of the revolution in Gerona, and Julio held back nothing. 'I don't like this one bit," Ayestarán commented.

Presently Julio said to him: "My dear friend, while we have the opportunity, could I talk to you about a personal matter?"

Don Carlos's expression changed. "But of course!" he exclaimed going to his desk and seating himself. "You know how highly I value you, Julio."

The policeman thanked him.

The subject was at once simple and complex. Julio wanted only to be a member of one of the provincial delegations that were going abroad to purchase arms, to deposit gold to be drawn on, and to inform international opinion...

Don Carlos turned his head. "We shall see. Be specific. You've mentioned three disparate things. Does that mean that your sole interest is to go abroad?"

Julio denied that. "Not by any means! What interests me is, first: to go with the men buying war matériel. I've named the other two reasons...so as not to inhibit you."

"Now..." Don Carlos folded his hands like one preparing to pray and lifted them to his lips as though to kiss the ends of his fingers. "Permit me one question: What do you know about war matériel?"

"Not a thing."

"Well, then..."

"It's quite simple. I'd like to go in the capacity of a policeman... I'm sure you grasp what I mean. I'd like to have some control over the deals made. How can I put it to you? Large sums of money are involved."

Don Carlos Ayestarán's face cleared. He had been afraid for a moment that Julio was trying to deceive him. Now he thought he understood the policeman. With sudden energy he said: "To sum it all up then... Unless I'm mistaken, what you want is to become a member of the Delegation in the capacity of a policeman without anyone knowing you are one..."

Julio reflected. "Well," he said, "what difference would it make if they did know?"

Don Carlos Ayesterán took a deep breath and leaned back. "I see," he whispered. "Well, that's plain enough."

It hardly seemed possible that everything could be resolved with such speed. That was Don Carlos Ayestarán's *modus operandi.* Once he was convinced of the good intentions of a person who was asking him for something, he would pick up his pen and sign on the dotted line. On this occasion, Julio's proposal was reasonable and worthy of being granted.

"Either I'm greatly mistaken," he said to Julio, "or you can count on being appointed." Julio spread his hands in a gesture of sincere gratitude.

Don Carlos Ayestarán asked him: "Of course you speak French?"

Julio looked at him and smiled. "*Oui, monsieur*," he replied, bobbing his head.

The interview came to an end. Julio rose, and his host rose with him. Don Carlos gazed at the policeman with affection. He admired him and would have liked to have him in Barcelona. Julio cut him short. "By no means! In Gerona they call me Don Julio. Here they'd drop the Don."

Don Carlos accompanied him to the door. On the way he asked: "How old are you, Julio?"

"Forty-seven. Why?"

"Would you like to go to Zaragoza with Durruti?"

"Not on your life."

Don Carlos smiled. "You're a devil."

"No, I'm not. I'm frank."

Don Carlos went on: "Don't you care for shooting?"

"I'd rather play dominoes."

"Why did you join the police force then?"

"For two reasons. First, because as a policeman I can shoot, too. Second, because policemen like to play dominoes."

Just then a knock came at the door, and it opened suddenly to let in a blond boy with a forceful nose and chin. He was carrying a beautiful hourglass in his hand. Don Carlos looked pleased and introduced the two men. "This is my nephew," he said. "He's a great help to me."

"How do you do? I'm Julio."

The boy's voice was clear and even. "My name is Feliciano, but I can't help that. Everyone calls me Moncho."

When Julio García left the Provincial Government office, he strolled through the Gothic quarter of Barcelona and then on to the Ramblas. He went into a café and asked to use the telephone in order to call the Hotel Majestic to arrange the third of the interviews he had planned, by far the most important to him, with Dr. Relken. While he was waiting for his connection, he noticed the title of a forthcoming work lettered on a placard outside: *Syphilis, or All of You for Me.*

Dr. Relken came to the telephone, and when he recognized Julio's voice he let out a jubilant and flattering "Eureka! Come over right away!" the doctor invited, and Julio hung up the receiver and lighted a cigarette with great satisfaction.

On his way to the hotel, Julio asked himself why Dr. Relken intimidated him. He was no superman, not in any way; and yet Julio seldom could behave naturally with him.

The doctor was waiting for him in the lobby of the hotel, and as soon as the two men caught sight of each other they hastened to meet and shook hands effusively with every sign of satisfaction. It seemed to Julio that the doctor was paler than he had been in Gerona, though his eyes were as bright as ever, and of course his hair was still very short. "Ah!" the doctor exclaimed, showing Julio to the dining room, where he had ordered tea for two. "It's a preventive measure. They won't shave my head again as long as it's like this."

The table he had chosen near the windows was quiet and amply ventilated with a fan. And while the doctor was summoning the waiter and tying his napkin around his neck, even for tea, he was recalling nostalgically the "superb dishes" that Doña Amparo Campo used to serve him in Gerona. "How is your wife? I hope she's well… And Colonel Muñoz? And the architects Massana and Ribas?" Gerona had won his heart! The doctor even recalled the regular nightly gatherings at the Neutral. "Do you remember, Julio, how each one of us looked like a thousand in the mirrors? …"

Julio suffered the shower of talk, at a loss to explain to himself the interest the doctor took in Gerona. "I don't know whether he's sincere or whether he's putting it all on." Indeed, the doctor spared him no detail, even asking about the water supply of the Oñar and the Ter and the fate of the Gerona choral group. "In times of war there's quite another kind of singing, isn't there?"

Julio was beginning to feel impatient. There he was in the Hotel Majestic, having tea with pastries only because he expected something to come of their conversation. The policeman felt certain that Dr. Relken, a veteran of so many revolutions, would hold a cool personal viewpoint regarding events in Spain. "We can't see the woods for the trees, you know."

The doctor was playing with him. He kept talking about trivia until after the waiter had served the table and gone away, his napkin over his shoulder. Then he looked at Julio, smiling. "Well, let's see now. What is it you want of me? What's on your mind?"

Julio set the cup of tea on the table because it was burning his fingers. He was preparing to answer Dr. Relken when he saw Axelrod and Goriev go through the hotel lobby with the dog that followed them everywhere.

"Those Russians..." Julio said.

Dr. Relken did not look at them. And he remarked as he took a pastry: "They don't talk to anyone. Only to the dog."

It seemed to Julio that the things that were being said about the Russians must be exaggerated. "I suppose they behave like anyone else," he said, studying Axelrod. "Sometimes they'll talk and sometimes not."

The doctor went on talking without looking toward the lobby. He knotted the napkin more tightly around his neck. "Don't kid yourself, Julio. The Russians don't behave like everyone else." He took another pastry. "Let me add, too, that they are not like everyone else."

The policeman paused a moment or two, and as soon as Axelrod and his escort had vanished inside an automobile, turned his attention again to his interlocutor. "I'd like to know the Russians," he said.

"That would be difficult," the doctor answered, smiling. "I lived in Russia for years and I never succeeded in knowing them."

Julio took a sip of his tea. "All right," he concluded. "Let's get back to what concerns us. Are you prepared for air raids? Thank you very much." Julio took a pastry. "Tell me, what do you think of the rebel soldiers? Let me make myself clear. What is your opinion of the *enemy*?"

The doctor nodded in recognition that the question was not an idle one. "They're not bad. What shall I say?" He reflected a moment. "As I see it, they'll be hard to beat."

Julio's expression showed that he agreed, and the doctor went on: "First of all, I've been very much struck by their stratagem of transporting troops to the Peninsula by air. That was a stroke of genius. It's the first time, to my knowledge, that this has been done in all military history."

Julio did not appear overly alarmed. "However..."

"I know," the doctor anticipated him, "you mean that this is only an opening move. Perhaps so... But don't expect an easy war. The brain that thought of that can think of other things."

Julio took another sip of tea and made a grimace of dislike. "Think of other things? ... I don't know what. They have hardly anything. No important port, no..."

"They have unity," Dr. Relken cut in quickly. "Does that seem to you like nothing? The rebels are united." He summoned the waiter and asked him for a glass of ice water. "Do you remember the importance I've always given to 'being united'? The rebels are united by religion."

Julio reflected, then agreed. "However..."

"Don't talk back to me." The doctor smiled. "You asked my opinion, didn't you? And I'm giving it to you after considerable thought. And there it is." The waiter brought the water. "There's a phrase by a leader of the Republic, Prieto, that has interested me very much. Prieto said that what scared him most in all the world was a Requeté who had just taken communion."

Julio had heard the phrase, but he laughed heartily. "Me, too. And that's the only thing I agree with Prieto about."

"You see?" said the doctor. "You're all dying to contradict one another. You'd give everything you have to prove that your neighbor is an idiot."

Julio agreed and suddenly turned thoughtful. "It's true," he admitted. And lighted a cigarette.

Dr. Relken slowly drank the ice water. Through the clear glass his lips looked enormous, monstrously magnified.

"Do you think then," asked Julio as the doctor set down the glass, "that the Spanish people are heroic?"

The doctor unhesitatingly agreed. "They unquestionably are. Very well, then," he added, "you've put it precisely. The Spanish *people* are heroic; therefore the 'Fascist' soldiers must be heroic, too."

"Why yes, of course..."

"Think what happened in the Alcázar in Toledo. Or in Oviedo. Don't you listen to the enemy radio?"

"No..."

"Well, you ought to. I advise you to."

Julio was showing more and more interest. "And what about our capacity for barbarity, for cruelty?"

"Aha!" exclaimed Dr. Relken with satisfaction. "I was waiting for that. Will I make you happy if I tell you that all countries are alike in that respect?"

"No," Julio denied. "I wouldn't be happy."

"Well, you might as well be, because that's how it is. All collectivities are the same. Where they differ is in the stimuli required by each country."

"But there are nations not capable of plunging themselves into a civil war."

"Is that so? History is long. Can you cite me one country that has not had a civil war?"

Julio frowned.

"England is a civilized nation, isn't it?" Dr. Relken went on with growing authority. "Then what have you to say about the Chamber of Horrors that's on exhibit in London and the archives of criminology at Scotland Yard?" Dr. Relken paused for a moment. "And what about Germany? Musicians, philosophers, all the geniuses you like. But is there a people crueler than the Germans? The Nazis are Germans, don't forget that... And what about the Japanese and the Chinese? Why must you all insist upon believing that the Spaniards are any worse than the rest?"

Julio did not look convinced. "It would seem that every race has certain tendencies of its own..."

"All right! I grant you that..." Dr. Relken was perspiring, and he glanced at the still blades of the fan. "In that respect, my dear friend, you're right. Your people's tendencies are...how shall I say it? Ah, yes! Primitive. They're most primordial."

Julio frowned again.

"How shall I explain it?" added Dr. Relken. "For example...the way you kill. Have you ever noticed that? You kill...capriciously, without any reflection." The doctor stared fixedly at the policeman. "Or, better, you kill without recourse to science."

Julio recoiled. "To science?"

"Oh now, please don't be angry with me! Listen to me, Julio. I'm talking to you in confidence. And I feel close to Doña Amparo... Your people have even gone so far as to shoot a man and then eat his kidneys, fried, there in the province of Cordova." Julio made a face of disgust. "And it seems that when a boy in Madrid goes through the streets shouting, 'Fresh water and cognac!' that means there'll be a shooting at dawn on the meadow of...."

"Of San Isidro?" Julio asked.

"That's it! Of San Isidro. The saints are mixed up in everything, you know."

Julio stubbed out his cigarette in the ashtray.

"That...and many other examples, like the patrol that always selected a poetic spot, with flowers if possible, for its killings. That, my dear Julio...is not of the slightest interest!" The doctor concluded: "Now what is interesting is psychological torture."

Julio sat motionless. The doctor snatched the napkin off his neck and mopped up his perspiration with it. Julio chose not to pursue his questioning, though he did not know why. He intended to keep in memory the strange mien of the doctor as he spoke the words "psychological torture" with such deliberation.

A silence ensued. Julio asked himself again: "Who is this man?" They were alone in the dining room. The waiter had sat down in a corner with his napkin across his knees, settling himself for a nap.

The doctor was growing increasingly agitated. His face had flushed. But his lips were trembling as if he were forcing himself to an extreme. He no longer waited for Julio to ask him questions. He was anticipating them and the replies as well. Indeed, Julio felt a constantly mounting astonishment. What a character the doctor was! Could he be a Communist? What were Axelrod and Gorki doing in the Majestic?

The doctor went on to give him valuable information. He confirmed that the British lighthouses on Gibraltar were aiding rebel ships and that the FAI in Barcelona—which the bellboy in the hotel called the "Federation of Automobiles Impotent"—had seized with a sure instinct four important services: the telephone company, the amusements, the streetcars, and the courts. "How do you like to have the Anarchists holding the scales of justice?" Then he added that, as surely as he sweated rivers, Hitler would try by any and all means to convert Spain into a ground for experimental warfare, while Stalin, for his part, would try to turn Hitler loose on the Western democracies instead of on Russia. "Hitler is Stalin's obsession," he emphasized. If Zaragoza were taken and the rebel resistance put down, nothing would happen; but if the war should last long, the fatherland of his dear friend, Julio, would see the invasion of combatants of all races. "And that would turn out to be very hard on you people." The prostitutes in Barcelona had formed the "Love Syndicate." An announcement in a leftist Barcelonan daily said: "The *democracy* of the silks is in the Cut-Rate Store." The ignorance and lack of discipline of the militia who had left for Aragón were such that several companies had been formed by fives because their officers did not know how to count above that number. Innumerable details he had observed had led him to the conclusion that something visceral—he repeated the word—visceral in Spain was anti-republican; for example, the phrase "to eat à la republic" was synonymous with eating abundantly and poorly, and even the vocabulary of the Spanish atheists was sprinkled with religious references: "Comrades of the UGT, the quota must be paid religiously." Yes, the Spanish people were an astonishing and picturesque lot, a people of short men and tall mountains, a contrast he frequently had noticed. While three leaders of the Estat Català were tossing a stack of Consecrated Hosts into the Ramblas from a rooftop, like bits of paper, a Nationalist in Bilbao, debarred from taking communion because he had inadvertently eaten bread and chocolate, left the church, and putting a finger down his throat, had made himself vomit.

"Hundreds of murderers are emerging in Spain, Julio. You know that as well as I do. But I don't happen to remember the normal figures. It's often been said that certain illnesses predispose people to criminality: schizophrenia—is that it?—hereditary syphilis, paralysis, obesity in combination with a yellow face, a triangular-shaped head, and so on. But then criminals who don't fit into that kind of classification can be seen on every street corner in Spain. In Spain there is a deep need to kill, as it were, perhaps because it is believed here that death is not an end, but merely a stage in the journey to another imagined life that is eternal. Do you know what struck me most in Gerona? That a mother would say to her son as she gave him a pinch: 'Ah, I could kill you.' And that one time when I asked Cosme Vila, 'Hi, Cosme, what are you doing here?' he said to me, 'Killing time.'"

Julio kept shifting from one state of mind to another as he listened to the doctor. Suddenly he grew angry, as if what he was hearing were being said by a man who had been drinking. Dr. Relken came to his peroration by adding that those days had been very intense ones for him, days favorable to his hobbies. He had done a great deal of walking, sniffing here and there. For politics and collective upheavals held a sweeping interest for half of his nature, but only half; the other half would always prefer the minute detail, as, for example, that the hotel maids could sing every morning as if nothing had happened, and that, on the other hand, the animals in the Zoo seemed as upset as if they understood such calamities. Ah, yes, the street was a veritable show, and each man wore his feeling of shock printed on his retina and in his smile, his wish for something vast, and at the same time his nostalgia for a quiet life. Possibly even the plants and inanimate things "were aware" in some way that man was unleashed; but that was another question...

At this point the doctor suddenly passed his hand over his forehead and rose to his feet. Julio, on the contrary, remained riveted to his chair. The doctor looked like a giant standing in front of him. And yet, he was saying that he had risen because he did not feel well.

"As a matter of fact I've not been in good health ever since I came to Barcelona," he explained. He stretched his legs as if to increase the circulation of his blood and added: "That olive oil! And the heat!" And then: "Excuse me, Julio, I have to go to the men's room for a moment."

Alone, Julio was thinking that the doctor did indeed look ill. And for the nth time he asked himself who the man really was. The only thing he knew about him was that he was a Jew from Prague, a naturalized German, and had been expelled by the Nazis. But was it enough for him to live, as he often said, by "interesting myself in minute details" and by theorizing? What about his heart? And his past? What was he seeking? To be sure, it was a pleasure to listen to him; it was not such a pleasure at times to look into his eyes.

When the doctor came back, his pallor had increased to a degree that alarmed Julio, who suggested accompanying him to his room and leaving him alone; but the doctor rejected that with a gesture. "I spend so many hours alone!" he declared abruptly. And he sat down again.

Julio forgot "events" then and devoted himself to the doctor. And for the first time, his interest finally opened a breach in the doctor's armor. The horizontal blades of the fan were turning now, sending cool air over the head of the sleeping waiter.

"Have you any friends, Doctor?"

This was the entering wedge. And Julio had said it without malice, without passing judgment, out of a sincere compassion.

"I think not," replied the doctor. "I don't think even you are one." He crushed his napkin in his hand. "We're together...by chance. And to kill time."

Julio protested. He swore "by all his saints" that he could be considered a true friend and he challenged the doctor to put this to the test under any circumstances. "Ask me for anything whatsoever at any time and you'll see." The doctor grimaced and Julio, understanding, stopped short. He recalled that the doctor had once said to him that in Spain constant proofs of friendship are demanded, whereas friendship was something hidden and perceptive that would endure even through absence and beyond the passing of years. "But don't go to the other extreme now, Doctor. Don't draw the conclusion that any palpable proof of friendship is worthless. You have a dangerous tendency to feel dissatisfied with yourself," Julio went on. "That's the worst of pessimists, I think. The same thing happens to me, and I've fought against it and overcome it. Now I operate on the theory that any mistakes I make could be made by anyone else, from my wife, Amparo Campo—who really adores you—to the mysterious Russian delegate, Axelrod. Listen! The democracy of silks may be in the Cut-Rate stores, but true equality, the democracy of defects, lies in our poor everyday life."

The doctor looked unconvinced. He seemed to be going through a moment of deep demoralization. He was staring at each object on the table as if he could find nothing to relieve him. Not so much as a glass of water! He was suffering. Perhaps he was in worse health than anyone had suspected.

Julio kept quiet, sensing that the only words that could relieve the man would be words spoken by himself. Dr. Relken needed to vomit, like the Nationalist from Bilbao who had made himself do so.

Finally he seemed to recover somewhat. He asked Julio for a cigarette.

"Take it, have a smoke..."

The doctor lighted it and smiled. "Thank you." Then he added: "Dear Julio, my drama is simple enough. I don't know who I am. Do you understand? People take me for an impossible man. Nonsense! Who could classify me? In Gerona I was aware that I was considered an eccentric, or a spy, or a homosexual... I have such an unusual head! But the fact is that I am none of those things. The truth is as I've just said, I don't know who I am. Here I am a man without roots. Expelled from my adopted country, which means I have no place I can call home. Divorced from my wife, which means I have no heart. Voluntarily sterile, that is, a coward. Ah, yes, perhaps my greatest tragedy lies in that, in not having children! You know something about that, too, don't you, Julio? Sometimes it's terrible to think that one will come to an end in one's own self. What am I to do then? To go on to wherever my temperament dictates... Mine has led me to travel, and here I am, occupying a hotel room wherever I am. I spoke earlier of my 'analytical curiosity.' What will become of an individual like me? How does the map look today? I'm always asking myself that. I wander over the world asking, and no one has ever given me an answer. I speak seven languages, but I don't know how to talk to children or old people in any of them. I'm interested in art and I spend my time nowadays buying stolen *objets d'art* without a qualm. I'm an engineer, but I've never built a bridge. All this lacks coherence, doesn't it? Would you like me to make you a prophecy, Julio? I'm going to die soon...and far away from Germany. I don't want the Nazis to kill me. No, I don't want that! They're even worse than a 'Requeté who has just taken communion.' I don't accuse them because that would profit no one; my mind repays me. I say that to you because I know them and because I am sure of what I'm saying. Although...would I be any happier without them? We carry all manner of things inside us, don't you think so, Julio? The misfortune of men like you and me is that we keep needing greater and greater subtleties for our enjoyment. As children we could enjoy watching a frog jump into a pond; now we need many stimulants or a revolution... How can one struggle against this? See here... There's that waiter over there, napping. Look at his legs, his shoes... He's sleeping the sleep of simple souls. The fan makes him happy. When he wakes up, he'll be happy calling me doctor and serving my dinner. He thinks I'm a personage. I have such an unusual head! Neither you nor I serve meals to anyone, and perhaps that's our mistake. However much... Why am I talking to you like this? Yes, I want to live! Ah, yes, believe me, Julio! I go through times like this often; but I soon come out of them. Give me another cigarette, please!"

Julio had not missed a syllable this time either. He had been listening attentively, blowing out mouthfuls of smoke and he kept thinking: "I'm like that, too... That happens to me, too." He, too, was a difficult kind of man, however often his wife might tell him: "A saint, that's what you are." Yes, he lived within himself, true enough. Now he was keeping to himself the idea of going to Paris with a Provincial delegation, to purchase arms. He differed from the doctor in one thing, however: it did not seem terrible to him, quite the contrary, to come to an end with himself. Why pass along to children so much disappointment, so much brooding? To be sure, this was the first time the doctor had spoken to him of death, a word that aroused true horror in Julio. On the other hand, one sentence had pleased him extraordinarily: "My brain repays me." And also this other: "How does the map look today?" And why repudiate analytical curiosity? Was it better to sing in the mornings like the hotel maids or to drowse like the waiter? Undoubtedly the doctor was a sentimental man, his impassivity a pose. He was lucky that his periods of depression were fleeting. Yet, why had he specified "psychological torture" when mentioning tortures? His colleagues, the police, had already hinted that something of that sort was going on. And where did he get the idea that serving others might be the key to success? Millions of servants on every continent were all tears and ulcers from head to foot, tears meaning self-disgust, and ulcers mediocrity itself.

The doctor suddenly rose, interrupting Julio's caviling. He thanked him again for his "human warmth." He was feeling completely recovered now. He hoped to see Julio again, very soon. Meanwhile, say hello to Gerona and everything within its walls!

"Drink my health in a glass of water... And my deepest respects to Doña Amparo."

SEVEN

DURING those weeks, the Alvears had received two letters. One addressed to Matías, at the Telegraph Office, bearing the date of August 3rd, 1936.

Dear Uncle Matías:

We'd like so much to hear from you. How are you? I trust that nothing bad has happened to you and that you're all keeping cool in the midst of everything.

We're all well, particularly my father, who doesn't age. I hurt my nose. But I don't even have a scar from it. I'd like to see you, but it's impossible right now. If we go on to the Aragón front, who knows what might happen?

It might be a good idea not to show this letter to Aunt Carmen. Remember me to her, and to Pilar and César. Give Ignacio a hug and don't let his foolish nonsense bother you.

See you soon. Greetings!

José

The second letter had been addressed to Ignacio in Barcelona on August 5th, 1936.

Dearest Ignacio:

I haven't forgotten you, in spite of your disappearance... I'm eager to know if you're well, if everyone in your house is well. I am as ever, although we've moved and my father is away from us for a time. Write to me, even if it's only a few lines, at the following address: Gaspar Ley (for Ana María), 13 Fernando Street, Barcelona 13, Tel.: 14351.

Ana María

The August sun, burning and pitiless, affecting the brains and the earth, decreed that the uprising should definitively become a war, thus bearing out the prophetic fears of the military men in Gerona who had rejected a mere "mutiny." The rebels began to call themselves "Nationalists" and to use the term "Reds" to designate the "defenders of the Republic." "Nationalists" and "Reds," face to face and aiming at each other's hearts. On the 6th of August, Franco was transported from Tetuán to the Peninsula—he landed at the Seville airport—to take personal command of the troops, in search of the "unity" of which Dr. Relken had spoken. Franco had left the Canary Islands on the 17th of July, and had apparently landed at Casablanca, where it was rumored that he had disguised himself as a Moorish woman in order to pass through that city unrecognized. General Sanjurjo's death in an accident had left the responsibility for operations and for the organization of the home front in the hands of Franco and General Mola. After the conquest of the city of Huelva, the Southern column pursued its advance along the Portuguese frontier toward Badajoz while the units coming down from the North had been checked in Somosierra and the Guadarrama Mountains by the Communists and Socialists dispatched from Madrid. Mola was advancing toward Irún and asking for ammunition. He wanted to reach the Cantabrian Coast and cut the enemy communications with France through Hendaye.

The Republican Government could count on several competent commanders; outstanding among them were General Miaja, Colonel Villalba, Colonels Rojo and Mangada. The column of the last-named was nicknamed the "Nitwit" Column by its own militiamen, owing to the reverses it had suffered. Regular officers and provisional commandants were in short supply, while "finger-made" officers were a glut; and so, above all, were political commissars, who created a dual command and consequent confusion. A Government decree had just set aside ten pesetas a day for the militiamen's pay, and they were elated. Many political commissars, however, managed to convince their men that they ought to toss their pay "into the Party kitty."

Gerona was hanging suspensefully on every move, thanks to the radio, the press, and rumor. The city learned of the sentencing to death and the execution of the rebel soldiers in Barcelona before the Council of War, and of the repeated attempts by General Goded to commit suicide. It learned that the monument to the Sacred Heart of Jesus, erected on the Cerro de los Angeles in the exact geographic center of the Iberian Peninsula had been fired upon and blown up, and also of the resistance, not only of the Alcázar in Toledo and of Oviedo, but also of Huesca and the Sanctuary of Nuestra Señora de la Cabeza.

A climate of war was emphasized by the daily dispatches from the Ministry of the Army, the news of bombings, the huge posters that Ezequiel had praised so highly—"What are you doing to win the war?"—and particularly by the echo of the footsteps of the Soviet delegates on the sidewalks of Gerona, alongside those of Cosme Vila.

From the first moment, Axelrod, Vasiliev's successor, stood out among the Russian delegates, with his pirate's eyepatch and his dog, which would often go up to Dr. Relken in the Hotel Majestic and sniff at his legs. *El Proletario* published several chapters of a so-called biography of Axelrod, a man scarred by smallpox, a native of Tiflis, an old-guard Communist. All kinds of versions were current concerning the loss of his left eye. Cosme Vila swore that he had donated it to a clinic in Moscow where they were experimenting on the possibility of transplanting corneas, but others attributed it to an accident with a pistol. Professor Morales, for his part, thought he knew that when Axelrod appeared with a black patch, that meant an ill wind was blowing through the Party, and when he wore a white patch, the opposite was true. Goriev followed Axelrod everywhere, always his second, though El Responsable kept saying that this was a fiction and that Goriev was actually the boss. Goriev never talked, but confined himself to listening, to taking snuff, and to popping green tablets into his mouth.

The people opened their eyes in puzzlement on the day that Axelrod addressed the populace through the medium of the Gerona radio. He exhorted them to militarize the factories and build air-raid shelters, in addition to installing searchlights on Mountjuich and the Pedreras Mountains. Air-raid shelters! The words struck deep. Were the skies over Gerona going to be visited by bombers, then? Would they be coming any minute? Axelrod said that the searchlights for Gerona would be given by Russia, and from the point of view that they would "put an end to the darkness," they would turn out to be symbolic.

Another person who evoked the climate of war in the city was Gorki. Gorki was sending to *El Proletario* news stories entitled: "Diary of a Militiaman in the Field." Invariably he datelined them "somewhere on the Aragón Front." This former perfumer, this titular mayor of Gerona, described the first skirmishes of the Ortiz, Durruti, and Ascaso columns. The last-named was his. The dispatches gave an impression of firsthand experience, and on the day he described Teo's courage with a machine gun, Raimundo, the barber, read the report at least four times to his militia clientele whom he was still shaving gratis. Gorki's texts were also full of telling expressions: "The last cuckold who was sleeping with your mother last night could have told you that"; "The Big

Kid," referring to the sun; and "Drink up, drink up, the Pope's out walking on Muhammad's arm today."

The decree that the official salute thenceforth would be the clenched emplace anti-aircraft searchlights. His preferred spot, however, was in the Dehesa, a spot next to the swimming pool now converted into a junkyard. Indeed, this junkyard, lying among tall trees with thick green foliage attracted him, he did not know why. The place was expanding every day, for the militia were wrecking cars, trucks, and even railroad coaches. Ignacio had found an ideal spot for meditation in this graveyard—the cab of a ruined truck with no doors. He would slide into the cab and become the owner of the vehicle, studying himself in the rearview mirror, which portrayed the lines in his face day after day and gave him an accurate daily report on his color and the sadness in his face. As he sat motionless behind the wheel, Ignacio's loneliness was boundless, and the scrap iron on one side of him and the trees on the other surrounded him with rare peace. He knew that he could step on the accelerator and nothing would happen. He knew that he could bear down on the brake without altering the rigid posture of the truck. In the cab of the dead truck, there was something definitive, something that seemed to hold his mind fast, too. This adventure, which never failed to arouse his emotions, reached its climax one afternoon when a summer storm surprised him in the cab. Red streaks crossed the sky as clouds began to mass over the city and to form a close, impenetrable ceiling. Ignacio crossed himself. Some of the leaves suddenly were starting to curl. And then the rain came. Water that awakened an indescribable lament in the junkyard. A dramatic downpour, drumming luxuriantly on the top of the cab. Ignacio was not sure whether he was to bear it or enjoy it. He could not see what was around him, and this brought on an intense anxiety; on the other hand, he felt that he was participating in something immense, perhaps excessive. Ignacio waited in vain to recover control of himself, while the storm increased in violence. Little by little, he seemed to shrivel within himself, until he felt worthless, a child, almost non-existent. When the rain stopped, the ground was a sheet of water, a lake, and Ignacio's heart was throbbing with a desperate weakness.

Sometimes he used to take a walk with Pilar. But something strange had happened to them. At such times, the brother and sister who always had carried on an affectionate dialogue at home, hardly spoke to each other when they went out. They had nothing to say to each other in the street, and could find no reasonable explanation for it.

Ignacio missed Marta. As long as the girl had been in the school, he had known she was near: now Barcelona seemed to him another place of exile toward which he yearned for her. He often contrasted his love for Marta with Pilar's love for Mateo, and could not help thinking about the difference. Pilar loved with the whole heart, monolithically, unreservedly. Ignacio could never feel that he was giving himself completely. His critical sense forced him to analyze Marta pitilessly. And ambiguous and vacillating zones of sensitivity in him disconcerted all who lived with him. One time Olga had said to him: "There's always something in you that's dying." Nevertheless, it was not unusual for Ignacio to be so moved while thinking of Marta that he would weep. Then his knowledge that Marta was living on the Calle de Verdi now would lead him to tune the radio given them by Jaime in search of an Italian broadcast. And when he came upon the number 315 in the bank, the number of the house in which Marta was living, he would repeat it to himself with delight. On one of the visits he made to Marta's mother in her apartment on the Calle de la Platería, he was invited by the major's wife to look at the sunny room that had been her daughter's. Ignacio accepted. And when he reached the threshold, he stopped, slowly studied the furniture piece by piece, then the wallpaper; and he felt a sweet and unexpected lump in his throat.

On the 20th of August his thoughts were especially attuned to Marta, for it was then that the Anti-Fascist Committee opened the trials of the twenty imprisoned soldiers of Gerona. It was a day of breathless tension, for as soon as it was known where the hearings were to be held—in the Court House on the Plaza de la Catedral—the stairway to the church was packed with people awaiting the arrival of the officers, who were being brought in pairs from the prison to the courtroom. Against the advice of his family, Ignacio joined the crowd. At exactly five o'clock in the afternoon, he saw Lieutenant Martín step out of the first vehicle, followed immediately by Major Martínez de Soria. A glance was enough to remind him once more how closely the father and daughter resembled each other. He could think of nothing else. The major's shoulders were Marta's shoulders; his nose, her nose; and that bearing, half noble, half haughty, was very much theirs. With clenched fists raised, the crowd yelled insults at the rebel officers. The square was in an uproar, and the only reason the watchers refrained from throwing stones was that they feared to injure the guards. No one fired point-blank because they all were expecting the death sentence to be passed.

The court, presided over by Colonel Muñoz, was composed of Cosme Vila, El Responsable, Antonio Casal, David, and the architect Ribas. They would hand their verdict to a duly constituted magistrate from Barcelona who was present by virtue of his office to interpret the code and pronounce sentence. From the beginning it was obvious that Major Martínez de Soria and Lieutenant Martín would be sentenced to death. The examination, to last a week, could be followed from outside the courtroom owing to the installation of loudspeakers. Ignacio never missed a session. Every day he sat on the same step of the stairway to the Cathedral and listened to the whisky voice of Marta's father. For the most part, the major's replies displeased him. He was dignified and he made no attempt to extenuate himself; but he had himself barely under control, and a trace of high-sounding rhetoric dominated his manner of speaking.

At the close of each session, Ignacio usually would go home with the feeling that he had missed something of what had taken place. A half-gypsy woman said to him one day: "You're going to be left without a father-in-law! Aren't you, kid?" Ignacio pretended to take it calmly, but darted away.

One fact kept disturbing him. He realized, with no room for doubt, that the major's death mattered very little to him, perhaps not at all. He had tried very hard to pity him, but in vain. Ah, the treachery of the heart! This was Marta's father, and he had always shown an understanding of Ignacio. Yet it made no difference.

Pilar, on the other hand, was following the trial with all her soul, and she had vowed on the first day of it that if the major's life should be spared by some miracle, she would climb to the hermitage of Los Angeles in her bare feet. Ignacio had laid aside his lawbooks. He had not studied a single lesson all summer long. He was distracted, and besides, the mere word "law" sounded to him ironical in that time of upheaval.

Yet if the war should turn out to be a long one, what was he to do? If only he could find some formula that would interest him in something, in something he could study! He would ask himself at times whether he might not like to study anatomy. Against the background of this question, he would often see the oval head of Julio. On a certain occasion the policeman had said something that remained engraved on his mind: "Everything originates in the brain. If I am an easygoing man, I owe it to my brain. If you're sentimentally inclined and you work in the bank, it's owing to your mind. If Axelrod is as he is, and César was as he was, that, too, is owing to their minds." This comment, plus a diagram of the human skull that he had seen in a drugstore, had made an impression on him and awakened his curiosity.

But he had no desire to subject himself to rigorous discipline. His mother tried to give him some advice: "Study whatever you can, son, whatever you can. It would be better for you to be studying than always to be going out."

Matías shared her opinion, but with one exception: Study whatever you like except anatomy. "Why do you want to open up heads and see what's inside them? Aren't they made closed? There must be a reason..."

MOSÉN Francisco and Ignacio were face to face again. At crucial moments in Ignacio's life, Mosén Francisco always had intervened without a specific proposal from either of them. One time when Ignacio had been weary of inner lack of balance and of sleeping with his legs apart, he had gone to confession to the priest and for a time afterward, the boy had glimpsed another way of life. Now he felt impelled to call on him. The priest had sent a message from his hiding place in the apartment of Pilar's dressmakers, the Campistol sisters, saying that the boy should come to see him. Mosén Francisco was planning to interview the relatives of all the men who had been shot on the first night, to tell them that he had given the men absolution and in the cases of some, including César, he even had given them Communion.

Ignacio received the message in the bank from the lips of one of the Campistol sisters. His surprise was immense, for he had heard nothing of Mosén Francisco since the 18th of July. Ignorant of what the priest might have to say, he preferred not to alert the household. Accordingly he went alone and greatly excited to keep the engagement, for Mosén Francisco represented to him something genuine, someone without any tricks or snares, a man of good will.

Once more Ignacio walked along the Calle de la Barca to the Plaza de San Pedro, now called the Plaza Bakunin. In the Oñar some little boys were paddling through a pool while a sad, dark man was playing a hand organ under the windows. He saw La Andaluza in one of the windows with a rose in her hair, fanning herself. That quarter of the city held a great deal of meaning for him, because it was there he had first discovered anger in the hearts of men. He would never forget the phrase: "Keep on, and they'll tar and feather you."

He had hardly touched the bell when the door opened, an indication that the Campistol sisters were waiting for him. Then he was walking through a long hallway hung with mirrors, and so into the separate, inner room occupied by the priest.

As soon as he saw the boy, Mosén Francisco went to meet him and embraced him. Ignacio responded sluggishly. He had never known how to give an embrace. He would always hesitate a second longer than was proper and the arms of the other would seem to imprison him. The priest was wearing a blue smock and was unshaved. With darkly circled eyes, he looked ill. He was wearing *espadrilles,* but his eyes were bright with energy and decision. Ignacio saw a wardrobe, a cup of coffee on the little night table, and a carpenter's or plumber's tool chest in one corner.

"How glad I am, Ignacio! How glad I am to see you!"

"Everything's all right now... At last we've found out something about you! Another embrace from the whole family..."

That last was a lie. Ignacio's family knew nothing about the visit. Why had he lied unnecessarily?

"Well, well," the priest said, "let's make ourselves comfortable." He drew the chair up to the bed. "Would you rather sit on the bed or in the chair?"

"I don't care."

"Go on! Sit in the chair, it's more comfortable."

Ignacio obeyed, and Mosén Francisco sat on the edge of the bed with the naturalness of old habit, as naturally as Don Emilio Santos would sit on César's bed now.

Suddenly the vicar of San Félix rose and went to the little table for his cigarettes. "Would you like a smoke?"

"No, thank you."

Ignacio did not know why he had refused. Actually he would have been glad to have a cigarette.

Mosén Francisco lighted his and sat down facing the boy, looking into his eyes through the first mouthful of smoke. He seemed to read Ignacio's innermost thoughts. The priest had told the Campistol sisters that doubtless his incarceration would prove useful in that it would prevent him from seeing people routinely as mere shapes. Weeks would go by with no other faces around him except those of the Campistol sisters. Ignacio's seemed much as it used to be, expressing a curious state of virginity.

Mosén Francisco broke the silence to say: "I get the impression that you're feeling somewhat depressed..."

"That's true," Ignacio agreed.

Mosén Francisco had no intention of preaching to the boy. He wanted to speak briefly. He told Ignacio that he had summoned him to tell him that César had died like a saint. He himself had been foolish enough to go into the cemetery and look at the victims, one by one, and had ministered to them. "Your brother was able even to take Communion. You know"—he pointed to his wrist-watch—"this was my ciborium. César closed his eyes and his face expressed perfect serenity."

Ignacio felt stunned. So Mosén Francisco was not above lying. He was on the point of exclaiming: "That's a lie! My brother's face was monstrously distorted!" But the pure gratification in the priest's eyes conquered him, and he kept silent. Mosén Francisco went on, giving details... And Ignacio admired the vicar all the more in the end for being capable of a small sin and, shamefacedly, for being good.

"I'll take one of your cigarettes now."

Mosén Francisco obliged, and the two of them sat quietly, face to face. A deep silence reigned in the apartment, for the Campistol sisters discreetly had gone out on the balcony.

"How are your parents, Ignacio? And Pilar?"

"Fine, very well…"

Ignacio was answering him automatically. Suddenly it struck him that the vicar was disguising his true self and that he would have been capable of dying with an "Alleluia" on his lips for reasons both opposite to and identical with those which impelled certain of the people in Gerona to enlist in the Durruti Column. Those people were promising man an earthly paradise whereas Mosén Francisco promised them life everlasting. All in all, men were dying and killing to convert the ideal of happiness into actual fact.

"Mosén Francisco… Why do you think men kill one another?"

The priest was slow to answer. For some moments he sat motionless, staring at a point on the floor. "I don't know what to tell you, Ignacio." Then he added, "I know more about love than hate."

Ignacio reckoned that the reply failed to resolve the question. He returned to the charge and pressed closer to his theme. "Why do you think they killed César?"

The vicar spread his arms in a gesture of helplessness. "I don't know, Ignacio." He pondered. "There's something hidden in God's designs… Man might wish that his salvation could come more easily, but it is written that we have to earn it."

Now it was Ignacio's turn to stare at the floor. "I'd like to know," he repeated, stammering, "why they killed César."

Mosén Francisco made a grimace of displeasure. He would have liked the interview to take another course. Ignacio interested him so much! Ever since that confession… Ever since the boy and his mother, Carmen Elgazu, had entered San Félix Church, their steps ringing on the tiles.

Finally the vicar answered Ignacio. In his opinion, the conflict could not be considered an individual matter. The hatred was not being directed against persons, but against symbols. "They are killing with their eyes blindfolded. They kill the landowner, not Don Jorge. They kill the doctor, not Dr. So-and-So. They kill the seminarian, not César."

"Well…"

The vicar was silent again.

"Well then," he said after a time. "This is dangerous. Do you understand, Ignacio? A man is not much, and we must all admit that hating a man may be, I don't know, unmotivated, unjust. Look at the case of Jesus. But when the people have hated certain institutions for years and years, they may easily come to the conclusion that those institutions are not above circumstances."

The priest was making a direct allusion. He knew in detail the accusation against the Church that Ignacio had made, and he did not believe the boy had restated the question to himself since the 18th of July, in the terms of the counterthrust Mosén Alberto had stated when he said: "If persecution comes, the sinner priests will fall just the same as the saintly priests..."

Yet the force of that argument was obvious. Mosén Francisco was a saint who wholeheartedly had given away everything he possessed. And he would do it again a hundred times over. But neither Blasco, the bootblack, nor Cosme Vila, nor Gorki, nor Murillo would make any distinction whatever between him and some priest with an income.

Ignacio grasped the intention of the vicar, but refused to enter the argument, in spite of the fact that the time had passed for uttering threats against the Vatican or ridiculing the Bible. Now César had been taken from him, and consequently the conflict had assumed another dimension.

"I know what you mean," he said. "But...don't you think that serious mistakes have been made? The religion that we profess in Spain has always been terribly sad and defensive."

Mosén Francisco did not care for the subject, but Ignacio, who always succeeded in captivating the vicar, clung to it insistently.

"Defensive perhaps," the vicar argued. "For sin does exist, you may be certain of that. As for the sadness, I think you're wrong there. What happens is that the commandments of God's law are 'soap that won't wash' because they run contrary to instinct, and in a country like ours, sensual by nature, they may become intolerable."

"In the Seminary we used to chew over two obsessive ideas: that the earth is a vale of tears and that the body must be despised."

"I have never said that," Mosén Francisco stated. "One may enjoy a good laugh on earth. You've had a good laugh yourself sometimes; and it's very shortsighted to despise the body, for we must take into account the mystery of the Resurrection."

Ignacio stared at the vicar, and mimicking Mosén Alberto's voice, he evoked the man himself. "What shall it profit a man to gain the whole world if he suffer the loss of his soul? If it's put that way, that's an invitation to fatalism, to making no effort here below, to folding your arms. That's not very consoling." Ignacio added quickly: "Do you know what an employee in the bank, Tower of Babel, said to me one time?"

"No, I don't know."

"He said that if you close your eyes and think of the Spanish church, you'll see just two colors: black for mourning and yellow for gold."

Mosén Francisco reacted to that. He dropped his cigarette stub and stared toward the window, from which he could see the bell towers. For a moment he forgot Ignacio and admitted that, in very truth, they ought to attempt another parlance, to rise above routine on the day when the present persecution should cease. For, as he had said to the Campistol sisters, "All persecutions have to come to an end someday." He himself had discovered that whenever he cited some little-known phase of the life of Jesus from the pulpit or in the confessional, everyone paid close attention. After all, it was a difficult problem! The Spaniard lacked contact with animals and plants, that is, with everything not human, everything that by its very lowliness in the scale of life invited generosity, invited man to soften its everyday existence.

But, as usual, Ignacio was exaggerating, for there was a discrepancy between his thirst for truth and his actual experience. Mosén Francisco told Ignacio that the Spanish religion owned many other colors than black and yellow. There was white, for the undeniable chastity of the majority of its priests. There was gray, for the numberless parish priests who carried on their work anonymously in obscure villages and churches. There was blue, for the missionaries who crossed and recrossed the seas endlessly, and for the scholars. Finally, there was red, for the blood they had shed.

"There's no deceit here, Ignacio. We Spanish priests do give our lives for our faith. We may be wrong in detail, but we have preached the Gospel plain, and those of us who are being burned now will be metamorphosed into torches for God. Besides, I think that as we review history, the Conquests, and as we consider the aridity of our soil, we priests do constitute a worthy militia. And I am sure that in difficult times like these we receive the help of the Holy Spirit. You will see this come to pass, Ignacio, and that the Church will be reborn, brilliantly. You'll see that our way is the eternal way and that the guns will fall silent. And, added to that, it is a privilege that we can exercise our vocation in a spot of earth where the people admonish the priests by saying: 'Be perfect, for if you're not, you will feel our anger!' Doesn't that seem a privilege to you? As time goes on, it ought to make us sprout wings from our ribs. Don't let your eyes deceive you, Ignacio. It's not true that everyone who kills does so for a reason. Again I say that sin does exist, and Satan does exist. Besides, no man has the right to punish a selected group of people, *en bloc.* That is the prerogative of God."

The sun was setting. Ignacio felt tired and was asking himself whether or not that was why he could find no valid arguments to oppose to the burning words of Mosén Francisco. His faculties as a debater had been declining for quite awhile, as he had recognized in his discussion with David and Olga—as if he had come to doubt the efficacy of words for transmitting thought and clarifying the obscure. Which was the more beautiful of two trees? Which the better of two doctrines? Mosén Francisco seemed to be right, at the moment. Nonetheless, Ignacio felt that if he closed his eyes and thought about the Spanish church, he would still see only the two colors mentioned by Tower of Babel: black for funerals or mourning and yellow for gold.

He got to his feet.

"I haven't convinced you, have I?"

"No, it's not that," replied Ignacio. "It's just… I have to go."

"I understand."

The floor was littered with cigarette stubs. Mosén Francisco rose, too. He gazed at the boy with such a longing to be understood that Ignacio was touched. He promised the vicar that he would come to see him from time to time provided that his presence on the stairway would not arouse suspicion. Mosén Francisco brushed this aside with a shake of his head. "Come whenever you can, whenever you like." The vicar was in such need of friendship that he even dared to invite Ignacio's mother and Pilar to the Mass he was thinking of saying in his room on the coming Sunday. "Tell them to come. At ten. They can receive Communion, too."

In the vestibule they embraced again. Without his broad-brimmed priest's hat, Mosén Francisco looked like another person. To some degree that made him a trifle ridiculous; on the other hand, it made him still more worthy of respect. He confessed to Ignacio that he had been constantly and deeply afraid, of course, and as a consequence had not known whether or not to try to leave Gerona. Meanwhile, he was here, praying and learning how to sew! The Campistol sisters were teaching him their needle trade. "We've started to embroider a tablecloth."

Ignacio said goodbye. Someone had written a woman's name, Luisa, on the staircase five or six times. He went out into the street. A militiaman was sitting on the front sidewalk with a bottle of soda pop beside him, powerless to see through the walls of the dressmakers' house and discover Mosén Francisco. So meager is the range of the human eye!

Ignacio walked on. The proprietor of the Crocodile was fanning himself with a fly swatter as he leaned against the doorpost of his shabby tavern. "Hi…" he said, seeing Ignacio. The sun was setting, ablaze above the small clouds yonder that quivered like desire. The motion picture houses had reopened their doors. In Raimundo's barbershop three or four men were carrying on a heated discussion. Ignacio entered the Rambla. Laura was taking a walk beneath the arches, arm in arm with Dr. Roselló's daughters. Laura was the Costas' sister. Ignacio had been told that she had been given back her apartment—Warning Voice's apartment—and that with the help of some girls from Olot she was busy organizing the caravans of fugitives escaping to France through the mountains.

At home he found his mother, her hair loose after a shampoo, and Don Emilio Santos. His mother was leafing through a book on anatomy that Ignacio had bought, and when she came to the diagrams of the brain, she exclaimed several times: "Good Lord!" Don Emilio Santos, half-hidden in the corner where the fishing pole still stood, was staring at the river. Don Emilio Santos had been going through some disturbed days and had failed a good deal. Now that Mateo had escaped, he had begun to worry about his other son, Antonio, in Cartagena, from whom he had not heard a word. He was mulling over the problem of how to leave the Alvears to themselves and go to Barcelona, to start from there to try to find his son.

Pilar arrived a few minutes later.

"Where have you been?" Carmen Elgazu asked her when her daughter greeted her with a kiss.

"Nowhere, here..."

By "here," she meant the Plaza de la Estación. Pilar would go there whenever she could, just to sit awhile in front of the house where Mateo had lived, looking at the POUM sign, and waiting to see if some militiaman would emerge wearing an article of Mateo's clothing.

Matías Alvear came home with the last of the daylight. He said he had been walking along the railroad tracks to San Feliu with his colleague, Jaime. But in fact he had been alone in the cemetery. Several days ago he had succumbed to the temptation that had assailed him suddenly as he left the house: to go to the cemetery. He went there and asked the gravedigger's wife for a plot marked Casellas Family. The moment he stood before the headstone, surrounded by cypresses, Matías Alvear, who never dared to wear a hat, passed his hand over his head. He stood rigid as a statue upon the little walk of gilded gravel. Then he left the cemetery and went home along the banks of the Oñar, fearing that the little boys in the streets and in the water might notice that he was weeping.

EIGHT

THE repressive system was following its course. In the suburbs of the provincial capitals, ditches were being dug to bury the dead, and not infrequently an "executed" man merely was wounded and could make his way through the woods, either to bleed to death or to find refuge in some hut. The life of a nephew of the notary Noguer was saved in this manner. In certain places, as in the province of Ciudad Real, the dead were buried in coffins improvised from condensed milk cans. Such coffins displayed the warning: "*Keep in a cool place.*" In Figueras, one woman, being told that her husband's body was lying unburied in the cemetery, herself made a coffin and crossed the entire city carrying it on her back. Throughout the land, tribunals of all kinds proliferated, employing a pantomime and jargon comprehensible to no one but the wardens of the towns in which the trials were held. Thus a committee for a certain quarter in Valencia, headed by a man of Italian origin, imitated the Romans. Whenever they acquitted the accused, they turned thumbs up, and when they condemned him, they turned thumbs down. Cosme Vila and El Responsable changed their procedures as often as they changed their minds. Frequently they would send a couple of militiamen to the prisons, particularly to the village jails, to claim a prisoner for interrogation in Gerona. If the name was marked with a cross, it meant that the prisoner was to be shot along the way; if there was an L, he was to be taken to Gerona without touching a hair of his head. The letters, the symbols, the crosses all counted. Certain prisoners were shot because someone did not like their names; others were spared because of their names. Gorki took pity on a man named Manuel Tocino. "Let him alone," he ordered. "With the name bacon he has enough to bear."

Ezequiel used to say that if all the places equipped as jails or prisons could be photographed from the air, they would constitute an extraordinary display. Numerous prison ships lay in the harbors—the *Villa de Madrid* and the *Uruguay* in Barcelona; the *España Número 3* in Cartagena; the *Sister* in Gijón; the

Altuna-Mendi and *Cabo Quilates* in Bilbao; the *Isla de Menorca* in El Grao; and so on. On the door leading to the prison holds of the *Sister*, a quotation from Dante read: "Abandon hope, all ye who enter here." As a rule, the prisoners on the ships were locked up in the holds or the tween-decks while their guards were installed above in the first-class cabins. Generally an oil slick surrounded these ships. In Cartagena, the prisoners used to take turns sitting in the sun that came through the holes or slits that had been opened along the strakes by shells. The prisoners in Almería were forced to go out on deck to relieve themselves, and the militiamen standing guard along the wharves made fun of them while the militiawomen watched them through binoculars.

Throughout the fighting zone, the churches and convents constituted most of the buildings converted into prisons, first because they were undamaged, second because their peculiar construction almost seemed planned for such use. The convent cells and those in the Gerona Seminary could be adapted readily. The indispensable patio already was there; the chapel became the "courtroom" with the main altar as the judge's podium. The prisoners occupied the benches, the public the choir stalls. The officers of the court could retire to the sacristy to deliberate or to refresh themselves. Some of the nuns and monks imprisoned there had not needed to move from their old quarters; they had simply exchanged their habits for prison garb and their peace for anxiety.

In Lérida, the Astoria Cinema was converted into a prison. The detainees installed in the pit and the boxes could sleep comfortably in their seats, while those in the regular seats protested. In front of the proscenium, in place of the screen was the eternal bulletin board, which became an obsession. In various bathhouses, the compartments were filled, and the prisoner who could sleep in a bathtub considered himself a privileged character. Advertisements for the establishment, with a list of the sick people who had been healed there lent splashes of color to the cells of those sentenced to death. In the office of the commandant of a small barracks in Albacete, a curious inscription could be read: "*Happy are the priests and the soldiers who never see beneath the surface of things.*" The mattresses in a dungeon in Sagunto were so thin that they were called "cats' tongues." Aside from the rotten food, the worst tortures were the stench of the latrines and the loud snoring of some of the prisoners. While, outdoors, harmony reigned over the vault of the sky, the prisoners were suffering from nightmares; kicking one another, trying to strangle their fellows, and thus arousing others, who awakened with eyes starting from their heads. A soldier who had escaped from Nationalist territory swore that the "Fascists" in the Zaragoza prison used to torture the men by putting in their mouths rubber balls of constantly increasing size.

The newspapers frequently boasted of the repressive work of the three leaders of the revolution: Aurelio Fernández in Barcelona; García Altadeli in Madrid; and Vicente Apellániz in Valencia. Each of the three had his own "Dawn Squadron," in addition to other "vigilante" forces, some of whose members sported spectacular uniforms. According to information in the hands of Brother Julián Cervera, the Police Commissioner in Gerona, García Altadeli was executing only the bourgeoisie, the professional soldiers, and the priests; while in Barcelona, Aurelio Fernández had had his political rivals shot, too, and even the provincial policemen. In Altarazanas the destruction of the "*maquereaux*" had been ordered and it was being said that in the "special prisons" methods of torture were being tried out.

The Chekas! The word was becoming popular, even though few people were certain just what lay hidden beneath it, and there were still a great many who supposed it to be sheer "Fascist" invention. Inspector Bermúdez had given Julio a hint of it on the day when he had visited the police station in Barcelona. Bermúdez had mentioned a place that had been set up at 321 Calle de Muntaner, under Communist control, where several chess boards had been drawn on the walls, plus geometric figures in all colors, which had brought on acute nervous attacks among the prisoners. He had also spoken of the "water torture" in a Cheka in the Calle de Ganduxer, and of wooden cabinets with room for only one person. Inside the cabinets a bell kept ringing and a metronome ticking in never-ending alternation. At the time Julio had supposed that Dr. Relken was exaggerating when he spoke of the lack of scientific method in the Spanish prison system, and he was full of curiosity concerning what was going on in the special Cheka prisons that had begun to operate in Gerona. One of them had been set up on the Calle de Pedret, under Cosme Vila's orders, and was visited by Axelrod in person. A sign on the front of it said: Lime Kiln. Another in the Station section, under El Responsable, occupied a former garage. Its inscription read: Woodworkers' Syndicate. Professor Morales would smile whenever anyone asked him about the Lime Kiln. Only once, when speaking to a waiter at the Peninsular Hotel, did he reveal anything. "It's not so much," he said. "We have a couple of priests there. They're sitting in front of a wall on which the good Crespo, the chauffeur, has written that famous phrase of Henry Deman's: 'Religion would fare better if the Church fared worse.'"

Professor Morales was in his glory, and he used to say to Antonio Casal, who sometimes stared at him as though tortured by his thoughts: "Don't worry. It's always been like this. The history of great men centers around their periods of exile or imprisonment. Remember Socrates, Dante, Leonardo, Michelangelo,

Cervantes, Dostoevsky, Lenin! And let's not leave out David and Olga, if they keep on asking so many questions..."

Apart from the Chekas and the improvised jails, there were other regular prisons, like the "model prisons" in Madrid and Barcelona. Those institutions formed a complete world in themselves, and reinforced El Responsable's theory that aside from the five hundred prisoners, a jail was like a village, with people of all classes and a "barber on every tier."

Professor Civil was still in the Gerona prison in the Seminary, the dean of it, and thanks to his optimism and serenity was often the man who kept up the morale of his companions, though he kept lamenting his inability to use the piano in his house. "I'd teach you who Chopin is!" Not infrequently a new "recruit" from some provincial village would take Professor Civil for a priest and would press him insistently for all kinds of advice and even to hear his confession, but Civil, the dean, would shake his head. "You're quite wrong, son! I'm just an ordinary professor. But we have three real priests here, from the Asilo. Go up to the next tier and ask for The Three Musketeers."

In the Gerona prison it became fashionable to play "naval battles." Everyone took part in them, even several boatowners from the fishing fleet of San Feliu de Guixols and Pálamos. Chess players abounded—El Rubio was tired of being checkmated. They had made their own chessboards from sheets of cardboard and had carved their men out of bottle corks. They also played "Nonsense" and then everyone put on his particular stunt, of course. El Rubio could move the little finger of his left hand in very comical ways. A man who ran a hostel could wiggle both ears without wrinkling his forehead or widening his eyes. One of the priests from the Asilo, the eldest, would tuck up his right sleeve and make a strange looking ball rise at his biceps. Teachers of French and Italian emerged, of voice, and of magic. Every day at the same time, a relative of the cashier in the Arús Bank would burst out singing *La Traviata.*

The "Judas goats," strange militiamen sent in disguised as prisoners, were given the cold shoulder they deserved. They were nicknamed "submarines," and Professor Civil began at once to harry them. The punishment lay in being ignored by the others, as if their physical presence did not exist. The prisoners would bump into them, blow smoke in their faces as if into empty air, and refuse to look at them. It was a rare "Judas goat" who could stand more than a week of such psychological nonentity.

As a consequence of the court-martial, the aspect of the prison changed. Major Martínez de Soria, Lieutenant Martín, and the thin second lieutenant, whose death sentence was confirmed, remained in the dungeons of the prison while the other officers and noncoms were moved to the Seminary in a chain gang. Thus three types of prisoners were mingled there: the soldiers, the civilians, and the common criminals.

The soldiers lightened the atmosphere of the prison, not only with their joy because their lives had been spared, but also because they could comment with professional knowledge on the war news that came to them daily in baskets of food or packages of cigarettes. The prisoners would watch, completely absorbed, while Captains Arias and Sandoval demonstrated on a chessboard that the Nationalist commands were constantly strengthening their position. The cork stoppers were used for everything... They played the part of generals, of batteries, of Moors, and of retreating Reds... "Now you see why it's impossible for Durruti to enter Zaragoza!" "It's a certainty that after San Sebastián is taken, Bilbao will fall with almost no resistance."

Several public officials in the Prison Corps of the Seminary, who had been swept outside during the first days, kept coming back to visit. Their presence ameliorated the lot of the secluded men. Two of them, with Republican sympathies, installed in the Corps thanks to the Costa brothers, would undertake to do errands on the outside. That was a wonderful help. They also organized the necessary services on the inside and convinced several militiamen that they could earn good pay without betraying the Revolution. Thus an Anarchist called The Necktie became a barber and even sold jars of cold cream. A cousin of Ideal called "Dynamite" became the librarian and brought to the jail several astonishing books he had stolen: many of Dumas's novels, Thiers' *The History of the French Revolution*, Father Coloma's *Jeromín,* and Renan's poetry. The Necktie, who was clever and enamored of one of La Andaluza's girls, conceived a curious business venture: to kill the bedbugs infesting the prison. He offered to burn them out with a blowtorch for the modest price of a dollar per cell. The deal was closed and The Necktie went to work...but, according to El Rubio, only half did it. Indeed El Rubio declared that the man would overlook one nest on purpose to keep his business going.

The prisoners in the Seminary saw just six kinds of living creatures: bedbugs, lice, and flies in the cells; cats and ants on the adobe walls and in the patio; birds in the sky.

The cats! They were a much greater attraction in the prison than even the naval battles and *The Count of Monte Cristo.* Their amusing tricks were followed with exuberant mirth. They symbolized the unexpected, the dance on the tightrope which might affect even a man's personal destiny. Each of them was familiarly known; their black, white, or brown markings were recognized. Captain Arias divided them into "Fascists" and "Reds." The "Reds" were the unfriendly ones, the ones that arched their backs; the "Fascists" those which permitted themselves to be petted. Captain Sandoval claimed that the opportunistic cats would as soon fight on one side as the other. As for the birds, they made the heart rejoice at times; but as a rule, they aroused envy. The birds had at their disposal immense space and freedom.

All of a sudden the jail would be plunged into despair. What was going to happen? Would any of them survive? Even if the Nationalists were to advance, might they not be shot in reprisal?

There came nights when fear settled down on their shoulders. Some of the prisoners would finally go to sit in the semidarkness leaning their heads against the wall. Then their thoughts began their dance. First the men would think of their families, their relatives, one by one. Then they would call up happy memories of childhood and youth. Particularly their school days and their first kisses. Then the rhythm would break and mental pictures throng writhing into their minds. This was anxiety. "What are you thinking about?" "Nothing... A lot of foolishness." Their mouths would go dry, and they would have given a fortune at such times to be able to walk through the woods or to suck on a lemon drop.

Fear came most frequently, too, with twilight. From the windows of the cells facing outward they could see through the bars the Mountains of Rocaborda in the distance and even the foothills of the Pyrenees. Other windows permitted them to scan the roofs of that section of the city. Some of the prisoners would stand looking out as if turned to stone, as if bidding goodbye to it all. Others, on the contrary, would stay in their own corner for hours and hours. Some would get hiccups; some took their pulse, and some changed their position every half minute. Those last would suddenly get up then and start to walk, only to come to a complete standstill and breathe deeply. In the women's wing, the drama was more intense. The lack of hygiene affected the women much more. They seemed more irritable and less able to find ways of distracting their minds.

One of the wardens of the Prison Corps told El Rubio on one occasion that the sick and the wounded might possibly not have to "take a walk." He mentioned the names of two representatives of a champagne company who had been spared because they were in the infirmary at the time. This item aroused a commotion. On the nights of fear the prisoners would long to contract an illness, and they would concoct stories based on formulas appropriate to such and such symptoms. Two chocolate manufacturers from Bajo Ampurdán vowed to each other that in case they were called out during the night, they would injure each other remorselessly. It was being said, too, that the insane were respected, and as a result, the most circumspect man in one cell suddenly began to claim that he was the Cid Campeador. Another came out of the bathroom naked, on all fours.

In the Seminary it was learned that a work brigade would soon be formed to go out through the city every day to make repairs and clean up the streets. "Chances are I'll have to work in front of my own house!" "My children will come to see me!" Others were thinking: "What kind of repairs can I make?" They did not feel able to lift a pick or move a shovel.

There was also talk of labor battalions. It seemed that five such gangs had been formed in the Red territory; three in Catalonia, one in Tarancón, and another in Torrejón. "If they put the bee on me, I'll sign the petition and be on my way." "Don't talk nonsense." "I'll have a better chance to escape." "To escape? You've been seeing too many movies."

Several people in the city realized that something ought to be done on behalf of the prisoners, to try to help them, for they were completely helpless. Laura was one of those people. She still was making up caravans of fugitives, through her contact with the girls in Olot and Figueras, girls with monarchist leanings. She decided to organize a prison service, too.

"Isn't there a Red Relief? Well, we'll set up a White Relief!"

The deputies Costa, with fear always at their backs, tried to stop their sister, but Laura was stubborn. "If my husband were here, he'd be all for my decision."

"Have it your way," the Costas replied. "But in a week you'll find yourself in Cosme Vila's Cheka, and then you'll be telling us what to do to get you out of there."

Cheka! The word was indeed coming into common use. And Cosme Vila and El Responsable alike systematically avoided any discussion of the subject. Julio came right out and asked Cosme Vila about it and the Communist leader replied: "What are you talking about? In the Calle de Pedret? As far as I know, the only thing we have there is the lime kiln. Haven't you seen its sign?"

WHAT about the Nationalist zone? The soldiers along the Extremadura and Aragón fronts talked constantly of hair-raising happenings, impossible to confirm from the Red zone. Julio believed them, however, without a moment's doubt. "I know my people." One time after returning from the Telegraph Office, where he had gone to chat awhile with Matías Alvear, he said to Doña Amparo: "I wouldn't give a nickel for the life of Matías's brother in Burgos."

"What makes you say that?"

"Well, think! He's one of the heads of the UGT..."

NINE

THE three prongs into which Durruti's column in the Aragón territory had been divided were having varied luck. The first had split off toward the North under the command of the Anarchist Ascaso, with Huesca as its objective. The second branched toward the South under the command of the Anarchist Ortiz, with Teruel as objective. The third, under Durruti himself and Major Pérez Farrás, was advancing along the main highway, objective Zaragoza.

Ascaso and his men moved northward toward Huesca in a wide variety of vehicles, from the small open car to reconnaissance cars and heavy trucks, many of them protected with mattresses, and with green branches hiding the radiators. The backbone of the column was Anarchists, the majority in its complement of more than a thousand men. The Communists were in the great minority: they made up two centurions, small companies called "Lenin" and "Karl Marx." The officers and noncoms had been appointed "by finger" and even "by merit." In fact before Ascaso left Durruti, he had presented him with a written list of the men capable of commanding. "Here is the equivalent of a major, three captains, and five lieutenants." Durruti had run his hand over his unshaven face. "All right." Gorki, now a political commissar, was appointed captain by this method, as were two of the foreign athletes who had come to Barcelona to take part in the abortive People's Olympic Games. The twinkling stars on Gorki's cap had evoked loud horselaughs from Teo and La Valenciana. Indeed, it would have been hard to imagine a less martial figure than Gorki, with his short neck, his paunch, and his waddle. And yet something dedicated, something potent, in the former Aragónese perfumer lent him an air of authority.

The march of the Ascaso column was slow. Not merely because the militiamen kept halting here and there at their whim, particularly in the villages, but also because, as they advanced, small enemy concentrations that had remained in the zone surrendered or fled before them. These enemy concentrations were almost invariably made up of Civil Guards.

At the same time the column was constantly receiving reinforcements. Aragónese peasants of all ages, members of some district organization or syndicate, would climb aboard the moving trucks carrying shotguns, sickles, or simply blankets. The women and children bade them goodbye with the clenched-fist salute. And they replied by waving their berets until the vehicles disappeared in a cloud of dust.

The line halted in the village of Pina, where Ascaso failed to gain a single volunteer. The villagers had interpreted Communism in their own way, reckoning that if "everyone gets into someone else's backyard, it would be a story that has no end." As they understood the situation, they said to Ascaso, the "Fascists" ought to be punished, but not in Pina. "They never did anything to us, and so we let them go." All that Pina asked was to be allowed to live in peace. Consequently, instead of spending their money on gunpowder, what the villagers had done was to change things about: to combine the stores into an "economy supermarket" and to make the Town Hall a place for meetings and social gatherings. Ah, yes, the village wore an almost idyllic look, with the men and women going about their business, the children bathing in the irrigation ditches, and the animals grazing! Ripe fruit was hanging from the trees, and in a little more than a month the citizens had acquired a movie projector, fumigants, phosphates, and farm equipment. Ascaso experienced a moment of indecision at the spectacle... Suddenly he shouted "Forward!" thinking that later he would send a detachment to wake up those idiots. And as he gave the order, a boy sitting on a bench in the square began to run and climbed into a truck, Teo's truck. He was a red-haired boy whom the village called "Puppy" because he knew how to imitate every kind of dog. Teo helped him up, saying: "Come, come along! Stout fellow!"

In Barbastro the column received an important addition in Colonel Villalba, who became the military legal counselor. Colonel Villalba informed Ascaso that the enemy had dug in behind the walls of the village of Siétamo, a few kilometers from Huesca, with the intention of defending it as a fort, and that it would be advisable to study the plan of attack. Ascaso realized that, but it would be a difficult thing to do. More and more the column was breaking up into small groups... "Hey, boys, this way! " "Milk!" "What's the hurry?" Many of the vehicles were breaking down and being left behind. The militiamen would stop for target practice at the slightest pretext, using the prisoners from the jails or the Civil Guards' tricorns as bull's-eyes whenever possible. Ascaso recognized, however, that the groupings of his men made a fine sight, for they filled the ditches and the open fields with shadows and fluttering banners.

Ascaso was an unusual man. He seldom spoke. He carried a pair of huge, black binoculars that formerly had belonged to the Abbot of Montserrat. He constantly kept scanning the horizon through them. Then he would draw aside from everyone and light a cigarette. He was a hard man, though it cost him some effort to be hard. Sometimes he would pick up a stone and weigh it in his hand. If he saw a lizard, he would quickly stamp on its tail, hold it motionless awhile, then let it go.

From the beginning, Colonel Villalba aroused a mingling of respect and envy in Ascaso. A professional soldier! What was going on in his brain? Someone had told him that the colonel had been a personal friend of Franco. He was on the point of ordering him to the home front, wrapped in cellophane; but his General Staff counseled him not to. The two foreign athletes, in particular, considered that precisely what was most needed was to coordinate all the disparate elements. The athletes feared that as soon as contact was made with the enemy in Siétamo or anywhere else, there would be desertions. They spoke from experience. They had fought in Ethiopia against the Italians. One of them was named Sidlo. He was a Pole and a javelin-thrower. Owing to his low stature, he always stood on tiptoe. His dream was to kill a Fascist with a javelin throw. The other was a Bulgarian who went around like a madman looking for yoghurt, his basic food. The Anarchists christened him "Pulverin" because of the number of weapons he carried at his belt. He was a shot-putter with extraordinary strength in his right arm. Sometimes he appeared to be cross-eyed, other times not.

Both Sidlo and Pulverin were Communists, but they had the good sense to speak of the FAI with respect. Whenever they sat down to write a letter, the militiamen would approach them from behind, and breathing down their necks, would study the written Polish and Bulgarian words. "Those words have lots of guts." The two commissars would laugh: "It takes guts to drink out of a wineskin, too."

Gorki, with his little belly and his dark woolen sash, often cursed the sedentary work that had stiffened his muscles years before. He could not manage his body. Nevertheless, the former perfumer moved as if all the proletariat in the universe were watching him. And he went on sending news stories to Gerona and secret reports to Cosme Vila. "As soon as it can be done, I'm going to set up a library and organize classes for the illiterates." "You ought to try to have Gerona send us clothing, tobacco, books by Baroja, Pedro Mata, and Pitigrilli." "We also need prophylactics, but not for me, as you know." "Couldn't you arrange to have Axelrod pay us a visit?"

Gorki was not accompanied by any woman, though the ardent commissar could not decide whether that was a good or a bad thing. The athletes, Sidlo and Pulverin, considered it suicidal to permit the enlistment of women in the militia. But when they became convinced that no one was paying any attention to their dicta, they shrugged their shoulders and joyously went in for suicide. Sidlo, the champion javelin-thrower, linked his fortunes to a girl from Tarragona, a somewhat tragic type who kept saying she wanted to die young. Pulverin came to terms with a prostitute from Gerona who prayed daily to San Pancracio that she should not lack employment. Ascaso performed some marriages, for the Anarchist code pledged the contracting parties to mutual faithfulness, a stipulation that, in La Valencia's opinion, proved the Anarchists' meager understanding of the world. In the course of the ceremony, Ascaso would say: "You, man, are forbidden to have another woman. But, just in case, you'd better repudiate this one first, so turn her loose."

Certain sights had made a special impression on Ascaso's men. First, the boundary crosses always erected in the most prominent places in the villages, which formed capital Ts outlined against the sky. Second, the plastic appearance of the lice in the seams of their clothing and their armpits. Third, the silence that reigned over the village of Tamarite as they entered it. The entire village had fled in tenor to the woods and fields. Only one inhabitant had remained in the village: a man of some fifty years, unshaved and looking like a beggar. He was waiting for the militia in the plaza, playing the saxophone.

Finally the column neared its objective: Siétamo. It lay only a gunshot away, barring the road to Huesca. Ascaso gave the order to make camp, then withdrew, and did not return until after he had stepped on the biggest lizard yet. What was about to happen on the following day? No one knew, and everyone settled down to fill the hours of waiting as best he could.

Gorki took refuge in his dispatches to *El Proletario,* as usual. He felt particularly inspired by the light of an oil lantern—the lantern was a sardine can—and he composed a beautiful treatise on blood and thirst. He said that human blood was sweet and that if no man had ever emptied his red veins, poppies would never have sprung up amid the corn and flags could never have been designed. Then he declared that the worst torture of the front lines was thirst… In that corner of the Aragónese earth, ever in the hands of capitalists, thirst was sometimes as deep as truth. It was so great that the militiamen were not able to sing. They could express themselves only by drumming on their aluminum plates and cooking utensils.

From time to time, Puppy would come up to him and ask: "When are you going to teach me to read?" Puppy had, in fact, become the mascot, not alone for Gorki and La Valenciana, but for the entire column. The boy never before had left his village of Pina. This was the great adventure of his youth. He did not know against whom he was to fight, but that did not matter. If so many men "hated" someone, they must have their reasons, and the pacifists in his village might as well be living on the moon.

Ascaso himself was particularly fond of the boy and he would often pat him on the head. He did not want to issue arms to him; but he gave him a comet to make up for it. Puppy was to be the bugler for the column. He could play reveille on it, and perhaps even a charge. And later, during rest periods, and in the truck, he could lend gaiety to the atmosphere by imitating dogs as only he in all Aragón could do it.

The body of troops heading toward the South, toward Teruel, was moving under precisely the same conditions, under the command of the Anarchist Ortiz, a carpenter by trade. It also kept enrolling many peasant volunteers, who never tired of reiterating their gratitude to Catalonia for sending the column to their rescue. They seemed more timorous and doubtful than the men from the Province of Huesca, and many of them were even more poverty-stricken. At every village along the road, a committee was waiting for them, offering very humble provisions, which it handed over to the commissary as it went past. "*¡Salud!*" "*¡Salud!*" From time to time a dead body could be seen lying in a culvert or on a corner. Ortiz would halt and if the body lay prone, he would turn it over to look at the face.

When this force had left Barcelona, it had been composed almost entirely of Anarchists, some German and Italian athletes, and the contingent from Gerona assembled by Murillo and Canela, by Major Campos—who had not yet revealed his rank—and by the colony of Murcians. To Ortiz's great satisfaction, however, he soon began to receive considerable reinforcements. These were made up of the common prisoners released from the jail in Valencia, already formed into companies called "Iron" and "Ghost" when they reported to him. Elated by their recent release and by strong drink, these prisoners proved very hard to discipline and seemed to be waiting eagerly for combat, which they called "the ball game." Many of them displayed arms tattooed with seamen's motifs or with indistinct forms that took on an erotic meaning when the arm was flexed. They arrived loaded down with victuals, especially all kinds of fruit, and a great deal to drink. Murillo and Canela made friends with them, and the girl was in her glory eating oranges and showering her face and chest with their juice.

These former prisoners in the "Iron" and "Ghost" companies were the ones who came to give the column its particular character. They kept jumping on and off the tracks and never stopped talking about their stay in jail. "Remember, Cerillita, that 'stew' we used to have for breakfast?" "How could anyone forget shit?" As they passed through the villages, they made it a point to visit each jail, and amid horselaughs they would parody their old habits by urinating in some corner of the patio or something of that sort. When the time came to leave the village, they would either shoot the prisoners or leave them in peace, depending upon their own humor or the suggestions of the wardens. Cerillita, who stood out from all the others, and who was called Little Candle because of his thinness and the shape of his head, had adopted the custom of jumping on the prisoners' bare feet, as his own feet often had been jumped on. He was a strange boy who carried a leather-cutter's knife in his bedroll and threatened everyone with it. He also carried a small, stubby Communion chalice that he used for drinking and shaving. Ortiz permitted all his misbehavior because he could not do otherwise, and because one of his maxims was "Anything goes."

The foreign athletes, for their part, had an obsession about bathing. They would have liked to follow the course of the Ebro, the father of Spanish rivers. Lacking a common language, they made themselves understood by signs to the militia, and their shower pantomime was seen more often than any other of their subtleties for making themselves comfortable in an open encampment. Their ex-officio leader was the Italian Gerardi, hairy and apelike. Gerardi and his own men were veteran guerrilla fighters, and they longed to impose discipline on the column and to advise Ortiz. But Ortiz proved intransigent, and furthermore was not lacking in ideas of his own. It bothered him that the athletes were German and Italian, and before long he was giving them the same sidelong glances as those Ascaso was giving Colonel Villalba. He would warn the militiawomen who formed liaisons with them, "All right. But watch your step!"

The two principal preoccupations of Ortiz were the artillery and the requisitioning of animals for hauling and carrying packs. He was well aware that the fieldpieces were jewels, and that, properly handled, each of those mouths was worth a battalion. When he noticed that the militiamen did not even know what a range-finder was, or how to direct the fire, and that they would climb all over the cannon as if they were carnival rides, he was in despair. One of the men, Sidonio by name, was from Almeria, where he had seen a human cannonball in the circus, and he had taken it into his head that he should be shot out of a big gun like the circus woman. "I'd come down on the Fascists, and bang!"

The requisitioning of animals as food or beasts of burden was entirely necessary, but it gave rise to painful scenes. The owners of the mud and adobe huts loved their rabbits and hens, and especially their mules and burros. Furthermore, buried as they were in the stony red soil, they never even had heard of the revolution. Their eyes would bulge with astonishment at the sight of a lot of men in breechclouts, with pirates' scarves on their heads, and then at hearing them demand that the animals be turned over to them. "*¡Salud!*" "Here, good people!" "The Jackals of Progress." "We're on our way to Teruel!" "Long live the FAI!" "Long live Durruti!" They could make nothing of such jargon, and the mule or the burro or the goat would stir uneasily.

Later, in the trucks, the animals slaughtered for food seemed to be asleep, while the mules and burros, future beasts of burden, brayed anxiously. Moments would come when the men longed to fire a bullet into their heads. At close range, traces of an atavistic sadness could be read in the tendons of the neck and in the eyes, especially in the eyes. They were mules or burros that almost never had seen green grass. Their hides were like stone made skin, and the twitching of their ears seemed to be marking time. The goats, for their part, tried to escape. In the trucks, their front legs were raised so that their teats were generously offered to the militiamen. Cerillita tied empty tin cans to their tails or dazzled their eyes from a distance with a mirror.

The column was meeting no organized resistance, so that when Ortiz called a halt and spread his enormous map out on the ground, everyone laughed at him. "What's he doing that for? He must be a nut!" With their objective, Teruel, in sight, however, Ortiz gave the order to make camp. He intended to send his scouts to reconnoiter the enemy terrain during the night and to attack at dawn in accordance with what he learned from them. The militiamen, primed to fight, kept urging one another forward. Gerardi tried to reason with them with no better results. Fortunately, several Assault Guards, deserters from Teruel, reported to Ortiz at the critical moment, and their statements changed everyone's mind. The number of the city's defenders had grown, and, contrary to appearances, all the surrounding prominences were manned and the machine guns and rifles at the ready. "You'll find yourself in a pickle unless you lay down a heavy artillery barrage." A pickle! At that word, Ortiz clenched his fists and threw out his chest.

He tried immediately to impose his authority. Using the megaphone that had belonged to a swimming instructor, the same one Future had used, he summoned his commanding officers and noncoms and ordered them to fan out so as to give him time to study the emplacements. But already a number of the militiamen had dispersed and some were far away, practicing at throwing hand grenades. "If they aren't a bunch of fools!" The members of the "Iron" and "Ghost" units in particular, egged on by Cerillita, seemed determined to take Teruel on their own and hand it to Ortiz as a gift. They advanced waving rags and singing "To the Barricades," and sometimes "Adiós, Pamplona." The jail, the recent jail, seemed to have addled their brains.

Night fell at last, tinging the motley camp spread over several miles with melancholy. The sky was clear and high. The headlights of the cars along the road were turned off. Weariness overtook them. Shadows moved along the lines, and the militiamen, seated on the ground, postponed the moment of lying down to sleep. No one lighted a fire. Everyone ate cold rations, but little by little the glow of cigarettes pierced the darkness. Cigarettes reassured them, for they signified the presence of comrades and that a man was himself a reality. A close look at the button of fire would reveal scraps of red and blue that seemed to exchange confidences before dying. When a cigarette went out, it left something behind. And after throwing his stub away, a militiaman would stay motionless for a time, sitting with his legs apart, as if meditating upon the great effort he must make at dawn.

It seemed strange to the Murcians who had come from Gerona not to hear the cries of their children or the murmur of the sea. They were accustomed to the summer nights of S'Agaró and other coastal villages. One of them, Hoyos by name, had a beautiful voice, and he would have poured from his throat all that he was feeling at that moment had it not been for the reports of the Assault Guards. The women who had linked their fate to that of the soldiers sought their men with lips and hands until they could feel their blood grow warm. Murillo and Canela, who feared the night dew, wrapped themselves in a banner that said MILITIAWOMEN OF THE POUM. One man fell asleep with his arms around the wheel of a truck. At midnight cheeks were pillowed on the most heterogeneous materials, from aluminum plates to leather cartridge belts. The foreign athletes demonstrated their skill at making themselves comfortable. Many of them had made beds of weeds and a blanket, and more than one acquired a mattress by taking possession of one of the pads used to protect the vehicles from bullets.

In that region, as old as war and hunger, the spaced silhouettes of the sentries appeared for the first time. Some of them hung their watches on olive trees. The watches swung as the sentries probed the silence before them, stretching ahead as far as Teruel. From time to time the goats would strain desperately against their tethers.

DURRUTI, Buenaventura Durruti, had followed the highway at the head of his column, with Zaragoza as his objective. His spearhead was aimed at this city in which he had accounts to settle, in which he had often been given delirious ovations and also had been persecuted.

The legendary Anarchist leader was forty years old. He had been born in León in 1896. At the age of twenty-one he had traversed Spain from top to bottom on a "crusade for social agitation." At thirty, he had taken part in the abortive attempt on Alfonso XIII's life in Paris. He had been imprisoned and exiled again and again. On the day of the uprising, he had directed the attack on the barracks in Barcelona and later on the armories and the arsenals of the ships anchored in the harbor. He was a man at once hard and sentimental, with an infallible talent for attracting to him other hard and sentimental men. He always used to say: "What's past is past." Because the past weighed too heavily on him. He had grand plans for the future, chief among which was the union of Portugal with Spain.

"I've had enough of Portugal not being Spain" was an old refrain he would utter as he ran his hand along his hairy cheek. Perhaps he would cross the Portuguese border with his own troops once Fascism had been downed.

His column was the best of the three, the only one that did not wear an obvious air of improvisation. A fair number of armored vehicles, fieldpieces, mortars, machine guns, and so on. Two ambulances at the disposal of Dr. Rosselló and his aide, Dr. Vega. Horses and many other animals requisitioned along the way. A band of musicians to inspire the men heading the march as well as those in the rear, the so-called "little red stoplights."

From time to time Durruti would stand on top of one of the vehicles to supervise the march of his column, observing that many men were left behind along the way, particularly in the villages. He had already taken this into account, so forward! The militiawomen added a note of color, as did Captain Culebra, so named because he carried a tame snake in a little box, and a thin boy nicknamed Rainbow because he was constantly appearing in some sort of disguise.

The makeup of the force was very heterogeneous. How could it be otherwise? The CNT-FAI, Anarchists from Barcelona under Captain Culebra's command were in the majority, together with the men from Gerona under Captain Future's command, two units of Communists, one composed of foreign athletes, and some regular soldiers, even some Civil Guards. In addition, they were joined at the crossroads near Osera by the reinforcements that had issued from Madrid, with José Alvear, Ignacio's cousin, among them. The reinforcements had freed many villages along their way, entering them with the shouted slogan of "Long live the Virgin of Pilar" as a lure. In each case, the enormous confusion of the defenders and their subsequent surrender had led many of the Madrid militia to suppose that they had found the touchstone to victory.

Immediately after leaving Barcelona, each man was able to occupy the post of his choice, for Durruti had ordered all the volunteers to fall in and select the weapon best suited to their tastes or aptitudes. He never forced anyone. "Volunteers for the Artillery, step forward one pace!" "Infantry, to the right!" "Communications and sappers, to the left!" And so on, until the fighting units were filled. Durruti realized that this was the most rational procedure, for he knew from experience that every soldier has his own likes and dislikes, which could turn him into a useful man or a nonentity. The jubilation of the militiamen proved him right. "Thanks, Durruti!" "Thanks, Chief!" "Give me a mortar that can sing." Durruti himself preferred the submachine gun. It was suited to his temperament, with its spasmodic bursts, like his own chattering manner. To him, cannon had one fault: there was no way of knowing whether what it shattered at the end of its trajectory was the enemy or a section of wall or trenches. The submachine gun, on the other hand, mowed down visible bodies.

The column was moving forward with almost no resistance, for its advance had been covered by light attacks upon Zaragoza from the air. It seemed that one of these had resulted in a direct hit on the gas works, for a huge tongue of fire and smoke rose into the air as far as the horizon.

Durruti's main concern was to combine individual initiative with efficiency in order to give the lie to those who declared that instinct, whether in peace or war, was the opposite of intelligence. Like El Responsable in Gerona, this man might have been said to be playing his stellar role at that moment. He was realizing a dream that went back to childhood. He always had aspired to occupy one of the main Spanish highways, well paved, with an objective in front of him, and an idealistic mass behind, singing hymns.

On the advice of Major Pérez Farrás, he adopted measures to assure insofar as possible the functioning of certain key services. He placed a Frenchman whom he had named Landru, whose trade was not known, in charge of communications. Landru linked together a perfect telephone network. A militiaman defined the Frenchman thus: "He knows how to say hello as well as anyone and he can hit you with a pie in four languages." The liaison men, selected without exception from Durruti's Anarchist friends, were supplied with motorcycles and crash helmets. Rainbow was put in charge of the camouflage of men and matériel—a mania with Durruti. Rainbow had learned the art of disguise in an establishment in which he had worked for fifteen years at the business of renting out all kinds of furnishings and clothing for amateur theatrical productions, masquerade balls, parades, and the like. Durruti put him to the test: in the twinkling of an eye Rainbow transformed a gasoline tank into a straw stack, a cannon into a tree trunk, a man into a sapling endowed with mobility. The Quartermaster's Corps was headed by several butchers who had joined up in Lérida, and Health was left entirely in the hands of Dr. Rosselló and his assistant, Dr. Vega. "Doctor, you will report to me on everything that pertains to health."

Everyone was pleased, including Dr. Rosselló, the one man whom Durruti addressed formally, perhaps because the first thing the doctor did every morning was to shave.

The doctor, who was trying on some surgical gloves from England in Durruti's presence, said to the Anarchist leader: "Don't worry...and take care of yourself. Don't forget that you're our leader."

Dr. Rosselló! The venture was increasingly reconciling him with his profession, as in Gerona he had hoped it would. Truth to tell, he had wavered in Barcelona and been on the point of backing out. The ingenuousness of the militiamen was boundless! But as soon as they all began to move along the highway, he realized that he had chosen wisely and that his work would be useful. Yes, it was obvious that the moment the weapons began to speak and the enemy to reply, he would be brought wounded bodies, bodies and minds to work on, for the doctor knew that machine guns could wound more than the flesh. How could he desert those people? Brother Julián Cervera had said to him: "Our motto is to help our neighbor." Oh, yes! The way lay clear before him. Dr. Rosselló could do good—he already had begun to do good. But in spite of that, the Frenchman Landru had said to him after he had been treated for a scratch on the leg, looking first at the doctor's face, then at his hands: "I don't know whether you're hot or cold."

Durruti also wanted to establish a system of rewards and punishments among his men. He was very detached about it, as always. Heroic deeds were rewarded with leave to the home front, with booty, with promotion, and with permits to sleep with the "Fascist" women being held in the local jails. Cowardly actions, desertion, and theft were punished with penalties that ranged from spitting in the face to a bullet in the belly.

"Where are you going to get the loot?" Future asked him.

"Don't you worry; everything requisitioned by my men is being kept intact, under guard, not far from here."

Consequently, everyone knew his place. Soon the order to encamp would be given. The line was moving more slowly now, in time to the majestic leisureliness of the sun, setting far beyond the smoke rising from the gas works in Zaragoza.

Future was one of the most satisfied of the men. He, too, had turned out to be a man of his word. He had married Merche, daughter of El Responsable. The wedding took place in Caspe, according to the rites of the column; he and his bride walking beneath a triumphal arch of clenched fists and rifles. Merche looked beautiful, with a white flower in her hair given her by El Cojo, who had plucked it from some unknown spot, perhaps from the foam on his lips. She came forward on Future's arm and, at the end of the arch both received the rough and comical blessings of a trio composed of Rainbow, a Romanian athlete, and Captain Culebra, who then signed and duly legalized the union.

Another of the satisfied men was Captain Culebra himself. He had married Milagros, the maid from Gerona, livelier than a pair of castanets, formerly a servant in the house of Noguer, the notary. Captain Culebra, who sported a coarse mustache, had a reputation for courage. They used to say he was brave enough to have been an Asturian miner. The snake that he kept in the box covered with a piece of linen added to his popularity. Captain Culebra had turned Anarchist on the day his first wife gave birth to a stillborn baby. Captain Culebra had spat out an oath, punched the wall, and become an Anarchist. Now he would say to Milagros: "No kids, eh?" Then he would add: "I love you." Milagros pretended not to believe him. "Get going with the kid. I want one with that mustache, and knowing how to talk!"

Dimas was another happy man, or almost happy; Dimas, the solitary one. Indeed, the head of the Salt Committee had hit upon a means for venting his black thoughts: the contemplation of flies and ants. Seated apart, with his rifle between his legs and his full canteen beside him, he would watch the circling of the flies and would make a bet with himself on the spot where each fly would alight—whether on the tip of a nose, the trigger of a rifle, or a stalk of grass. He could see through the tiny digestive sacs the transparency of their bodies; and he used to smile at the pirouettes of their feet. He enjoyed the subtle conformation of their wings. The flies were not to be harmed. And much less the ants. Yes, Dimas had suddenly begun to love the ants. This had come about when it first occurred to him to examine one of them singly, one entirely alone. He then discovered that this tenuous miniature lived in a universe as complete in itself, as fragile as the ideas surging through his own head, as the moon that made him nervous on many nights. The ant would advance with challenging speed, and a man never knew what he would do next. He might halt abruptly, retrace his steps, or climb a tiny twig. He seemed prey to terrible internal conflicts or to hereditary palpitations. Sometimes the ants would send forth an inexplicable and contagious zest for life, Dimas came to love the flies and the ants of Aragón so dearly that he sked himself whether his secret companions might not completely vanish from a world as paradisiacal and hygienic as that envisaged by the FAI.

There was one man, however, who could have given cards and spades to anyone in the Durruti column in matters of love and euphoria, and even camouflage! Durruti did not know him... He had not been assigned to any particular service; he was not called a key man; but there he was, sufficient unto himself, wearing a captain's bars. That man was José Alvear, nephew of Matías, the man whom Carmen Elgazu could not bring herself to forgive, the man who once had stood in the Gerona station with a suitcase filled with subversive pamphlets. The man who had once said to Ignacio: "Those vipers must be stamped out, and the mothers who bore them!"

José Alvear had arrived with the Anarchist reinforcements from Madrid. He never had aspired to "posts of command," for he hated adulation. Nevertheless, he was very well known to his own men, and would soon be well known throughout the column. Not alone for his vitality, but because in the entire Anti-Fascist Militia he was the one individual who wore a derby hat. Ah, indeed, Rainbow would nearly burst with jealousy when he heard about it! José Alvear had requisitioned the hat in Madrid, in one of the palaces along the Castellana, after taking part in the attack on the Montana barracks, in which he distinguished himself. Wearing the hat, he had been a member of the parade through the streets of Madrid in which the head of General López Ochoa was exhibited on the tip of a pole. He had worn it when he patrolled at night behind the wheel of a Fiat that "went like God," meting out justice from it, the justice he had learned from his father and the FAI, to many persons, two marchionesses among them, before "taking care of them" against a tree. Finally he had fought with the Mangada column in the Sierra, had saluted the "Fascist" trenches from afar, and had married three times since the outbreak of the revolution.

José Alvear admired Durruti, but refused to show it. Besides, he had arrived on the Aragón front somewhat tired, had climbed nimbly into the mobile canteen and lain down to sleep on a cat's-tongue mattress, covering even his head with a blanket.

He slept nine hours straight. And with the newborn day, he yawned, and as he left the mobile canteen to light his first cigarette, he saw someone who milled his peace of mind. A few steps away from him, he recognized El Cojo. There could be no doubt of that! There stood El Responsable's nephew, his pal from Gerona, next to a banner that said The Anti-Fascist Hyenas, rubbing his buttocks as usual and staring all around him as though seeking his own reason for being.

José Alvear recovered himself quickly and took note of the place, orienting himself. Of course, of course there were many volunteers from Gerona! He tossed away his cigarette and went directly to El Cojo. After a very brief preamble, he inquired about the Alvear family and saw El Cojo's lips tremble as he told him that the little priest in the family had been "rubbed out."

José felt a catch in his chest and was at a loss to know what to do. Unconsciously he took off his derby hat. He stared at El Cojo, then at Durruti's camouflaged lean-to, and finally turned completely around, facing Zaragoza, still enveloped with smoke from the burning gas works. He remembered clearly the entire family group surrounding César in the dining room in Gerona. He could see them individually, Ignacio somewhat absent-minded, and could hear again their "*Ora pro nobis.*" He turned back and went into his mobile canteen. There he sat down, tossed his hat into a corner, and spent a long time caressing his memories.

AFTER a skirmish just outside the village of Escatrón, the Durruti column had approached so close to Zaragoza that the city, with its sugar factories and its railroad equipment works, seemed within hand's reach. Lieutenant Colonel Díaz Sandino, head of the Catalan air force, was sending out from the Prat airfield in a steady stream all the aircraft at his disposal, with orders to bomb all the small enemy concentrations they could spot.

Díaz Sandino announced from the balcony of the City Hall that "the surrender of Zaragoza was imminent," and Major Pérez Farrás made a similar statement.

But the defenders, who had begun to inspire some hope of survival in the people of La Zaila and Azaila with the appearance of some cavalry units there, still were displaying activity in Quinto, Codo, and Belchite. This forced Durruti to plan a broad pincers movement. During the ensuing pause, it was relatively easy to slip from one camp to the other, and this was to change the basis of the operation. Indeed, a substantial number of Civil Guards went over to the rebels in a body. In return, fugitives from Zaragoza, particularly Assault Guards and regular soldiers, plus some farmers and their wives, began to present themselves to Durruti in greater numbers than at Teruel.

Their reasons for coming across the lines were similar to those of the Teruel deserters, but with one variation. They said that if Zaragoza had not thrown its doors wide open to Durruti, it was his own fault. The Assault Guards, their eyes still bulging with terror, considered that it had been folly to announce the advance of the column with bombers and a lot of racket, and especially stupid to urge the thirty thousand Syndicalists in Zaragoza by radio and pamphlets from the air to disobey the orders of the military and sabotage their efforts. The consequences had been swift and ruthless. Cabanellas, the rebel general, had launched a bloody "mop-up" that left an incalculable number of victims, even though he still had concluded his accusations with the cry of "Long live the Republic!" All the revolutionary units had been decimated and terror reigned among the poor families. The recruits themselves could not show their party or syndicate cards because they had thrown them away or burned them. To top it all, a thousand Navarrese Requetés had gone to the aid of Cabanellas. "Comrade Durruti, we're giving it to you straight. It was a mistake that cost us very dear. It cost the lives of many, many comrades. If you want names, we'll give them to you. Your own comrades Gil and Royo were shot yesterday while the gas works was burning..."

Major Pérez Farrás felt stricken at hearing such things, and Durruti paled at the mention of the names of his two companions in the FAI. The Anarchist leader realized, nonetheless, that it was futile to bewail inevitable mistakes, for the only way to organize the column speedily in Catalonia had been to give it publicity. Accordingly, he asked for more air cover, and with the support of the militia, particularly those on the Southern wing, some of whom had already begun to act on their own account, he gave the appropriate orders for an all-out attack on Zaragoza.

"Fire!"

This was the start of the first battle worthy of the name. The characteristic roar of all kinds of firearms discharging at once benumbed the militia. Durruti and Pérez Farrás aimed their batteries according to the information given by the deserters. Look out for the planes! The Anarchist volunteers flung themselves on the ground, tasting earth. What was happening in the world? To judge by facial expressions, the earth had been shot in the heart.

The shock was felt along a broken and arbitrary line. For lack of trenches and parapets, they made use of the accidental contours of the land, particularly the outcroppings and the hollows. Ah, it wasn't a question of target practice now, of aiming at tricorns nailed to gates, much less of slitting the bellies of priests or notaries in a culvert! This was a matter of facing men determined to kill. Regular soldiers, Popular Action, Falangists, Requetés—Navarrese Requetés!—and Civil Guards. Just where were they hidden? No one knew. Where they had expected strong resistance, there was none; where the terrain seemed open, heavy firing suddenly crashed forth.

From his observation post, Durruti had seen the face of the enemy. He had spotted red berets—the color red meant suicide during wartime—and blue shirts. Were the Falangists shooting arrows? And he had seen officers and troops crawling nimbly along the earth and skillfully moving into empty corners. The picture was clear. The right wing, led by Pérez Farrás himself, was making headway against the enemy; on the other hand, the left wing and center core, under General Mena of Tarragona, were running into unexpected difficulties.

Half an hour after the battle started, there was weeping in Aragón. Tears gushed from the cannon, from the machine guns, the rifles, the hand grenades. Gaps appeared in the lines. Where was this one, that one, the other one? A dark force was sucking in men, some of whom, Ideal among them, were fighting hand to hand, while others, Dimas among them, could see no enemy near them. The intermingling of troops on the plain was such that air cover and artillery both held back to keep from destroying their own front lines.

The bullets, and even the shrapnel seemed to go forth toward fixed destinations. But they had scarcely left the muzzles of the guns when, as if blinded by their own velocity, they would orient themselves capriciously and might as easily kill a worm as make a worm of a man or woman. The fire was widely strewn, contrary to the calculations that had been made.

Equally random was the valor and the generosity of the men. Individuals, whole platoons, such as that of the homosexuals from the Entertainment Syndicate, seemed to have forgotten that they wanted to go on living. Others were panic-stricken, and some, like the opportunistic cats in the Gerona prison, changed their minds about fighting at all. Of course the voice and bearing of the commanding officers and the fluttering of banners exerted a strong influence on the men. As for selflessness, what can be said? Generous deeds were continuous and anonymous. Rainbow placed a crown of laurel on his head, perhaps to honor them. "You wait here, I'll go ahead," was generosity. "Keep your head down, I'm just a poor devil," that was generosity. "Careful, Future, you're a bridegroom," was also generosity. The binoculars of the officers could not spot such things, for they occurred in low-voiced utterances and personal reactions. But there were those who gave their lives for their friends, those who gave their lives for strangers. Why did the pools of blood bubble with a croaking sound? Because the generous deeds were like fish jumping.

Durruti, still in his observation post, was furious. Communications were not functioning as Landru had promised. Foot liaison was unreasonably slow. The munitions supplies proved disagreeably surprising, for many cartons did not contain the material indicated by their labels. In fact, the only service that functioned satisfactorily was the Health Service directed by Dr. Rosselló, which skillfully covered the front lines. He had installed his field hospital at the edge of the highway in a "chauffeur's hostel," with booths in the dining room which served him as operating rooms.

Dr. Rosselló had given the orderlies their instructions: "The worst injuries are abdominal, next chest and head wounds, then limbs." The field and operating room orderlies had learned their lessons, and when they brought in a wounded man they would say "Abdominal," "Chest," or "Head," if not all three at the same time.

The men reacted variously to their wounds, each according to the code of the side for which he was fighting. On the Red side, many would spit out an oath; on the Nationalist side, most of them exclaimed, "Oh, God!" A boy from Tremp, in Captain Culebra's company, clenched his fists and said: "I'm out of gas." A dentist from Zaragoza who had fought with his scapulars swinging, scratched at his shirt and whispered: "Goodbye, Pamplona." Among those mortally wounded, the differences were stressed dramatically, for whereas on the Red side, a dying man usually had a woman at his side—his own or one of the militia floaters with no particular man—the dying men on the Nationalist side were generally attended by the field chaplain. It was obvious that in either case, a man could feel that he was not dying alone.

What was happening to the prisoners? Perhaps there could be no cruder fate than theirs. Suddenly they would find themselves surrounded by men who were not mere men, but rifles thirsting for their lives.

The confusion in the lines made possible the taking of many prisoners on both sides. Three Jackals of Progress on the Southern wing fell into the hands of a Falangist squadron. The Falangist corporal was from Zuera, and his name was Ayuso. He was loose-fleshed and flabby. The three Jackals were from Barcelona, very young, great billiard players. Corporal Ayuso, wearing immense arrows on his shirt, asked them if they had anything to say. Hands up and backs turned, the Jackals refused to answer. When they heard Ayuso loading his automatic rifle, one of the boys threw himself on the ground, while another started to shout: "Cowards, cowards! Murderers! Murd—" That was all. Ayuso fired coolly, and the three boys from Barcelona became motionless pawns of history.

At the same time the political commissar of the "Lenin" battalion captured two Requetés on a rise that had changed hands six times during the day. The commissar was a Communist from Tarrasa, a weaver by trade, nicknamed Commissar Siberia because he was always talking about Russia in Asia. Commissar Siberia disarmed the two Requetés and looked them up and down, surprised at the size of their berets and that they were not in uniform, but in their shirt-sleeves and *espadrilles*, as if they had just come from their village. Suddenly he noticed that someone had embroidered an emblem of the Sacred Heart on the shirt of the younger, just over the heart. It said: "*Stop, bullet.*" Siberia decided to put it to the test. He drew his pistol and calmly aimed at the emblem. He fired, and the bullet did not stop. It pierced the embroidery and the Requeté's heart. The man grimaced as if to say "How curious!" blew into the mouth of the gun, and, noting that the other Requeté had made an uneasy movement, got ready to fire again. But the boy, who had turned the color of parchment, bit his lip cruelly and said quickly: "I warn you that we've poisoned the waters of the Ebro."

He did not know why he said this, to the astonishment of Commissar Siberia and of the river itself, flowing below with an audible murmur. He said it either in the hope of extricating himself or for the pleasure of envisioning a catastrophe. Commissar Siberia ripped out a terrible oath, riddled the Requeté, who fell beside his comrade, and then headed straight for the nearest field telegraph to communicate the news to Durruti.

The face of the adjutant who received the message tightened in disbelief. Nevertheless, he stared at the Ebro, which was full of silt and within three hundred yards of emptying into the sea. Durruti asked him "What's up?" and when he was told, he ordered: "Bring me a glass of that water and I'll drink it." But it was too late to ward off fear. The rumor of poisoned water ran from mouth to mouth and village to village with dizzying speed. It ran along telegraph wires and on motorcycle saddles. "Don't drink water! Cap the tanks! Don't go near the riverbank!"

The battle was long and agonizing. All the frantic efforts of individuals failed to shape it into orderly combat. The day was far gone, and the militiamen feared to see the first tints of pink in the sky. "Up and at them!" But Zaragoza was not any closer... It was acquiring an increasingly hostile aspect with distance. "Forward!" But how?

José Alvear was the delight of the sector where he was fighting. He had both luck and imagination, and he waved his derby at the planes overhead which never had let up for a moment. Throughout the morning, his mission was to watch over and advise the greenhorns. "Take off the safety, you fool!" "Put your aluminum plate on your head!" In the afternoon he occupied a hill singlehanded and covered with machine-gun fire the advance of twelve of his men vainly seeking a hollow to dig themselves into. José Alvear, an ardent officer, even found the time to observe. He said to himself, "It's an odd thing how many bodies that are cut down form letters on the ground as they fall. That one looks like an X. The one over there with his legs apart like a V. The one with his arms out and his hands bent, like a T."

Captain Culebra was another imaginative man. José Alvear stimulated him. "Who's the guy?" he had asked, pointing to José's derby. "One of the Madrid FAI." Captain Culebra, though short and fleshy like Gorki, wanted to prove worthy of such a comrade. He rescued the wounded from no-man's-land, issued orders, and rationed out sips of cognac, planted the flag in the shoulder of a dead Civil Guard. From behind a billboard advertising sherry, he surprised the enemy by firing off rockets he had stolen from a fireworks store in Alcañiz.

"There she goes!" The blue, then the pink, swift fountains of fire shot through the open air ahead. Milagros stared upward: "What good is that?" "Women had better keep their mouths shut."

The day ineluctably ended, and the battle still showed no sign of going one way or the other. The Nationalists were only waiting for the shadows to take possession of Aragón. The dead bodies that formed letters were so many that read in sequence they composed an elegy, a song that had an irresistible drawing power for the hungry ants studied so lovingly by Dimas.

Future lay among the dead, despite the image he had carried with him of the Infant Jesus wearing a militiaman's cap and with a pair of pistols at his belt. Yes, the boy who had been a child of the Barcelona wharves would never be able to send General Cabanella's head to El Responsable as he had promised. Neither would he be able to keep Merche happy as he had promised on their wedding day. He died the victim of a random bullet fired by an amateur just for fun. It struck him in the abdomen and instantly El Cojo who was fighting at his side, open-mouthed as usual as if waiting for a bird to peck his gums, said to him: "What's the matter?"

Future died at sundown in the improvised hospital, attended by Dr. Rosselló. "Doctor, I don't want to die!" But an internal hemorrhage was draining him of life. "I don't want to die, Merche, Merche!" Merche was wiping away his sweat, while El Cojo, sobbing, was holding the charm of the Infant Jesus, not knowing whether to pray to it or stamp on it.

Finally, Captain Future ceased to breathe in the fullness of his twenty-six Anarchist years. Merche let out a delirious scream that caused the round, blue eyes of the Infant Jesus to open wide, while Dr. Rosselló who had been in the operating theater all day with his gloves never off, simply said: "Next!"

At the end of the day, Durruti and Major Pérez Farrás gave up the idea of taking Zaragoza. In the North, Ascaso had given up taking Huesca; and in the South, Ortiz had given up taking Teruel. Durruti and the major got busy carrying out their promise to the column to apportion the rewards and punishments. Durruti punished Landru, in communications, for his tardy field lines, and Dimas, whom he had found behind a rock studying a yo-yo given him by Rainbow. Pérez Farrás rewarded Future by providing an ambulance to carry him to Gerona in the coffin El Cojo had found for him, accompanied by Merche.

José Alvear and Captain Culebra were each awarded a pass that read "*Permit to sleep with a Fascist woman.*" Captain Alvear was given the El Burgo prison, where he could pick and choose among the women, and Captain Culebra the Alfajarín prison. They could ride in any vehicle that was evacuating wounded. They were to be back the next day at sunrise.

Night fell over Aragón. At the moment when the ambulance carrying Future started to roll toward the home front, José Alvear and Captain Culebra were climbing into the back of a truck from Administration, which took them, along with other heroes, to their reward.

The two captains were exhausted. They had had a hard day, and they lay down with their faces to the stars. José Alvear covered his face with his hat; Captain Culebra shaded his eyes with a handkerchief. The belt of stainless steel that José was wearing kept cutting into him as if it were a suction cup. Captain Culebra was worrying because he had to be back at sunrise.

The farther they went from the front, the less real it seemed. They could hear mortars firing at regular intervals in the distance. "Give me a cigarette." "Okay. Here it comes."

José Alvear tried to picture the women in the El Burgo prison, Captain Culebra those in the Alfajarín jail. They were exhausted. Occasionally they would mutter "Zaragoza." And an hour after the departure of the two captains they were lying dead to the world, each with his permit clasped in his hand.

TEN

NATIONALIST Spain was maintaining communications with France through a village in the Navarrese Pyrenees called Dancharinea. There were "Fascist" carabineers in Dancharinea, and the bicolor flag waved over it. To cross that borderline when coming from Red Spain was to enter another world. All the symbols that meant life in the Red zone meant death in Dancharinea and vice versa. A remarkable schism to occur within a single country.

The fugitives from Red Spain came by land or sea in legions. Some of them put the Civil War out of their minds as soon as they set foot in a foreign country and began to look for work or to seek economic aid from such business firms in France or England as had had dealings with them. Others moved to Italy or the Côte d'Azur, where they spent their days in hotels, listening avidly to newscasts or playing cards. But the great majority, not yet recovered from the terrors of their flight, turned to the Nationalist Spain of Dancharinea after making an obligatory stop at the Sanctuary of Lourdes, where they begged asylum of that Lady whose image they had been forced to destroy or burn.

All this confirmed the prophesies of Ezequiel. He had always said to Marta that war is like one of those pipes children use for blowing soap bubbles. Men were the bubbles. No one knew what was going to become of them, where they would come to rest, whether they would hide in a cell for the insane or drift across chains of mountains. No one knew whether they would grow to an important size or burst without pain or glory.

The Nationalist officials and carabineers who guarded the frontier at Dancharinea were hardened to the scenes of hysterical patriotism and the tears with which the fugitives from the Red zone greeted them. At the first glimpse of the bicolor waving over French soil, the refugees would lift their arms and shout: "Long live Spain! Up, Spain! Long live the nation's flag!" That scrap of cloth meant resurrection to them. They would run to it and kiss it and press it to them. "Long live Spain! Long live Spain!" Some of them knelt and kissed the ground as they crossed the border. They would embrace and kiss the officials and the carabineers, and they almost expected the woods, the trees, and the soil to share their jubilation. Ah, how near and yet how far were Cosme Vila and El Responsable, Durruti and Stalin! The uniforms of the soldiers looked like the garments of the gods and the coffee offered to them seemed like mead.

What had such wonders to do with reality? Dr. Relken would have said: "To each his own," and "It's all in the mind." So many lives, so many camps, so many anthems, and so many colors stretching from that village on the French border to Seville and into Africa! To reach Morocco they had to cross all of Navarre, then Castile, then Extremadura, and finally Andalusia, where they crossed the Straits of Gibraltar. To go up over the mesa and then down. More than a third of Spain. More than ten million human beings. Baptismal fonts and cemeteries. Minds and hearts. Laughing and suffering without end. Unity and diversity. Not all the carabineers bore the stamp of princes, nor was everyone drinking coffee fit for the gods. José Luis Martínez de Soria, Marta's brother, a volunteer in the Falangist Onésimo Redondo Company garrisoned in the mountainous region called Alto de León, was staring around him and thinking: "Castile is beautiful!" Paz Alvear, Pilar's cousin in Burgos, was in her home at 12 Calle de la Piedra, with her head shaved and castor oil in her stomach, and with the realization that her father, Matías's brother, had been shot on the 20th of July by the Blue Patrol. She lacked the strength even to utter a word, and she spent the hours bundled up in her kitchen, keeping her mother company.

All such things constituted the problem that was worrying Mosén Francisco in the Campistol sisters' apartment. Mosén Francisco always had believed that after so many millennia of human life, and especially after the more recent words of Jesus Christ, man had established his scale of values on earth, man knew what was permitted him and what was not, and just which grass should be mown. And now at the blast of a trumpet men were emerging from the awful caves of passion and ignorance in Spain, with guns in their hands that threatened everything. After so many millennia it could happen, then, that Cosme Vila and El Cojo and thousands of other men considered him, the vicar of San Félix, part of the grass that needed to be cut, along with the bishop and the Works delegate, and the assistant manager of the Arús Bank. On the other hand, a dentist nicknamed Warning Voice, a boy named Ignacio, and a couple of dressmakers named Campistol believed that the grass that should be cut was in the other field yonder: Cosme Vila, David and Olga, the deputies of the Left, the laborers in any syndicate or in the People's Houses. What was the meaning of this game of Russian roulette? Some called themselves ministers to the commonweal, and under the emblem of the hammer and sickle, they were firing upon X; others, who believed themselves account able to the Holy Spirit, with crosses and tapers as their symbols, were firing upon Y.

What had the seminarian César Alvear to do with such classifications of people? Was the brother of Matías, the one in Burgos, a murderer or not?

Nobody knew; everybody knew; nobody was defending anything; everyone was defending something. Those who were killing for the sake of killing were only a few; only a few those who knew why they were killing. The boundaries of the conscience had become amorphous. José Antonio Primo de Rivera once said in a speech that no one would fight over a swimming pool; Ilya Ehrenburg, the Russian poet, had written that no one would fight for abstract ideals, that the one thing man demanded was the satisfaction of his infantile appetites, of the deep selfish needs of the human being.

Mosén Francisco was suffering over these problems spread out before his eyes. But not everyone was as sensitive as he. Among those presumed accountable to the Holy Spirit, there was one who felt he knew beyond a shadow of a doubt where the truth lay: Warning Voice.

Warning Voice had fled Barcelona in a ship bound for Genoa. Within five minutes after he had stepped ashore, he learned of Dancharinea. He started immediately on his way to Nationalist Spain, annoyed because he had to cross France from east to west, that is, that he had to see the fruitful fields of the neighboring nation and its rivers a thousand times more copious than the Ter and the Oñar. Warning Voice was one of the thousands of fugitives who entered Nationalist Spain without doubting for an instant that everything there was wonderful and that all the shots being fired were justified.

Warning Voice was the first of the people from Gerona to kiss the bicolor flag in Dancharinea, as was only right and proper. He arrived there before Noguer, the notary, Mosén Alberto, Mateo and Jorge, the Estrada brothers, or anyone else. At the frontier he was not content to shout "Long live Spain." He had to embrace the flagstaff and burst into tears. He wept so abundantly, so wholeheartedly, that he communicated his emotion to the carabineers watching him from their barracks. An officer went up to him and, gently taking him by the arm, stood beside him. "Calm yourself, calm yourself... You're safe now. Come, you're among friends. We'll fill out your form and you'll be free."

The coffee revived him, and he was further revived by the thought that the officer was what an officer should be. He was a young boy, closely shaved, infinitely more of a gentleman than those militiamen who had been pillaging along the Barcelona wharves as he was going aboard ship. After ten minutes, Warning Voice felt sufficiently restored to speak.

Dear God! He told all that he had seen or imagined in the Red zone. The more he talked, the more he seemed like a hurricane. The drama of his words contrasted with his spotless white suit and linen hat, also white. His sentences always ended with the word "criminals" and his trip to Genoa took on the character of an epic.

Finally a pause came, but the officer failed to note it as such. Soon afterward, he cut him short: "All right, that's enough now. Where do you want to go?"

This upset Warning Voice. What was going on there? Why wouldn't they let him? ... But he checked himself. "To the front," he replied. "I'm a dentist."

"There are no dentists at the front," said the officer in a kindly tone, shaking his head.

Warning Voice's expression did not change. "Then... To Pamplona!" he opted. "I'd like to go to Pamplona and offer my services to the head of the Traditionalist Commune."

"Very well. I'll give you the papers you'll need and a safe-conduct. Wait outside here and we'll let you know when a truck will be leaving for Pamplona."

The officer shook hands. And again he said: "Calm yourself..."

An hour later, Laura's husband began his adventure into the interior of Nationalist Spain. The truck belonged to Administration. He was given a seat in the cab between the driver and a soldier. The driver was a talker. The truck carried an enormous bronze crucifix on the radiator.

Navarre, the seat of Monarchism, Traditionalism made flesh, the idea for which he had fought for twenty-eight years made flesh! "Would you like a smoke? Italian tobacco." "That would go good." "Here... Have one. What are your names?" "I'm Eustaquio." "I'm Lorenzo." How odd! Why weren't they named Fermín? Navarre was beautiful. Smooth hills, green grass. Warning Voice half-expected His Majesty the King to appear in the middle of the road any minute.

Before they reached Pamplona, he had been given some useful information. According to the soldier, the two axes of Nationalist Spain were Castile and Navarre. Castile was a sea of blue shirts, Navarre of red berets. The soldier pronounced blue and red in the same tone of voice, and that rubbed Warning Voice the wrong way. The 19th of July had broken as if by enchantment over the thousands of Falangists in Castile, and they had rushed off to the front. In Navarre the villages and the little houses were emptied. Every Carlist Club became a barracks. Bonfires were built with pictures of Azaña and the others, and the Requetés fell in line and gathered in Pamplona. There were families that had yielded up eleven volunteers: the grandfather, the father, and nine sons. There were women who apologized for having only five sons, or only six.

"What about the harvest? …" "There'll be lots of harvests, but there's only one Spain." "For God, for Country, and for King." The sweethearts and sisters hung scapulars and charms like shields on the Requetés' chests. The bells pealed. The priests heard the volunteers' confessions in the cafés before they marched off, and candles as long as their thoughts were lighted on the altars.

"You've got to change here and wait for the Zumalacárregui truck. See?"

Warning Voice tipped his white linen hat. He reminded himself that the original Requeté beret had been white, too. "But blood had dyed it red!" It was dyed so red that the dentist's first act upon reaching Pamplona was to buy himself an outsized red beret. A red beret and some puttees. Then he went to the Fénix Hotel on the Plaza del Castillo, and looked at himself in the mirror. If Laura only could see him now! If only his brothers-in-law could see him! One, two, one, two, his steps echoed through the room. If only El Responsable could see him!

He went next onto the balcony that commanded a view of the plaza. Serpentines were hanging from the façades of the buildings. Some children were marching to bugles and drums. The Falangist children were called "Arrows" and the Requeté children "Pelayos." The balcony overflowed with spectators drawn by the sound of the music. Catalans and Carlists alike applauded wildly. They were fugitives from the Red zone who had arrived even before Warning Voice. He began to talk with them, and later in the hotel lobby he pelted them with questions. They had come from Olot, from Figueras, from Barcelona. They were manufacturers, lawyers, professors. Some of them had brought their whole families with them. They were full of enthusiasm. They had decided to found an infantry regiment of Catalans under the protection of Our Lady of Montserrat, and to offer it to the supreme command. Two white Russians and three Frenchmen belonging to La Croix de Feu, also guests of the Fénix Hotel, wanted to enlist in La Unidad. For the time being, the head of the Traditionalist Commune in Pamplona, Don Anselmo Ichaso, was sponsoring their project.

Warning Voice blinked when he heard the name of the sponsor. He was sure he had met Don Anselmo Ichaso somewhere, perhaps at some gathering in Madrid.

"He's a tall man," they told him. "Quite fat. With a red face."

Warning Voice decided to pay a visit to Don Anselmo Ichaso straightaway. It turned out to be very difficult to make personal plans, however, to have a choice. News was constantly coming in from the streets, delaying one when he tried to do this or that, and in the end he confined himself to buying a toy bugle to make a noise with, and to going out on the balcony and shouting "Long live Spain!"

But in spite of everything, the interview between Don Anselmo Ichaso and Warning Voice did take place that same day, before supper. Laura's husband called the leader of the Traditionalist Commune, who said when he learned that his caller was a veteran Carlist escaped from the Red zone: "Come over at once."

Warning Voice adjusted his red beret in the style of the French mountain-climbers and, fortified by a brief visit to the Cathedral, found himself within an hour inside the office of the highest Monarchist authority in the region. Don Anselmo Ichaso received him all awash with cordiality, and his first words after the customary greetings threw Warning Voice into the greatest ferment. "Well, well! ... I never pictured the famous Warning Voice from Gerona looking like this," Don Anselmo Ichaso said. "Perhaps you'd be surprised to know that a dozen of your articles which appeared in *El Tradicionalista* have been read aloud in our Carlist Club."

Warning Voice, all puffed up with vanity, whispered: "It can't be possible..."

"Well, my friend, it's true... We're subscribers to *El Tradicionalista* of Gerona. Ah, Navarre has many surprises in store for Catalonia! Would you like a drop of cognac?"

Don Anselmo Ichaso... Tall and round-bellied... A perfect gentleman, with polished fingernails and an apoplectic temperament. He was an engineer by profession, and he seemed to whinny when he talked. His forefathers were Navarrese back to God knows when. He lived in a regal mansion, with portraits of Charles VII and Vázquez Mella in the study; in other words, an assemblage that would have given great pleasure to El Responsable and Captain Culebra, if they had been able to burst in upon it.

Ichaso had two sons and a grandson: a "Pelayo" who played the drum. His elder son was taking part in the advance on Irún under Colonel Beórlegui. His name was Germán, and it was he who had popularized among the Requetés the custom of painting rifle barrels yellow and red for the Spanish flag. The other son was named Javier. He had been sent home from the front on crutches... "He was with Ortiz de Zárate and fell in the fighting at Oyarzun, outside the village. He lost a leg."

Don Anselmo Ichaso had one fault: he never stopped talking. His voice was thunderous, loud enough to sink a bridge. He called the war "The Cause." He was still making occasional trips to the front in his professional capacity as an engineer, to lend a hand to the sappers... While willing to admit that in Catalonia and among the Supreme Command there had always been a restless Carlist minority—the present register of the Fénix Hotel testified to that—he declared that the Movement would have collapsed, as General Mola himself had recognized, had it not been for Navarre. Thanks to Don Anselmo, Warning Voice learned that the volunteers from the district now added up to twenty thousand, and that for two years, since 1934, the Navarrese Carlist Clubs actually had had military posts where the members were given officer training. Their excursions and pilgrimages had provided a cover for field practice, and appointments as corporals, sergeants, and officers were issued by the clubs, as in a military academy. "This is the key to the efficiency of our organization's contribution to The Cause. Within twenty-four hours we were able to offer Mola a disciplined corps, ready for combat." Six squads constituted a Requeté Company, three such companies an old-time regiment. When Warning Voice could get a word in edgewise, he asked about the problem of armament... Don Anselmo stated that this was the most difficult aspect of the question. They lacked arms and almost every kind of manufactured goods. Trubia, Toledo, Murcia, and so on, were all in the hands of the enemy.

Resolutely Warning Voice asked him: "What about the monarchy?"

Don Anselmo tapped one of his pointed fingernails. "That's not the point right now. The war will have to be won first."

Warning Voice blessed the moment when he had come to Pamplona and entered that house. And he was thankful as never before that he had edited his paper in Gerona. He and Don Anselmo saw eye to eye; they were congenial. The latter showed him the paintings he owned, his famous collection of Bibles, some Carlist relics, and, finally, the most precious treasure in his house: his collection of miniature electric trains—"I know there are more important collections in Barcelona." These were his great passion, and he remarked with a smile that the Republic might easily have suborned him by giving him trains. He had them mounted on a huge table in a large room next to his office. The table was the kind used for drawing because, owing to his paunch, Don Anselmo could not bend down to the floor. He always had several trains made up on the table, their locomotives carrying tiny national flags. Warning Voice noticed that one of the stations said *San Sebastián* and another *Madrid.*

"Those are the cities that are going to fall to us soon," explained Don Anselmo. "And on the day of the occupation I'll line up all the trains in front of them."

Then Don Anselmo turned on a switch and the miracle took place. Four very rapid lines of cars started to move on their tracks, crossing halfway and going into and out of tunnels like blasts of air.

"Wonderful! Marvelous!"

"Oh, now!" protested Don Anselmo.

"It's too bad you don't have a flag that says Gerona."

"All in good time, my friend, all in good time."

They went back into the study. And as soon as they had sat down again, Don Anselmo asked: "What are your plans?"

Warning Voice spun his red beret in his hands. "I don't known yet… In the hotel I heard that a Catalan regiment would be formed before long. I thought they might perhaps need a dentist…"

Don Anselmo whiffled. He seemed to be meditating. "Would you mind waiting awhile?"

Warning Voice blinked his eyes. "I don't know what you have in mind." Then he added, "But naturally I'm at your service."

Don Anselmo nodded. "Perhaps you could do…something more useful."

He stopped nibbling the tips of his fingers. Finally he said that for the time being Warning Voice could remain in Pamplona, in the Carlist Club, as a member of the local staff of the newspaper, *El Pensamiento Navarro.* "For the moment you could report on the Red zone. Or on Catalonia."

"And later? "

Don Anselmo was still noncommittal, but suddenly decided to end the guessing. "You'll see," he said, caressing a Bible on his desk. "The thing is that Mola needs information… We have no time to waste…" Warning Voice swelled his chest. "He has no maps whatsoever! All the military cartography remained in the hands of the Reds, in the Ministry of War in Madrid. He has to use Michelin tour maps and Taride guides. Mola was right here in this office day before yesterday, and he told me about his plan to set up a communications network across France into the Red zone." Warning Voice was staring at him. "Do you understand?"

Warning Voice was not prepared for that. "Well…not completely, I must admit."

Don Anselmo paid not the slightest attention to his interlocutor's hesitation. "Of course," he went on, "it's something that requires thought. But I gave Mola my word that I would organize the thing for him." Don Anselmo whiffled again. "Information, espionage, call it whatever you like… Time will determine the extent of it."

A silence ensued. Don Anselmo was wearing a ring that flashed in the light. "Will you let me know within twenty-four hours whether or not I can count on you?"

Warning Voice was as swift as an electric train. "I can tell you now, my dear friend. Yes, of course. I'm at your command from this moment on."

Don Anselmo nodded, satisfied. "You don't know how glad I am that I was not mistaken in you."

Warning Voice swelled with complacency. Don Anselmo's last remark had been most flattering. He felt that he was almost indispensable.

He was preparing to say something, but just then a knock came at the door. Don Anselmo shifted his attention, saying: "Come in."

It was Javier Ichaso, Don Anselmo's younger son who had been wounded just outside the village of Oyarzun. He was wearing his beret, but he took it off when he saw Warning Voice, not without difficulty because of his crutches. His body was athletic, broad-chested, but his left leg was missing below the thigh.

Warning Voice rose as though a general had just entered. He felt a profound respect for the veteran, and was almost ashamed of his own whole, sound legs. Don Anselmo introduced them. Javier Ichaso nodded. He was serious, painfully serious, and his eyes were so close together that they attracted attention immediately. He would be about twenty-two; his forehead, like Julio García's was slightly rounded, and he wore a beard like Balbo's. When he heard that Warning Voice was from Gerona, he remarked, "I've never been in Catalonia."

He had trouble sitting down in a chair near the door. He appeared to be sweating. "Please be seated," he said to Warning Voice. The latter obeyed, and Javier Ichaso ignored him, staring around as though looking for his lost leg. He must have been wandering through the house, sitting on chairs upholstered in red, and searching for his leg. Occasionally he would turn on the switch to watch the miniature locomotives run around.

Don Anselmo exclaimed: "Here's Javier! We call him 'the kid from Oyarzun.'"

Warning Voice replied, "I am honored."

Javier's voice, very like Don Anselmo's, echoed through the room.

"When did you arrive?"

"In Pamplona?" asked Warning Voice.

"Yes."

The dentist consulted his watch and answered with a smile: "Exactly five hours and twenty minutes ago."

"He wanted to go to the front to pull teeth," Don Anselmo explained. "But I got that out of his head. Wouldn't you have done the same, Javier?"

"I guess so."

Warning Voice asked himself whether Javier ever had said no to his father. He gave the impression of being ineradicably stamped with Don Anselmo's personality. His type was no novelty to Warning Voice. An admirable man to his comrades in arms, extremely dangerous to those on the opposite side.

Javier Ichaso showed much more curiosity than Don Anselmo had concerning events in the Red zone. He asked Warning Voice some very searching questions, seeking to correlate events.

Warning Voice felt driven, and he would not have admitted for anything in the world that he knew nothing about the Red zone because he had fled from it within forty-eight hours of the surrender of the regular soldiers. His report far outdid the one he had given the officer at the border. To please Don Anselmo he made a strenuous effort to build up the executions of the landowners. Truckling to Javier, he cited the killing of "every single well-born young man, after shaving their heads." He told of the rifling of the garrison's files, of the Espasa dictionaries tossed over the balconies, and so on. He even went so far as to distinguish between the committees from the coast and those from the mountains or the interior. "The coast committees are not so bloodthirsty, I don't know why. In short," he concluded, "the place is a hell. The zone has been invaded by 'death cars.'"

Don Anselmo gave signs of approval. "Too many of the rabble! We ought to have made a clean-up a long time ago. We're several years too late."

This time it was Warning Voice who indicated agreement. "I defended that theory in *El Tradicionalista.* We ought to have done it during the revolution of 1934."

"Clean-up..." For no particular reason, Warning Voice suddenly glanced inquisitively at Javier. And he caught a fleeting expression that transformed his face. Absurd though it might be, Warning Voice suspected that Javier personally had played a part in the "clean-up." He wondered whether the boy's eyes might not have been pulled together by dint of aiming at the hearts of the men he had killed.

Javier asked: "So they're called 'death cars'?"

"That's what the gentleman said, Javier. Why do you ask?"

Javier sat stiffly, avoiding his father's eye. "I was afraid I had not heard him right."

Warning Voice was aware that a subtle, complex thread was holding father and son both together and apart. He would have been glad to make their joining complete, but he could not think how to do it.

Then Don Anselmo brought the interview to a close with a question. Turning to the dentist, he asked: "Will you be free for lunch tomorrow? We'd be very pleased to have you with us. I'd like you to meet my wife."

Warning Voice could hardly conceal his pleasure. "Yes, of course I'm free, but..."

"Say no more." Don Anselmo cut him off.

Warning Voice realized that he must consider the interview ended, and he rose. He heard a bell ring in the house, followed by the sound of footsteps. Don Anselmo also rose, but with no sign of impatience. Finally Javier got up, with extreme difficulty.

Ah, yes, that meeting had been fruitful! Warning Voice went to the door feeling much more secure then before. As he went, he was admiring the paintings, the photographs, an enormous and very old map of Navarre. He would have liked to caress all those things. Behind him, Don Anselmo seemed to be pushing him ahead with his paunch. Javier lagged behind, limping.

When they came to the door, the three men shook hands. Warning Voice gazed affectionately at father and son. "I can't tell you how..."

The ring flashed on Don Anselmo's finger. "We're not doing it for your sake! ... We're doing it for Spain."

"Then I'm all the more grateful."

From the stairway, Don Anselmo's voice still could be heard. "As a matter of fact, I believe Mola was in Gerona... Yes, he was! He was there when he was a captain."

Warning Voice turned his head, deeply stirred.

"Oh, don't fool yourself! I know full well why the fellow looked a bit sad. He was missing the palm trees of Africa."

MATEO and Jorge, the Falangists, entered Nationalist Spain after Warning Voice, also during the first half of August. Their entry was less happy than his, for they had learned from some refugees in Perpignan what had happened in Gerona. When Mateo found out that César was dead and more than half the Falangists besides, he clenched his teeth until they hurt. After he had recovered a little, he straightened himself and stretching out his arm, cried, "They're present!" As for Jorge, his heart stood still at the news that he had lost his parents and his six brothers and sisters, and he collapsed at the table. His first thought was: "I'll kill myself." No one dared to speak to him, to touch him, and even the shoeshine boys approached him with sad faces.

Mateo had all he could do to arouse him and give him the necessary courage to drag himself out of the café and listen to the suggestion that they should go to Nationalist Spain. "You'll be more at home there. You'll feel more secure... We'll go on to Valladolid. Perhaps we'll find Marta's brother there."

Jorge did not answer. Secure! What did that mean? Jorge's depression was abysmal. The shoeshine boys stared at him, then went back to their work, shrugging their shoulders.

Mateo finally coaxed Jorge into talking. He used the name of God to do it.

He pronounced it fearfully. He was afraid that Jorge would answer him with a sacrilegious wrath toward Him who had made him a full orphan in an instant. But Jorge did not; he said, "Thank you, Mateo."

Mateo helped Jorge into the train. He intended to stop at Lourdes to pray to the Virgin for strength for himself and Jorge, and then to go on to Valladolid. Jorge absolutely refused to stop at Lourdes. "I wouldn't know what to say," he declared. But he did agree to go to Valladolid.

Mateo had chosen that city for two reasons. First, because he intended to look for Marta's brother there—José Luis Martínez de Soria, whom he had met with the other brother, Fernando, when they had visited in Gerona. Fernando, however, had been shot down in Valladolid, in the street where he was pasting up a Falange poster. José Luis doubtless would be useful to them and would help to orient them. In the second place, because that Castillian city was, to a degree, the Falangist Pamplona, and this was more important. Back in 1933, José Antonio Primo de Rivera had formulated his doctrine in a Valladolid address that Mateo knew by heart. Onésimo Redondo had come from Valladolid, and the first volunteer formations had been effected there on the 18th of July.

They crossed France from east to west a little to the south of the route Warning Voice had taken from Genoa. Mateo spent most of his time in the passageway so as not to be with Jorge whom he wanted to get some sleep. The rich, well-tended French countryside spread out before his eyes. Mateo felt toward it the same envy as had Warning Voice; but the Falangist boy tried to offset this from a rich store of mental counterarguments: from how difficult it was for a rich man to enter the kingdom of heaven to the danger that flaccidity would arise from prosperity. José Antonio himself had said to him: "When they want to call up the entire repertoire of insults against us, they call us cabaret boys." In a measure, France impressed Mateo as one immense cabaret where everyone ate enough for two, where they toasted one another in red wine, and where armies of cunning Communists and Masons, riding on the backs of frivolity and of Rousseau, were stifling the marvelous, intimate entities of the Gothic cathedrals. Mateo was never to forget the contrast he noted in Banyuls-sur-Mer: Jorge's stricken, parchment-colored face, surrounded on all sides by the rosy, country-boy cheeks of the gendarmes from the Roussillon.

Mateo had his mind made up to go to the first officer he came to once they had arrived in Dancharinea, and say to him: "Here we are, at your orders, one Falangist left alone on earth, and another Falangist whose very soul is blue." To him this moment seemed long delayed. And he saw, indeed he could not help seeing from the train, gentle Frenchmen fishing with a rod or bowling in the village squares. But at last the time came when they set foot on Spanish soil. Unfortunately, Jorge showed no reaction whatever. He crossed the line like an automaton, kissed the flag listlessly, and was totally incapable of responding to the officer on duty.

Mateo explained the situation to this officer, and the picture was so clear to him that he legalized their entry and handed them forthwith a safe-conduct to Valladolid. "Good luck! Up, Spain!"

"Did you hear that, Jorge? Good luck! Up, Spain." Jorge had heard nothing, and Mateo felt hurt, for he had so longed for that moment! He would have liked so much to feast his eyes on the Spanish countryside, to watch it unwind from the train like a motion picture film! And he could not, for Jorge needed him there at his side. Mateo kept glancing out the windows, reading the names of the stations. "Navarre is beautiful," he kept saying to himself. Soon he noticed that they were in Castile. Then Mateo could not contain himself. He instantly forgot all the orphans in the world, went out into the aisle, lowered the window, and let the air ruffle his hair and cool his skin. And then he stood looking. Simply looking. What an impressive display of grandeur! There was nothing of sweet and feminine France about this. Grandeur, poverty, earth that was the color of earth, and sadness that was the sadness of man and woman.

Mateo's exaltation was heightened when several platoons of soldiers climbed on the train at every stop, men who burst into song once they had wetted their whistles from their canteens. The songs were the familiar, simple ones, and the soldiers sang them very badly: "Adiós, Pamplona," "Riau-Riau," "Legionario, legionario." Nevertheless, they sent shivers up Mateo's spine and brought him to the brink of tears. At that very moment, as he stood in that dirty, slow, unpainted train, he felt a certainty that all would go well, that the Nationalist Movement would win despite the opposition of the French newspapers. He thought that, judging by those songs and the clatter of weapons, there would nevermore be orphans like Jorge in Spain, nor ignoramuses like Ideal and El Cojo. Someone might even discover underground waters! In spite of Ignacio's irony on a certain occasion when he had listened to this final prophecy from Mateo's lips. "If you were to find rivers like that and change the country into a garden by means of them, we'd end up getting as flabby as the French." Oh, yes! Mateo knew very well that they would have to struggle against skepticism in addition to everything else.

They came to Valladolid. Jorge went to the men's room and then stepped down, with Mateo's help. Mateo took a quick look all around the station and saw that the clock had stopped and that one of the railroad lines that doubtless had been mobilized, carried on its breast a miniature locomotive on a blanket of yellow baize. It would have bowled Don Anselmo Ichaso over with admiration.

They left the station and asked a small Arrow for directions to the Falangist barracks. The child showed them the way, and they started off on foot. Mateo noted that many cafés had their chairs painted in the colors of the national banners, the red and black of the Falange predominant. Jorge also noticed it. He even stopped for a moment before a toyshop window where the balls were red and black and several dolls were dressed to match. A man who looked like Blasco the bootblack was selling Falangist ties and belts on a street corner.

An hour later they were assigned adjoining cots in the Onésimo Redondo Barracks. Jorge lay down and fell asleep. Mateo seized the chance thus given him to make an appearance at Marta's house to inquire as to the whereabouts of José Luis Martínez de Soria.

No one was in the apartment except an aged servant. "The young gentleman, José Luis, is at the front, in the Alto del León." Mateo nodded with respect. José Luis was doing his duty... That was to be expected. Mateo went back to the barracks. On the way he met a parade headed by some squadrons of marching Arrows and Pelayos blowing bugles and ruffling drums. "The youth of tomorrow will belong to us," Mateo thought.

In the patio of the barracks some very young volunteers were being trained. He went upstairs and found Jorge depressed, leaning on his elbows at a window. "Buck up, Jorge. I know it's awful. But you must show yourself worthy of your dead family."

Jorge turned toward Mateo for a moment. "Father, mother, and my six brothers and sisters..."

"I know, I know. It's too much for one man to have to bear."

Jorge turned back. "Three little brothers. Three babies! That's it!"

Mateo did not know what to say. The Falange never had foreseen such radical extermination. Jorge was nibbling on something in his hand. Whenever he thought of it, he ate incessantly. Or he smoked. And Mateo could read an obsession in his eyes. Jorge was thinking of revenge.

"We'll soon leave for the front, Jorge. Come on. You'll be able to work it off there."

"Work it off? ... Go away. I don't want to talk."

That was it. He did not want to talk. Mateo felt at a loss when he was with his friend. Moreover, he knew himself incapable of giving as much attention to Jorge's drama as he should have. He, too, was bleeding, on behalf of the Falangists in Gerona who had been called to the sacrifice—and how they had responded!—and on behalf of César. He kept recalling César's voice: "What does the Falange stand for, Mateo?" And he was remembering Pilar. What was Pilar doing?

Added to that, he kept wondering whether he himself was an orphan. What had become of his father, Don Emilio Santos? He was far from robust, and he took so little care of himself... And Mateo loved him; he realized more every day how much he loved him. The boy was worried, too, about the fate of his brother, Antonio, a Falangist like himself, who had been imprisoned in Cartagena for a long time now. Two years had gone by since they had met. As children, they had gone everywhere together. Then they had drifted apart.

Mateo inquired for the local leader, and for the man who had drawn up in France a complete report on the Falangist activities in Gerona. The boy at the switchboard called Headquarters and spoke to this man. "Have him here in a half hour. The meeting will be over by then."

Mateo agreed to that. He said goodbye to Jorge—"I'll be back soon"—and went out to the street. He breathed in the Castillian air, which, some writer had said, had been made by men who knew how to whistle. For a moment he stared into the Pisuerga, the river, confirming his suspicion that the running water chilled the banks. At the appointed hour he entered the Provincial Headquarters—so many arrows, so many roses!—as devoutly as Mosén Francisco might have entered the Basilica of Saint Peter.

A boy on guard duty led him to an office on the second floor. It was almost bare except for a long, official-looking table at the rear. Mateo saw a group of comrades standing, waiting for him. Doubtless they were old hands, and they hailed him with upraised arm, then came to meet him, to bid him welcome, and even to embrace him as "the first provincial leader from the enemy zone."

Mateo turned somewhat shy and had a hard time with the introductions and the names. He grasped the fact, however, that the highest-ranking officer there was Second Lieutenant and Provincial Delegate of Syndicates, Comrade Salazar. This was a corpulent man with a walrus mustache like Murillo's, highly versed in social questions, risen from the JONS, and in close contact with several Germans who had come into the zone. He was stationed in the Alto del León and had come down on a twenty-four-hour pass.

It seemed to Mateo that a good many of the Falangists were replicas of one another, so similarly were they uniformed by the blue shirt, the bearing, and the black mustache. He fixed his attention, however, on a short boy who emanated impressive force. His hair was crewcut, and whenever anyone coined a felicitous phrase, he underlined it by exclaiming, "Bong!" He was covered with emblems and decorations. His name was Núñez Maza, and he was about to be appointed national director of the Propaganda Service, then in the process of organization.

Mateo also retained the names of Mendizábal and Montesinos, who were introduced to him as two of the "reliables." Mendizábal was the administrative officer, but owing to some mysterious lesion he could serve only in the auxiliary forces. But the person presented to Mateo as the most important in the gathering was María Victoria, a delegate from the Women's Section. She was a blond girl with an outgoing, lighthearted manner, always chewing gum until she got tired of it and stuck it on the nose of any chief of staff whose portrait was handy on a wall near her. María Victoria had been the sweetheart of José Luis Martínez de Soria for a good many years, and, obviously, she was not so stiff as Marta.

After his first shyness wore off, Mateo had himself under control, and within a scant quarter of an hour he was sitting in the seat of honor and had everyone eating out of his hand.

The group was impressed not only by Mateo's credentials from the Falange of Gerona, which he read out to them in a solemn silence, but also by his personality, for he wore an aura of secret heroism which only those who "had come from the other side" could aspire to, those who doubtless had struggled for months and months against "them" in a "hostile environment."

Núñez Maza made a persistent effort to learn the details. "Granted," he said, "that Soria, Burgos, or this city is a piece of cake for the Falange. Where it must be hard is in Alicante, or Madrid, or Gerona."

Mateo finished lighting a cigarette with his tow lighter, and nodded his head. "Naturally," he agreed. "When I first went there no one had heard either of the Leading Lights or the Vertical Syndicates. And they thought I was crazy."

Indeed Mateo kept astonishing them by his precision. He submitted data on each of the enemy political parties, revealing a capacity for synthesizing that had Núñez Maza hopping around the room like a monkey. He talked to them about Cosme Vila, El Responsable, David and Olga, and Dr. Relken. They all frowned when he told them that the commanding officer of the rebels in Gerona was the father of José Luis Martínez de Soria, and María Victoria stopped chewing her gum.

"What do you honestly think?" asked the girl. "Did they absolutely have to surrender?"

Mateo bit his lip. "I wouldn't dare to judge."

Then it came his turn to be given information. "Let the leaders' talk," he said, smiling at Núñez Maza and Salazar. "It must be so comfortable to obey!"

They told him a great many things. Núñez Maza, whose intelligence and fluency spilled over in his words, told him that the spirit of the Falange was winning the masses through sheer mimicry. "Without knowing it, they've found what they were looking for in our style. They imitate us in everything, even to our way of walking. They use our lexicon. It seems logical even to peasants to be treated like comrades. A kind of military collectivity similar to what is now proving viable in Germany, and which José Antonio forecast when he said: 'There'll come a moment when what seems nonsense now will seem completely natural to everyone.'"

Mateo had not heard that phrase by José Antonio, and asked for an explanation of it. Salazar, tall and somewhat flabby, complied. "You won't find it in any text. He said it to us one day, right here in this room."

Of course Mateo would find himself among men in Valladolid who had known José Antonio well! Núñez Maza, in particular, whose cross was the knowledge that his leader was imprisoned in Alicante. "We miss him a lot. We're disconsolate. If we had him with us on the Alto del León, we'd come running down and we wouldn't stop until we came to Madrid. And everything on the home front would be safer, more tightly bound."

"More tightly bound?"

"Yes..."

Montesinos and Mendizábal, the administrator, were speaking. Morale was very high, but obstacles were not lacking. Comrade Hedilla, José Antonio's provisional substitute, was falling over many stumbling blocks. The Requetés kept to themselves, and the soldiers to themselves, the same ones who had set up a Junta for Defense in Burgos which practically barred the men from the Falange. "As for the priests, they look at us as if we were going to rob them of God. They'd like us to go to our death singing, 'O Blessed Virgin, sweet heart!'"

Mateo soon became aware that they were all eying him in a strange fashion. Twelve or fourteen pairs of eyes kept looking him up and down. They were asking one another, "Where are we going to set this piece?" He was a good quality blue piece, with upstanding hair and a tow lighter. Núñez Maza, assigned by choice to Propaganda, was intending to set up some mobile units manned by electricians and equipped with loudspeakers which would tour the firing lines addressing the Reds. "That Santos would be ideal. A good voice, a good presence. He knows the enemy zone and he's got our line down better than the best." Salazar, for his part, was thinking of the Alto del León, where he had to report back the next day. "He'd be ideal there with José Luis Martínez de Soria. He's disciplined and intelligent. We'd make him an officer." Mendizábal, who took care of the administration of several small centurion companies, was thinking: "If only they'd leave him here with me..."

"What I'd like," Mateo said, "is to go to the front and take my comrade Jorge, whom I told you about, with me. But, I'll do whatever you want me to, naturally."

Nothing was decided immediately, and in the meantime they toasted him in La Rioja wine, a monarchical wine! Mateo was so happy he almost wept. He had been so alone in Gerona! How splendid it was to feel himself surrounded by congenial minds and arms, to be understood in the fewest words, to listen to them and be able to agree inwardly from the heart! "That's just it." "That's the way I see it." "I would have done the same thing."

He never wearied of staring at those comrades. Núñez Maza, a native of Soria, was an odd character. Often he would start to speak with a sneer, but soon he became so intoxicated with his own words that in two minutes he was "in spirits as high as the sky," and his pontifications surprised even him.

Mateo soon saw evidence of this. Núñez Maza began to tell them that on the preceding day in Salamanca some Falangists had been giving a group of small soldiers a ride around the city in a truck. The men had escaped from the barracks. The Falangists had dressed them in women's clothes, in skirts and gauzy bed hangings. Núñez Maza unexpectedly associated the anecdote with what he called "the people's thin skin." Speaking to Mateo, because he had just arrived from France, the boy said: "A man dressed in women's clothes is a joke to a Frenchman; to a Spaniard he's an object of loathing."

Mateo asked him: "Have you ever been in France?"

"No," Núñez Maza replied, suddenly serious.

Mateo was enjoying himself. Later, Montesinos suggested that they all go and see Jorge "to cheer him up."

Mateo was against it. "It's best to leave him alone and let time do its work."

Mendizábal asked Mateo: "Doesn't he talk to you? Won't he talk at all?"

"Very little."

"And what does he say?"

"All he can talk about is his little brothers. And, naturally, he talks about avenging them."

Salazar, who was smoking a pipe, took two or three violent puffs. "Do you think he'd like to join up with one of the firing squads?"

Mateo stared at him in astonishment. "What did you say?"

"Would he like to join up with a firing squad?"

Mateo bit his lip. Of course! Anyhow, that would be natural. There was a war on. "I suppose he'd like to," Mateo replied, measuring his words, "but for that very reason, I think we ought not to suggest it to him."

"Nonsense!" exclaimed Núñez Maza and Mendizábal in unison.

Salazar asked Mateo from behind the smoke from his pipe: "Correct me if I'm wrong. You did say his parents and six brothers and sisters, didn't you?"

"That's what I said," Mateo replied.

"Well! If they did that to me! ... Okay! I'd better keep still..." And Salazar turned himself completely around.

María Victoria quickly changed the subject. She turned to Mateo and asked for more details about Marta, "I was listening with both ears, you know, to everything Mateo has said about her. Marta has a brother buried here, in Valladolid," she went on. "His name was Fernando. If you like, I'll take you all to the cemetery to visit his grave."

Mateo accepted. "That would top it all off! I knew Fernando in Gerona, two years ago."

Núñez Maza suggested: "Let's all go together and sing 'Face to the Sun.'"

Face to the sun, in the cemetery... Mateo was reacting with the eyes and ears of the heart. He was thinking of César, of Pilar, of the Leading Lights and the Vertical Syndicates. He was still carrying the map of Spain over his heart. He had sworn to carry it as long as the war lasted.

Salazar, Núñez Maza, Montesinos, María Victoria, and Mateo all went together. The five of them fitted into the car with difficulty—Salazar took up enough room for two—but they got on well together. Núñez Maza drove very rapidly, as though Fernando Martínez de Soria might escape them, even though buried in the cemetery. Mateo was inwardly lamenting the fact that he was not wearing the Falangist uniform or, at the very least, the cap.

They came very shortly to the gates of the cemetery and Núñez Maza braked with chilling force. The gravedigger came out at once, visibly alarmed. Alighting, Salazar greeted him. The gravedigger was observing each of them as they got out of the car, and seeing a stranger dressed as a peasant, he opened his eyes in increased alarm and stared at Mateo with unconcealed pity.

Salazar, accustomed to dealing with the members of the Syndicates, reassured him with a gesture. "It's all right, Félix. We're just visiting."

The gravedigger nodded and went away. The group of five Falangists entered the cemetery and, caps in hand, turned to the niche along the left row where Fernando Martínez de Soria was buried.

They lined up there, looking at the white marble stone that seemed to reject, to cast back their gaze, like a jai-alai wall. Salazar stretched forth his arm and broke the silence with the first notes of "Face to the Sun." Everyone joined in with him. Five live Falangists, motionless, confronting a motionless dead Falangist. Along the eastern line of niches in the cemetery, other visitors—a couple and an old man—turned toward the singers when they recognized the Falangist anthem and also raised their arms timidly, mumbling the words.

"Comrade Fernando Martínez de Soria. Present!"

They turned to the exit where they met two children, dressed as Arrows but with small swastikas on their chests.

"Look who's here!" Núñez Maza cried jubilantly.

They were the sons of Herr Schubert, a delegate of the German Nazi Party in Spain. Two children who might have passed for Spanish except for their slower manner of walking. María Victoria told Mateo about them. She spoke of the great surprise the two boys had given them. They could be found at every turn, always unexpectedly, though the places they had chosen seemed to indicate a certain logic or objective.

"They're always in the most picturesque spots, where there's something they don't know about, something strange to Germany."

Montesinos, the least intellectual of the group asked: "And just what has this cemetery got that German cemeteries don't have?"

Núñez Maza was indignant. "Don't be so dumb. Don't you know that niches are peculiar to the South, southern?"

"Excuse me, chief, I didn't know that…"

They saluted the two boys with a lift of the arm and the boys returned the salute. Mateo smiled as they moved away. They were wearing miniature leggings and hobnailed boots, as though for a cold winter. María Victoria commented: "What I can't understand is why their father calls himself Schubert."

THE Estrada brothers, Alfonso and Sebastián, also were arriving in Nationalist Spain. Their guardian in Gerona had been La Andaluza, and through Laura, she had found a way to send the two sons of Don Santiago Estrada, the head of the CEDA, through the Pyrenees.

Once in Nationalist Spain, the two brothers parted. The elder, Alfonso, decided to enlist in the Regiment of Our Lady of Montserrat, since the idea, born in Pamplona, of forming this Catalan regiment had been carried out. Their main barracks were now in Zaragoza, in San Carlos Seminary, and the Requetés there were scheduled to be garrisoned on the Aragón front in the Belchite sector.

At the time when Alfonso Estrada enlisted in the new unit, he was told that the famous Frenchmen of the Croix de Feu and the White Russians whom Warning Voice had met in the Pamplona hotel formed a part of it. He asked about the French group, and a corporal told him: "They've got courage, but they always seem to be giving lessons in syntax." The White Russians kept very much to themselves, and there was not one among them who had not been a personal friend of the czar.

Sebastián, the younger of the Estradas, decided to enlist in the Navy. He expected to run into difficulties, but that was not the case. He was sent at once to the El Ferrol base, where he filled out an application with the necessary documentation. He was accepted immediately and told that he would be at sea within a week.

Yes, the words of Ezequiel were proving true: men were soap bubbles. None of them ever knew whether he would go to the front as a dentist, with a group of electricians from one Falangist stronghold to another, off to sea or to the mountains. The last man to enter Spain through Dancharinea—the last of the first wave—was Mosén Alberto. He, too, stopped over in Pamplona, unknown to Warning Voice. The bishop of the diocese saw that he was tired and appointed him chaplain to a convent of nuns of perpetual vigil, the Sisters of San José, who received him as if he were the Pope and listened to his first sermon with tears in their eyes. They treated Mosén Alberto so well that the priest felt remorseful. "I ought to be considered worse than the others," he said to himself. "A vast number of priests have died and yet here am I being served chocolate with toasted ham sandwiches again!" He intended at the first opportunity to visit Sister Teresa, Carmen Elgazu's sister, who was with the Salesian nuns in Pamplona. All around him the priest heard a jargon that displeased him with its aggressiveness, and a pacifist pastoral letter from the Portuguese Archbishop of Mitilene came to his hands, praying for charity and moderation.

On the day when, as he opened *El Pensamiento Navarro,* he read a dispatch on the Red zone signed by Warning Voice, he nearly jumped out of his chair. The dentist! Ah, yes, his style was unmistakable. "Criminals!" he shouted, and felt a surge of anger.

ELEVEN

"THERE'S never been such a sight," El Responsable declared.

He was referring to Future's funeral. This interment had been planned to galvanize the population of Gerona. The boy's body—his "remains" as his comrades called it—was shifted from truck to truck all the way from the firing line to Gerona, with Merche on perpetual guard. The wake was held in the Anarchist gymnasium. Blasco never moved from the spot, nor did Santi, tenacious as an acolyte.

Merche was inconsolable, El Responsable somewhat less so. El Responsable had not wept for many years. He always said he was too small to cry, that weeping suited big people like Teo better. When he saw the incredibly rachitic body of his comrade, he took off his cap, and there in the middle of the gymnasium, tears were born again in his eyes and fell steadily. Unconsciously, he drew himself up like a soldier. Future! He kept remembering the skull the boy had played with for awhile. How mysterious time was, what transformations it could bring about! What a mysterious thing a bullet was, what importance it could acquire inside a man, in his heart!

"There's never been such a sight."

Indeed that was true. A dragging, interminable funeral. All the authorities attended it. The cortège wound along the riverbank at sundown. Merche, at the head of the women's group, looked like a soul in torment. El Responsable was breathing with difficulty, feeling the loss of Future. Cosme Vila was at his side, of course, saying to him: "I'm awfully sorry'." Who could tell whether or not that was the truth. Cosme Vila was thinking vague thoughts; he was feeling the need of a hero from his own side, the Communist Party, to balance the situation, to provide an equivalent. The coffin was carried by pallbearers. The Anarchists spelled one another every three hundred yards, handing over the extinguished firebrand, soon to be ashes, which Future had become.

Obviously this was the most direct shock the people had felt since the trucks had gone off to the firing line. The presence of a coffin gave people new bearings. Until then such words as the Aragón front, reconnaissance flights, howitzers, fatigue, thirst, had all been mere symbols… Now they had a dead man among them. What had been was no longer. Someone who knew how to shoot was standing face to face with them. The enemy was real.

When they reached the cemetery, the cypresses stood at attention. The gravedigger pointed: "Over there…" As the coffin was being lowered into the grave, Merche kept her head turned. El Responsable, on the other hand, was staring fixedly at the box, wondering that the earth should serve such diverse needs as the harvest and the eternal concealment of Future. Antonio Casal's eyes were damp. David and Olga stood like statues. The Costas did not know where to look. At the final moment, Cosme Vila cried: "*¡Salud!* For the Revolution!" El Responsable was somewhat taken aback, but the militiamen all replied: "*¡Salud!*" Their hoarse cry ricocheted from each of the nearby crosses and was lost somewhere beyond the wall, in the blue. Merche felt sure that the echo of that shout would go whirling to the Aragón front and would resound there like a cannonade.

TWENTY-FOUR hours later Cosme Vila had available for exploitation the hero he had wished for. He had not had long to wait for his quid pro quo. Pedro, the dissenter, stupidly had crashed into a tree six miles outside Gerona, on the Vía Bañólas. The boy had been making his maiden trip as a driver, and had purposely avoided the San Feliu de Guixols road because he had taken part in several executions there and had said to himself that sometimes a thing like that could make you nervous. Pedro killed himself. No one would ever know what mistake he had made. They wrapped him in a flag and set up their wake in the Party Hall.

Cosme Vila was infinitely chagrined that he had no heroic photograph of Pedro—*El Demócrata* had published one of Future in connection with his death, showing the young Anarchist addressing his men from the top of a truck, and another in which an arrow with the word Zaragoza on it could be read perfectly on his rifle. Cosme Vila had no choice but to invent some heroic action himself: Pedro had died while pursuing a carful of Fascists trying to escape. The Fascists had opened fire, a tire had burst, and the boy had been thrown against a tree.

Of course his funeral lacked the spontaneity of Future's, and there were even some who asked: "Why wasn't that Pedro at the front?" But at least Cosme Vila could fly the flag at half-mast on the balcony, and *El Proletario* could publish the boy's obituary, with the following good wishes: "May the earth lie lightly over him." This phrase infuriated El Responsable, for it was the Anarchists who referred to the Earth in many of their utterances, even to the point of calling it often "The Great Mother of the World."

But even so, the excitement was great. El Responsable, wearing a black armband on his shirt, said to the Committee: "We have to make some decisions," and it was done. No one would have dared to contravene him. "A tooth for a tooth." Cosme Vila added: "We've got to prove that the blood of the people must be paid for dearly."

In a tense meeting, in few words, the resolution was unanimously adopted: the soldiers. That would be most appropriate, it was what everyone was waiting for. Why so much delay? Three death sentences were passed with the final motion: those of Major Martínez de Soria, Lieutenant Martín, and Second Lieutenant Delgado. Thereafter the condemned men were chained to their places in the prison at all times. Why shouldn't those men, already condemned, occupy their proper places? The gates of the cemetery were wide open.

The date of the executions was announced officially. The militiamen burst into stentorian "hurrahs." Still, many of them could not understand why the lives of the other noncoms and officers were being spared, after all. Why? El Responsable said again and again to various people: "That's Cosme Vila's doing. The Russian with the black eyepatch has given him that kind of orders."

The three condemned men were notified. On their last night, their nearest relatives were granted permission to visit them, thanks to the intervention of Colonel Muñoz. The bars of the cells were far enough apart so that they could even exchange kisses.

Lieutenant Martín had no visitors. His parents lived in Palencia, in Nationalist territory. It seemed strange to him that no one came to say goodbye when he was so soon to leave this world. He was realizing that one could be an orphan even when dead, and during the visit of Second Lieutenant Delgado's father, Lieutenant Martín could not bear to watch, and burst into tears of desolation and envy.

Second Lieutenant Delgado's father came down the stairway to the dungeon on unsteady feet. He was a man so bent over that when he went up to the bars, it looked as though he would slide between them to embrace his son. The latter bore himself with dignity. He said: "We made our play and we lost."

As for Major Martínez, pale, spent, and with mothballs still in his pockets, he received his wife's visit exactly at midnight. She was escorted by a guard with an automatic rifle.

The interview was so charged with feeling that the few minutes permitted by regulations seemed to them a second on the one hand and an eternity on the other. The major, hands gripping the bars, stared at his wife, unable to credit the idea that she was to go on living. A fact like that was difficult to grasp. They had always been together in everything! Why should hearts be severed though one of them should cease to beat?

His wife, already in mourning, could only kiss his fingers and moan. Kiss patches of the flesh of that man she had loved and who kept saying to her: "Do you think I did wrong? Do you think I ought to have held out?" By the body of Christ, this was no time to judge! Or perhaps it was... But how could she? "Where is Marta? Where is my little girl? Embrace her, give her a big hug for me... And José Luis, too, when you see him... Darling! I'm a soldier, but I feel myself weakening. This is hard. It's hard to die, to leave you, to say goodbye to everything. Long live Spain! Be brave. Give Marta and José Luis a hug for me..."

When the guard separated them, the major noticed that his wife had left in his hand a photograph and a package of cigarettes. By the light of the bulb on the staircase, he studied the photograph, and his heart beat faster. He saw Marta on horseback on the railroad tracks, with José Luis and Fernando beside her, looking at her. The major pressed the back of the photograph to his breast as if he could imprint it on himself. Then he began to sob, like Lieutenant Martín. The calmest of the three was Second Lieutenant Delgado, who had sat down on the straw with his head in his hands.

The sentence was carried out the following day. The firing squad was made up of militiamen from all the parties, with El Responsable as a reinforcement. He aimed only at Major Martínez de Soria. Everything was done according to rule, with the book of regulations in hand and even the proper affidavit drawn up. Julio García was at the cemetery, escorting an English newspaper-woman, Fanny by name, who had arrived in Gerona the previous afternoon and who had wanted to witness the spectacle. Julio García remained outside and stood listening to the volleys, staring toward the river with his cigarette-holder between his lips.

The major smoked until the final moment, then took leave of his officers, shouting "Long live Spain!" with a slight lift of his left shoulder. Second Lieutenant Delgado lost his nerve at the last moment; his legs scarcely would hold him up. As for Lieutenant Martín, he refused the bandage over his eyes and asked: "How do you do your murders, in the front or the back?"

The second decision taken by the Committee was to search for the Bishop. "First, the soldiers, now the Bishop." It was known that many bishops already had fallen victim to the people's justice: the ones from Jaén, from Almeria, from

Ciudad Real. Where was the Gerona bishop, a native of Olot, elderly, very well versed in finance and country estates, according to the manager of the Arús Bank. Axelrod, the man born in Tiflis, had asked Cosme Vila about him again and again, and the latter had not known what to tell him.

The impression had arisen that he had not left the city. "Maybe there are such things as magic wands like those that find water!" In this case, Merche was the dowser. Her intuition, her widowhood, had inspired her to keep insisting that one of the Costa brothers must have hidden him in his house. Antonio Casal, who felt a curious respect for the Bishop, cried: "Don't talk nonsense!"

At nightfall, a patrol captained by El Responsable burst like a waterspout into the apartment of one of the Costas and there found the Bishop sitting in the dining room playing solitaire. An overflowing ashtray sat beside him, whether or not he had filled it. "Hands up!" The Bishop shuddered. He had hidden his episcopal ring on top of the water tank. If only he could wear it! But they gave him no time for that. He feared for the Costa brothers, and he could see the maid drying her eyes on a corner of her apron. El Responsable shoved him toward the door and then downstairs. The Bishop felt dizzy and clutched the banister. "Don't be afraid! It'll only take a minute!"

Actually, it took four and a half hours. Four and a half hours of waiting in the Anarchist Cheka, formerly a garage near the station. The Bishop was given time to hear the confessions of those who were languishing there: two landowners, a manufacturer of images, and a chauffeur. At midnight, they manacled him, to his great distress, for he could not lift his hand to grant absolution. He was then taken to the cemetery in a black car. The car traversed the main avenue, striking terror among the niches and in the boy cradling the celluloid duck whose photograph César so often had looked at. They got out of the car and placed the Bishop on the still-unsettled earth that covered Future's body. They blindfolded him while he whispered short prayers. The rifles were invisible, the snick of the bolts inaudible. Everything went off like a rite in a Black Mass. A voice threatened him: "I'll bet you don't call yourself a Catholic now!"

The Bishop was surprised and said: "Why not? Of course I am."

Then he noticed that the lantern light was shining on his chest. And he glimpsed a knife. And felt them unbutton his shirt and slash his flesh lightly twice. A vertical cut, then a horizontal one. There was a pause until the blood began to show, at first in timid and arbitrary beads, then more and more visible, joining until they formed two exact paths that finally shaped a cross.

Voices were heard again, among them a woman's. The Bishop was at a loss to understand it all. The dizziness! The cross. The lantern. Where was he? A volley rang out, and the Bishop fell above Future.

Meanwhile, the place he had occupied in the Cheka was being taken by the traitor Costa, a deputy of Izquierda Republicana. Blasco himself was stationed on guard over him, and he would ask from time to time: "Shine? Want a shine?"

The third decision taken by the Committee was to create the necessary climate of war in the city. The work would start with the people and end with the factories. The men could take their choice of two ideal places in which to prove their manhood: the Aragón front and Mallorca. The Aragón front was in need of reinforcements—of course! But, it happened that the Catalan command was also getting ready to invade Mallorca, under Captain Bayo... The force was to consist almost entirely of Catalans, who were to sail from Barcelona harbor. "On to Mallorca! On to Mallorca!" That island in the Mediterranean suddenly had taken on the character of a symbol, something El Responsable could exploit, for there was something epical about crossing the sea. Little Santi volunteered for the expedition, together with about twenty other militiamen! Some thirty Communists also joined up, and, somewhat unexpectedly, the entire union of waiters. The waiters, carried away by enthusiasm, had agreed to enlist as such, in a body. This somewhat singular decision moved the entire city to emotion. It would offer Ramón of the Café Neutral in particular his opportunity to become acquainted with new lands. Raimundo, the barber, for his part, parodied the formula used by the waiters in Mallorca: "What would the gentleman like? A bomb of anise or a mortar with soda?" Professor Morales increased his propaganda over the radio, and the word spread rapidly that other Syndicates were inclined to imitate the example of the waiters. Owing to this, Ignacio spent several anxious hours, for the employees of the bank had held a general meeting to decide whether or not to enlist. Luckily, they decided not to. On the other hand, the members of the Construction Syndicate announced that for the time being the younger members at least would offer themselves to the Anti-Fascist forces.

Mallorca, Aragón, the Alcázar in Toledo. The Government was ready to mine the foundations of that great fortress and blow it up unless its defenders would surrender. Commissar Gorki's dispatches and all the other events were convulsing the minds of the people in Gerona. Cosme Vila realized that the moment had come to apply Axelrod's theories, and accordingly he set about directing his psychological offensive.

His first act was to forbid gambling, except for the lottery, because gambling was "bourgeois." At the same time, in emulation of Barcelona, he ordered the pawnshops to return their pledges to their owners, and that led to a good deal of cheating and altercation. Many people had lost their tickets, but on the other hand there were some sharpers like Blasco, who laid claim to a typewriter.

With El Responsable, Cosme Vila then visited the banks one by one—it was high time to do something about them—and forced the managers to open the private strongboxes and turn over their contents to the Committee. Finally he drew up a list of girls from the prosperous families of Gerona who were thenceforth to scrub the floors and the toilets of the local Anti-Fascist headquarters. "The women who used to do that have gone to the front, so..." The Communist local was assigned to the two daughters of the proprietor of the Peninsular Hotel, on the night shift.

Then came the master stroke. They planned to take over the labor force and to militarize all the industries that could be converted into war plants to produce war matériel. And they succeeded. "The manufacture of belts, garters, and bicycle parts must hereby cease. Arms, ammunition, armor-plate, spare parts must be manufactured instead." The Soler factory was the first to be converted; it was to produce tires, leggings, and every other kind of rubber product. Next the Costa Foundries! "I tell you, the time is ripe..." The workmen were glad of the change, for it made them feel they were making an effective reply to the sign that said: *What are you doing to win the war?* One by one the factories were changing their signs, and the men who worked in them were soon to go home dyed another color. They were going to breathe in other alloys. Antonio Casal was appointed to organize the collection of scrap metal all over the province, scraps that could be melted down in the foundry. That operation called forth all his skill. Trucks went streaming along the highways as in the days of the Food Cooperative, and each of them came back with a load of the most heterogeneous objects. Many bells, gangways, communion rails, garden gates, and beams began to pile up on the outskirts of the villages, on vacant lots, on football fields, or old, disused millponds. So much iron, so much bronze! Cosme Vila oversaw the unloading of the trucks and harangued the troops. "More! You've got to get more! Do you or don't you want to win the war?" But the moment came when more was hard to come by. Artistic door-knockers from country mansions, palaces, and convents in the province. Door-knockers in the shapes of lizards or serpents, lion heads, or hands. The militiamen would laugh when they found them. There were serpents with forked tongues showing and hands of incredible weight. There were convulsed faces like Merche's when the volley was fired at the Bishop. "More! You've got to get more!" Then Cosme Vila's father-in-law, the grade-crossing guard, suggested two sources: old railroad coaches and zinc and copper coffins. Coffins! They spaded up the ground among the cypresses. The coffins were melted down, bones and all.

"Now what about the specialized technicians to operate the factories? Why don't we talk to Axelrod?"

"You'll have them without delay," Axelrod promised.

The next drive, assigned to David and Olga, was to collect donations for the front. "Clothing for the front." "The nights are cold on the firing line." People were asked to give blankets, knapsacks, binoculars, rainwear, gloves. "For the Anti-Fascist Militiamen!" From everywhere came mountains of all kinds of garments, some of which took on the haunting look of living beings as they lay on the piles. Carmen Elgazu gave nothing to any collection center; on the other hand, faithful to her old custom, she gave a vest belonging to Matías and two pairs of Ignacio's trousers to some needy neighbors. Matías always had loathed meeting someone wearing a sweater or a necktie that had been his. He felt uncomfortable and vaguely guilty of something or other. It was the opposite with Pilar, who felt touched when she found that some militiaman of the POUM was wearing something that had belonged to Mateo.

But in the final analysis, the most spectacular request was for mattresses. Each family was asked to donate a mattress. And they did so. Militiamen went from house to house collecting them, sniffing as they passed through the dining rooms and bedrooms, and the factories of San Feliu de Guixols and its region began to turn out mattresses of cork wool. Cosme Vila experienced a special joy at giving up his own mattress. He gave the mattress off his bed, the only one he and his wife had, and used a grass pad as a substitute. La Andaluza, on the other hand, had mattresses to spare. "Choose, choose!" she screamed. "They all tell the same story!" Garment-making shops much more productive than the Campistol sisters' blossomed forth. A large number of women volunteered to run requisitioned Singer sewing machines, and the enormous quantities of linen found in the convents were put to use. Antonio Casal's wife helped with this work.

The publication in the press of the so-called "Militiaman's Mailbox" was initiated and became enormously popular. The fighting men would send to this column a note specifying their needs or wishes, or just their addresses: "*I should appreciate a pair of rubber-soled shoes. Comrade Epifanio Grau, 'Germ' Battalion, 4th Company, Huesca Sector.*" Or field glasses, or books, or a special brand of pipe tobacco. The corresponding gifts were assembled in the UGT and reached their destination more or less promptly. Professor Morales often said that the idea was touching, but it had one drawback: it told the enemy where the troops were situated. "All they need is to be patient awhile, and thanks to this lovely mailbox, they'll be able to draw a perfect diagram within two weeks of the whereabouts of all the battalions, one after another."

Actually the fifth plan, for defending the home front, related to that very thing. The enemy was taking a breather—for how long?—and it was essential to keep them from coordinating their forces. The warning of Professor Morales was heeded to some degree. A succession of sandwich men, anonymous inside their signs, began to roam the streets and stop at meeting places to eavesdrop. If what they overheard sounded suspicious, they reported it. Similarly, the militiamen were ordered to approach from the rear people who were walking together and separate them, then question each privately on "what they were talking about." If their versions failed to agree, they were reported. Methods for establishing identity also were being perfected. How were they to make certain, for example, whether a certain hunched-over traveler on a train was or was not a priest? Goriev proposed a trick that had been used in Russia, so he said. It was worked by suddenly tossing a light object into the lap of the traveler, between his thighs. If he were a priest, and accordingly accustomed to wearing a soutane with a long skirt, he would be likely to react like a woman, separating his legs. If he were not a priest, and therefore used to wearing trousers, he did what men did to catch an object: brought his legs together. As for the nuns, many of them would hesitate before going through narrow doors. Accustomed to wearing starched coifs, they would pass through in profile.

The basic phase of the defensive operation, however, lay in the establishment of censorship of the press and of letters and telegrams. The natural resistance to the first type was overcome thanks to the example of the Madrid and Barcelona papers, which came out daily with censored blank rectangles, columns that tempted the resourceful to look at the back of the page to see if anything could be read there. But the work of censoring letters and telegrams became impassioned! David and Olga, who appeared to have acquired the gift of ubiquity, organized the censorship of the mails, and they tried to coerce almost analphabetic militiamen to do it. A fascinating task to open the letters and read between the lines, to find things out! What surprises were in store! What odd phrases men exchanged among themselves! How they would threaten one another, and how they loved one another, and how they longed for companionship! The correspondence coming from abroad awakened a particular interest, for there were some impossible languages. Olga kept a check on the number of letters Julio García received from beyond the Pyrenees. And two envelopes prettily addressed to "General Francisco Franco, Ministry of War, Madrid," came into her hands. Could they have been meant as a joke? Equally fascinating was the control over telegrams... Jaime and Matías Alvear had to put up with the presence of a succession of sentries who stood watch during working hours and who kept asking them: "That bit about 'Uncle Andrés has met Dolores,' what does it mean?" One day Professor Morales himself made an appearance in this branch. And seeing the black armband that Matías was wearing on his office jacket, he touched his spectacles and said: "Unless I'm mistaken, there's a ban on the wearing of mourning."

Matías eyed him steadily, not at all dismayed. "In that case, you'll have to take it off me."

Professor Morales blinked, wavered. Finally he turned around and went away. The strings were being drawn tighter and tighter, to such a point that Cosme Vila grew alarmed. "Brains have to have oxygen," he said. He laid out a program for amusements and sports. Once more the free-for-alls, the strong devouring the weak—dances, *sardanas,* and outdoor movies on the Rambla! With the screen in the middle and the public on both sides of it half the people saw figures in reverse.

True, those outdoor movie-showings—the screen hung between the Alvears' balcony and the front of the Café Neutral—were densely and spectacularly attended, for everyone knew that the mild nights soon would come to an end, that the cold soon would sweep the Rambla clean. Meanwhile, the titles of the films were attractive: *The Cruiser Potemkin, The Sailors of the Kronstadt, Professor Mambok.* Cosme Vila attended the showings and took personal charge of the loudspeakers through which he made pointed commentaries from time to time.

But his crowning, almost triumphal moment came at the intermission, that is to say when the pause was announced in immense letters on the screen. Then Cosme Vila would fling into the air the first majestic strains of the "Internationale." The public rose immediately, and hundreds of clenched fists seemed to threaten the stars. Finally the audience was singing the anthem in chorus, although they used a Spanish version that the radio and pamphlets had made popular:

> "Arise, ye prisoners of starvation,
> Arise, ye wretched of the earth.
> For justice thunders condemnation.
> A better world's in birth.
> No more tradition's chains shall bind us.
> Arise, ye slaves, no more in thrall.
> The earth shall rise on new foundations,
> We have been naught. We shall be all!"

Everyone did the best he could, for Fascism meant death. Nevertheless there were fighters with imagination and others without it. Antonio Casal, whose capacity for admiration was growing constantly, reviewed the local heroes of the revolution and arrived at the conclusion that the most imaginative of them all, by far, was Julio García.

Perhaps he was right. The policeman's smile always hinted at something hidden. Deeds in themselves failed to satisfy him; he always wanted to know their consequences. In this period that the city was going through, he displayed not intelligence alone, but gallantry as well, which would have delighted Doña Amparo Campo, except that a rival to her had appeared.

Julio García believed that opinion in the foreign press, the great newspapers, was most important, much more important than the garbled dispatches Gorki was sending from the Aragón front. And accordingly, he had constituted himself protocol chief and escort to all the newspapermen who stopped in Gerona on their way from France. And behold, one of those newspaper people, the very one who had witnessed the execution of Major Martínez de Soria and his two subordinates, was named Fanny. She was writing for an English-speaking newspaper chain, and she seemed to be not insensitive to the policeman's ironic utterances.

Everyone noticed it, for Fanny was very conspicuous, and Doña Amparo Campo had no recourse against her but to add more black make-up to her eyes and reveal more of her arms. The journalist enkindled Julio from the first moment with her reddish-blond hair, her way of saying, "*Merci*, Julio," and the three wedding bands she wore on her ring finger to match her three husbands.

Julio escorted Fanny, as he was later to escort many other correspondents, on her visit to the Cathedral to find out whether the people "were respecting works of art." Then he went with her to the Dehesa, to see the century-old trees beneath which the volunteers from the Construction Syndicate were puffing out their chests and saying "One, two; one, two," and he even took her to the monastery of Montserrat, still intact thanks to the care of the Provincial Department of Culture. Fanny's worst fault was turning out to be her insatiable curiosity... Of course she would not be a newspaperwoman otherwise. Fortunately, Julio was quite able to look out for himself. "Fanny, for God's sake! Not that... Beautiful women don't ask about such things..."

Julio was proving that he was imaginative, and, thanks to his knowledge of French and English, he was really the only man in Gerona capable of handling the journalists. Fanny knew that, and she told him of the forthcoming arrival of several friends of hers, European correspondents, among them Raymond Bolen, a Belgian and one of the most aggressive pens she knew. "For a fact," said Fanny, "Raymond told me in his last letter that he was bringing with him a mobile printing press, a gift from the International Commission of Writers to the Provincial Government of Catalonia." Julio smiled. "Your fourth husband?" he asked. Fanny made a face and answered, "*Peut être.*"

This success of Julio's that was disputed by no one, brought with it a sequel... Suddenly the press of Barcelona was hit amidships by a bombshell. The Provincial Government had appointed the Gerona policeman special assistant to the commissions delegated to go abroad, mainly to France and England, to buy arms, medical supplies, and whatever else was essential. Don Carlos Ayestarán, the brother in the Northeastern Iberian Lodge, with an obsession about hygiene, had turned the trick!

Julio seemed to be begging everyone's pardon as he confirmed the news at the Neutral bar, the Ovid Lodge, and Police Headquarters. "My mission won't be technical, you understand. I'm simply going in my capacity as a policeman."

Antonio Casal was dumbstruck. Cosme Vila slowly ran his hand over his bald head, and El Responsable, for his part, thought of Future and was angry. "So it's France and England, is it?"

Julio García sensed the animosity, but he stood up to all the leaders who were accusing him of "running away from the fire," in particular Cosme Vila, who declared that the thing was utter folly because the Western democracies would not provide any help whatsoever: Russia alone would help them.

The policeman heard them out, smiled, and sought comfort in Fanny's good judgment and knowledge of the world. She took his part. Julio said that of all the conclusions drawn by the Anti-Fascists in Gerona stemming from Future's death, hers was doubtless the soundest. "As you know, I believe more in intelligence than in instinct." He added that he considered it laudable, poetic even, that the Committee should dedicate itself to militarizing the city, to melting down hands and serpents, to opening its neighbor's letters, and to providing motion picture showings. But as things were going—what was happening on the Aragón front might serve as a sample—the only worthwhile move was to obtain important, decisive foreign aid. "We must purchase matériel in massive quantities. We need airplanes, tanks... Otherwise, the Moors will descend upon us here by surprise while we're singing the 'Internationale' and sewing up underdrawers for the waiters who'll be leaving for Mallorca."

Fanny emphatically agreed. "Forgive me," she said with that accent which seemed adorable to Julio, "but the gentleman is right... If you don't get that kind of aid, *pouf*, you'll lose everything."

Doña Amparo Campo was told of the English newspaperwoman's role, and she stamped her foot with rage. "I'll teach her to put her two cents' worth in where she's got no call to." She caught her breath and went on, "I'll teach her in Spanish, and I'll teach her in English..."

TWELVE

WHEN Ignacio conveyed to Pilar and his mother Mosén Francisco's invitation to hear Mass in the Campistol sisters' apartment, the two women were overjoyed. "It won't amount to much," Matías Alvear muttered slyly. But in fact Ignacio's mother had been attempting the impossible ever since the 18th of July: trying to find some priest who was clandestinely carrying on the sacrifice on the altar. She had not succeeded. She had had to resign herself to picking up an occasional Mass broadcast over the Nationalist stations and to hearing the solemn Office rebroadcast from Radio Vatican. Millions of families in the Red zone listened to it with fervor. Matías did not care to kneel in front of a radio, but Carmen Elgazu drove him to it with a glance half forceful, half tender, and the man could not refuse her.

Mosén Francisco's invitation seemed rash to Matías. "What! In that particular part of the city... There are seven militiamen to every house!" "So what?" Carmen Elgazu replied. "There are also two dressmakers, aren't there?"

Matías was opposed to it, but in the end he yielded. In matters like that, the least little thing would annoy his wife! Although actually it was not the ceremony of the Mass that frightened Matías; he was afraid of the consequences of it. He did not doubt for a minute that little by little Carmen Elgazu would work herself into becoming Mosén Francisco's sexton, his acolyte, his bearer of candles and holy wafers, and his maker of albs, girdles, maniples, and chasubles. See if she wouldn't!

"Go on, you little coward, nothing's going to happen. Do you hear?"

Matías Alvear opened the balcony window to let in fresh air. "You do whatever you wish. If something happens to you, I'll have a Mass said for you."

Carmen Elgazu and Pilar went, more dressed up than usual. They were not carrying candles, but they were carrying two very clean white handkerchiefs in their handbags. It was Sunday. Just a month to the day since César had died. The sun shone on the militiamen's red neckerchiefs, as if setting little fires on their necks. Three sandwich men were walking the street with a sign that said: Big Dance at the Swimming Pool This Afternoon. Carmen Elgazu and Pilar had agreed upon a story in case some patrol should separate them and question as to what they were talking about: they were talking about the summer they had spent in San Feliu de Guixols. "You were telling me that your flowered bathing suit didn't suit you very well, and I was saying that that was a lot of nonsense, that it was very becoming."

They strolled toward the Pedret section. As they were going along the Calle de la Barca, they saw a boy writing on a wall: "Long live me!" Then they heard a newsboy crying the news. He was selling *El Proletario,* shouting: "*Proletario!* Letters from a canon to his sweetheart! *El Proletario!* ... He paused a moment then cried again: "*Proletario!* Letters from a canon!" Carmen Elgazu went past the boy with her head down and Pilar warned her: "Be natural, Mother. Don't be silly."

As soon as they started to climb the Campistols' stairs, Carmen Elgazu crossed herself. "My God, such things!" Pilar ran ahead, stopped in front of the door, and rang the bell. Carmen Elgazu said: "What a pity the men wouldn't come."

Soon they were standing in the vestibule with the mirrors and then in the back room, which Mosén Francisco had arranged like a chapel. The priest was touched when he saw the two women, and all the more so when he realized that Carmen Elgazu was approaching him with the intention of kissing his hand.

"For Heaven's sake, woman..."

"Yes, Mosén Francisco... It's been more than a month since I've been able to. Now it's your turn, Pilar!"

Carmen Elgazu saw the altar all prepared, but she begged the former vicar to hear her confession so that she could take Communion. Mosén Francisco agreed. Left alone with Carmen Elgazu, he sat on a chair in shadow while she knelt at his feet. Carmen Elgazu confessed how little she was reconciled to César's death. "It's awful, Father, but I can't resign myself." Then she confessed she was guilty of hatred, genuine hatred, toward a number of people. "I hate a militiaman on sight, Father, and I can't help myself." The penance Mosén Francisco gave her was to say three times a day for a week: "Dear Jesus, I am ready to yield up my other children to Thee, if it be Thy will."

Pilar was also brief. It seemed strange to the girl to kneel at the feet of the priest without a confessional booth between them and to see that Mosén Francisco had almost closed the shutters. She confessed to the same sins as her mother: "I'm hardly resigned at all to César being dead and Mateo being away, and I hate the enemy." Then she added: "And I've got quite a sweet tooth when no one can see me." Mosén Francisco gave her a penance of three "Our Fathers" and told her to try not to give in to her appetite for one day of the week.

The Campistol sisters already had confessed, so that everything was ready for the opening of the Mass.

The altar was a table covered with a viaticum cloth embroidered with a dove. A champagne glass served as the Communion cup, a prayer book as the Missal, the Host was made of small pieces of bread, the water and the wine were poured. Praise be Our Blessed Lord! Mosén Francisco, half boy, half thinker in his blue coverall, with deeply circled eyes, went to the table and bowed his head, unaware that the mirrors reflected to infinity the room they all had helped to arrange.

Perhaps this Mass was the one that Carmen Elgazu would later remember as the most moving in all her life, even more moving than her nuptial Mass. One of the Campistol sisters stood guard in the vestibule, alert to the slightest sound on the stairway. The other sister had opened the window so that the sun shone on the back of Mosén Francisco's neck. Carmen Elgazu and Pilar, their heads lightly covered in white, had knelt between the bed and the wardrobe. They both felt the strangeness of that altar, that little sputtering candlestick, the prayer book serving as Missal, and the absence of an acolyte. They would rather not have had to pray in Latin, but to cry out instead in their own language: "I will go unto the altar of God. Unto God who giveth joy to my youth."

Mosén Francisco looked now like a taper, now like a torch, and when he beat his breast it seemed to send forth an echo. The Campistol sisters made the replies to the priest in very soft voices. Carmen Elgazu and Pilar were not able to accompany them because they did not know the Latin text of the Mass.

But that did not matter. Carmen Elgazu prayed for a great many things at once, although she missed having her Rosary twined between her fingers. When she saw the priest move to the left side of the altar and heard the word "Epistle," she thought of Saint Paul and prayed to him: "Protect us!" When Mosén Francisco moved to the right side and spoke the word "Gospel," Carmen Elgazu thought of Jesus and prayed: "I want to love Thee as Thou hast never been loved." When the priest, unattended, washed his hands in a small basin, she understood as never before that the Mass was a sacrifice.

Mosén Francisco next offered up the bread. He elevated it, looking upward. It was ordinary bread, not the Host, and therefore seemed more truly "our daily bread," given us this day. Immediately afterward the priest offered up the chalice... Oh, Lord, it was not a chalice, but a crystal goblet; that is, it was transparent... Carmen Elgazu's eyes were fixed on that marvel. This was the first time she ever had seen the wine of the Offertory, the wine of the Consecration. The gold and silver of the Communion cups were beautiful, but opaque; the humble champagne glass let one participate directly in that peerless mystery.

Mosén Francisco turned toward the women. "Pray, brethren, that this my sacrifice and yours..."

He spread his arms as if measuring with them his capacity for love. Carmen Elgazu had glanced at Pilar from time to time to see if she was paying attention. Her knees hurt, but what did that matter? Jesus had suffered much worse pain. Suddenly—where were the bells?—"*Sanctus, Sanctus, Sanctus,* Lord God of Hosts—of Hosts!—Heaven and earth are full of Thy glory." Mosén Francisco concluded this canticle and lapsed into a deep silence. Only God could hear him. People were going up and down the stairway.

At the moment of the Elevation, Mosén Francisco's stature seemed doubled, while Carmen Elgazu seemed to shrink. She could see the bread made Flesh and then the goblet of wine made Blood. It seemed to her that the blood was the blood of César mingled with the blood of Jesus. "As often as ye shall do these things, ye shall do them in remembrance of Me." Ah, yes, Carmen Elgazu was there, between the bed and the wardrobe, motionless, in remembrance of César and of Jesus! May Jesus forgive her her sins, especially the sin of hate, and teach her to renounce them. Carmen Elgazu now felt absolute certainty that Christ in person was lying upon the altar. "Jesus, protect my family, save my country, forgive those who make war on Thee." "I love Thee, my God, with all my heart."

Mosén Francisco was barely moving and yet he was filling the altar. "Vouchsafe to grant us some part and fellowship with Thy Holy apostles and martyrs, John, Stephen, Matthew, Barnabas, Ignatius!" Mosén Francisco joined his hands and made the Sign of the Cross three times over the Host and the chalice. The candlestick was the only erect witness to the ceremony. Soon they heard him say: "Thy will be done on earth as it is in Heaven..."

At the Communion, Mosén Francisco turned, holding a piece of white cloth that contained four tiny pieces of bread. Pilar was the first to pray, "Lord, I am not worthy..." Carmen Elgazu joined her, and then the two Campistol sisters. "O Lord, I am not worthy that Thou shouldst come to me..." Carmen Elgazu wanted to be the last communicant. First came the Campistol sisters, one of whom—the one who had remained in the vestibule—was limping visibly. Then Pilar received Communion. The girl clasped her hands and went back to her place. Carmen Elgazu did not need to rise and move forward; Mosén Francisco came to her. When still on her knees, she saw his intention, closed her eyes, and, raising her head, offered her tongue to that Bread, the food of eternal life.

The Bread seemed to fill her breast until the end of the ceremony and long afterward. She was sure that Christ now dwelt within her as her children had dwelt there before their birth. And she was thinking that she preferred the bread of her children, for the Host was dissolved too quickly. She could feel Christ spreading through her, even to the tips of her fingers and toes. "I can do anything, because He comforteth me." For the first time since the outbreak of the revolution, since the bugles had sounded in the Rambla, she felt mistress of herself. And for the first time since César had died, she felt a kind of sweet consolation in her soul. Yes, in the instant when she murmured, "I can do anything…" it seemed to her that she could make, as he meant her to, the penance given her by the vicar, and that she could offer her son to the Lord without despair. "Yes, yes, I will see him again. I will see him again in Heaven." "Lord, Lord, I offer César to Thee, forgive me." "Spare the world and my country, protect Matías, Ignacio, and Pilar."

At the conclusion of the Mass, Pilar helped her mother to rise. There was a radiance on Carmen Elgazu's face. Even Mosén Francisco could see it. When he had blown out the candle, he turned, and his face looked radiant, too.

"Many thanks, Mosén Francisco…"

The vicar smiled. "Don't call me by my name aloud, like that. Someone may hear us."

"Oh my God, that's right."

Pilar added: "And don't say 'my God' either.'"

Everyone laughed.

"Are you happy?" the Campistol sisters asked Carmen Elgazu.

"Indeed I am. Many thanks."

"And you, Pilar?"

"I am, too. I've missed going to Communion."

Carmen Elgazu looked down at her knees, fearing that she had soiled her stockings. Matías always used to say that her trick of lifting first one foot then the other to look at her shoes or stockings was performed with inimitable grace. Her knees were clean, and Carmen Elgazu said: "Good, they're all right."

One of the dressmakers opened the window and the sun poured in.

"Look, Mama, what a beautiful day!"

"Yes, yes, it is, child. Come, let's go."

They made their goodbyes. The Campistol sisters took them to the door. Not Mosén Francisco, who never left his room, and who now wanted to say a prayer of thanksgiving. "Come back whenever you can, you know."

"May we really come back?"

"On Sunday, of course..."

"All right. Many thanks again."

"Remember me to Matías and Ignacio."

The door closed behind them. The stairway was empty. Carmen Elgazu began to run down it with an agility that surprised Pilar. "Mama, I won't be able to keep up with you if you go so fast..."

Outside, the sky was the same color as the sea.

THIRTEEN

"I'M completely overwhelmed just now... Nothing matters to me now, Ignacio... I've lost the desire to go on living! But I still have two children left, you know. I'll have to go on with the struggle. I'll have to try to save myself and Marta..."

Major Martínez de Soria's widow had spoken the above words to Ignacio on the day following the execution of the officers. The boy had gone to see her and found her in a state of extreme despondency. With Assault Guards as her bodyguard, protecting her. It was impossible to protect the heart.

Ignacio suggested that she try to leave Spain with the help of some consulate. Marta's mother already had thought of that and presumed that Colonel Muñoz, who had sent her an eloquent letter of condolence, would not refuse his help. But it was not yet time. For the moment she could think of nothing, and nothing mattered to her. She could not even pray.

"The only thing I ask of you is that you go and talk to Marta as soon as you can. You go to Barcelona. I don't feel up to it."

Ignacio did not insist. Behind the woman an enormous map of Spain was hanging on the wall, with some smudges on it that had been left by the major's index finger. Marta's mother aroused a great pity in the boy; on the other hand, he could scarcely call the major to mind. The death of this man had affected everyone in the Alvear home, especially Pilar. He, on the contrary, had read all the details of the execution in the newspaper as though it had had to do with a stranger. At the last moment, Marta's mother said to him: "I trust you, Ignacio. My daughter loves you very much." Then she said again, with a searching look, "I trust you."

Those words followed Ignacio throughout the day and into the following morning, when he climbed on the train that was to take him to Barcelona. "I trust you..." What a strange feeling to know that someone trusted him! What a curious responsibility! How absurd and capricious man's subconscious is. He had dreamed all night of a handsome cigarette-holder that had belonged to the major, and had been wondering whether they would give it to him now.

A cigarette-holder, the train, "My daughter loves you very much," Barcelona! He could not pull himself together. The train was crowded. He had intended to think of Marta all through the trip, but had not been able to. He was carrying his UGT card in his wallet. Twice he had been asked for his papers. "Identification!" A paper was more valuable than a man. The train was coming from the frontier and was carrying some foreign journalists whose faces and manner reminded him of Fanny. At every station militiamen came aboard and began to sing: "*La cucaracha, la cucaracha, ya no puede caminar...*" The song began to haunt Ignacio so that he could not sit still. He roamed the corridors, stared at the outdoors, where the countryside looked abandoned. Near the washroom a coach with the little curtains drawn said: Reserved. Ignacio said to himself: "What stupidity... There's no mystery in wartime, except killing."

Halfway through the trip, he calmed down a little and laid out a plan. First he would go to Ezequiel's photographic establishment to find out how Marta was. He did not know Ezequiel, but that was all the same to him. Then he would go to see Marta... Marta! "I love you very much, I love you, too, and another piece of stupidity was for me to dream about the cigarette-holder." Of course he would like to meet the family with whom Marta was living. Julio had said to him: "Manolín is in love with Marta, he's jealous of you!" He would stay and have lunch with them. Then, before taking the train back, he would telephone Ana María. Why not? He ought to do it. It was nearing the end of August. He had met Ana María in August in San Feliu de Guixols; and the girl had written him a nice letter. "I trust you." A crushing responsibility!

Ignacio arrived in Barcelona. He was surprised that he was not exhausted. His body felt nothing, except that his nostrils were a little inflamed. Suddenly, this fact lent him a deep sense of security.

He left the station. Barcelona! In this city he had taken his examinations in two law courses. In this city he once had delivered a Falangist envelope, at Marta's request. Thousands of houses, thousands of men, thousands of maps... Everything around the station smelled of coal smoke, of a produce market, of low-quality gasoline. Fortunately, the Vía Layetana was nearby. The look of the people was sad or frenetic. A large luggage shop said: Clearance Sale, but not a single suitcase was to be seen, and at the Post Office an enormous board gave the postal rates for sending packages and money orders to the front. After treading upon some snow-white letters that said UHP, he found himself in the Vía Layetana, which smelled entirely different. It smelled of ship cargoes and paper.

"Photomaton!" Fifty yards away from Police Headquarters. He entered the establishment and saw Ezequiel—tall, long-haired, wearing a string tie, and holding between his hands the live head of a militiaman who just had sat down in one of the three booths. Ezequiel was correcting the pose of the head, saying: "Hold still! As if you were on parade!" The militiaman, who looked timid, blinked his eyes and stared at the designated point in tenor as if it were a cannon's mouth. Another booth gave a rattle on its own account, and just as Ignacio looked at it, it spat out the requisite strip of six photographs along its tiny toboggan slide.

Ignacio waited, unconsciously humming "La Cucaracha"...and, when the shop was empty, went up to Ezequiel and said: "I'm Ignacio. I've just got here from Gerona."

Ezequiel stared at him fixedly... He was on the point of saying: "Identification!" But suddenly the former caricaturist felt easy. He was remembering Marta's description, and finally said: "Yes, it's you."

Ignacio smiled. But there was something forced in his smile that told Ezequiel at once that this boy was the bearer of bad news. After a moment's pause, he asked: "Has something happened?"

Ignacio said yes, nodding affirmation.

When the photographer learned what the matter was, he closed his eyes and raised a hand to his brow. Then he said: "It was inevitable, but..."

"No, no miracle occurred."

"When did it happen?"

"Day before yesterday."

Ezequiel would have liked to close the shop and go with Ignacio to the Calle de Verdi, but dared not do it. "That would attract attention." The blow would be a hard one to Marta. The girl was well, but as was only natural, she was afraid. Although she had behaved marvelously. "She has what is known as class, believe me." Ezequiel had seated himself on the stool in the second booth and was biting on his dead pipe. Ignacio thanked him for his interest. Ezequiel, brushing that aside, said: "Well, it can't be helped. You've got to go and tell her." Then he added, on a note of conviction: "She loves you very much."

Ignacio nodded.

"I'll be able to close up soon, and then I'll be with you." He paused. "You'll stay to lunch?"

"I'll be glad to."

Three militiawomen appeared in the doorway, rifles at their shoulders. "Hey, boss. Are those machines working?"

Without rising or taking the pipe out of his mouth, Ezequiel answered: "Ten minutes."

"Go ahead, then."

The militiawomen entered and placed the three rifles in the booth with practiced ease. Ezequiel rose and spared Ignacio a glance that meant: "I'm sorry."

Ezequiel had told the truth. Marta was behaving herself very well. In Gerona, Ignacio had been mistaken in suspecting that her political beliefs would lead her to do something foolish. Only on two or three occasions had she tried to proselytize Manolín, telling him about the Falange as if the child was capable of understanding the significance of Vertical Syndicalism and the meaning of hierarchies. Aside from that, she never entered the patio during the day and never once tried to make contact with anyone. She helped Rosita around the house, exchanged lessons in arithmetic with Manolín for lessons in shadow figures, studied Italian diligently, and spent hours glued to the radio, trying to bring in the broadcasts from Jaca, from Burgos, and so on. And of course, she listened to Queipo de Llano every night. His ideology was curiously like Ezequiel's, according to Rosita.

Marta's behavior had won her the affection of them all. Ezequiel would often say to her: "You'll see what will happen when that sweetheart of yours—I suppose he wears a mustache—tries to drag you away from us. You'll see what a fight we'll put up." Rosita was convinced that Marta's every gesture was a token of good breeding. As for Manolín, Julio was right. Marta's presence had awakened precocious desires in the boy, and it was evident that he would have let himself be torn limb from limb to please her.

When the girl heard the doorbell ring at a quarter of twelve, she felt alarmed, though she did not know why. Rosita signaled to her that she was going to answer, and Marta hid. A few seconds later, she recognized Ignacio's voice unerringly, and, beside herself, ran into the vestibule to meet him. When she saw him, she dropped the gray cat she was carrying in her arms, suddenly overcome by anxiety. "Ignacio!" She flung herself at him in a rush of feeling unusual for her. Ignacio could not speak, and Marta was torn between longing and fearing to hear what he had to say. Ignacio pressed her to him and said nothing. There was no need for words. His hands spoke for him. Indeed, Marta was beginning to realize from the way he began to smooth her hair, ever more gently, that Ignacio was the bearer of bad news. "They've killed my father, haven't they?"

"Yes," Ignacio admitted.

Marta fell prey to a moment of despair. She struck Ignacio in the chest as if he had some remedy hidden there inside him. Then she burst into sobs and clasped her hands in a gesture of prayer. Finally, she slowly released herself from the boy's arms, turned quickly, and, avoiding a chair, started to run upstairs to her room.

Ignacio looked at Rosita, who indicated with her head that he should follow Marta. He charged the stairs resolutely and guided by the weeping, which could be heard all over the house, went to the girl's room. Marta had thrown herself on the bed. The sun was streaming in, playing over the wallpaper that was patterned with flowers and birds.

He sat down on the bed beside the girl. "Marta, Marta." He felt a profound love for that creature who lay there face down, and thought how very unfair everything was. The world was unfair and so was the wallpaper. And it was unfair that he craved a cigarette just then and that the streetcars were following their usual routes painted black and red, the colors of the FAI and the Falange. As for Manolín, he was asking his mother: "Why did they kill him?"

Ignacio found broken phrases of consolation. He told Marta she need not worry about her mother, that he was looking after her, and that for the time being she was in no danger whatever. He told her that her father had kept with him "that picture of you on horseback." That they knew where the major was buried... Finally he stopped talking. He was waiting for the girl to have done with her healing tears and recover herself enough to look at him and speak. After a long time, Marta did look at him. She turned her head, buried in the pillow until then, and gave him a look of gratitude, saying: "I have no one but you..."

Ignacio protested. "Don't say that, Marta. You have your mother and José Luis."

"No, no. I have no one but you."

Marta asked Ignacio to close the shutters. They stayed there a long time in the semidarkness, she lying on the bed, he sitting beside her on a chair. Marta seemed to doze at times, but soon he would feel her hand eagerly seeking his.

"Ignacio! It's all so hard, so cruel!"

Whenever anyone passed in the street, his silhouette was thrown into the room through the shaft of light from the window.

Marta passed through several phases. In one of them, it was as though she was laughing. In another, she kept turning restlessly, her breathing rapid, and she confessed to him in a tone he could not recall ever to have heard her use that she was afraid of something within her, that inwardly she was filled with hatred.

Ignacio felt uneasy. "Be brave, Marta... Cast away such thoughts... Please try hard..."

"I am trying hard. But I can't help it! I hate that rabble, Ignacio..."

"Marta, be quiet. I beg you."

"However hard I try, I can't get that kitchen out of my mind. Nor David and Olga... Nor the militiamen I used to see in the road. And I don't trust Julio García! Oh, Ignacio, I'm afraid they'll put my mother in prison, and she knows this address. I'm afraid..."

Ignacio leaned over her and kissed her on the forehead. He was at a loss to know what to do. Her words offered a clue to her unhappiness. The face of the grief-stricken girl was ghostly in the gloom.

Ezequiel came home for the lunch hour, not venturing to greet everyone with a film title this time. At first the girl would not hear of going down to the dining room, but Ezequiel and Ignacio managed to persuade her to come after she had gone to the washroom and reappeared wearing dark glasses.

She sat down at the table with the others, and immediately Rosita brought in the hot soup. The steam went straight to Marta's eyes, and she rose and said, "Excuse me, I can't..." then left the table to sit in a corner some distance away from it.

Everyone respected her wishes, and they arranged themselves so that no one had his back to her. It was a luncheon at once short and eternal. Every noise sounded like gunfire. Conversation had died, and if an occasional word was spoken, it sounded spectral. From time to time they could hear a hymn from some neighbor's radio, and Ezequiel would try then to distract their attention. He and his family appealed to Ignacio. They were a trio that hovered over Marta with love. A man with a whisky voice had been shot in Gerona, and this had caused Manolín to rise and go to Marta, laying the cat gently in her lap. And Rosita to say to her, "How about an omelet? Would you like me to make you an omelet?" And Ezequiel to mull over in his mind caricatures of sorrow, many caricatures, none of which satisfied him.

Ignacio was feeling that he had suffered one more defeat. Truly, nothing was coming out right. He had dreamed of a quiet valley for Marta, and especially of freeing her of that excessive seriousness which sometimes made her unattractive. And then the war! The war came to justify her prevailing mood...

By the time dessert was served, an unexpected peace had spread itself within the boy. Ezequiel reminded him a little of his father, and each time that Rosita went out to the kitchen, he could hear her from the dining room making sounds identical with those made by Carmen Elgazu in the apartment in Gerona. Were it not for the news he had brought... If she had not suddenly found herself orphaned...

Ignacio would have liked to stay in the dining room. He was sorry he could be there only for a visit. Under normal circumstances, it must be fine to stay in that house, modest and clean and shut off from the outside world. With an ever more complicated Meccano set in Manolín's room, with the giant pines in the patio. It must be fine to open the shutters from time to time and sit holding the cat and smoking while Ezequiel told gossipy anecdotes or foretold the future: "Before the year 2000, sea water will be potable!" Must there be a Gerona, an El Responsable, and a brain that was an everlasting anthill?

After the coffee, which was all that Marta would have, everyone vanished and the two young people were alone again. Then Marta went to Ignacio and kissed his hand and wrist again and again, then flung herself on his neck and pressed her cheek against his. And finally, she gave him a quick unexpected kiss on the lips... Ignacio noticed that the girl's body was trembling. "Marta, Marta..."

"Forgive me for what I said awhile ago, Ignacio."

"Don't worry about it. I know what you're going through. I understand it only too well."

"I ought to be braver."

"All right! Do you suppose I'm satisfied with myself?"

"Don't say that."

"Why not? I ought...to be more effectual. I ought to be able to take care of everything for you."

"You do the best you can."

Ignacio bit his lip. "That isn't very much... I can't do anything."

IGNACIO'S visit lasted another hour. Marta had slept for a good quarter of an hour of that time, and they spent the rest of it talking. Marta felt comforted by the boy's presence and the tenderness he sometimes showed, a tenderness that Carmen Elgazu knew by heart and that out of all the things of this world was one that gave her the greatest pleasure.

Marta could not grasp the idea of death. She had realized what it was when her brother died in Valladolid, and now the realization had to be reaffirmed. What was death? Did the soul actually depart from the body? Was it possible for the soul to move from a particular place, to be displaced? Had it a form, then? Where might the spirit that had given living reality to her father be now? Why did people stare upward toward the stars when they pondered such things? Had Lazarus really risen from the dead? Was that because he had not yet come to judgment? Was judgment beyond appeal in the next life then?

"I'm afraid, Ignacio."

Ignacio tried to picture the major dead. Since his visit to the cemetery, he could visualize death with much greater fidelity than when he had seen the corpse of his billiard opponent, Don Pedro Oriol's son. He fancied that the major would be smiling now from his grave. For the major used to smile at the most serious moments, as a means of self-defense. He had been tall, and now he was horizontal. He had been a drinking man, and now he had evil deeds and even eternity to quaff. The archangels would appoint him a major in their glorious hosts, and as commander of them he would soon descend into that absurdly papered room and give back the color to Marta's cheeks, a normal beat to her pulse, the will to live and to win the war…

"Don't be afraid, Marta. I'm here beside you. And your father sees us…"

IGNACIO left the house at four o'clock in the afternoon. The train for Gerona would not leave until six-thirty, so that he could have stayed with Marta for a while yet. But tension had pulled his nerves taut, and he longed to feel free and to breathe. He said goodbye to Marta with an embrace that brought tears to Rosita's eyes. As for Ezequiel, he came forth with one of his prophecies: "You're going to be happy, children. I can see that! You're going to be as happy as Rosita and I have been…"

Once in the street, Ignacio began to walk down from that section toward the center of the city. He knew that he had something more to do to telephone Ana María—but he was not thinking about it. He was not thinking about anything. He had lighted a cigarette and the cigarette was doing his thinking for him.

Barcelona under the banner of revolution! He was not looking at anything, yet no detail escaped him. He would have liked to inventory the city. On one door he read a sheet of paper: "A foreign subject lives here." On one corner an excavation was being dug; the men were building an air-raid shelter. Ignacio kept walking, now rapidly, now slowly, according to whether he was in the sun or the shade. His hair was long and the heat had bleached the circles under his eyes. He was wearing navy blue and his trousers were wrinkled.

As he was passing a fountain, his mind started to function and he began to think of unconnected things: that he was twenty years old, that he was a man, that there were many dogs in Barcelona, that the dogs would have to die, too, that Axelrod, the Russian, had a weather-beaten skin, that the air was stifling, that his feet hurt. Why should his feet hurt? "It's hard to say why things hurt." A few steps farther, and his blood felt hot. And then he began to be hurt by the trees he was caressing with his hand as he passed them, by the oppressive hour of the siesta. His tongue hurt him a little, and so did all the dirt, and all the tremors, and all the hopes of that almost unknown city.

He climbed into a streetcar, and this act snuffed out his mood. He was heading down toward the heart of the city. "You'll be happy, children. I can see that!" The conductor collected the fare and gave him his change. He was a man with a bird-face who resembled Padrosa in the bank. None of the passengers was wearing a hat or a necktie. None of the women was wearing jewels or high heels. Adornment might attract attention. "So much filth!" "Everything must be of the people." "The people have decreed the death of..." He got off the streetcar for no reason and then noticed that his cigarette had gone out, that it was no longer doing his thinking for him.

He reached the Plaza de Cataluña. Immense sheets were hanging from the façades, all saying the same things as the little sheets in Gerona. How was Ana María? What a long time had gone by! He entered the Ramblas, toward Colón, and felt benumbed. It was like a beehive. A frenetic crowd was in motion, dragging its feet beneath the trees and treading ovals of sunlight underfoot. And what were the components of that crowd? Men like Ezequiel, women like Rosita, and kids with a Marta somewhere and a telegrapher for a father and wrinkles in their trousers. The women were bare-necked and the men unshaven. "Yes, there's baseness here, and complacency about baseness." And a swarm of street vendors. Everything was for sale except the heart. From badges—for what Syndicate, for what road to salvation?—to a cure for mothers-in-law, preventives, and slices of watermelon and other melons.

Ignacio stopped at the book and newspaper kiosks. The headlines proclaimed: OVIEDO ON POINT OF SURRENDER! HUESCA WITHIN RANGE OF ASCASO'S FORCES! Postcards of the heroes of all the revolutions: Russian heroes, Hungarian, Czech, French! ... Caricatures of La Pasionaria, of Margarita Nelken, of Garcia-Oliver, of Durruti! Three adjoining playhouses advertised: *The Women, You Touch Them,* and *Who Cares?*—titles that, read consecutively, formed a whole sentence. Militiamen for the Red Relief were offering all kinds of pamphlets, from how to protect yourself against flak in case of air raids to the pedagogical slogan: "To be inwardly free, the teacher must slay the priest." Ignacio said to himself: "I'd better go into a bar and telephone Ana María."

He went on down the Ramblas. The shoeshine boys were doing as their opposite numbers did in Gerona: lacking shoes to shine, they were polishing puttees and Sam Browne belts. Not a single door was showing a sign that said: Attorney-at-Law or Doctor or Real Estate Agent. Those and other like titles would arouse the gravest suspicions *per se.* In the high school, taken over by the Provincial Government, a concert by the tenor, Lázaro, was announced. And at about that point the kingdom of the street photographers started. Ignacio thought of Ezequiel. The militiamen were flocking to them as if mesmerized. They did not want their photographs for identity cards so much as for keepsakes. They wanted a permanent record of their last hours on the home front or their first hours of splendor. They would strike martial poses or crouch like football players. Some held up a thumb or a clenched fist so as to be immortalized not only as subjects for photography, but also as members of the revolution.

Ignacio came to the top of the Calle de Fernando, where Ana María was living. He was about to telephone when a seismic movement swept the crowd. The passersby divided into halves to make way for some people who wanted to parade. But the curious thing was that no band music nor shouts were heard. Something was approaching, silent and solemn. Perhaps a lone madman with a beard, pleading for peace!

Ignacio stepped back and stationed himself in the front row. The parade was composed of women in blue coveralls and lopsided caps. They were carrying signs and wearing neckerchiefs. They marched in platoons, and each platoon represented an idea. "Rights for Anti-Fascist Women." "Loyalty to the New Principles." "Blood Donors." "Free Love." "Advice on Abortion." "Long Live the Universal Proletariat."

The onlookers reacted unexpectedly... Many of them laughed. Some militiamen forgot about being photographed and began to make great sport of the "Free Love" platoon. "Hi, girlies," they cried. "Why don't you make it obligatory?"

For some reason the women did not laugh. They went by sober-faced on their way to the new world they were helping to shape, and as they went they ran head on into the vendors of badges. Ignacio had not moved. Women had always inspired a deep and indefinable respect in him. He had spoken of it once to Olga, and she had alluded to the Oedipus complex, excessive chastity, what not. Ignacio did not know what to think now. He stared at those women and felt a deep pity for them. They distressed him as had the streetcar conductor with the bird-face. He thought of Carmen Elgazu, of course, of Pilar, of Marta, of Marta's mother. "I trust you..." He thought of Rosita—"You're going to be happy..."—and of Ana María. "Blood Donors." He thought of Dimas and of how his own blood was in ferment. Why were those women with signs making a parade of love through the Ramblas, between rows of rifles and caricatures of La Pasionaria? "You touch them, who cares?" Love was never free. Love was a delight and a torture, a stimulus and a fatigue. It was a law of life. Those women would behave prudently on their way back to their homes, if indeed they had homes, and would wait there for some shirt-sleeved man to approach them with the rough hands of timidity.

Ana María was having her siesta less than three hundred yards from the telephone booth that Ignacio just had entered. She was at Number 27 Calle de Fernando, third floor. A bourgeois apartment. Her bed was more comfortable than Marta's and was surrounded with flowers, but not with birds.

The flat was the property of Gaspar Ley, commonly known as Gaspar, an intimate friend of the girl's father. Gaspar had owned, and now was "responsible for" the Chiqui Jai-Alai Court. Ana María's father, an ardent fan of regattas for small boats, was a manufacturer of sports goods, from footballs and boxing gloves to tennis racquets. For years he had supplied Gaspar with equipment for the court. The two men had become fast friends. During the first week of the revolution, Ana María's father had been arrested by two of his employees and taken to the Modelo Prison. A placard saying "Commission for Aid to the Front" had been placed on his door. The mother had gone into hiding in a country house, and Ana María had accepted Gaspar's hospitality. He was a young man married to a Valencian woman named Charo. They had no children.

Ana María no longer was wearing buns of hair at each side of her face. She had had an ordinary permanent wave, though she always covered her hair with a scarf when she went out, for fear that some workman from the factory might recognize her. She would have preferred to live in a quieter section farther from the Barrio Chino. But on the whole, she considered herself fortunate, for both Gaspar and his wife, Charo, treated her like a daughter. Like Marta, she was learning to cook, and she, too, spent hours glued to the radio, and she read a good deal. On the other hand, she was not studying Italian, for she did not care for Mussolini. Apart from that, she went to the Modelo Prison every day to take a basket of food to her father, and she had become very adept at inserting into it a slip of paper with news of the outside, news that soon went flying along the tiers of cells like bits of springtime.

When the telephone rang in the house, Ana María was startled. Gaspar had been a member of the Liga Catalana, and the telephone constituted a perpetual threat, particularly as some of the jai-alai players at the court looked at him askance. The beautiful Charo lifted the receiver, and when she heard Ignacio's name she put on an almost coquettish air and said: "Yes, she's here." Ana María had told her that she had written to Gerona. "If a boy named Ignacio calls, please let me know."

Ana María went somewhat shakily to the telephone. Ignacio! Three years had gone by since their meeting in San Feliu de Guixols. Blue balloons had been floating in the air then, and rich children had strolled about lazily with their "gang" saying "It's the living end" and other fashionable phrases, and thereby making Ignacio nervous. Ana María picked up the receiver...and was instantly enchanted. Ignacio's voice moved straight to her heart. The voice sounded worried, but at the same time forceful and affectionate. A man's voice.

"Ignacio! ..."

Ignacio wanted to see her. He was in Barcelona, three hundred yards away, and he wanted to see her!

"How marvelous, Ignacio! Five minutes... Well, ten—ten minutes and I'll be there."

"Where shall we meet?"

"In front of the Chiqui Jai-Alai Court."

"The Chiqui Jai-Alai Court?"

"Yes, go there. I'll explain it later."

Ignacio hung up and began to walk slowly toward the Chiqui Court, which was not far away. A fly bit him on the forehead, as quickly as one may be struck down with some illness. "*La Soli,* Private Letters of Alfonso XIII! *La Soli-i-i-i—!*" The thought of seeing Ana María awakened sleeping echoes in Ignacio.

The court was closed. In a little while it would be very lively, for money flowed freely there and the betting was heavy. The names of the players shown on the billboard were Basque, and doubtless they would have brought tears to Carmen Elgazu's eyes.

The two young people stood gazing at each other, overcome. They began to move toward a meeting point on the sidewalk, like two birds on a horizontal limb. Neither was sure whether this actually was happening or was not. Ana María was thinking: "Unless he vanishes, he'll take both my hands, as he used to do, both hands." Ignacio was thinking: "Why does she have her head covered?" Then they came face to face, in wonderment, unable to speak a word. How everything had changed! And yet nothing had changed. They stood and stared. Ignacio's eyes were still dark and lustrous. Ana María's were still green. "Lord, how pale he is!" "Ana María has grown into a woman."

Ignacio said: "Excuse me for not wearing a dinner jacket."

Ana María said: "Excuse me for wearing *espadrilles.*"

They both felt astonished at their own joking words. And with all they had on their minds, too, weighing on their hearts!

The sun was very strong, and Ana María suggested that they move out if it into a quiet café next to the court, owned by a man who thought he was Gaspar's niece. Ignacio agreed; they went in and took seats at the back, between a billiard table and the scoreboard, where they could still read the figures of the last championship game.

They still felt confused, and they kept staring at each other. Ignacio was afraid that, out of their usual orbit, he would feel strange with Ana María, but he did not. The girl still wore her air of serenity, her unmistakable mixture of astuteness and ingenuousness. Apart from that, she was certainly not wearing make-up, and she had on a simple percale frock. But her class was beyond question, dangerous even, Ignacio feared. The revolution had not changed in any way her manner of seating herself. Any militiaman whatsoever might have arrested her and shouted in her honor: "Death to Fascism!"

"But I just can't believe it, Ignacio! How did you happen to think of coming to see me?"

"I was in Barcelona, and it seemed the natural thing to do."

"Natural? It seems supernatural to me!"

They would have liked to relive those conversations in the water when Ignacio caught her by one leg and she called him "Octopus" or "Satyr." But there was something more pressing. They knew nothing about each other, nor about what had happened to their respective families. They had to clear up this point straightaway so as to know whether they could go on joking or must change to weeping.

On Ana María's side, the situation was not hopeless! They had lost everything, but they were all still alive, and the reason she had suggested a meeting at this spot was that she felt relatively safe in the street where the Chiqui Court was situated, thanks to Gaspar. "We're all alive, Ignacio... And I'm just the same. Except for a terrible aversion to these people, perhaps...an aversion that sometimes makes me feel ill. We are all alive, and I can even believe that Gaspar will come out of it without losing anything, and may even get my father out of prison. Now what about you, Ignacio? Tell me!"

Ignacio bit his lip. He was on the point of concealing the truth from her. But it was impossible, and he told her of César's death. Ana María's face expressed horror. She gave a kind of cry that shot out into the street and was lost. The girl took a sip of coffee, her hand shaking. Two sailors had come in and clapped their hands to summon the owner. Ignacio was afraid someone might notice them. He begged her to be careful.

"How awful, Ignacio!" she stammered. "César!"

Ignacio did not know what to say. His brother's face seemed to materialize in the mirrors. Ana María whispered, drawing out the syllables: "I'm so sorry, Ignacio...with all my heart."

Ignacio turned paler. There was something indefinably sweet about Ana María. It was there when she spoke of sorrow and even when she pronounced the word "aversion."

They sat in silence for a time, while the sailors at the bar were talking about the *Uruguay*, the ship on which the soldiers were imprisoned. Then, little by little their nerves began to subside. They ordered another coffee, and the interruption of the waiter, and the wheezing of the espresso machine calmed their thoughts. Ana María merely commented: "Of course, naturally it's all a part of their system… They won't forgive my father for having succeeded. And they wouldn't forgive César for being a saint."

Ignacio considered that the facts were complicated beyond that, but he lacked the spirit to argue.

Ten minutes later they began to talk about themselves again. Ana María chided him for never having written her a single line. "The least you could do was to ask your father to send me a telegram. The worst of it is that I keep thinking of you every time I pass a bank… And you? Of course you'll be thinking of me whenever you look at the sea. But it's my bad luck that there's no sea in Gerona."

Ignacio remarked that strange things could happen in the world. He was far more interested in what Ana María was saying than in the war. He would have liked to stare at the sailors and shout, "I'm fed up with the war…and with the *Uruguay*!" But he knew better. Someone had turned on the radio and two Assault Guards had entered the café. While they were heading toward the billiard table to begin a game, they were whistling, "La Cucaracha"…

Ana María kept hoping that it would all be over before long, and that "*they* would collapse." She believed that with a blind faith. "What about you, Ignacio? Don't you think so, too?"

Ignacio's reply came after a moment's delay. Then he began to talk impromptu. This was what always happened: with Marta he stuck to facts and gave no rein to his imagination. With Ana María—how beautifully she moved her wrists—he enjoyed playing the poet, arousing in her a little thrill of fear. He told her that the struggle was tremendous because it had to do with two opposing conceptions of life. The one of "It's the living end," which tended to ignore suffering, and the one of "I'm hungry," which resulted in imprisoning those who had tasted success. And above all, it had to do with Spain, now like a sea shell in the depths of which the roar of the whole world could be heard.

"We're a kind of summation, you see… We have our greatnesses and our faults. We never change and we're about as useful as our toes are. We conquered America, yes, but out of that came nothing worthwhile. Fatalism, the knife, and the loaded revolver. And why did we conquer America? For the same reasons that we're fighting this war now. Three reasons, Ana María, remember them: for God, for the devil, and for no reason."

The conversation went on. They touched on a thousand themes. Ana María declared that she liked to cook and that Charo was teaching her to sew in the afternoons. As for the Chiqui Court, its atmosphere was strange. Gaspar was earning his living from it, and he always used to say that it would be an ideal spot for espionage. "Can't you picture it? The scorekeeper could tell whatever it was he had to tell and the players could pass it on while they were batting the ball. So could the men selling the balls! The wrappings around the balls could contain a message or a note."

"I think Gaspar has something there."

It surprised Ignacio to hear Ana María speak about such things, and for a moment he asked himself if... It would be funny if the one who got involved in plots were Ana María instead of Marta.

Ana María was gazing sweetly at Ignacio again, and she said: "Naturally... I wasn't made for war either, you know. I was born...to lead a quiet life."

Ignacio felt a wrench. He lighted a cigarette, the match singeing his eyebrows a little, and he felt stimulated. His phrases were punctuated by the *crock* of the billiard balls shot by the two Assault Guards and the *sprt* of the espresso coffee-maker on the counter. Ignacio told Ana María that every time she had asked him, "Do you remember?" he had been touched. "You're a little like a seashell to me. All my befores echo when I see you." "Even though centuries might go by, you'd still be steering that boat in San Feliu de Guixols." Yet how strange it was that after such a long time nothing had changed! Wasn't the brain capable of evolving? He had a double impression with regard to it: sometimes he felt that he was a child again, other times he could not admit that he had ever been a child. And what about the war? Perhaps not even that would modify anything substantially. Perhaps the war would accomplish nothing except to convert hidden inclinations into deeds. He was a man who doubted; that is, he was an easy prey to suffering. With the war, his doubts had reached their peak and sometimes he felt that the bombs and even the trees and the house fronts were hurting him... The brain! What exactly did it contain? Did each man's destiny, and his goodness, and his ferocity reside in his brain? With the coming of the war, brains had ceased to be cloisters and had become militia who killed or idealists who buried their heads in the sand. Ah, no! There was no logic in it all, and behind each person's eyes lay a great mystery like that in Ana María's pronouncement: "I was born to lead a quiet life." It went without saying that he would not make so bold as to prophesy; a friend of his named Ezequiel was taking care of that. Nevertheless, he was sure of two things: that he was not going to die in the war and that love was the most important thing in life. "What happens is that it's hard to love truly. My mother doesn't think so, but it seems to me it's very hard." "You women have settled that question by natural law, but it comes harder to us men." In Gerona, to go no farther, that policeman named Julio wanted to fall in love and he had succeeded only occasionally. And there was an Anarchist boy named Santi who would have been happy to be loved. But he had been left an orphan, and the only people who caressed him were other men carrying rifles. Incompatibility, being excluded, these were the misfortunes of being human. To love one thing implied to abhor another, and to be a Communist implied annihilating the individual. If only there were nothing but love over all the earth for a moment, just one moment! What a beautiful sight that would be! People embracing one another in the streets, the sailors shaking hands with the waiters. The example would spread and in the end even the billiard cues and other inanimate objects would love one another. "Can you imagine it, Ana María? The doors of the prisons would open of themselves and would say to your father, 'Go on, you may go... Your wife and daughter are waiting for you.' Can you imagine bullets being converted to love? And machine guns refusing to shoot anything but lottery tickets or green leaves? And ships chatting with the fish, and ulcers healing themselves? Can you imagine me finding myself and saying to you: 'My darling Ana María, I know why I am here, why my feet hurt, and why I cry when women go by carrying signs.' Can you imagine it? It would be wonderful, yes, and my flesh wouldn't be yammering so often for its ration of flesh... I could sit beside you and look into the depths of your eyes without shame."

Ana María was bewitched, as she had been in San Feliu de Guixols. She took one of Ignacio's hands in hers and pressed it. She was sorry there was not a drop of coffee left in her cup for a toast. And she was sorry that the time was all too short and that she was not wearing rolls of hair at each side of her face this afternoon. But she felt uncomfortable when Ignacio spoke of his "ration of flesh." Gaspar was always saying that war raised a special dust so stimulating that everything was condoned and everyone degraded. But why was Ignacio not above such usage? Perhaps he was like the rest, like everyone else. Then why was he the only one who could say things like "machine guns shooting green leaves" or "ships chatting with the fish?"

And why did Ignacio insist that it was difficult for men to love truly? What about his father, Matías Alvear? And Gaspar, so much in love with Charo? There was something concerning Ignacio that he was keeping back, she did not know why.

Ana María was silent for a moment. Then she asked the unexpected: "Tell me something, Ignacio... Have you a sweetheart?"

"Sweetheart? Why do you ask that?"

"I don't know." Ana María shrugged... "Tell me, yes or no."

Ignacio blew out a mouthful of smoke and replied, "No."

Ana María made an odd face. Another long silence fell. Finally the girl reacted. "You mustn't mind me," she said. "But I'm happy when I'm with you."

An hour later, Ignacio was on the train going back to Gerona. Two messengers loaded down with bundles were dozing beside him. Next to the toilet, a sign on a coach said Reserved, and the curtains were drawn. The August sun was setting beyond the mountains. "You are going to be happy… I can just see it." The wheels of the train seemed to be in love with the rails, and the telegraph wires kept kissing, parting, then kissing again.

PART TWO

September 1, 1936 to March 31, 1937

FOURTEEN

THROUGH the months of September and October important events took place in both the military field and the psychological. In the first place, the Nationalist forces that had left Galicia intending to rendezvous with General Aranda, who was besieged inside Oviedo, surrounded by the miners, succeeded in opening a breach, breaking the siege and entering the capital of Asturias. This feat was of supreme importance, for it demonstrated that the miners were not invincible. The siege of Huesca also failed to bring about the occupation of the city. Huesca was still holding out. Teo was there, deeply attached to La Valenciana, but there was nothing on which he could employ his remarkable endowments. Ascaso stated as a fact that the Nationalists had disinterred Galán and García Hernández and had shot them again. With this and other like news, the Anarchist leader kept his men at fighting pitch, but still Huesca would not surrender. A Catalan volunteer, a pal of Teo's, remarked: "Well, they'll have to be shot all over again. But as for me, I've cut all but the pee for pig out of the word priest."

In the second place, the Nationalists had occupied Irún and San Sebastián. General Mola's forces were rolling back the Basque army corps in order to cut off the border with France. This struggle was a dramatic one which had begun virtually on the first day of the revolution. The Basques were defending themselves with ardor and confidence. The athletic prowess of the race permitted them to make almost superhuman efforts. There were moments, in Peñas de Ayala, in San Marcial, when what rose from the ground was not smoke alone, but earth and smoke, and when the bodies of the men stuck to their machine guns and parapets like leeches. The knowledge that those fighting men were brothers was terrible. If the battleground could have been seen from an airplane, what conclusions could have been drawn? The red berets, with Germán Ichaso's conspicuous among them, were like bloody wads of cotton scattered over the Pyrenees. The fighting men were brothers! The Basques stonewalled against the advance of the Requetés shouting "Long live Christ the King" had nothing whatever to do with Durruti and Axelrod. They were a part of the Popular Front. Mixed in with them were some perfectly disciplined French and Belgian volunteers. Nevertheless, the backbone of the squadrons were the Basque Nationalists, ultra-Catholic. Jaime Elgazu of San Sebastián, the croupier from the Kursaal, the brother of Carmen Elgazu herself, was with them, singing anthems in the line. When the Requetés fired, therefore, they were shooting at men who said the same prayers they did and sang the same songs: "Riau, Riau," "La Sequía," "Adiós, Pamplona..." They were even shooting at priests. For there were in fact Separatist priests who could handle a gun with the best of them and who kept throwing grenades even as they were ministering to the dying. Those priests were doing what their conscience bade them, and, like the orator whom Mosén Francisco used to listen to on the radio, they believed they were defending the cause of the people, as Christ Himself had done. "Christ rose from the people," the Basque President Aguirre had declared. And that is how the priests understood matters, and accordingly they preferred fighting alongside the "Gudaris" to standing on the side of Don Anselmo Ichaso. What conclusions could be drawn by a man looking down from an airplane? That the moment of love entreated by Ignacio had not yet come, that the war was awful, and that the winds of madness were blowing over the legendary Cantabrian Coast.

A part of the defeated Basque army fell back toward Bilbao, carrying with it many women as hostages. But there were units that could go nowhere but to France. The battles on the bridge at the Hendaye border and in Bidasoa were bloodcurdling. The crack of bullets pursued those trying to cross the river by swimming or in rowboats, and fugitives on the international bridge were shot down at the very moment they set foot on the dividing line. They fell dead into France, and their bodies found true sanctuary there. A crowd of French people and diplomatic envoys was witnessing the carnage from the heights, as the English had witnessed naval combat through binoculars from the heights of Gibraltar. The onlookers understood little of the causes of the struggle, and they cried: "*Ah, ces espagnols!*" There were women who tore a button off the refugees' unies to keep them as souvenirs.

Irán was set afire. Houses collapsed. San Sebastián remained almost intact, still offering the beauty of her bay to her people. The small Nationalist navy had acted as a timely auxiliary along the coast while the Red navy was sheltering in the Mediterranean.

After the *Te Deum* in the cathedral in Pamplona, Don Anselmo Ichaso threw the switch on his miniature railroad and all the little trains, flying pennants, drew up in front of the "San Sebastián Station" in the presence of his amputee son, Javier Ichaso, and Warning Voice, who had been invited to the ceremony. His other son, Germán Ichaso had entered the capital of Guipúzcoa with the Cayuela Column. He had promised to take a swim in La Conchà, but he did not. Instead, as a gesture of jubilation, he threw all his hand grenades into the water. They sent up a lugubrious echo. Many Requetés imitated him while the fish were spreading the tremulous news beneath the water. The Navarrese Companies were reformed into brigades and later into divisions.

The victory of General Mola in such a strategic sector as the province of Guipúzcoa unleashed an outburst of enthusiasm throughout the Nationalist zone from Galicia and Castile to Extremadura and Andalusia. Queipo de Llano said in his broadcast: "We gave them a kick in a place I know all about." Mateo, who had been stationed at the front on the Alto del León, where he had joined José Luis Martínez de Soria, stretched his arm until it seemed he could touch a star. His comrade Núñez Maza, now fully committed to the Propaganda Service, was shouting into his loudspeakers and María Victoria took a special chew of gum in Valladolid. In the Red zone, on the other hand, the defeat was a grievous surprise. The Government could not find the words to square the facts. Axelrod, the native of Tiflis, and the Russian soldiers who were working at his side, were indignant with the Ministry of War. In Barcelona, Ana María managed to slip the news to her father in his basket of food, as usual. Her father, still in the Modelo Prison, realized the significance of it. In Gerona, Colonel Muñoz spent an afternoon staring out through the ventilators.

The third important military fact during that month of September was the capture of Badajoz and the consequent union of the Nationalist armies of the North and South along the Portuguese border, a linking of forces that was to have an important influence on the march of events. Indeed, it permitted the coordination of the campaign under a single command and the dispatch of troops toward Madrid and Toledo, where the Alcázar was still holding out. Franco was in command of these troops. The Moors had proved to be most effective on the offensive, particularly if the Legionnaires were treading on their heels. Their wild, strange shouts disconcerted the militia, some of whom were convinced that the Moors were not really Moors, but monks in disguise. The attempt to free the Alcázar of Toledo became a race against the clock, of the greatest importance to morale. Everyone, whatever his allegiance, was asking: "Will they get there in time?" Attempts had been made to set the fortress afire with gasoline, but they had failed. Now expert dynamiters were tunneling beneath it to blow it up. Two huge mines had been made ready, one by the

Communists, the other by the Anarchists, and several men with movie cameras, among them Fanny's friend, Raymond Bolen, were awaiting the moment. The artillery, emplaced almost at the foot of the walls, was rooting up sections of wall. Inside, the place must have been a graveyard. The Government in Madrid announced again and again that surrender was imminent. "It's inhuman to hold out!" "At least let the women and children leave!" The woman revolutionary leaders—Margarita Nelken, Victoria Kent, Federica Montseny, and La Pasionaria—declared that Colonel Moscardó, the defending officer, was a criminal. Olga strongly shared that opinion. Dr. Relken, on the other hand, held that the defense was a notable military feat, quite typical of the strong spirit of the race, and that it constituted a major problem for the ingenuous Supreme Command in Madrid.

The fourth military event of that month of September was the unaccountable failure of the Catalonian expedition to Mallorca under Captain Bayo. The expeditionary force was made up of some fourteen thousand men, Santi and many other Gerundians among them, as well as of the volunteer waiters' guild. Captain Bayo, determined that the operation was to be carried forward under the flag of the Provincial Government of Catalonia and not under the flag of the Republic, weighed anchor in the harbor of Barcelona and disembarked south of Porto Cristo on the coast of Mallorca, in the Bay of Madrona, and later in Morlando Bay, without any great difficulties. The island was scantily garrisoned and confusion reigned over most of it, though the natural ports of Sóller, Pollensa, and Alcudia had been fortified with the cannon from the parks. The landing of the Catalonia Militia sowed panic everywhere. The battle would have lacked color if disciplined, war-hardened troops had been involved. But the militiamen gloried in their improvisations and lack of foresight, and they were insatiable looters. Consequently they gave the defenders time to react and to organize. The jai-alai players from the Balear Court fought with distinction. Another factor in the militia's defeat was the arrival over Mallorca of an unopposed Italian air squadron, which paralyzed the reflexes of the expeditionary force.

Captain Bayo had to order his men back to the ships and return to Barcelona. They left behind them in Mallorca many dead and many who had been captured; in exchange they brought back to Catalonia some regular soldiers who were incorporated into their ranks. The anger of the defeated men was unanimously directed against the Italians for their intervention. "Mussolini, the pimp!" "He scorched us the way he did those little Negroes!" The Barcelona papers had little to say about the action, but what they did report was avidly devoured in the Arús Bank, for it confirmed that the Balearic Island was at the mercy of the caprices of a fabulous Roman horseman, Count Aldo Rossi, attorney by profession, and an outstanding member of the Fascist Party. He was said to ride around in shorts on a white horse, wearing bracelets with bangles of buckshot, and carrying a small arsenal of knives and hand grenades at his belt. According to *El Diluvio*, Count Aldo Rossi was imposing his will, both sportive and homicidal, on the weak-kneed Fascist authorities of Mallorca as recompense for the aid given them. "*Fusílate subito*"—"Shoot yourself right now"—was his favorite expression. "Some countrywomen," *El Diluvio* said, "thought he was a kind of reincarnation of Saint Michael whenever they saw him galloping along the dusty roads of the island at night."

The foregoing events were plain as daylight, and they operated to jell public opinion. Those who wanted to see the Nationalists win paid little heed to the means used, and found firm ground for their hopes. Those who had faith in the smashing triumph of the Government of the Republic realized at last that "the enemy was strong," as Prieto had recognized in his speeches and Dr. Relken in his conversation with Julio. Everywhere there was talk of the lack of discipline and a surfeit of "everyone doing as he pleases." The General's theories were being borne out daily. But the General suddenly had disappeared from Gerona with his daughters, mysteriously summoned by the Ministry of War. If the Basque Separatists, first-class fighters, could not halt General Mola, how were Durruti's big-bellied militiamen going to prevail against the defenders of Zaragoza? And how were they going to halt the advance on Madrid? The best thing to do would be to start again at the bottom, to think a thousand times more about the front lines and a thousand times less about what was going on behind the lines. What were so many cars doing, driving around everywhere on patrol? Why had the men of the Iron Column quit the Teruel front in a body, saying they intended to "watch the forward march of the Revolution?" War first, revolution next. That was the open sesame, to the annoyance of El Responsable. He considered it possible to bring both to a successful conclusion at the same time.

SETBACKS like that failed to open even the smallest crack in the morale of the Red zone, however. The chances for victory still were very great, and in many phases of the war the Nationalists had very little to fight with other then technique, discipline, and faith in the enemy's capacity for making mistakes. *El Demócrata,* the vehicle for the meticulous statistics of the Socialist leader, Antonio Casal, kept publishing very precise data on enemy resources. "The Bank of Spain's reserves are still ours, and the industrial regions of the country and the big war plants are ours, too. Practically the entire Navy is fighting on our side—fifty units including twelve submarines—and all the Mediterranean ports and most of the Northern ones are in our power, intact. Something similar may be said of the Air Force. Our network of airfields is being perfected, so that the enemy network is bottled up in the interior with landing fields either very distant or poorly manned. Control of the air belongs to the Rebels along the disengaged Guipúzcoa front, but along the broad Aragón and Southern fronts it is undisputedly ours." All these and other like figures demonstrated to the people of Gerona that, despite the reverses to be expected in any far-reaching undertaking, the final outcome left no room for doubt.

Colonel Muñoz, with his characteristic objectivity, was alone in assessing circumstances differently. Since the 18th of July, Colonel Muñoz had gone around in peasant dress, but that detracted nothing from his competence in military affairs. His opinion, often expressed in the Café Neutral, which he patronized in the company of several employees of the Arús Bank, was that the gold reserves Antonio Casal talked about and that actually existed in the Bank of Spain—probably the third largest gold reserve in the world—might or might not be used wisely. "If there's such a thing as honesty, and if it could be converted into armaments, Antonio Casal's estimates are accurate. But if the money is being used to play roulette at Monte Carlo, everything will be lost." The initial advantage of owning the industrial region of the country was a fact, though the agricultural regions would prove very important, too, if the war should last long. "What scares me is the paucity of technicians in war plants like the Soler. How right Cosme Vila is when he says it's one thing to manufacture a button and another to turn out a bomb. And what about our lack of certain essential materials? Antonio offers our mastery of the sea as an answer to that problem... In actual practice it's not that simple! We are now going to have to pay for the shooting of so many officers in Cartagena... Yes, I don't worry about their being able men, and so I say this: it was a monstrous thing. In the recent battle of San Sebastián, our powerful Navy shamefully retreated to the Mediterranean because no orders were being issued, and left the Cantabrian Coast to a few enemy feluccas. And if my information doesn't lie, the crews of our twelve submarines don't dare to submerge because they're afraid they wouldn't know how to surface." Colonel Muñoz declared that something similar was happening to the Air Force. For the moment the Government was superior in the number of aircraft; but the planes were of a thousand different makes, which made it difficult to coordinate them properly, and, besides, the number of competent Spanish pilots was very low. "Needless to say, we've hired French and North American pilots with high enlistment pay plus a generous bonus for any plane they shoot down; but I'm not at all sure that money will turn a man into a hero, and I'm also afraid that before long Hitler and Mussolini will turn over to Franco an air fleet superior to ours. If you will permit me to state my opinion," Colonel Muñoz concluded, "the Nationalists have won the first round."

The opinions of Colonel Muñoz made little impression. Very few people shared his pessimism, even though Fanny, the English newspaperwoman who was often at the Neutral with Julio García, insistently declared that the colonel's words were true. Indeed the feeling of the majority was expressed by Tower of Babel's invariable reply to Colonel Muñoz. "Colonel, nothing you say can alter the crux of the matter. The gold is still in our hands, and even we humble employees of the bank know what that means. The first round can be won without money, but not the second. In spite of the joke about the submarines that don't want to get wet, and the thousand makes of airplanes, the Fascists will be overthrown. Neither Alfonso XIII nor the pirate Juan March can save Franco. Well, I think..."

The fact is that each man in the driver's seat tried to prove that from where he sat the general optimism was justified. At times they brought forth arguments that were mouth-watering. For example, at the end of September, *El Demócrata* triumphantly announced that the long-awaited heavy buying of war matériel abroad was actually about to be made. "Comrade Julio García is on the eve of departure for France and England to purchase arms, as a member of an official commission appointed by the Provincial Government. We salute the Government! We salute the Government Commission! We salute Comrade Julio García!" *El Demócrata* went on to say that the members of the commission were almost all the same men who had obtained the fifty Potez planes from Léon Blum and Pierre Cot, the French Air Minister, in the early days of the revolution.

Julio was offering a toast to Doña Ampara in the built-in bar at home. "Your health, darling!"

Doña Amparo's eyebrows shot upward. "Why do you let them call you comrade?"

Cosme Vila, too, was compiling optimistic arguments. Of course, he refused to grant the slightest importance to the coming journey of Julio García and his "pals." "England and France will sell arms to the highest bidder." "If Franco offers more than the Government, they'll sell to Franco." Cosme Vila's optimism was based on Russian aid. Russia had taken the part of the Spanish people without any need for commissions or policemen. "The shipments by sea of technical personnel and matériel of all kinds have already started and will be attuned to the rhythm of events." Within the past week four merchant vessels—the *Rostok*, the *Never*, the *Volga*, and the *Brahmil*—have sailed from Odessa and other ports in the Soviet Union, with Cartagena as their port of arrival. On their return voyage those same ships will carry two hundred Spanish volunteers who will be certified as pilots, or bombardiers, or fighter pilots after completing the necessary training in Russia."

Cosme Vila added that Russia had decided to violate the "Non-Intervention Agreement" with regard to Spain which she had recently signed in London, having found out that the said accord was an artifice adopted by the democracies in order to favor Franco. *El Proletario* stigmatized Chamberlain as an "unfrocked Jesuit" and Roosevelt as "a spiritual paralytic." Cosme Vila reminded his readers that Franco had proclaimed Pétain his mentor, and went on to say that the Pope was sending gold to the rebels. Finally, in referring to the military balance of the scales, the first round, he trotted out the old argument that it was salutary to suffer some reverses because they would act as reagents. The people, prone to be flabby and sentimental, would now begin to evaluate Fascism correctly. They would learn now that the Italians were prepared to kill the Spanish people over the length and breadth of the land, as they had killed Ethiopians in Ethiopia. And the same must be said of the Germans. By this time the Extremaduran peasants must have come to know at firsthand the daggers of the Moors, and many of their wives and daughters must have been raped. All Spaniards, from the Basque coast to the Gibraltar line had had impressed on them that the slogan uttered by Prieto of "mercy for the conquered" was a cruel trap laid by a weak spirit.

El Responsable had his Anarchist reasons, too, for never doubting the final victory; so did Alfredo the Andalusian, Murillo's substitute in the POUM, and the architects Massana and Ribas of the Estat Catalá, and David and Olga, plus each and every one of the men and women who raised their clenched fists when the flags went by.

On the other hand, if it was true that very grave deficiencies did indeed exist, which could not be argued away, deficiencies perhaps even graver than those pointed out by Colonel Muñoz, it was equally true that these were being compensated for by feats of efficiency and dedication as abundant behind the lines as at the front.

The home front! To the growing success of the "Militiaman's Mailbox" and the decision of the manager of the Arús Bank to turn over to the Red Relief the contents of the private strongboxes entrusted to his care could be added the almost miraculous adaptation of many people to the needs created by war. This adaptation was important, for it signified the triumph of a dynamism that embraced the little kitchen garden patch of tobacco grown by Cosme Vila's father-in-law, the crossing guard, the spontaneous offer of some of the women to drive trucks and trolleys, the large number of young people of both sexes who had started to study Russian, and the furnishing of the Duran Asylum to re-educate Fascist orphans and former seminarians.

As for the front itself, any summary of the actual data would be interminable. In Barbastro, one of Ascaso's militiamen appeared at the village jail to see his father, who had been arrested as a Carlist, and fired two shots into the old man the moment they met face to face. "Death squadrons" were formed, so named because their members had vowed to infiltrate enemy territory and not to return until they could bring back a machine gun or three heads. Shepherds communicated news from Nationalist territory through the medium of their flocks, grouping the sheep or separating them according to a code agreed upon. Slaughterers in the Supply Department who butchered beasts for the front lines made use not only of the flesh, but of the blood, too, which was invaluable to the hospitals for Wassermann tests and cultures; of the entrails, essential to making catgut; of the fat for industrial use, for war pyrotechnics, and so on. There were other touching examples, like the one set by the members of the "Germ" Battalion in the Teruel sector, who used their spare time to make crutches and canes for the old and for the young amputee victims of bombings. Truly it was heartwarming to see those men felling trees, sawing up the logs, and later polishing the wood under the direction of a corporal. Each cane bore the initials of its maker, which was why Julio García asked for one to add to his private museum, recently enriched by an antique candle snuffer with a silver cone.

Ah, no, nothing was being wasted! How could it be wasted! Then, too, the marching lines of volunteers were increasingly able to keep in rhythm. And to top it all, veteran international fighters were being recruited in several European capitals and would soon be offering their experienced help. This fact was transcendental, for it demonstrated the widespread repercussions of the Spanish struggle. Police Commissioner Brother Julián Cervera, back from a short trip to Perpignan, brought with him the news that in the South of France he already had met several lots of soldiers waiting to enter. The groups were not made up entirely of Communists and Socialists: there was one of Jews expelled from Germany who were coming "as a protest against the expulsion of their race, which had been Isabel the Catholic's objective." Those Jews spoke in Yiddish, though there were many Poles and Palestinian Arabs among them.

On the other side, the Fascists had also made mistakes and done stupid things. They also squandered their resources and were making enemies. Merely to listen to their broadcasts was enough to prove this, as were reading their papers and, especially, interrogating their soldiers at random. The latest idiocy broadcast by Queipo de Llano was: "We shall make a city of Madrid, a factory of Bilbao, a solarium of Barcelona." What an inspiring prospect! Judging by the items in the newspapers, the summer norms of public morality dated back to the beginning of the century, and it would seem that the showing of painted or sculptured nudes was prohibited. Soldiers were saying, indeed they never tired of declaring that the "daughters of respectable families," like those put to work scrubbing floors and toilets in Gerona, were being turned over to the Moors in Zaragoza and other Nationalist cities. The French press described the rebel territory as "the reincarnation of the Middle Ages."

Autumn brought with it two additional news items of such significance that they seemed to confirm all the other evidence. The first was a pastoral letter issued by Cardinal Gomá; the second was the execution of García Lorca. Merely to stand on a rooftop those days and gaze at the melancholy and the yellowing of autumn should have predisposed the mind to moderation. But it could not abate the anger arising among all the Anti-Fascist Spaniards. Cardinal Gomá, Archbishop of Toledo and Primate of the Spanish-speaking world, characterized the conflict in his pastoral letter as "a true crusade for the Catholic religion" and gave assurance that "if it was God's will that the Nationalist Army should triumph," the workers "would definitely be on the way to obtaining their just deserts."

Crusade! What about the murders in the Canary Islands? What about the presence of the Moors? And the promise to turn over the Riff mines to Hitler, whose Nazi doctrine condemned Catholicism and was persecuting it to the death? Christ had said: "My peace I leave ye, my peace I give ye." Christ never had proclaimed a state of war in the deserts and valleys of Israel.

As for the second item of news, it took the wind out of half of Spain. Yes, the enemy on both sides was taking pains to awaken the soul. García Lorca shot by the rebels in Granada! Could it be possible? García Lorca murdered! No one could see any reason for such a crime. The gypsy head and the olive-skinned face of the writer cried to the four winds for vengeance. Immediately the Civil Guards were blamed for the deed. It was said that they had come upon García Lorca hidden in a friend's house and that they had taken him to an olive grove at night, and there by the silver light of the moon, which he had called "my sentimental story," had shot him down. But then it became known that the Civil Guards had merely carried out orders, that a "rightist" deputy had drawn up the charges against the poet, probably for personal reasons. David, who often had pointed out that the majority of the intellectuals had remained loyal to the Government, listened to a foreign broadcast to the military in which it was claimed that the poet had carried a Communist Party card. But Professor Morales, and later Axelrod, denied that. Professor Morales had met García Lorca when the poet had been visiting Cadaques, a village in the province. García Lorca had made a deep impression on him because "he had that shimmer in his eyes and words often possessed by the great and the humble." He went on to state that the Fascists had killed the poet simply for that, simply because he was the opposite of Queipo de Llano and Millán Astray, because he stood for sensitivity and ideas. "García Lorca wrote *Bodas de Sangre* and the Fascists spilled his blood for a wedding toast."

Julio García made a statement in the Café Neutral that puzzled everyone. He said the poet was of such a different stamp, he hated so much to be pigeonholed, that not only was he a personal friend of José Antonio Primo de Rivera, but also he had been offered the task of composing the Poem for the Falange and had accepted! "Only Federico can do this," the Fascist founder had said. Julio García adduced some eloquent data to back his thesis: "García Lorca had been hiding in the house of some of his Falangist friends from the 18th of July on. At the end, he was in the house of the poet Luis Rosales."

The policeman's words aroused the indignation of his listeners. Everyone reminded him of "The Ballad of the Spanish Civil Guard" and other works of its type. "Don't be silly!" Julio insisted. "The Civil Guards were only the executioners. García Lorca had friends even in the Episcopal Palace."

In vain. Besides, what difference did it make whether the circumstances were this or that? García Lorca was dead, and his death had made a hero and a mythical figure of the poet. Fanny and Raymond Bolen each sent their respective newspaper chains a moving obituary. People who had never read a word of García Lorca's, shouted: "War without quarter!" Many tricorns could be seen in the streets again. And Jaime, in the Telegraph Office, thought of the Flower Games and admitted to Matías Alvear that it was an outrage. Jaime had always greatly admired García Lorca. "They'll never kill me for my verses," he said wistfully. The poems of Federico's that he liked most were not those about the gypsies, nor those about New York, but the ones about Nature. He always carried "Autumn Song" in his notebook, and on the day when General Mola entered San Sebastián, Jaime could not forbear reading the first stanza to Ignacio's father and the militiaman censoring telegrams at his side:

"In my heart I feel now
A vague shimmer from the stars
And all the roses
Are white as my sorrow."

FIFTEEN

EZEQUIEL was right. Men were soap bubbles. Who could tell whether they would expand with the war or quickly burst? Their course was unpredictable.

To be sure, it was not only at the front that the span of man's generosity broadened. It was happening on the home front, too. Many people felt awakening within them the need to do good. Diverse people, acting from opposing reasons.

One of them was the proprietor of the Crocodile. In his Barrio de la Barca, not everyone had profited by the attack on the "bourgeois" sections of the city or by the revolution. There were God-fearing families who were poorer than ever now. The proprietor of the Crocodile knew every one of them, and the door of his bar was always open to them. "Hi, take that bottle of wine and a couple of those herrings." "You, have some of those tomatoes. I hope you like them."

The proprietor's daughter was another, even though she was still shut up in the madhouse. After years and years when she could utter nothing but the stammered syllable "bo...bo...bo" she suddenly wrote the word "*Thanks*" on a piece of paper and went the rounds of the courtyard and the rooms showing it to everyone. El Responsable's wife, also still there in her usual place, saying the Rosary and recognizing no one, quieted instantly when she saw the paper and then, looking toward the window, smiled.

The architects Ribas and Massana were doing good works, too. Axelrod's remarks on the need for bomb shelters found an echo in the professional consciences of the two architects. They took the job in hand with the help of the City. The work was easy for them in the old quarter, so full of cellars and convent "catacombs," but in the modern section they had to begin at the beginning, opening narrow entrances. One such shelter was built very near the Alvear house, behind the Café Neutral, and the prisoners from the Seminary helped build it with pick and shovel! The sight did many hearts good. The employees of the Arús Bank said: "Work is good for the arteries," but in the end the architects themselves were made unhappy by it. They excused old or ailing prisoners from the labor.

Ribas and Massana also proposed to safeguard the artworks of the province, as they had saved the Cathedral on the first day. Their efforts were rewarded. They made the rounds of the villages in the name of the Cultural Commission of the Catalonian Government. They would pick up a seventeenth-century canvas here, a sarcophagus or mosaic there. Thanks to their efforts, the ruins of Ampurias were kept well guarded. Sometimes they had to confront militiamen who would corner them muttering: "You touch that and you'll smell something burning!" But they were tireless, and they seldom went back to Gerona empty-handed. They broke only one rule: they refused to turn over to the Government the little bells they found in the sacristies. Some of them were as curious as the candle snuffer acquired by Julio. They collected bells, and the policeman said that thanks to them the bells could serve as warning sirens. "When planes are approaching, ring the bells, and into the shelters with every living soul."

Colonel Muñoz was another sentimental man. He could not rid his mind of the shooting of his friend and adversary, Major Martínez de Soria, and the letter he had written to the widow had been sincere. He became the patron of the permanently imprisoned soldiers in the Seminary, Captains Arias and Sandoval among them, and he was able to prevent their transfer to either Cosme Vila's Cheka or El Responsable's. The relatives of the soldiers thanked the colonel with all their hearts for this generous deed, and to the lonely man's astonishment, they sent him gifts of homemade pastries and boxes of Havana cigars.

Laura, too, was wearing herself out in her neighbors' behalf. To be sure, she kept feeling a shock similar to that which had led her to adopt the singers and the stonecutters during the Revolution of October 1934. As soon as Laura learned that Warning Voice was safe, she gave all her time and energy to organizing the White Relief in the city and the province. There was so much to do! For the time being, she needed help. And she showed an instinctive wisdom. In less than a month she had won the allegiance of Don Pedro Oriol's widow and several of her friends, of the Campistol sisters even, and of La Andaluza herself and Dr. Rosselló's daughters. She had likewise enlisted the valuable help of the railway engineers—a link with France and Barcelona had to be established—and of the gravedigger. The last named was a complex man, a movie usher in his time, and he often used to think those days of his former job as he was making the rounds of the cemetery at night with his lantern.

Laura enjoyed organizing the White Relief. Whenever she was walking along the street and saw the signs: Denounce the Defeatists! Look Out for the Wastrels! she would smile and nod her tiny head that resembled a handball. One of the signs showed a huge red ear and it said: Rumor Is Sabotage. Rumor... That was true. The White Relief was dedicated to helping refugees and prisoners, but its special task was to spread false rumors meant to sow confusion.

After a few weeks of activity, Laura and her co-workers from Olot and Figueras had led no fewer than two hundred persons to the snug harbor of France by the use of smuggled forms and the stamps of Izquierda Republicana. The sons of Don Santiago Estrada were the first of them. Laura's masterstroke, however, was to save one of her twin brothers, the one who had kept the Bishop hidden. Her brother was being held in El Responsable's prison, though not incommunicado, in Blasco's custody. With great effort, she succeeded in convincing him that Blasco could be bribed. "I tell you I know him." The Costas would not have risked it, but Laura persisted. And was proved right. A thick sheaf of bills accomplished the miracle of converting the Anarchist bootblack to a soldier in the White Relief. And not to do things by halves, the two deputies and their respective wives escaped to France. Blasco and a couple of acolytes accompanied the party to Perthus in a car belonging to the FAI. What about El Responsable? Blasco answered, "I'll see what I can do."

To be sure, not all the soap bubbles mentioned by Ezequiel were turning to benevolent works. There were people who felt drawn ever more strongly to evil, thus confirming the thesis of schizophrenia and hereditary syphilis which Dr. Relken had expounded to Julio. Santi provided a good example of that. This former pupil of David and Olga had had seizures of fury ever since returning from the expedition to Mallorca. He did not look normal; even El Responsable had noticed that. One day Santi told Merche that he wanted to go to Barcelona to shoot the elephant in the Zoo with a single shot.

"Why?" Merche asked him.

"I don't know."

In some cranny of his mind, Santi must have hated everything massive, slow, traditional. Probably elephants seemed to him bourgeois because they lived long lives while his disordered existence seemed so short.

Axelrod was another of the people tending more and more to the perverse. A veteran Communist, native of Tiflis, he had come to Spain on a special mission. "At home" they had ordered him to keep the Spaniards happy "with kind words" insofar as that was possible, to lead them to believe that Russia even was ready to intervene directly in order to help the Spanish people. That meant lying and lying and lying. Lying when he promised Cosme Vila many ships; lying when the rifles left over from the Crimean War were delivered in Cartagena for the price of new ones; lying when he washed himself and chomped down floods of lies three times a day. Lying so cleverly that not even Goriev, his right arm, knew that he was lying, not even the beautiful Ukrainian dog that was his mascot and the Hotel Majestic's. To behave in such a way, so imbued with lies, that in all his being, in the total Axelrod, there was nothing true except his distress from the onset of an attack of asthma and the black patch he wore over his left eye.

The perversity that was beginning to possess him was subtle. Up to the time of his arrival in Spain, Axelrod had served the Party on innumerable occasions, always either with pleasure or with sorrow over violating his personal standards. Now none of that mattered to him; the Spanish conflict was nothing to him. Nor was the loss of San Sebastián. Yet in spite of that, he carried out his assignments scrupulously and knew full well that he would carry them out until the end. Axelrod was forty-five years of age. He could not have said at what moment he had turned so cold. Perhaps it was the southern food or the temptations that arose from thinking. "The feeling must be implanted that every Russian child is participating in the Spanish drama." "It would be advisable to appropriate an Italian or German plane that was shot down so as to study its construction and how it functions." Bah! Why bother? Why was Goriev here and the Kremlin so far away? Why was he living, and what was happening on the other side after all the whys? What did Barcelona and Dr. Relken and Cosme Vila matter? What did the Virgin Mary and flamenco dancing and the Photomaton matter? Not at all. And yet, Axelrod was aware that he would do his duty to the end.

There were people, too, who alternated enthusiastic activity with sick examinations of conscience. The teachers, David and Olga, could be placed in this category. They carried on endless dialogues sitting on the rim of the fountain in the school garden, or in the Post Office while they were waiting for the letters they had to censor.

"I feel depressed and I don't know why."

"Because it's all enough to make you sad."

They had been discussing the military reverses. In addition to their work in the Post Office, the teachers were overseeing the shops where clothing was being made for the front, and they kept busy with a hundred other tasks. Lately they and their pupils had organized an "Exposition of Anti-Fascist Children's Drawings." The exhibition, with its uncertain and ingenuous drawings of bears as generals, crows as Falangists, buildings destroyed by bombs, corpses, and a great profusion of Hitlers and Mussolinis, became very popular. Every day when the hour to close the exhibition came, David and Olga stayed there to sweep the place. Sometimes they would stare at the drawings and ask one another whether it was a good thing to encourage the aggressive instincts of the children.

"Why not? Sometimes hatred is necessary. And in this case it is."

"Yes, David, but..."

Little by little they would start to talk about themselves. They both felt they were aging rapidly.

"You'll never grow old, Olga."

"Why not? I'm like anyone else."

"No, no. You'll never grow old."

David would go to her and put his arm around her waist or caress her wrist.

"You're very sweet, David."

"No, I'm not. But I don't want you to feel discouraged."

"I'm not discouraged. I believe in victory more than ever."

David told himself that he, too, had faith. His ideas were sane and some day they would prevail in Spain and all over the world, he did not know how. "But in the meantime, let me tell you that I love you."

"Tell me then."

"I love you, Olga."

"And I love you."

"We've been together a long time, haven't we?"

"Years."

"Ages."

"And always the same."

"And it always will be the same."

THE men at the front were soap bubbles, too. On all the fronts. From the quiet one of Cordova, where the bullets were olive pits, to the seething one of Toledo, where there was all-out fighting. From the peaks of Navacerrada to the Cantabrian shores along which General Mola was advancing. Many unsung fighters were laboring constantly without a breathing spell; others stood out in sharp relief. Among the latter were a former Gallegan singer named Lister and an Extremaduran guerrilla fighter named El Campesino. Both commanded brigades and were born leaders.

On the Aragón front, Durruti was still lord and master. But the days dragged slowly by, and any man had a chance to inch his way upward. The same was true in Huesca, in Zaragoza, in Teruel, where the line had been stabilized, trenches dug, and wires strung. The Nationalist trenches were in a zigzag line, in obedience to a plan; the Red trenches in a straight line, which did not take advantage of the strategic dead angles.

Cerillita was developing. Not outwardly, but inwardly. He deplored the failure to erect gallows and gibbets in Valencia at the exits of the prison, as had been the first intention of the Iron column. Now he was a threat to everyone with his leather-worker's knife and his joking countersigns like those of the Gerundian militia: "Franco is an old crone." "The Borgias were on the up and up." "Screw yourself, brother."

El Cojo was another who had developed. Suddenly one night, he felt that the world had been rediscovered. He began to notice details, something he had never done, and came to the conclusion that the earth and the night were very big. He would stare at Aragón and exclaim: "Gosh, what a lot of land there is!" He would gaze at the night and say to Ideal: "It's imposing, isn't it?" El Cojo had inherited the toy Infant Jesus that had been Future's, the charm with the astonished eyes. He had made a small round hole in its mouth and would often put his lighted cigarette into it. "If you're God, pull on it! Suck!" he would say, laughing.

While he was shelling acorns, Dimas, the sickly Dimas, the student of flies and ants, now would agonize over the little things being destroyed by the war. He was indifferent to the dead. He did not care if they belched or if their wrist-watches were still running. Dimas cared only for the little things killed by the war... A curious aberration! When a fieldpiece fired, he would think, "A wall torn down..." "Windows broken." When the airplanes zoomed by, he would say to himself: "Roofs, railroad crossings, bridges!" He felt a special pain for ruined bridges, for the posts of the sheepfolds, and for water pipes. He mourned the bridges with the sorrow of one who wanted to cross over to the other side. Dimas could be numbered among the inert who succumb helplessly, and when Dr. Rosselló became interested in his state of mind, Dimas told him: "I'm living from day to day. Leave me alone."

Gorki, Commissar Gorki, *El Proletario's* correspondent, had developed—but within the narrowest orthodoxy. His Karl Marx Battalion had occupied the northern sector of the Huesca cemetery and had entrenched there. The front seemed likely to stay quiet, but that was no reason to be idle. Gorki carried on his personal war in a model theater. The bifurcations of the trenches had names like streets: Progress, Science, Moscow, The People were their names. Cleanliness was rated essential, and Papa Pistols, the Bulgarian, used to say you could eat off the ground. The crypts of a mausoleum became a "Culture Corner" that had a library stocked with books sent from Gerona and an abundance of pamphlets giving instructions in warfare. "How to protect yourself from enemy air attack," "How to correct your shooting," and other how-to's. And it was in this "corner," which the militiawomen kept supplied with flowers, that Gorki was giving lessons in reading. He had a respectable number of pupils. While he was teaching, Gorki sat on the ground as César used to do in the Calle de la Barca. Ah, the men of the militia! Bearded men spelling aloud and straggling with the alphabet. "These letters sure have a lot of curlicues!" Gorki was tireless. He wanted them to learn to read rapidly for themselves such words as "Lenin, Stalin, proletariat, peace" and to nourish their minds with the bulletin-board news stories put out by the battalion. Sidlo and Papa Pistols attended the sessions as auditors and began to feel a stir of admiration for Spain and her men, something quite different from what Axelrod was feeling. "These people are as revolutionary as the Hungarians or even the Czechs," Sidlo remarked. Teo waxed indignant with the foreigners because they had a mania for making comparisons, and La Valenciana muttered: "Those pinheads don't matter a damn to me."

Puppy, the bugler and clown, was living his moment of glory. He was the adopted son not of La Valenciana alone, but of all the militiawomen in the sector. The boy was almost frightened by so many caresses, for he noticed something abnormal about some of them. Like a stray dog, he liked to sniff in colorful places: the kitchen, the improvised barbershop, the infirmary, and so on. He had not changed, but his neighbors had. Indeed, his present comrades took his imitations of dogs as a joke, and the harder they laughed, the worse became the plight of the dog he was imitating. In his own town the contrary reaction was the rule. Eyes would turn to him with a look of infinite sadness. Puppy could not comprehend the difference, and one day he asked Gorki which reaction he should respond to. Gorki told him that the war was such a hard thing to bear that "Alongside of it the calamities of a dog seem foolish."

Another soap bubble that had expanded was Dr. Rosselló. He had found at the front the humility needed to treat without distinction anyone brought to his surgery, and he never yielded to the facile lure of making surgical experiments at the expense of the nameless wounded. Everyone noticed the growing nobility of his face, and Durruti found more and more justification for using the formal style of address with him, and even gave him a list of supplies from which to provide himself from any establishment in the zone with whatever he needed from scissors or strychnine to an automobile.

One of the doctor's most serious worries was the increase in venereal disease, something that might have been foreseen even without Ezequiel's gift of prophecy. Dr. Rosselló affirmed that on the Aragón front some militiawomen were causing more casualties than the enemy mortars. The militiamen were beginning to call them "machine guns," a nickname Murillo refused to accept because he declared that the damage they caused was "noiseless."

Dr. Rosselló's recreation was chess. Teams had been formed by a couple of English doctors and an anesthetist, and the four of them organized championship matches as soon as they took off their gloves. The matches were played with excessive, almost comic solemnity. The doctor also enjoyed listening to music. He did honor to his post of president of the Musical Association of Gerona. He had a record player and records, and, listening with eyes closed, he would go into ecstasies over the harmonies that filled the air, most of them German. The English doctors used to listen with him. Ideal, on the other hand, murmured: "You'd think we were in the theater!"

Rainbow was developing, too. This former clerk in the costume-rental business became the creator of any kind of camouflage the situation demanded. Durruti himself hailed him for transforming his General Headquarters into a dense wood. Rainbow, who had only to hear the word "war" to burst into loud laughter, had thought of a way to steal a march on the "Fascists" on guard duty opposite them, and to that end he carved wooden silhouettes of the FAI militiamen, activated by strings like marionettes. He had the dummies placed at intervals along the parapet, thus forcing the sentries on the enemy side to waste dozens of cartridges. He also conceived the idea of the so-called "vegetable battery" consisting of four tree trunks, painted with matchless cunning and emplaced some distance away like fieldpieces. Strangely enough, they aroused the wrath of the enemy artillery.

José Alvear and Captain Culebra, inseparable since the night Durruti had granted them permits to choose any woman they wanted in the jails of El Burgo and Alfajarín, had also developed. The fact that they had both slept like logs in the truck taking them there had sealed their alliance.

"You're no Anarchist nor anything else," Captain Culebra said, wearing his snake wound around his neck. "You're just my friend."

José Alvear took off his flexible belt and made the steel links roll up by themselves in honor of his friend. "Whatever you say, fellow, whatever you say."

The two captains had felt the impact of the latest military reverses, and they could not understand why Durruti did not either ask for reinforcements or make up his mind once and for all to take Zaragoza. "A waiting room, that's what this is. I had enough of that in the railroad station in my home town," Captain Culebra declared. "It's all right the way it is, isn't it?" Dr. Rosselló asked with an insinuating smile. They shook their heads. Like Puppy, they wanted something to brag about.

Nevertheless, unless and until the "Supreme Command" woke up from its nap, they had to adjust themselves to listening in on two very different extensions: the barrage and the loudspeakers addressing the enemy.

Culebra and Alvear organized gambling games of *padre* and *muy señor mío* there in the trenches. Winning or losing was all the same to them, because, for one thing, they almost always gambled with worthless paper money put out by some Aragónese People's Committee. On the other hand, they took delight in shouting "Bitch" when a queen came up, and "Durruti" when a king was dealt.

Broadcasts over the loudspeakers were an old story by now. The Nationalists had been the first to use this propaganda medium and within twenty-four hours Durruti had been answering them with a more powerful installation.

As a rule, all the dialogues sounded much alike: "Hey, Reds, you big cuckolds! Are you asleep, or what?"

"Asleep? You'll soon find out. You'd better write to your family."

"What about those two pepperings we gave you yesterday? Did they hot you up?"

"One of them killed a beetle and the other was a dud. There was a piece of paper inside that said 'Death to Fascism.'"

"Oh, yeah? We can smell the cold meat from here."

"Tell that to the last old goat that slept with your mother."

Sometimes a sentimental note was struck. "Hey, Fascists! Sons of Mussolini!"

"Now what is it? Make it short because we're sleepy."

"Is there anyone there from Alcañiz?"

A voice spoke out. "Yes, I'm from Alcañiz. What's up?"

"Yesterday some girl in your village had a litter. A twenty-year-old sweetheart had twins."

"What? The hell you say! Tell me her name! What's her name?"

"An everyday name...very common. Margarita! That's it... Margarita Iguacen."

"I know her, I know her... Listen..."

"What do you want?"

"If you go back there, if one of our stray bullets doesn't get you today, remember me to her, remember Eustaquio... She'll know..."

"Are you the father or what? Sure, I'll do that..."

Sometimes the sentimental note was struck by a fair interchange of news from one side to the other. Every Monday the Nationalists told the Reds what had happened during the bullfights held in their territory, and the Reds returned the favor by giving the results of the football games held in theirs.

On the 26th of September, Captains José Alvear and Culebra, respectively disguised as Don Quixote and Sancho, the former with a lance, the latter looking the part of a shrewd peasant, decided to stir things up. Knowing that the Nationalist trenches were well manned with Falangists and Civil Guards, they went up to the microphones and launched into the first lines of "Face to the Sun," parodying the words. They said "dirty shirt" instead of "new shirt," and instead of "springtime will laugh again," they said "Primo de Rivera will be slain," and a few seconds later recited the "Ballad of the Spanish Civil Guard" by García Lorca from beginning to end:

"They have skulls made of lead
That's why they never weep
With their souls of patent-leather
They come along the highway."

Everyone took it for granted that the rebels would reply with a shelling. Rainbow, forewarned and forearmed, had put a green-painted helmet on his head. But something quite unexpected occurred. The Fascist reply came in words instead of shells. The orotund voice of a professional speaker said: "Attention, Reds, attention! We've heard enough verses! Toledo is ours! Toledo belongs to Spain! The Alcázar has been liberated! Up, Spain! Scum, pigs! Toledo belongs to Spain. Now we'll go on to Madrid! Tarantara, tarantara!"

The militiamen in the sector, particularly Captain Culebra and José Alvear stopped dead, as if turned to stone. Many times when similar announcements had been made, they had replied: "Lies, Fascist cheats! Lies! I hope you get it in the balls!" But for some reason they had a presentiment this time that the news was true. "Damn it!" And again there was silence. Captain Culebra, dressed as Sancho, left the microphone and picked up the box with his little snake in it. José Alvear, dressed as Quixote, laid down his lance and took off his hat. They started to walk away. They walked away with drooping shoulders, for their heads were not made of wood. Very slowly, for even their legs felt weak. Unconsciously they drifted toward the open space where the "vegetable battery" was aiming at the enemy. The distance was about a kilometer, perhaps more. Neither of the two men had a word to say, and the snake was asleep in its little box, which its master was holding loosely.

Meanwhile the enemy was playing "Legionario, Legionario," "Oriamendi," and "Face to the Sun." The Legionnaires were proclaiming that their "sweetheart was death," the Requetés were chanting "union," and the Falangists were saying, as Mateo had said when he arrived in Gerona, that dawn was beginning to break. And as they were so declaring, the thoughts of Quixote and Sancho were dark, and the first ghostly shadows were falling over the Aragón plain, shadows as sick as Dimas, as caressing as Merche's hand on Future as he lay dying.

Captain Culebra and José Alvear came to the emplacement of the four tree trunks camouflaged as cannon. And they sat down there at the foot of the mock-ups. José Alvear sighed as he pulled out his package of cigarettes with a jerk. "Makes you want to screw yourself."

And Captain Culebra replied: "I shit on Mussolini and Hitler a thousand times over."

They lighted cigarettes. The paper was trademarked Job. After awhile the two fanatical acrobats were busy obliterating ants and more ants with their feet.

"The thing that really killed me," José Alvear said suddenly, "was that 'tarantara, tarantara.'"

WHAT had impressed Durruti most deeply, even more deeply than the loss of Toledo and its famous munitions plant, more than the news that the Moors and Legionnaires were allegedly making an uncontested advance on Madrid, was the defeat of the Basques in the North. Durruti admired the strong, and the Basques were that to a superlative degree. He often used to say to the foreign athletes: "Any time you think you're supermen, let me know. I'll bring you a dozen Basques and you'll eat crow." Then what did the Requetés have that they were able to conquer the "Gudaris" and take Irún and San Sebastián?

Durruti had developed. He no longer cherished any illusions. His men, the Anarchists, magnificent fighters on the barricades, left much to be desired at the front. "Freedom and discipline are taught by blows," Pérez Farrás used to say to him. He was getting bad news constantly, not only from the Aragón front, but also from the others. Reports that told him even of shameful desertions. Buenaventura Durruti, who had once said in a speech: "We relinquish everything but victory," realized that a decision had to be made, and he made it: to set an example by his siege of Aragón that would serve as a guide for the entire People's Army.

That could be done in many ways; he chose the one best suited to his temperament. And his temperament advised him to take the most direct course within the bounds of reason and with due caution. He called into consultation his colleagues Ascaso and Ortiz, who told him that the Communists Lister and El Campesino were already employing the procedure of personal example and tenor to win the obedience of their troops. "All right! I don't understand Russian. They can do whatever they want to. I'll act in my own way." Durruti hated the Communists, especially since they had tried to capture him for the Party with honeyed words.

"I'll do it my way." And so he did. He toured the front from end to end in an armored car, from Teruel to Huesca, and came back furious. He had learned that there were sentries who sang on duty. There were men who would report themselves as volunteers in a company, receive their plate, their blanket and poncho, and then go immediately to a second line where they sold it all, only to report to another company and repeat the ploy. There was someone who used to make the rounds of the front line at night with a lighted lantern. "Comrade Durruti, something's got to be done!" In his staff quarters in the vicinity of Siétamo, Colonel Villalba said to him: "I don't feel up to making soldiers of that lot."

Durruti was not a man of long-range plans. He had one fault: the irrepressible desire to live would suddenly be born in him, as in the ants. He was a man of action, and indeed Gerardi, a bearded, apelike Italian, had said that Durruti would have made a great headman of a desert tribe. After his tour of the lines he demonstrated that. Among the manifold irregularities to be corrected in his fighting forces, irregularities he had noted down on the back of a publicity photograph of Marlene Dietrich, he judged that two were the most urgent. Two anomalies that his much-admired Dr. Rosselló had pointed out to him at last! They were the epidemic of homosexuality which was spreading through the trenches, and the already well-known venereal diseases that were threatening to decimate his column.

"Comrade Durruti, I'm sorry to say this. The homosexuals are a danger that has been demonstrated in every war. And as for venereal diseases, I don't think it's necessary to show you the statistics."

Durruti, a veritable human tower, who looked even burlier in his autumn outfit, decided to start there. He pushed back the cap with the ear flaps tied on top, and, as usual, gazed at distant Zaragoza. Then he ordered a listing of all the homosexuals and all the diseased militiawomen. All those on the list were to be disarmed and marched to the Bujaraloz Station.

Carrying out such an order presented its own difficulties, for three sectors were involved: Teruel, Zaragoza, and Huesca. But Durruti was adamant. "Forty-eight hours will be more than enough. When you're all ready, let me know."

Dr. Vega went to work with a will. And turned up many surprises. More than half of the complement of the Spectacle Syndicate were homosexuals. And the Romanian athlete who had been a witness at the wedding of Future and Merche also was disarmed. The infected militiawomen were many and constituted a major problem because some were falsely accused by militiamen who wanted to change women. Altogether, twenty-one were disarmed, amid painful scenes, and many of the women fought against evacuation. La Valenciana was one of the most conspicuous. She screamed insults, but Dr. Vega was implacable. La Valenciana had to climb into the truck for Bujaraloz, despite Teo's protests and the astonishment of Puppy.

At the Bujaraloz Station, the catch from both nets was impressive. Everyone supposed that Durruti intended to have the prisoners returned to the home front. But the Anarchist leader privately had decided otherwise. As soon as Health informed him that his order had been carried out, Durruti picked up his submachine gun and went to Bujaraloz in his armored car. On the way he kept repeating to himself, "The past doesn't count. We must relinquish everything except victory."

The car came to a halt at the station exit facing the passage to track level. The persons under guard, totaling thirty-seven, had been locked inside freight cars on a siding. Cars marked "*3,000 kilogram cap'y*," painted a dirty vermilion, and with sliding doors. Durruti made a sign, and two militiamen from his personal suite posted themselves beside the door of the first car, whereupon he approached and took a favorable position. Shouts were coming from the inside: "Hey, we're not mules!" "Did I shoot you, or what?"

Durruti did not turn a hair as he adjusted his submachine gun to his right side and ordered the door opened.

The car door screeched and the faces of the prisoners inside appeared… Durruti opened fire. A perfect single line of fire that transformed living bodies into terror-stricken dolls. The fallen revealed those who had crowded to the rear or crouched in the corners.

The maneuver was repeated in the other cars with the trapped people helpless to prevent it. At his orders the two militiamen slid the door to the left, and *bang!* Altogether the operation took a scant five minutes. And no one was in a position to voice an objection.

His work done, Durruti lowered the submachine gun, gave the necessary instructions, and got back into his car. "Go ahead," he ordered. And went straight back to his headquarters, where he sat down and ordered a cup of coffee.

"Comrade Durruti, something has got to be done!" The news of what had done flew from mouth to mouth like the rumor of the poisoned waters of the Ebro. From trench to trench, from the Alcubierre Mountains to the Pyrenees. Teo, who had taken on the job of sweeper in Culture Corner," was the last to learn of the happening. Gorki told him, adding: "La Valenciana, too!"

Teo gave a loud cry and dropped his broom. "Bastard!" He lifted his arms like a prophet. He pictured Durruti's face and swore in the name of La Valenciana that he would find a way to avenge her.

SIXTEEN

THE Nationalist column that had left Galicia to free the defenders of Oviedo, besieged by the miners, achieved its objective. The forces occupying San Sebastián continued their advance along the Northern front, toward Bilbao. The Alcázar had been liberated and the Sanctuary of Nuestra Señora de la Cabeza still was holding out. Consequently, the balance in the campaign had tipped in favor of Nationalist Spain.

In the Nationalist zone the military command breathed an air of confidence. Their confidence was merited, and all the stationery shops in the territory had sold out their maps of the Iberian Peninsula so that the course of the war could be followed on them. Spain appeared dirty or new-minted, according to the individual map, vigorous or limp, with many or few highways. Colored maps looked bright on the wall, even though the white or red patches did not coincide with the territories held by the belligerents. The maps of the productive regions of Spain were charming. They showed olive trees, orange trees, hearths, peasant girls tending cows, and so on. The sea bordered these maps with sportive fishes here and there, cutting through the blue. All the maps were dotted with little flags as if Spain were an insect on a pin. Portugal was not marked with little flags on any map; it looked idyllic, bound together in enviable unity.

Perhaps the most popular victory was the capture of Toledo and the liberation of the Alcázar. With the passing of the days and the emergence of detail, the saga of the defenders of the fortress went on acquiring the aura of myth. People talked of the "Numantine spirit" reborn within those walls, and some newspapers published the life story of one of the defenders who died there, Angel Ribera, who, according to his comrades was an archetypal saint, an exemplary spirit able to smile amid the mortar shells and the dynamite. The Nationalists wanted also to free the defenders of the Sanctuary of Nuestra Señora de la Cabeza, but it was so far away that the operation did not seem feasible. Meanwhile, it was supplied from the air insofar as possible, and communication was kept open by means of messenger pigeons.

Don Anselmo Ichaso lined up all his trains in front of the station marked "Toledo." The Carlist leader, however, charged the supreme command with sentimentality in this case, because they had been deflected from their main object, the road to Madrid, and had rushed to liberate the Alcázar. That had cost them time that might never be recovered. All told, the mortal wound was visible, and the foreign papers, unanimous in giving a respectful account of the deed, were circulated from hand to hand.

Núñez Maza and his four Falangist assistants had a movie camera, thanks to the German Schubert. He filmed the Nationalist soldiers entering the city. On the Red side, the Belgian newspaperman, Raymond Bolen, Fanny's friend, was filming the militia fleeing. José Alvear's father was in Toledo, and, like his comrades, he had fired upon the Alcázar again and again.

On the whole, the war was still a war of skirmishing, well suited to the Moors and the militia. Yet the course taken by both sides was leading fatally to a real war, a big war.

The Nationalist command was undoubtedly making ready for that, as was demonstrated by the creation of academies for the training of "provisional" sergeants and corporals, academies wisely conceived, among whose instructors were Germans who had served in South America and had some command of Spanish. The applicants for enrollment in the short courses for corporal were young boys as a rule, with firm, open faces. They were intoxicated with the idea of wearing a star on their chests.

Another evidence of the magnification of the war was what was happening in the two basic arms: Air and Navy, discussed by Casal in *El Demócrata* and Colonel Muñoz in the Café Neutral. The number of airplanes was increasing daily in both zones, although the Reds still were leading in the proportion of four to one, thanks in part to the campaign initiated in France, to which Julio García was privy, with the slogan of "*Des avions pour l'Espagne!*" Thanks, too, to the creation of the International Esquadrille of Volunteers, enthusiastically commanded by André Malraux, the writer. At the end of October 1936 it was estimated that the Nationalists could count on eighty airplanes to their adversaries' three hundred twenty-three. The Red planes were still of the most diverse origin, and the greater number of the pilots were foreigners working for a salary. They tried to avoid imprisonment in the enemy camps and more or less confined themselves to defensive fighting. This worried their commandants, who were forced to admit that they must look to Russia, as Cosme Vila had said. Russia had already sent her small quota, of course, a token force. One of its members was said to be a girl of less than twenty years whose plane was hit by anti-aircraft fire in the Talavera sector. She was forced to parachute down and surrender to the Nationalists.

The pilot Rexach was still the Red ace, still keeping to his own course in the Red air force that had been christened "La Gloriosa" by the newspapers. Equally outstanding were the Frenchmen Gilles and Bourjois and the Englishmen Griffith and Martin Drew. Many of their planes were decorated with a big red patch, and many of the pilots who were fathers adopted the popular automobile custom of carrying the youngest child's shoe in a corner of the windshield. García Morato soon distinguished himself in the Nationalist air force. He was as unwearying aloft as Captain Carlos de la Haya. García Morato's slogan was: "Ceiling unlimited, good luck, and go for the bull." His popularity even among the Red pilots was so great that many of them would salute one another as they peeled off: "I hope you don't run up against García Morato's group."

Carlos de la Haya had to his credit countless missions to the Sanctuary of Nuestra Señora de la Cabeza to drop supplies to its defenders, and his technical mastery was considered unequalled.

As for the Navy, the numerical superiority of the Red units still was crushing, but their activity was very slight. On the other hand, the Nationalists were proving efficient at keeping a guard over the enemy ports Sebastián Estrada was patrolling aboard Torpedo Boat 19—and the cruiser *Canarias* had been launched from El Ferrol shipyard and was being fitted out. The construction of another cruiser, the *Baleares,* was being speeded up in the hope that she soon would be ready to launch. English observers conjectured that, given the length of the Spanish coastline, "whichever of the two adversaries has control of the sea will win."

The war was spreading constantly. A civil war with innumerable contrasts and paradoxes. In the Monastery of Guadalupe, the investing militiamen came upon friars and Moors inside the church singing the same chants. Jorge de Batlle, the Falangist orphan who had applied for enlistment in the Air Force so as to satisfy his thirst for revenge—perhaps he would bomb Gerona some day!—knew that one of the best of the Nationalist pilots in García Morato's squadron was called "Satan," while a dynamiter on the Cordova front was nicknamed "Archangel." A militiawoman in Almería used to say to her little son, "Let's see you make the face the Fascists make in La Playa when they're being killed, cutie." Meanwhile, in Gerona, the wife of a militiaman in the Calle de la Barca dressed her children in mourning every time a doctor was executed in the province. In Asturias, the "People's Volunteers" who had no firearms were fighting with scythes; on the Huesca front, the Falangists who lacked weapons would beat rhythmically on their pots and plates to simulate the noise of machine guns. In Barcelona, the women letter-carriers, several of whom were friends of Ezequiel, were spending their August among the mothers and sweethearts of the Red fighters; in Andalusia, Queipo de Llano failed to register the gypsies because they kept disappearing along short cuts, hurling Pharaonic curses at the barracks or trenches. The Reds had decided that it was important to remove the treasure from the Bank of Spain and put it in a safe place, and accordingly a commission went to Valencia and Catalonia in search of such a hiding place. The Nationalists believed in the importance of getting the mail to the soldiers on time, and they never quibbled over the efforts that had to be made day after day to adapt the communication network to the meanderings of the firing line.

The pendulum kept swinging. Each side often influenced the other and frequently one copied the other. Yet in every man's depths, more operative than ever, was Dr. Relken's phrase that had impressed Julio García: "My brain repays me."

On the Red side, authority was scattered, opinion suppressed. On the Nationalist side the Joint Chiefs of Staff installed in Burgos decided to name a single head, a head of Government who would centralize responsibility in his own hands. After some casualties, the appointment fell to General Franco because it was thought that he combined in his person youth, coolness, and a long acquaintance with Moroccan affairs, a basic asset at that moment, when Moorish forces were pouring onto the battlefields.

The decree read:

> *His Excellency Señor General Don Francisco Franco Bahamonde is hereby named Head of the Government of the Spanish State, and will assume the powers of the new State. He is likewise named Generalissimo of the Forces of Land, Sea, and Air, and the office of Commander in Chief of the Active Army is hereby conferred on him.*

The Army of the North remained under the command of General Mola and that of the South under General Queipo de Llano. General Moscardó, defender of the Alcázar, was appointed to the command of the division being organized in Soria.

IN line with the march of events, the number of refugees from the Red zone into Nationalist Spain was growing by the day. After the occupation of San Sebastián there was no longer any point in using the pass to Dancharinea, and everyone crossed the border at Hendaye, which had been opened to the public immediately.

The occupation of Guipúzcoa left many people without an orbit, like the comets. Among these were all the Guipúzcoans who had fled to France or toward Bilbao. On the other hand, it settled the lives of many other people, among them Warning Voice and Javier Ichaso, the amputee son of Don Anselmo Ichaso.

With the occupation of San Sebastián, Don Anselmo judged that the time had come to put into official form his plans for the organization of an Information Service. The service would be espionage, but this word was too high-sounding, and more especially, pejorative. "SIFNE" was the preferred word: "Service of Investigation for the Northeast of Spain."

Warning Voice, with his huge red beret and his puttees, was given the appropriate instructions. He was to be installed in San Sebastián in a flat with a moderate rental, and, as Javier Ichaso was incapacitated for duty at the front, he was to take the boy with him. Don Anselmo would be the supreme head, of course. He was to make periodic trips to San Sebastián. Warning Voice would be his delegate, and Javier the dentist's good right arm.

The first job they were given was to organize a corps of colleagues of proved loyalty, most of whom were to be chosen from the fugitives from the Red zone. The budget would be slim, and yet it was essential that the colleagues should be men well endowed in their own right. As the Service began to stretch out its tentacles, it would need more and more specialists, but for the moment the more discreetly it could carry out its mission, the better.

"Naturally, there are a number of urgent requirements: listening to the radio, reading the newspapers, personal search at the frontier, disguise, decoding, patrol of French ports, and counter-espionage. I shall expect you to be outstanding in this role. Organize the communication lines with France immediately, and, after that, with Gerona, Barcelona, and Madrid. Please don't forget that Mola still has to use Michelin and Taride Guide maps exclusively."

Warning Voice was exalted. His enthusiasm was boundless and it never entered his head for a minute that his mission could fail. During the first days, when all he could see of Navarre had seemed strange to him, he had smoked many cigarettes as he stared at the horizon, but that was history now.

He made rapid calculations, so that before leaving for San Sebastián he already had given Don Anselmo the names of two possible collaborators: Noguer, the notary, in France; Laura, in the Red zone. Warning Voice did not know how much Laura already was aiding him in Gerona. Don Anselmo gave his blessing. "I'm leaving it in your hands."

Within four days he had made the journey to San Sebastián. The rented flat in the Calle de Alsasua was spacious. What a pity that La Concha, the bay, could not be seen from it. Javier said so several times: "It's too bad." A young servant girl named Jesusha, well known to Ichaso, came with them. Don Anselmo saw them off at the station, and gave them some firm advice. "You, my dear dentist, must read the text of Joshua 2 in the Old Testament before you start to work." "You, my son, don't forget that in God's eyes no hero is anonymous." "And you, Jesusha, starve the gentlemen...but slowly." The train pulled out just then and Don Anselmo, enveloped in smoke, said to himself: "I like miniature trains better."

As soon as they had settled into the flat on the Calle de Alsasua—the front part to be used as an office, the rear as living quarters—Warning Voice and Javier Ichaso sat down in their respective chairs and read the text of Joshua 2:1, as recommended by the father of the Requeté amputee. It said: "And Joshua the son of Nun sent from Setim two men to spy secretly.... They went and entered into the house of a woman that was a harlot named Rahab, and lodged with her."

What had Don Anselmo meant to imply by that? It was easy enough to guess. He meant to convince them that the work to which they were dedicating themselves dated back to very remote times, that it was older than Masonry, older even than Christianity.

"So you see, Javier," said the dentist, "We're the two men from Shittim, ready to spy secretly... Too bad we didn't find the harlot named Rahab here!"

The amputee rolled his eyes and they both laughed: "I'll tell my father."

Later they went out for a short walk to get acquainted with the section. Autumn was lighting bonfires in the sky over San Sebastián at sunrise and sunset, and the water of the bay was no longer mere water, but a coverlet over the hidden life of fish, algae, sunken ships, and a million other worlds living out their span in the unplumbed depths. Warning Voice was happy to learn that a church and a pastry shop were near their house. Javier was happy to see that the nearest cafés offered comfortable armchairs.

Then they started to work, with success. In two weeks the network across France to Barcelona and Madrid had begun to take shape. In San Juan de Luz, a French monarchist, the headwaiter in the Fénix Hotel, was to be their secret agent. He would be in contact with the agent in Perpignan, who was in fact the notary, Noguer. A railroad engineer was to link up with Laura in Gerona, and Laura with Barcelona, Valencia, and Madrid. In the interior of Nationalist Spain, groups or cells would be set up to handle counter-espionage, and to brief the agents who were required by the Service to cross the lines and operate in the Red zone.

Counter-espionage was needed because the Reds already had their own organization. Don Anselmo Ichaso thought he knew that at the moment the head of their organization was a young man called Dionisio. Nothing more was known about him.

"Well," Warning Voice commented as he fondled the pile of blue envelopes just delivered to him, "let's hope we'll find this Dionisio before the war's over."

Their first objective was to have the cartography in the Ministry of War in Madrid photostated. Military maps, diagrams by the Geographical Institute at one to fifty thousand, charts of the coastal waters at one to twenty thousand, plans of the large Red cities, and so on. Warning Voice thought he was asking for the moon, but he was wrong. Notary Noguer reported to him that "the Service was getting under way with all possible speed." Warning Voice touched his gold-rimmed eyeglasses and thought that Laura doubtless had had a hand in that. The thought of collaborating with Laura from a distance had pleased him from the beginning, though he feared that in the end the Committee of Gerona would catch up with his wife.

Javier Ichaso was in charge of making a conscientious summary of the newspapers from the Red zone and to listening to the radio. He was to note down everything that caught his attention. The "Militiamen's Mailbox" published by Labor Solidarity became his immediate and most direct source of information regarding the location of the forces in Aragón, thus confirming the fears of Professor Morales. Javier also noted down the flood of foreign visitors being welcomed to the Red zone.

Listening to the radio became very burdensome; after a time the interference, the knobs, and the lighted strip made him nervous. "This damned leg!" he swore at times, his brow dark with gloomy memories.

The scanning of foreign newspapers and listening to French, English, and Italian broadcasts was the task of Warning Voice himself, assisted by the former director of an Academy for Languages from Lisbon with whom they had made contact. This man, whose name was Mouro, was nearly sixty years old. He possessed infinite patience, and he never shirked an hour of service. He was slightly deaf, so that the diligence and precision with which he caught the radio messages within range were surprising. Exactly a week after the study of the foreign press had begun, it was evident that they could count on two invaluable sources of military information in the dispatches sent to Paris from Madrid and Barcelona by the French observers Armengaud and Rieu Vernet. Their commentaries on the Red front and the home front were prodigies of objectivity and common sense.

SIFNE lacked coders and decoders; it lacked men trained to block and sabotage shipments of arms leaving French ports for the east coast of Spain, thus belying Cosme Vila's skepticism about French aid. It lacked broadcasting apparatus; it lacked experience; it lacked money! But it did not lack willingness, and the important thing was not to lose courage, to guard thoughts, and to be meticulous.

Don Anselmo Ichaso had supplied Warning Voice with every kind of document that could be useful in his work, and had written to all of the authorities in San Sebastián and at the frontier asking them to lend him facilities without interfering with the work. All this was a two-edged sword to the dentist. On the one hand, it flattered him; on the other, it burdened him with responsibility. At about that time, he received an unexpected visit from a balding German who carried a note from Don Anselmo. This German represented himself as an old espionage agent from the World War of 1914. Soon Warning Voice and Javier Ichaso were hypnotized by his talk, for he substantiated his claim by pointing out to them a complex of procedures and tasks, each more cunning than the last, for getting out the news and receiving it. One means of "penetrating" the offices of the ministries and the General Staff was to bribe the cleaning women, whose duty it would be to empty the wastebaskets every morning and deliver their contents to him. Another effective ploy was to bribe the stenographers in the particular office chosen as objective. Their trick would be to change the sheet of carbon paper "every time," lay it aside, and keep the used sheets, which could easily be read later in reverse against a light. The German mentioned that the backs of stamps were handy places for writing down and sending messages by mail. News could also be passed with surprising impunity by simply folding newspapers with their margins written on. Another means of passing news was in diplomatic dispatch cases, advertisements in specified newspapers, and so on. The most laborious task, in his opinion, was to obtain accurate news concerning ship convoys, owing to the difficulty of gaining access to the piers, the falsification of schedules, and the changing of flags on the high seas. He put them on their guard against "mercenary" double agents who might go over to the enemy at the crucial moment, against charlatans—"The Spanish are charlatans by temperament"—and against drunks. And he counseled the use of women, not overly intelligent if possible, but levelheaded and capable of putting on an act, and with babies in their arms.

A fascinating field for action! "Be very careful," the German advised them in conclusion, "not to mistake the spectacular for the useful..." With those words he vanished, leaving them a telephone number right in San Sebastián where they could call him at any moment.

Warning Voice and Javier Ichaso were left speechless for a time, and when they could open their mouths it was only to put a cigarette in them.

"What do you think?"

"With your permission, I take off my beret."

Warning Voice smiled with satisfaction... He had got off on the right foot. "Joshua the son of Nun sent from Setim two men to spy secretly..." Warning Voice had not changed. He still had his *philias* and his *phobias.* Before long he would be walking through the streets of the marvelous city of San Sebastián, strutting like an admiral, and would mingle with high society, with the "pearls" as well as the girls who waited on table in the improvised dining room of the Kursaal.

Of course he liked the Cantabrian Coast because it was mightier than his own spirit. He wrote a long letter to Mosén Alberto in Pamplona, who had paid him a call before he had left there. At the conclusion of the visit, he had said to the priest: "I'm ashamed to confess it to you, Father, but I'm almost happy." The very thing Mosén Alberto reproached himself with every time they served him chocolate in the nunnery! Added to that, Warning Voice had become without wishing to, the automatic "counsel" for all the refugees from Gerona and its province who arrived in San Sebastián feeling disoriented. They would come to him immediately, or rather come upon his beret, for it was the largest in the city and everyone knew that it belonged to "the distinguished Catalan dentist." He would give the refugees his own version of the news... He told them that the Requetés were carrying the full burden of the war at the fronts, that the Falange was in deep water, that many generals wanted the monarchy, and so on. And naturally he censured the many Catalans whose first thought was to go with a woman the minute they arrived in the Nationalist zone from Lourdes. Their second thought was to start feeling that they were "Separatists," and their third to take a look around with the idea of finding a favorable spot for starting a business or setting up a factory.

His relations with his secretary, Javier Ichaso, were complex. Sometimes he would stare at the twenty-one-year-old boy and think, "I'd like to have a son that age." A son with a less obsessive look, of course, more elastic, and with a better sense of humor. The figure of Javier, with crutches, wearing the two chevrons for his wounds embroidered on his sleeve, reminded him ceaselessly that living was an arduous, a serious task.

Javier Ichaso frankly admired the dentist. He realized that Warning Voice had broadened his mental horizon. Javier Ichaso, like Jorge, was the victim of an authoritarian father with an authoritative and striking paunch, whose ideas were circumscribed by Navarre, by Spain, and by the desire to be ruled by a king.

"I'm telling you the truth. Before I talked with you, I had Zumalacárregui confused with Napoleon."

Javier's kind of mind found in Warning Voice the flattering intellectual justification for many of the attitudes and ideas it had adopted by instinct all his life, including the identical idea of monarchy. Indeed, Warning Voice had given this idea a broader geographical dimension. He would list all the things the human community owed to kings beneath whose patronage most of the conquests by every country had been made. "They inspire respect and authority; they are agglutinates, and a natural hierarchy emanates from them. On the other hand, it would be very hard for you to distinguish who is the president of the Republic and who is the head of the Falange at a meeting where no uniforms were worn."

Javier Ichaso also felt like a child when he went into the office headed by Mouro, the multilingual Portuguese, and found that self-same dentist there catching all the broadcasts or making a running translation from *The Times* or *Le Figaro* without making an error. Javier Ichaso spoke nothing but Spanish, with a Navarrese accent. "Of course, of course," he would say to himself pensively, "there are other countries besides Navarre and Spain."

Such lands seemed to the boy enormous... And even more enormous whenever he remembered as he got to his feet that he was dependent on crutches.

Much the same thing happened to him with regard to religion. Warning Voice said to Javier one day at the conclusion of a parade that they had both been watching from the balcony of their house: "Let's see now, you've just sung out 'For God, for Country, and for King' ten times. What is God to you?" Javier looked abashed. He did not know what to answer. Shrugging his shoulders, he said: "Everything." But he knew it was not an honest answer.

Strangely enough, Javier Ichaso held such a deep religious faith that he would have let himself be killed for it; yet it never occurred to him to question his beliefs inwardly, any more than it had ever occurred to Carmen Elgazu. Javier had inherited his faith as he had his name. And Warning Voice told him that faith was something more important than the inheritance of a nose or ears. He ought to reason out the conception of God lest he become an ignoramus or a despot. The dentist was a fine one to talk about despotism! Nevertheless, Javier Ichaso's admiration stimulated Warning Voice, and he would accuse the boy of faults that he himself was guilty of to an extraordinary degree.

"God is not just a scapular and a candle. Your religion is one of fear. It is a religion based on scruples. You sin, and then you can't rest until you've gone to confession… Do you really think a man can offend God with infinite malice?"

Because he was not completely obtuse and because he had a vague intuition that his hereditary convictions often lent him great inner strength, Javier Ichaso would defend himself. But now he realized that he was wearing the red beret because he had been born in Pamplona, and that if he had been born in Peiping or Melbourne, he would be wearing another kind of headgear and might even have his two legs.

In his heart, Warning Voice delighted in baiting Javier. "I bet you don't know who invented the clenched fist salute?"

"Well… I don't know."

"You ought to know. A German, Edgar André. He founded the Society of Red Fighters. His group imitated him, and later the salute was required."

Javier was sitting, holding his crutches between his legs.

"I'll bet you don't know," the dentist went on, "where the Virgin, the Mother of Jesus, died?"

"No, I don't know."

"There are two schools of thought. Some say she died in Ephesus; others in Jerusalem. So!"

Javier Ichaso went so far as to rate Warning Voice as a "great gentleman." The Navarrese ate ravenously, voraciously; the dentist very little, just enough, except when some victory was being celebrated. Warning Voice could wear a white hat naturally, and his toothbrush always looked unused. Javier's, on the other hand, was ruined after a few days.

Actually Warning Voice reciprocated; that is, he admired Javier. First, because he was young. Twenty-one years old! That was certainly to employ an important idiom… Second, because he had a voice as powerful as Don Anselmo's, whereas the dentist's voice was reedy. "I could extract teeth without instruments if I had that voice." And, finally, because Javier was affected easily. Yes, his eyes would soon spread apart to the normal breadth, and then the boy's expression would be frank and kindly in spite of the executions in Pamplona. "Sometimes you look like the good Samaritan."

Warning Voice was another breed of man. Since the age of four, his inner self had been overlaid with coldness. Often, in Gerona, he had had to recognize that he loved nothing but *El Tradicionalista,* Laura, and the harm he could do his enemies; now, in San Sebastián, he felt no attachment for anything but espionage and his servant Jesusha, who called him "*señorito*" though she used the familiar form of address to Javier. Yes, it was the same with Jesusha as it had been with Dolores in Gerona! He was fond of her, and when he saw her go out on Sunday, all dressed up, carrying an outsized handbag, he felt tender toward her. "I must be a very timid man," the dentist would think, "to let the people who wait on me, who work for me, inhibit me this way."

SEVENTEEN

THERE was one in the rebel zone who had forgotten the meaning of happiness: Jorge Batlle, the orphan. He finally had been granted permission to join a firing squad. Yet, as Marta had predicted, this completely failed to console him. Jorge could not be satisfied with seeing a single man fall. He needed to shoot at least as many victims as there were members of his family in Gerona.

Yet the news of his admittance to the training courses for the Air Force did gladden him. Twenty-four hours after receiving the appointment, he was ready at long last to report to the Tablada airfield in Seville within forty-eight hours. Not only would his commission as pilot give him a chance to take revenge, but also flying could be equated with fleeing, with escaping through space. María Victoria, who had been very cordial to Jorge, maintained that when anyone had suffered as this boy was suffering, he had the alternatives of being very great or very petty, "either a mystic or an alcoholic."

Mateo said goodbye to Jorge at the station. To the latter's astonishment, Mateo did not call him "comrade," but "brother" at the last goodbye. "So long, brother!" Jorge was touched, and for a moment admitted that a friend actually could become a brother in time and, on the basis of common memories, a substitute for blood brothers. But no sooner had the train pulled out, leaving the station platform behind, than Jorge felt alone again, alone with a ridiculous suitcase that María Victoria had given him.

When Mateo had said "brother" he had been thinking of his own brother imprisoned in Cartagena and of his father, too. As soon as the train was lost to sight, Mateo turned and slowly went back to the barracks, wondering why his comrades Rosselló and Octavio had not arrived in San Sebastián yet. They also had left Gerona on the 19th of July. What had happened? Were he and Jorge the only ones left out of the whole Gerundian Falange?

Mateo had been spending some days of exaltation in the barracks courtyard learning rifle drill and the various makes of hand grenades, for until then he had never done any shooting except with a pistol. Now, with Jorge gone and his instruction over, he could leave very shortly for the place he had chosen: the Alto del León, on the road to Madrid, where his Second Lieutenant Salazar and Marta's brother, José Luis Martínez de Soria, were expecting him.

He meant to join them immediately, but he did not want to leave without fulfilling an obligation he thought he could not evade. This was to pay a visit to the Alvear family in Burgos. Pilar herself earnestly had recommended it. "Do go, so you can tell me how my cousin is. Remember, her name is Paz."

Paz… Mateo obtained the necessary permit and got on the train for Burgos, the Castilian city that virtually had become the capital of the territory under military control. In the station he bought a copy of a recently founded weekly to read on his trip. It was called *La Ametralladora* (*The Machine-Gunner*), a magazine with a new and sane kind of humor that lightly satirized a great number of topical subjects and old customs. Schubert, the German Nazi with whom Mateo had established cordial relations in Valladolid, was of the opinion that *The Machine-Gunner* was stupid; on the other hand, Núñez Maza, Mendizábal, María Victoria, and especially Lieutenant Salazar, would burst out laughing at the mere sight of a tree drawn by Tono. Mateo settled himself comfortably on the train, and after crossing himself, he began to laugh with *The Machine-Gunner*, to the astonishment of a peasant woman with an overflowing basket of eggs in her lap.

As the train went along, Mateo was torn between staring at the Castilian landscape, reading *The Machine-Gunner*, and chatting with the woman with the basket of eggs. He finally decided to attend to each thing in its turn, and even had time left over to call to mind his Falangist comrades in Valladolid, as well as Schubert, the German, and Berti, the Italian Fascist delegate, whom he had also met. Berti was a very quick man; it always seemed as though he was afraid of missing the boat. It amused Mateo to notice that Schubert pronounced the name of Mussolini with respect, while Berti uttered Hitler's name with a hint of ridicule.

In Burgos, where they arrived about midday, Mateo consulted the address he had with him on a slip of paper: 12 Calle de la Piedra. It was in a separate, lonely section. He went there, feeling the name Alvear beating like a hammer in his temples. What would the Alvear family in Burgos be like, in mysterious Burgos? How often Matías had spoken to him about his "brother in Burgos," also a telegrapher! A head official or something of the sort, of the UGT… What had become of him? And of Paz, Pilar's cousin? And her mother and brother?

Pilar's aunt was the one who opened the door. She was a dried-up woman, disheveled-looking. Mateo introduced himself. "My name is Mateo. I come from Gerona… I'm a great friend of Ignacio, and Pilar's my sweetheart."

The woman fixed her faded eyes on Mateo's blue shirt. "How do I know that's true?"

Mateo cooly handed her a photograph of Pilar that he had brought in readiness for that question. "My intention was to carry greetings and to find out..."

The woman invited him in. Mateo had hardly entered the dining room before he felt his first very strong impression: a girl a little older than Pilar, perhaps nineteen, was sitting in an armchair. Her head was shaved and her face the color of parchment.

She was Paz, Pilar's cousin, daughter of that desiccated woman and the telegrapher, the leader or something like it of the UGT. A girl with a noble bearing who reminded him a little of Olga, and of whom Matías had talked, saying: "She distributes fliers for the Organization. She helps her father." Here she was now, offering unmistakable proof that the winds of a harsh fate had lashed that home. Paz said nothing; she stared at Mateo with a wild intentness, and suddenly sprang up as though terror-stricken.

Her mother soothed her. "Don't be afraid... He says he's from Gerona... That he's Pilar's sweetheart."

Paz stiffened and went back to her armchair. Then the mother, bursting into sobs, explained to Mateo: "Some Falangists took my husband away on the first day and we've never heard a word about him since. Oh, if you only knew!" She paused. "They must have shot him! They must have shot him!"

She had made all sorts of inquiries and always had been given the same answer: "He's been arrested." All the families of the workmen in Burgos were answered in the same way.

As for Paz, they had beaten her badly, made her swallow half a liter of castor oil, and then shaved her head with a razor, as he could see. "It's horrible, it's horrible!" The thirteen-year-old boy was in the country, in the house of some relatives.

Mateo was speechless. It was all very hard, very cruel. What was he to think? He had no time for analyses nor theories.

"Please help us... You are one of *theirs,* and you love Pilar. Try and see if you can find my husband, if you can find out something. This is horrible! I can't stand it any longer!"

Mateo felt deeply troubled. "You are one of *theirs.*" He left the house as best he could, struck by the appearance of Paz, by her parchment color. Before he went, he gave the two women his word that he would do whatever lay within his power to find out something and to protect them. At that moment he would have given anything if the UGT and the principles he was defending had not become irreconcilably opposed.

His pilgrimage had been a senseless failure. He walked among boys playing drums and flags, asking questions, showing his identity card. "Arturo Alvear, of the UGT. He was a telegrapher. Let's have a look at the lists."

The lists were looked at. "He not here, kid. You can see for yourself..."

Mateo made the rounds from one place to another.

"No. No, I don't see his name here. Alvear, you said? No..."

In one of the Falange barracks, a mature man, his blue shirt rounded over his chest as though swollen by his breathing, stared at him curiously. "Did you say he belonged to the UGT?" He shook his head. "Rubbed out..."

Rubbed out... The expression struck into Mateo's mind and would stay there. Within two hours he was distressingly sure of what had happened. Arturo Alvear, Socialist, local Secretary of the Syndicate, had been shot on the second night by one of the mop-up squads. He had been buried in the cemetery in the common grave of those killed during the first few days. They showed Mateo the name on the list with a cross beside it.

"But..." Mateo stammered.

"Why are you interested in that guy?"

"A relative."

"He was an out-and-out Red."

"Out-and-out?" Were there out-and-outs? Mateo felt ashamed. The war was a knife of a thousand colors. He did not know what to do. He hardly dared to go back to the Calle de la Piedra to confront that dried-up woman and Pilar's cousin.

Under his heavy black hair, inside his mind, he kept shouting: "I was interested in that 'guy' because he was a man!"

Once more he was walking like a somnambulist, with a cigarette in the corner of his mouth. What was the purpose of it all? He kept thinking disconnected thoughts and remembering Matías's description: "My brother is rather reserved."

Well, he had run into the situation head on, and had seen with his own eyes how it was with the two women, and the sight had pierced him with remorse as though he had been the leader of the firing squad on the second night. They had stared at his blue shirt and his cap with unconcealed hatred.

Paz had muttered: "You're all scum."

Mateo had kept his composure. He would not let himself be downcast, or pass judgment. He had not told them about César or Jorge, nor about the smoke of Gerona which had reached high into the sky. He had wanted to stay there as long as necessary in order to protect them, at least. For an instant he pictured Paz with her hair grown out; it would probably be the color of Castilian wheat. What was it about Paz that had reduced him to silence?

Mateo said to them: "I would give anything to have got here in time."

He could do nothing on behalf of the two women beyond discreetly leaving his Valladolid address and all the money he had with him on a chair. He would need to stay several days in Burgos in order to find adequate work for them or anything else that would relieve their situation, but he could not do that: he was expected on the Alto del León. Mateo wondered whether some member of the Falange Company he was joining in the Siena might by any chance have been a member of the "mop-up" squad that shot Arturo Alvear.

A thousand thoughts were milling around in his head as he left the house. The whole thing seemed to him both logical and incomprehensible. Until he had climbed that stairway he had believed that he had resolved his doubts as to whether or not the war was licit… Of course it was! And now suddenly…

His nerves were strung up tightly, as seldom before. Every picture that came into his mind was like a lash. "You're all scum!" "If you only knew!" Absent-mindedly Mateo had taken a direction away from the station, and he found himself on a deserted corner, feeling a pressing need to unburden himself any way he could.

He thought quickly of where that could be done: either in a church or in a brothel. As María Victoria had said, "the great or the petty." It bothered him to set both places on the same plane; and yet, from all the evidence, that was how things were inside him.

The Cathedral! It must be beautiful… He was walking aimlessly. He had never been with a woman. He thought of Ignacio and felt stunned. "There are prophylactics, you know." What about Pilar? Why was he remembering Pilar so clearly just now?

Little by little a sense of his manhood was arising in him, a manhood too great for him, an excessive and exuberant manhood. That seemed to him a bad sign, as he generally went to church in quite another frame of mind, with rejoicing and the wish to be humble.

Several soldiers went by, singing. Their appearance suggested to him that they were "going," not "returning." Ignacio had pointed out to him one day in the Calle de la Barca that when the soldiers were "going" they sang one way and when they were "returning" they sang another way. Well, he was a soldier and he was not singing any way.

Instinct urged him to follow those soldiers, and within five minutes he found himself before a vestibule with a chocolate-colored door that seemed discreetly ajar. On one adjoining wall a lantern had been hung above an image of Our Lady surrounded by flowers. Mateo threw away his cigarette and, casting aside many other things with it, pushed open the partly disguised door of the house. "Did you say he belonged to the UGT? Rubbed out..." Before long, Mateo was returning, still not singing a note.

The train took him back to Valladolid. He ate ravenously in the Falange canteen. Castile was immense... Sometimes from the train window it had looked like a horizontal miracle.

In Mateo's compartment two soldiers were playing chess on a charming miniature set. They had placed the board between them, above the seat, cleverly holding it with their thighs. Their fingers were bigger than the king, and it seemed impossible that either player did not knock down all his opponent's men. At Mateo's side an old woman was nodding while the Burgos paper, with its yokes and arrows was sliding off her lap to the floor.

Mateo arrived very late in Valladolid. On his way to the barracks from the station, he was halted three times. He slept well, for he had managed to stop thinking. He slept nine hours until someone woke him, saying: "We're leaving for Alto del León at twelve."

Oh, of course! ... The Alto del León. This was the day he was to join up at the front. Well, he was ready... His mouth felt dry, and he drank from his canteen.

He barely had time to visit María Victoria in the Falange Headquarters. She hung a scapular around his neck and tried to cheer him up... "Don't worry. My boyfriend and Salazar have already killed off all the enemy army!" Yes, of course! Her sweetheart was José Luis Martínez de Soria, and Salazar was the tall second lieutenant, fat and onion-shaped, knowledgeable about the Syndicates, and a friend of the Nazi agent called Schubert, no one knew why.

"Thank you, beautiful. And...what shall I tell José Luis?"

María Victoria took her gum out of her mouth with a quick gesture and stuck it on Mateo's hand. "Give him this." Then she added. "And tell him if he doesn't come and see me soon I'll run off with a colonel."

Mateo smiled, at a loss to know what to do with the gum on his hand.

"I wouldn't worry about that if I were you."

"Why not?"

"Well, gum is a binder, isn't it?"

"Oh, you! ..." cried María Victoria. "So you're fastidious."

Five minutes later, he had an opportunity to say goodbye to Berti, the Italian Fascist delegate, faultlessly uniformed. He was a very belligerent-looking man with a large face. Anyone might take him for an Italian emigrant to America with prospects of making a large fortune. The myopic Nazi delegate, Schubert, was his opposite. He looked more like someone who had been expelled from America after losing everything there except his intelligence and his tenacity.

In the presence of María Victoria, Mateo asked Berti if it was true that Count Aldo Rossi, a member of the Roman Fascist Party, had "had his way" in Mallorca... Berti fixed his eyes on Mateo. "I don't know what you mean by 'having his way.' I can only tell you that my dear friend Aldo Rossi has spent several weeks in the Balearic Islands carrying out the Party's orders and for the benefit of Spain, naturally."

Mateo did not dispute that. Driven by the need to avoid thinking about himself, he asked Berti whether the rumors concerning the arrival in Spain in the near future of Italian and German soldiers were true. Berti looked confident. "I think so. The Italians, at least. Infantry..."

María Victoria interrupted with a smile. "The Germans will arrive, too. Technical services..."

Mateo nodded, and Berti said: "You see. She knows more than we do."

The hour had come, and Mateo left Headquarters after saying goodbye to María Victoria, Berti, and everyone else. In the barracks he picked up his knapsack, his blanket, and the rest of his things. Soon he was climbing into the back of a supply truck marked L-1, meaning front line, together with other Falangists.

The Falangists with him were feeling a little exalted because that morning they had attended a solemn requiem Mass in Valladolid for the soul of Ricardo Zamora, the great football player who was said to have been shot in the Red zone. After a few miles the truck was swiftly passed by the car and troupe of Torerito de Triana on his way to a bullfight somewhere.

Yes, Mateo had decided on the Alto del León... Núñez Maza, the short little fellow from Soria and the head, more or less, of the Propaganda Services, had made every effort to lure him into his unit. They would tour the fronts; they would install the best modern loudspeakers. Mateo declined. He wanted to make the lowly acquaintance of the trenches, the mud, and his own fear.

"You'd be plenty scared with us, too," Núñez Maza argued. "We almost always exchange a few shots in the end. That's why our officers don't look too friendly when they see us coming."

Mateo declined. The die was cast, and Salazar was expecting him on the Alto del León.

The highway followed by the L-1, the Madrid highway, was overlooked by large towers standing on the hills. In bygone days they had been used for transmitting signals. The countryside was lean and spare. Signs could be read on the walls: Join the Falange! Now or Never! No Hearth without a Fire, No Spaniard without Bread! Nitrate from Chile! Mateo was sitting on top of some bags of cement with his legs hanging over the side of the truck, and the wind brought him well-being as it whipped past his face.

As they began to climb the Alto del León, some five thousand, nine hundred feet high, they could hear the boom of howitzers. They were startled. It was their baptism of fire. They could see soldiers and mules, strings of pack mules moving along the trails. The light was very strange, like snow-light, and patches of white seemed to imitate Rainbow's camouflage.

They came to the height where the trenches were, and the parapets—the huts were in the sheltered spots—and Mateo jumped down and suddenly felt disheartened. This was not war, only a parody of war. The defenses, the barbed wire, the sentry boxes all looked like toys. One machine-gun nest actually looked like a mailbox. The truck driver stepped down from his cab, munching on a fabulous sausage sandwich. He noticed the perplexity of the novice and said: "Don't fool yourself, see. There's enough here for you to cook with."

"To cook with..." An apt expression, as apt as Pilar's and the words "rubbed out..."

He asked where Lieutenant Salazar was quartered, and at first they hardly knew whom he was talking about. "Ah, yes! The Elephant! Salazar! The smart fellow! That hut in the rear."

Mateo followed directions, and in a couple of minutes he was facing Salazar, who had come to the door to receive him wrapped up in a tentlike gray cape that almost swept the floor. Mateo understood the "elephant," a trumpeting elephant who did a heel dance in the doorway of the hut because he was freezing. "Come in. Welcome, son of the tobacco official. Come on in. Have some coffee."

Mateo entered the hut and felt at once that everything about Salazar was voluminous, colossal. A colossal stove, colossal women pasted on the wall, colossal camp bed, colossal pipe that would have torn off Mateo's lower lip. Salazar was an extrovert, of course. His poncho, his shirt, and his cap were covered with badges and emblems and he was carrying on a correspondence with six godmothers at once. He was very boisterous, a great advocate of action. His father was an agent of the Bourse in Salamanca and it seemed that "only the important negotiations exhilarated him." As for Salazar, he thought the important job in Spain was to put an end, once and for all, to the idleness and backwardness of the means of production. He talked like Antonio Casal, though instead of Casal's wad of cotton, he had stuck in his ear a roll of paper carrying the letterhead of the Falange.

"Here I am, doing a jig with the cold, and holding up those longbeards"—pointing to two Falangists who had put their heads out the door—"to see whether we can finally do away with the national siesta through the Vertical Syndicates and the whiplash. This war is the result of too much talking. Look at me, I never stop… First, we talked about sex and football. Then we started calling each other sons-of-bitches, then all of a sudden, *bang bang*, fruit salad."

Salazar admired the Germans for their capacity for work. He admitted that the Nazi agent, Schubert, had made an impression on him in Burgos with his theories. "The Germans work; nobody here turns a hand. Do you see this hut? We could even have central heating, yes, yes. But instead we're beating our gums, and then the siesta."

Salazar introduced the two Falangists, who had come in rubbing their hands. Mateo could not retain their names.

"How do you do? Up, Spain!"

Mateo felt a real affection for Salazar, especially because the Salamancan lieutenant could burst into frequent shouts of laughter, laughter that shook his walrus mustache, so like Murillo's. If the echo was right, he probably could be heard as far as the Red parapets.

Mateo was given precise instructions. He was to stay with the Onésimo Redondo Company in the same squadron as José Luis Martínez de Soria. "José Luis is a corporal. He's a corporal with a lot of self-confidence."

Self-confidence? Were there corporals with self-confidence?

"Get some rifle practice. I see you carry yours as if it were a baby. There's not much ammunition, so you'd better not miss. The worst thing here is the cold, the sentry duty. No, don't throw the lantern at me! Tomorrow you'll be saying… But we can stand anything because on clear days we can see Madrid from here…"

Salazar went with Mateo to the advance post where José Luis Martínez de Soria was corporal. The second lieutenant started ahead of Mateo, emitting through his soft fat noises that might have been words, yawns, or oaths.

Mateo was soon face to face with José Luis, Marta's brother. Salazar already had announced the visit to José Luis, so that he was prepared for the meeting. He jumped up from the pallet beside the stove, where he had been pondering for an hour, thinking of ghosts, and, after greeting the lieutenant, he went to the newcomer. "Mateo!"

"The same."

"I wouldn't have known you, boy." He was harking back to their first meeting in Gerona.

The two Falangists embraced, and Salazar took advantage of it to say, "I'm going… I don't want to be a bother…"

José Luis and Mateo hailed each other as comrades, lighted cigarettes, and sat down in Gandhi's pose, both on the same pallet. A gasoline lantern was hanging in one corner, and beside it a calendar stood out like a beacon. It showed a dazzling blonde in the bathtub.

"Would you like some cognac?"

"Sounds good."

José Luis handed him the canteen as a joke. "Go on—you didn't really think it was cognac?"

As Mateo took a long pull at the canteen, he drew his shoulders together and tried to stand up to the drink without closing his eyes or coughing.

"I'm going to recommend you for the Military Medal this very day." They laughed. Their meeting was turning out well. Mateo had decided that José Luis had a tinge of the intellectual, the opposite of Salazar. He seemed reserved, a searcher, probably a skeptic. Although, if he were a skeptic, would he have gone up to the Alto del León on the first day?

He was somewhat shorter than Mateo and very sensitive to cold. He kept filling the stove, which looked like two eye sockets with spectacles and a tiny pipe. Compared with the lieutenant's, this pipe looked like a baby's pacifier. But Mateo noticed that José Luis's mouth was firm and that his wrists were strong. For no apparent reason, wrists were as important to Mateo as ears to Carmen Elgazu. And they were to become more important in the future when, in line with the practice of the Company, he would clasp on his own left wrist the oval disc with his number, so that he could be identified in case he was wounded or killed.

They spent the first few minutes in impersonal talk, as if sizing each other up. But, as with Ignacio and Ana María when they met in front of the jai-alai court in Barcelona, the sizing up did not take more than five minutes. It opened the way for the subject of Gerona. José Luis himself brought it into focus. After a glance at a photograph of María Victoria thumbtacked to the wall, he looked Mateo in the eye and asked him to bring up to date his own family's situation.

Mateo suddenly realized his almost complete ignorance of what had happened, for he had left Gerona only an hour and a half after the surrender of the regular soldiers. Indeed, the only thing he knew was what he had been told in Perpignan by other refugees, and naturally that had all had to do with the capitulation.

Mateo told José Luis about it, adding: "You must understand… Of course the names of your parents and Marta were not on the list of the executed they showed me in Perpignan. Your mother is probably staying in her apartment. Marta must be in hiding somewhere. As for your father, it's as I said; he's in prison, waiting to be tried."

José Luis Martínez de Soria gave a little sigh. Sometimes he had feared the worst for his family. Everything was not lost then! To be sure, there was a dark shadow over it all, some unknown that must be deciphered. Mateo had said clearly: "Your father surrendered unconditionally."

"Tell me one thing," José Luis said. "That unconditional surrender... Was there no other way out for my father?"

Mateo answered him cautiously, as he had María Victoria when she had asked the same question in Valladolid. "Naturally, I don't know... I'm not a professional soldier." Then he added, "Perhaps there wasn't."

José Luis turned his head toward the door as if he might find out the truth beyond it. A pause came. Finally he remarked: "One day this will have to be cleared up."

Mateo was glad to have got by that dangerous topic, and he plucked up courage to anticipate José Luis's inevitable next question. "The thing in doubt right now is what is going to happen to your father and the other officers and noncoms who were arrested. In my opinion," Mateo lowered his voice, "there isn't much hope for them."

José Luis concealed the shock these words gave him, thus confirming what Julio García had said about the Falangists and the Communists: "Weeping is not allowed. They consider it a weakness..."

"What about the other Falangists? Your comrades..."

"Almost all of them are dead," Mateo replied.

José Luis Martínez de Soria stared at Mateo, again measuring the boy. Mateo's expression did not alter and he began to talk about Marta, praising her. "She's a kind of María Victoria, but serious," he opined with a smile. And he told how she had run outdoors on the day of the uprising, carrying a first-aid kit that said CAFÉ.

"And my mother?"

"She didn't go out... She stayed in the apartment."

"And where did Marta go then? Ah, yes, you told me! She must be in hiding somewhere..."

There was something about José Luis which overawed Mateo. A strange aureole of integrity. Of course he had changed a good deal since his trip to Gerona. Salazar called him "Kant" because he was always cudgeling his brain. His corner of the hut looked like Gorki's, though it was much dirtier: musty books, a map of the zodiac, and a lantern. Both lantern and abstractions flickering there, as tall as Navarrese candles. Well, the two of them were going to get along well together! José Luis Martínez de Soria did not care for the colossal, and the size of things left him cold. His only war godmother was his sweetheart, the lively María Victoria. Nazism stuck in his throat; he was much more interested in Italian Fascism. He did not attribute the maladies of Spain to laziness, but rather to ignorance. If he was a Falangist, and consequently a totalitarian, that was because he considered the masses of the country incapable of democracy, incapable of profiting from elections and a parliament. "Democracy would be suicide here." And if he loved Spain and uttered her name several times a day, it was not, as in Núñez Maza's case, from a desire for empire harking back to America and believing the Spanish human type superior, but from the contrary, "because everything is still to be done in Spain." A phrase of José Antonio's that he could not swallow was: "To be Spanish is one of the few important things anyone can be in life." "I'm sorry," José Luis would say, "but José Antonio made an idiotic statement that time. Any person of any country is important, from the poorest Albanian peasant to the most astute militiaman fighting against us."

José Luis was not fanatical about "action for the sake of action." "I believe in intelligence. At the front the intelligent prove to be even the best marksmen."

José Luis Martínez de Soria made a good impression on Mateo. Perhaps he was a little bit haughty...but so were all his family. Mateo was to realize later that Marta's brother was a man of unbreakable will and that, without in any way resembling Kant, he actually lived in a separate world of the mind. Instead of having a good time, as almost all the other soldiers did, he read steadily and wrote to María Victoria or studied. He read books on politics; he wrote "I love you" to María Victoria; he studied to become a judge. Indeed anything juridical fascinated him, although he recognized that there were two things in creation whose dimensions were unknown: the intention of a man and the heavens, the starry heavens. "When this is all over, men who know how to judge will be needed. Who know how to judge...their own fathers." Exceptional self-assurance!

José Luis Martínez de Soria was trained. He assigned Mateo to guard duty—two hours in an advanced post—but as this was the first time his friend had stood a guard, he had the delicacy to stay with him the whole time. There they had a chance to go on talking and to see Madrid in the background, through clouds and distance and civil war.

Naturally they grew confidential... "What about you, José Luis? Why are you a Falangist? What won you over to the Falange?"

José Luis narrowed his eyes as he stared at the horizon, and finally gave an unexpected reply: "The Woman's Section."

Mateo laughed. He knew that he was over-serious himself. Matías once had said to him rightly in reproach that he was always "mixing serious things even into the soup." José Luis had just set him an example.

At the end of the guard duty they went back to the hut and to thinking that the good thing about the Falange was to unite the most disparate people, people as opposite as Salazar and José Luis Martínez de Soria.

They found Padre Marcos at the hut waiting for them. "I heard the family had grown."

Mateo would have liked to be glad to see Padre Marcos, the chaplain of the unit, but he could not. The uneasiness he had felt ever since he had pushed open the chocolate-colored door in Burgos became almost unbearable in the presence of Padre Marcos. Added to that, he was not yet ready to go to confession.

Padre Marcos observed that Mateo was staring at him as if confused, but he attributed it to the strangeness of the first day. "You'll like it here. You'll see."

Why shouldn't he like it? Padre Marcos left, and as José Luis Martínez de Soria had some duties as corporal to perform, Mateo was alone for awhile, until a Falangist came in, and after opening a can of sardines and eating them, used the oil to rub on his face. "Your skin gets chapped from the cold, so oil is a help."

Lying side by side that night, Mateo and José Luis Martínez de Soria went on talking and Mateo learned a number of things. That Salazar had come up from the JONS with political ambitions. That Germany was not willing to recognize the Military Government of Burgos, but only the Falange. That if Marta could pass over into Nationalist Spain, she would be a great help to María Victoria, who was organizing a Social Auxiliary. Finally Mateo learned that the Falange had under study a plan to liberate José Antonio from the prison in Alicante.

"What's that? What did you say?"

"Just what you heard."

"But..."

"This time everything has been carefully planned. Better than you might think."

"Why do you say *this* time?"

José Luis Martínez de Soria stared at Mateo. "Because up to now, every attempt that's been made has failed."

EIGHTEEN

PILAR had stopped keeping her diary. She did not dare to leave a written record of her impressions, for they revolved around a forbidden name, a name that was taboo: Mateo. She was thinking of the boy with obsessive frequency, relating everything to him, and absence and time had only magnified the halo around the young man on the Alto del León.

Mateo was able to see Madrid through haze; Pilar was able to see Mateo with almost palpable clarity. And her memory of him was making the girl a better person, was motivating her inwardly to such a degree that Carmen Elgazu, sitting in her little rocker at the rear of the dining room, next to the balcony, often used to stare at her daughter and think that the danger of frivolity had been swept away forever. The austerity of the clothes they were forced to wear had something to do with it. They wore *espadrilles* instead of high-heeled shoes; they never penciled their eyebrows or used eyeshadow. Pilar was wearing only one showy item: the earrings that swung gracefully as she was taking the plates off the table, or scrubbing the floor, or standing on tiptoe to kiss her father.

Pilar had fallen into the habit of reading newspapers, for she could deduce a good deal between the lines. In the street she avoided the places where anthems were being played, and whenever militiamen went past her, she turned her back, pretending to look into a shop window. When she would see the prisoners from the Seminary working with pick and shovel in the most unexpected places, she would make three crosses on the palm of her hand. She was the first to tune in Radio Seville at night in order to listen to Queipo de Llano, who sometimes reminded her of certain set phrases used by Martínez de Soria.

One day Pilar did an impetuous thing: she went up to the apartment where Mateo used to live. It had been requisitioned by the POUM. The idea had come to her suddenly when she had found herself in the Plaza de la Estación. She saw the sign POUM on the house front, thought of Mateo, and went upstairs. She felt sure that some valid excuse would occur to her on the stairway, and it did; she asked for Murillo's address on the Aragón front. Her figure was conspicuous among the rifles in the apartment, the maps, and the rubber stamps. The militiamen were not suspicious; they took her for a member of the leader's family or a former sweetheart. They did not give her the address. But what did that matter! Pilar had a chance to study what had been the dining room for a few minutes, and to see through a half-opened door what had been Mateo's study: the desk, the armchairs, the bookcase. How it all smelled of tenacity, of the blue shirt! Not even the charts and graphs, not even the firearms and the rubber stamps had been able to replace the old scent. Pilar dallied as long as she could, breathed deeply, turned around, felt half happy, half tearful, and finally ran down the stairs, thinking that Mateo's hand prints were still on the banister.

Life for Pilar was going on in this fashion, with a calm that became monotonous as time went by, until on the fifth of October, the day the SIM began to function in Madrid and Barcelona and millions of leaves, withered by autumn, began to fall in the Dehesa of Gerona, the girl met the Rosselló sisters in the Rambla, under the arcades. They asked her flatly whether she would like to join the White Relief, the work being managed by Laura, with the purpose of helping the prisoners and facilitating the escape of the persecuted.

"You can't refuse us, Pilar. They've killed a brother of yours, and Mateo was the head of the Falange here. Those are things that count, aren't they?"

Pilar was struck dumb. She felt a panic so great that she felt ashamed. Life for her was becoming an enterprise of uncommon responsibility. A voice deep within her said, "I'm no good for anything like that." But the Rosselló sisters, less attractive than she, yet with an enviable firmness in their glance, questioned her hopefully, ready to pretend that one of their *espadrilles* had come untied, in case a militiaman should approach them.

Pilar's breathing quieted and she managed to stammer: "I'll have to think about it. I'll let you know."

"They killed one of your brothers."

She left them, crossed the sidewalk of the Rambla, and went upstairs to the apartment in perplexity. She spoke to her mother, handed Don Emilio Santos a package of cigarettes she had bought for him, then went to her room. There she bit her fist and thought. She imagined herself a spy in disguise, with papers hidden in her watch—as Mosén Francisco had hidden the wafers of the Host—in the neck of her dress, inside a false tooth… She pictured herself cornered by Cosme Vila and El Responsable, or by Olga, and screaming: "I don't know anything. I don't know anything!" Well, that would be the truth. She did not know anything either of the world or of herself. All she knew about was César, was Mateo, and the uncertain beating of her heart.

When Ignacio came home from the bank with his hair very long and another package of cigarettes for Don Emilio Santos, she called him cautiously and told him what had happened. "Tell me what to do. I don't know what to tell them. I'm afraid. I'll do whatever you tell me."

Ignacio was instantly indignant. "But what were those stupid girls thinking of? Tell them to let you alone."

"But maybe they're right. I'm not happy doing nothing either."

"You weren't made for such things."

"Then what was I made for?"

"To go on the way you've been up to now, helping everyone at home."

"I don't know whether that's a compliment or not..." Pilar wrung her hands. "What would Mateo say?"

"Mateo... Mateo would probably get you into the mess."

Pilar clenched her fists. "You see?"

"The only thing that's important to Mateo is to be a hero, and I'm tired of seeing that word everywhere." Ignacio paused. "Besides, what would you have to do? Did they tell you?"

"I don't know. Help people who're trying to get away. The prisoners..."

"People who are trying to get away?" Ignacio stared long and hard at his sister. She had grown, she had developed, she was a woman. But she still had about her the aroma of fresh bread, of childhood. "No, she won't do for that," he thought. And he felt that he loved her, that he did not want to lose her, and that he ought not to let her get into the fight.

"I don't want to lose you, Pilar... Leave it alone. It will all turn out the same without you."

"Then... I'm just a useless creature."

"Why do you say that?"

"Marta would agree with me. Marta went out on the 18th of July with her first-aid kit."

"That's not the same thing. Are you crazy to start singing 'Face to the Sun'?"

"I wasn't, no."

"And not now either. You're all sentiment now; you want this to end. But neither you nor I are crazy about 'Face to the Sun.'"

Pilar lowered her head and Ignacio went to her and took hold of her wrists. The girl was trembling. She was trembling from head to foot. A spy! She was trembling with shame and thinking that if she bungled that, she would be despised by Laura, the Rosselló sisters, Queipo de Llano, Spain, and Mateo!

"If I could only talk to Mateo..."

Ignacio put his arms around her and kissed her on the forehead. "Run along, little one...our mother needs you."

Carmen Elgazu was frightened, for it was rumored that many draft contingents were about to be called up, Ignacio's among them. Ignacio with a rifle! Ignacio with Durruti on the Aragón front! It was more than she could grasp.

"If that happens, it would be better for you to go into hiding somewhere, to go away...anything but report for duty."

Matías Alvear shared Carmen's opinion, and they both lived under the burden of this weight. They would look at their son as if he might vanish from one moment to the next. Particularly at night, when they would wake up terrified, as if groping in the dark. Matías concealed his fear. He had begun to fish the river from the balcony again, the Oñar flowing so muddy then from the first rains that it seemed the fish ought to come out livid. But his mind was filled with Ignacio. Naturally, the boy would follow in the footsteps of Mateo and many others who had escaped to France; but he had heard that during the past few days carabineers had surprised three parties in the Pyrenees.

Added to that, Carmen Elgazu had suffered a serious loss in Mosén Francisco. The priest had made up his mind to escape and go into hiding in Barcelona. Consequently Carmen Elgazu had been deprived of the Mass, of spiritual comfort, left "like a savage," as she put it. And at the very moment, too, when she was planning to make the divine little white discs at home, as the Campistol sisters had suggested. "Perhaps this is my punishment," she told herself, "for intending to make them without Matías's knowledge." It pained her to feel deprived of that direct road to sanctification. But Mosén Francisco had decided to flee because his hiding place no longer had been safe after the moment when some tatterdemalion had written on the dressmakers' staircase in charcoal: "*There's a priest here!*" Ignacio had gone to say goodbye to the vicar and the latter had admitted to him that he knew no one in Barcelona and did not know where to go. "I'm not worried about the trip," he said. "That's all prepared. I don't know whether I'm to go as a woman or a political commissar, but there's no danger. In Barcelona, on the other hand..."

Ignacio hesitated, then told him that if he could find no solution of his own, he should go to Ezequiel's photography establishment. "In front of Police Headquarters. You'll see 'Photomaton.' Mention my name and I'm sure Ezequiel will take you in." He also gave him Ana María's telephone number and explained that Marta was at Number 326 Calle de Verdi.

Carmen Elgazu had witnessed that departure of one she loved with sadness. No one knew what was going to happen. The Provincial Government had just issued ration cards. The decree was published on the 13th of October, Tuesday the 13th! But that did not worry her. "I can manage things in the kitchen." She would not fail! That was what she had been born for, to love and to support them all in anxious moments. When Matías went back on the day shift, she and her husband began to go out for an occasional airing, for Carmen Elgazu had gained a good deal of weight. She was losing her light grace and needed to walk. They would turn to the Dehesa from force of habit. She would go to the Telegraph Office to pick up Matías, and then both would head toward the Dehesa with the innumerable trees where they once had sat on a bench and decided to buy a hat-rack, and where Future, wearing a breechclout and holding a microphone, had harangued his men before going off to die.

"Do you remember, Carmen, those bicycle races, the bowling championship matches, and the amateur painters?"

One afternoon they saw a crowd gathered in the Dehesa and became alarmed. But it had nothing to do with a demonstration. It was the fakir Campoy again. The man had promised, as before, to let himself be buried for several hours and then to be resurrected. The grave, deep as in a Biblical tale, was already being dug and the fakir was drinking lemon juice. When Carmen Elgazu saw the skeleton-like man, unshaved, she drew crosses on her hand and thought of the cemetery and César. Ah, if only César could also! … She felt an overwhelming desire to go to the cemetery and she told Matías about it. He hesitated, concealing from her that it would make the fourth time he had visited it. Then he yielded. They turned and, walking along the muddy river with the livid-looking fish, went to the cemetery, where Carmen Elgazu wept disconsolately, where even her arms and her eyebrows seemed to weep before the passive niches and the headstone marked Casellas Family. What a strange cemetery! The chapel had become the "Pantheon of the Martyrs to Freedom," and the mingled remains of men who had hated one another lay sleeping in their plots of earth. Matías felt on his back that the sun was dying, too, and he said to his wife: "Let's go…" And at that moment the birds were singing and Carmen Elgazu longed to hear the voice of César saying to her at the Collell: "Mother, I tried to play tennis, but it tired me too much."

When they returned home, they were met with another surprise they never would have anticipated: Don Emilio Santos had gone away, too. He had disappeared like the fakir Campoy. For at least two weeks Mateo's father had kept insisting: "I don't want to endanger you any longer. This is enough. I'd like to learn something about my son Alfonso, go to Cartagena to inquire about him." In the end he had won over Ignacio, who with the help of the cashier of the Arús Bank had obtained a false safe-conduct for him and a seat in the cab of an ambulance. Don Emilio Santos had gone, and Carmen Elgazu hardly had laid eyes on his empty bed, once César's, before she had a presentiment that something bad was going to happen to their friend. Mateo's father had not forgotten to leave a bouquet of flowers for Carmen Elgazu—what would she do with them?—and a note saying: "*Forever.*" Matías was a little ashamed to have to admit to himself that he was glad. "We can breathe easier."

The next day Matías went to the Telegraph Office somewhat calmer. The presence of the militia guard hardly mattered to him now; on the other hand, he was increasingly sad because telegrams of glad tidings never came in anymore.

Ah, the Telegraph Office, the Post Office! A small world... The sorters would laughingly throw into the wastebasket many letters addressed to "Fascists," and the men at the stamp window accepted tips for properly wrapping what was sent to the firing line by way of the Militiaman's Mailbox, which also had opened a money order service for the militiamen. Matías could not help musing silently at the sight of those lines of skeletal women with babies in their arms, sending twenty pesetas, fifteen pesetas, ten, to their sons or husbands at the front. Could anything be more poverty-stricken? The stone lion's head presiding over the façade seemed to shake its mane and roar.

David and Olga still were opening and reading the foreign mail every day, as well as what was on its way through the province of Gerona. They, too, were horrified at the poor, the miserable printing or handwriting on the envelopes. After reading letters by the hundreds, they had acquired a sixth sense for translating the cryptic phrases employed. "Don't forget to say hello to Juan's mother," meant "Don't forget to pray to the Virgin." "When you receive this, Mama's birthday will be coming up," meant "Don't forget that the feast of the Virgin is coming soon." "On Christmas Day I had my fill of nougat, as I used to," meant "I took Communion on Christmas Day, as I always used to do." The Virgin was "Mama." "To drink champagne," to take a tonic, "to contemplate the beautiful, round moon" was to receive Communion. To succeed in crossing over into the other zone was "to pass the examination," or "to get over the grippe." Not to succeed was "to have the same toothache," "to need to poultice the leg again."

David and Olga grew angry at such messages, as if feeling a kind of shame. And indeed, in October 1934, when they both had been in prison, they too had sent keyed letters through the prison personnel. "I'm not sure, but I seem to remember that on the 15th of December last year, we went to the country," had meant "There's a rumor that they'll let us out on the 15th of December."

Occasionally the schoolteachers would go to speak to Matías even though he treated them with the greatest coolness and almost invariably gave the excuse that "he had work to do." They wanted to ingratiate themselves with him and all his family, if they could. They failed to do so. Matías's mourning armband was the ditch that lay between them.

On the day the ration cards were issued, Olga hastened to pay Matías a visit and tell him: "Don't worry about that. Carmen Elgazu will lack nothing... if we have anything to say about it."

Matías stared at Olga. "And why should you make any distinctions?"

The teacher did not know what to say. She had spoken because increasingly tight restrictions could be foreseen, as Antonio Casal had prophesied. Casal had said: "The Fascists will be lacking in heavy industry and we'll be lacking bread."

Matías would break his silence with the teachers only when he could give them bad news—of the uncontainable Nationalist advance on Madrid, for example. He would add that all such nonsense as censoring letters, mailing packages, and killing seminarians would not alter the course of the war, for wars were never won by disorder and pillaging.

"You will lose on that account—on account of the disorder, the thieving, the sabotage. Besides... Look here! You're going to read this telegram..." They went to the teletype and Matías took the strip into his hand with the ease of long practice. "No, this isn't the one, but it's all the same. You already know the contents of most of them, don't you? 'Grandfather Juan has gone to Aunt Dolores...'"

David and Olga replied, "The soldiers kill people, too."

"I don't know about that..."

Sometimes Ignacio went to the Telegraph Office to see his father. The two men had mutual need of each other, more so than ever before. Matías could no longer spend an evening talking in the Neutral, and Ignacio had no friends of his own left, nor even his junkyard. They walked along the railroad track through force of habit. They could not hear the anthems or meet militiamen there. They crossed the iron bridge toward the quarries and sat there in the sun, seeing at their feet the waters of the Ter, the bell towers to their right, and the march of the rails into the distance seemed to them a hopeful image.

"Your mother needs our love, Ignacio."

"I know."

"So does Pilar."

"Am I not behaving all right?"

"Naturally you are. But be consistent, for once..."

"What if my quota is called up?"

"You ought to speak to Julio about that."

"There's nothing he could do. I'll have to go."

"I hope you'll find another solution."

Matías offered his son a cigarette. Ignacio accepted and waited with the cigarette between his lips for his father to give him a light. Matías's hand was trembling as he held the match. The flame was a caress, a warm expression of the love Matías felt for his son. The smoke was the words he would have liked to speak but could not summon. The two men soon went on, sucking in the tobacco with voluptuous enjoyment, though it was of such poor quality now that it attacked and irritated the bronchial tubes. It was a tobacco that smelled of war, of war and the black market in some sort of ratio. At times they would suddenly hear the puffing of the train coming from the frontier and soon after they would see the iron worm shoot around the curve that paralleled the meandering of the Ter in that spot. Father and son tried to get off the track on the same side, but they did not always do it. Frequently the clatter of the train divided them, one on each side of the tracks. Then as cars and more cars rumbled by in an endless line, Matías and Ignacio would feel uneasy until the metal serpent had passed and they could see each other again. They would smile, breathe a sigh of relief, and exhume from their grief the family slogan of the Michelin tires.

NINETEEN

THE series of reverses suffered by the Loyalist forces was so evident to the eye that everyone agreed that steps had to be taken. The government fell, and the Socialist leader, Largo Caballero, became President, replacing Giral and also taking over the Ministry of War. In this government the portfolios of Industry, Commerce, Justice, and Health were officially assigned to the FAI, and, to the astonishment of Dr. Relken, the Basque Nationalists were admitted. A government much more revolutionary and energetic than the preceding one. Except among the Communist ranks, it inspired public confidence at once. In fact, Largo Caballero was nicknamed the Spanish Lenin, not the Spanish Stalin. Purely Marxist, its entire course demonstrated that its aim was to implant in Spain the dictatorship of the proletariat, that is Marxism, but independent of Moscow. A Spanish Marxism, adapted to the temperament of the people and the nation's current circumstances. Consequently the orthodox Communists were placed on the defensive, and as Cosme Vila put it, "We're still swimming in two waters." The Secretary of Labor, who had known the new head of the government for a long time, said that he was a contemplative and stubborn man, a great organizer, and famous for his long silences. He was cooler than the others, yet he possessed more vitality and decisiveness. His given name was Francisco, the same as General Franco's, which evoked from Professor Morales the comment that "The battle is going to be waged between the two Franciscos." Seemingly, Largo Caballero was a symbol of contradictions. Some people considered him plebeian because he was of humble birth and had been a labor foreman and plasterer. Others considered him a gentleman. In Burgos they were saying, "He's got a lot that's *largo* and very little that's *caballero*." And *The Machine-Gunner* published a caricature of him so apt that it would have delighted Ezequiel. In it Stalin was portrayed with mustaches that were hammers hitting Largo Caballero on the head.

The change seemed to indicate, however, that the new leader meant to begin his work at the bottom. The decree unifying the militia was read at the front. "All dispersion and autonomous forces are hereby ended. A single Militia under a single command. All the members of the Militia of all parties henceforth will obey the same voice." On the home front, the decree dissolving the Anti-Fascist Committees was published. "The People's Committees now acting autonomously and not accountable to anyone are hereby abolished." Oh, how subversive all that was! One step forward, one step back, according to Olga, a terrible step back, according to El Responsable, who said to Merche as he stood in a corner of Don Jorge's flat where the arms were stacked: "It's only a step from this to Fascism."

That was not true. The truth was simply that Largo Caballero, like Matías Alvear, attributed the reverses in large measure to disorder and mismanagement, and when he made his first speech he uttered a gemlike sentence in support of his theory: "The impetuosity of the race makes the Spaniards efficient when they obey, but exceedingly dangerous when they command." That was it. Those militiamen and militiawomen, if properly channeled and wisely "commanded" would be capable of building a new Spain. (Like the Masons, Largo Caballero was fond of using the terminology of construction.) But as soon as they got hold of a rifle and power, they offered a dismal spectacle.

Largo Caballero's first decision was to insure the efficient functioning of Supply. "Though there is food to spare on the Aragón front, there are militiamen on the Southern front who have nothing to eat but raw tomatoes with salt and olive oil." Then he ordered the chiefs of the United Armies to make a rigorous inventory of their commands. "In one sector of the Sierra, fifteen hundred men are fighting, but they have been assigned rations for four thousand and they have a supply of war matériel more than sufficient to fill one Army Corps to the brim."

The second decision was to set in motion a massive collection of every kind of weapon still on the home front "guarding the Revolution." The success of this collection surpassed even the estimates that Antonio Casal had enthusiastically published in *El Demócrata.* From the most unlikely places veritable arsenals of shells, rifles, machine guns came forth, and even half a dozen artillery batteries that had been concealed.

Some militiamen rebelled against the order, especially in Catalonia. They chose to throw away their weapons rather than turn them in. A stupid kind of initiative which endangered the peace of the countryside and the children who played there. A son of one of the jai-alai players at the Chiqui Court, Ana María's court, was killed instantly when a grenade exploded in his hand.

The third decision was meant to put an end to acts of "unjustified" terrorism at the front. Commanders and other officers were ordered to produce witnesses and make investigations of all denunciations. "The militiamen have been guilty of tossing prisoners in a blanket with a pencil in their right hand and of forcing them to write their names on the ceiling, one letter for every toss." Largo Caballero was dreaming of a clean war on the firing lines. He believed that "to fight" must equate with "to be unified." On nights when he could not sleep—his insomnia was as proverbial as his silences—he would picture to himself the People's Volunteers growing ever more austere, increasingly able to control themselves. Whenever anyone raised the objection that such optimism ran counter to Karl Marx's concept of the "proletariat," he would say: "Marx did not know the Spanish man."

Another decision affected the officers in Health. Dr. Rosselló was one of those consulted by emissaries of the government. All the reports received by Largo Caballero agreed that Health was functioning satisfactorily. But it would have to be perfected, for it was a key service upon which the lives of so many combatants depended. Largo Caballero took effective steps. A number of Pullman cars from the main railway lines and as many ambulances as were available were converted into mobile hospitals. Sleeping bags were issued, and campaign medical kits with rubber tubes for tourniquets; surgical instruments, Kocher and Pean forceps; surgical scissors and anti-tetanus and anti-gangrene sera. Several buildings situated at strategic points in the territory were assigned to Health; for example the Monastery of Covadonga in Asturias was equipped as a leprosarium. The deadliest enemy was dirt, filth. How could they combat it? They would have had to control even the elements. In Gerona itself, the Río Oñar was a threat to health; so was the sea at many points along the coast where no one dared to fish in certain zones for fear that the fish had been feeding upon human flesh, the flesh of the "Fascists" who had been cast into the water there.

The fifth decision, of a precautionary nature, had to do with the White Relief. It was urgent to smash it, to keep a watch on all the Lauras, all the Rosselló sisters, all the Campistol sisters… Largo Caballero had the fronts of buildings, the villages, the roads blanketed with signs exhorting vigilance. WATCH OUT FOR RUMOR. THE ENEMY MAY LURK IN YOUR OWN HOME. A TRUE REVOLUTIONARY DOES NOT TRANSMIT MILITARY SECRETS EVEN TO HIS MOTHER, OR HIS SISTER, OR HIS SWEETHEART. Largo Caballero labeled the spreaders of false rumors *fabricators of defeat.* He kept the existing Chekas open and permitted the opening of many more. The Anarchist García-Oliver, his Minister of Justice, helped him in this task. "Justice must have teeth," the minister declared. "Justice must be living, not moldering in the forms of a profession. Justice must not only be popular, but primordial..." In Valencia, the Russian terrorist Leo Ledaraum was starting to operate. In Madrid, the so-called Blue Auxiliary was born, organized by Falangist girls and attached to the White Relief.

Yet Largo Caballero was a realist, so much a realist that he seemed to think like Julio García in many ways. He realized that all the foregoing measures would be ineffectual unless he could make fantastic purchases of war matériel, especially of airplanes and tanks. Tanks were as much of an obsession with Largo Caballero as machine guns were with Durruti. He particularly wanted tanks. Indeed foreign purchases became his main objective once it was clear from the arrival of only a few Russian ships that Russian aid would be insignificant. A number of delegations were sent abroad with varied and plenary powers. Finally, "The mobilization of all the workers of the world must be achieved. All the workers of the world must be consolidated in our heroic struggle."

When Colonel Muñoz had glanced over this program, he made a grimace. "This is all very well," he declared. "But what about the militiamen? A race of people doesn't change because some articles of a Code of Laws has been changed."

THE intervention of Don Carlos Ayestarán on behalf of Julio was decisive. *El Demócrata* had not lied; the policeman was leaving for Paris and London as a member of the Provincial Delegation whose mission it was not only to buy and pay for armament, but also to observe at firsthand the progress of the recruitment of the international volunteers prepared to leave for Spain. Their main recruiting stations were in the French capital. Julio's original idea of remaining anonymous could not be carried out. The Ovid Lodge felt it was an honor, a source of prestige, to broadcast the news that one of its members had been chosen for a mission of such import.

As he was leaving Gerona, Julio García promised Doña Amparo Campo that he would bring her back a couple of "European" gifts. He fitted easily into the ironical mold of the Delegation, composed in great part of skeptical men who took their mission very seriously and considered it a sacrilege to enjoy the trip by going to shows and cabarets. "Being courteous detracts nothing from courage," Julio would tell them as he dragged them out for a night on the town.

In London the policeman soon found an inseparable companion in Fanny, the English newspaperwoman. A woman taller, more scintillating, and more cosmopolitan than Doña Amparo Campo. Julio preferred her company to that of the Catalan delegation; not to mention that she was very useful to their work. Julio García was crazy about Fanny, though he tried not to carry it to excess. He found himself staring constantly, like a schoolboy, at that woman with the blond hair and the troubled eyes.

"Why are you looking at me like that?"

"Because I like you."

Yes, he liked Fanny. He liked her when she said she was not a Communist, nor an Anarchist, nor a Socialist; that she was not anything, that she was a simple journalist in love with the classics and that she longed for the triumph of the weak, that is, of the worker, the universal worker. He was glad Fanny had had three husbands and that she wore three wedding bands on her ring finger and was keeping a place for a fourth. He liked her because she could drink as much as he could, more than he could, and because sometimes she would tactfully take his cigarette out of his mouth. He liked her because she had been born in London and never bragged about it, because she had a voice like absinthe, and because she could quote Keats and Baudelaire. What he did not like was for her to call him "Spaniard" in a tone suitable for calling a cat or a child. "Please call me Julio!" All right, Fanny would please him, pronouncing the J adorably.

Even though aware that he was behaving like a child, Julio García had all he could do to keep any secrets from Fanny. He could not help it. Fanny had only to look at him to stir him, and he was ready to betray all the signs Largo Caballero had stuck up across Spain.

The secrets that Julio passed on to the English newspaperwoman those days could not be called monotonous. Things seemed to be moving ahead, and to tell the truth everything being accomplished could be attributed not to the Delegation of which he was a member, but rather to previous negotiations. The avalanche of aid to "Republican Spain" already had started. Up to then, almost all the matériel being received had carried French or Czech trademarks, and the first ship to dock in a Loyalist port had been the Mexican freighter *América*; but lately the sources of supply had begun to proliferate in many European countries—the Non-Intervention Pact was flouted at will—and of course in Russia, though Julio García suspected that Russia would not send first-class arms. Her weapons would more likely be weapons rejected by her own Army. In any case, a network of commercial banking and manufacturing firms scattered over the Continent was receiving orders paid for in advance out of the national Spanish fund, filling them, and guaranteeing the arrival of their shipments at the Spanish frontier. Julio knew by heart the location of those firms, at least the most outstanding of them: Paris, London, Copenhagen, Amsterdam, Zurich, Warsaw, and Prague. "Seven cities," he said to Fanny, "for the seven deadly sins." Julio even tried to learn where the ships sailed from and what sea routes they followed. "Port of Gdynia, in Poland, via the North Sea. Greek ports on Mediterranean waters, Fanny, waters as Latin as I am… English and French ports, all kinds of ports! And all kinds of ships, many of them under English flags, S. Navigation flags, or French, or changing their flags on the high seas whenever necessary."

Gold! Julio pronounced the syllable as if he were making a smoke ring as round as the wedding bands on Fanny's finger. And, according to the policeman, the balance was something to think about. During the first month of the war, five thousand kilos of gold had left Madrid by air for Paris. Shipments had been made at the same rate up to that very day in October when necessity had forced them to dig deeper; half a million kilos of gold just had been loaded in Cartagena on a ship whose port was Odessa. "Not less than seven thousand, five hundred cases, Fanny. Add to that the ingots we brought with us and those brought by the other delegations making the rounds here. Do you understand what I'm getting at? My country, my poor blessed country, which has created I don't know how many nations in America without being asked to, is now throwing its wealth overboard, exchanging the gold for cartridges and airplanes. But what difference does it make after all? It used to be exchanged for Communion cups and monstrances. In the Cathedral in Gerona… Well, why go on?"

Fanny kept listening to the policeman with a mixture of scorn and admiration, as Dr. Relken had listened to him. She was sure that Julio García had few scruples and that he would get in on the take from the work he was doing if he could. For in a moment of euphoria the policeman suddenly had said: "My dear Fanny, I don't think I'm forbidden to own records, turtles, or strongboxes, nor to buy huge bracelets for my lawful wife."

Fanny was convinced that she could not understand Spaniards. The days she had spent in Gerona had disconcerted her. "All of a sudden you seem like peasants, primitives; then all of a sudden you seem to be made of good stuff. That Responsable, for instance, who is he? Sometimes he can look like a king. No Englishman can do that. And Cosme Vila's head! It's the very head of Lenin! And those schoolteachers, and the elegant Colonel Muñoz… Not to mention you, you shrewd policeman. You look at me as if you were undressing me while you're talking about giving bracelets to your wife."

Fanny could not understand the Spaniards, and with her décolletage, her absinthe voice, and her Keats, she doubted the blessings to come from that Civil War, whoever the winner might be. Something about Julio bothered her: he was blind to the beauties of London. He greatly preferred Paris. "The

Thames is a bellicose river, an oil slick; but the Seine is decadent and *charmant.*" Julio kept catching cold in the English climate, and he disliked "the gregarious spirit of the people." "You don't need a Hitler here to make you all equal." In all England nothing interested him except Fanny, Bernard Shaw, and Scotland Yard. He visited Scotland Yard and remarked as he came out: "I pity the English criminals. These people would be quite capable of finding out that my esteemed chief, Commissioner Julián Cervera, is a born fool."

At the conclusion of its work in London, the Delegation went on to Paris. Fanny went with Julio because she wanted to be in Spain again. She did not forget her portable typewriter. In Paris a curious adventure awaited them, connected with the International Volunteers. Their recruitment for the Spanish war had been going on for several weeks. According to information given Julio by Don Carlos Ayestarán, the Russian Ambassador in Madrid, Rosenberg, had reported the gravity of the situation to Stalin. And Stalin, amid his framed canvasses, had assigned to the French Communist Party the task of forming the International Brigades, because of its nearness to Spain. Thorez appointed André Marty to head this mission, and André Malraux, an intellectual and art expert, was appointed adviser on whatever had to do with the air arm. Largo Caballero would have liked such foreign volunteers to be inducted into Spanish units, but as he could not offer them a suitable squadron, he had to yield.

Recruitment offices were opened through the International Communists in many countries besides France—practically all over the United States and in northern and central Europe. But France was the amalgam, with offices not only in Paris, but also in Lyon, Marseille, Bordeaux, Toulouse, and distant Oran. In Paris, the most important recruiting station was in the Syndicates' House on the avenue Mathurin Moreau. Julio and Fanny were registered in a hotel very nearby, the Progress Hotel. From its balcony they could see the lines of men who came unendingly with suitcases like the one José Alvear had brought with him on his trip to Gerona.

The plan was to recruit men from every country, to form them into so-called mixed brigades—self-sustaining in operation—which might become the pioneers of an international Communist army prepared to intervene in Europe and America. Thorez, the Czech Gottwald, and the Italians Palmiro Togliatti and Luigi Longo constantly were making the rounds of the recruiting stations, acting on the advice in military matters of the Soviet general Walter and other professional Russian commanders.

Julio García very soon ascertained that the recruitment was a success and that enthusiasm was growing. A kind of contagion had set in, and the Gerundian policeman himself fell victim to it. Instead of using his time to enjoy the

French capital with all its color, scents, and mystery, he scarcely moved from the avenue Mathurin Moreau. In his opinion such success could be ascribed first of all to clever propaganda, and second to the excellent pay offered the enlisted men, particularly the technicians.

The technicians were the first to cross the Spanish border. Workmen trained in shipbuilding already had left for Valencia and Cartagena; aviation mechanics, radio operators, anti-aircraft technicians, and so on, many of them of Russian origin, or trained in Russia, went to work in Madrid. Axelrod, in Barcelona, doubled his liaison work, and Dr. Relken could see his divinations inexorably confirmed merely by taking a walk in the neighborhood of the Majestic. The French Popular Front was providing the facilities needed to elude the formal obstacles implied by the existing Non-Intervention Pact. The volunteers would turn in their passports and be given Spanish passports in exchange, with Spanish names on them, or equivalent documents to present in Perpignan and later at the frontier. The withdrawn passports then were sent to Moscow where the GPU was prepared to supply them to their spies, a subtlety that would have scandalized Warning Voice. Of course they valued most highly the passports of the American Volunteers because they opened the way to planting agents in the United States.

Volunteers were pouring from everywhere, from every country. Sometimes they were sent by their local Communist Party, sometimes on their own account and at their own risk. In every country the pontiffs of propaganda were emerging. In England these were members of the Labor Party and the Duchess of Atholl. In Belgium, the president of the Second International, Debruchère, and others. The general administrator, Maurice Thorez, proved meticulous about everything that had to do with the financial arrangements for such an international corps, perhaps modeling his plan on the Cómpagnies Blanches of the French adventurer, Bertrand Duguesclin. Of course the fundamental, the basic source of payment would be the "Spanish national treasure" in the gold that Julio García had talked about. It was estimated, however, that this would not be anywhere near enough, and accordingly public collections were solicited everywhere, from the individual factories in Russia to the exits of motion picture houses and stadiums and circuses, whether in Czechoslovakia or in New York. "Help the Spanish people!" Help our Spanish brothers!" The organizations were many and the collection centers various. Czechoslovakia organized choirs of Marxist youths who toured the cities and villages singing for "The Freedom Volunteers" about to leave for Spain. Pablo Casals traveled hundreds of miles with his marvelous violoncello for the same cause. The writers were mobilized, too: Ralph Fox, English; Ludwig Renn, German;

the above-mentioned Malraux, and of course Ilya Ehrenburg, Pravda's indefatigable correspondent. Ilya Ehrenburg announced that the biggest collection was the one from the colossus, Russia. Not only the factories had made their contribution; the schools and even the chess clubs had, too.

Who could doubt that it was becoming an international war? Lines were forming outside the recruiting stations in Paris. Julio García and Fanny were living with the miracle every minute. Such a heterogeneous mass of races and origins could not fail to possess a certain grandeur. Yes, there was something grand and legendary in the fact that those lines were forming. From the most distant points of the globe, from the Arctic to South Africa, and from Mexico City to Vladivostok, fanatical or desperate men, sincere or mercenary men, professors or common fugitives from justice, all met in Paris, ready to "overthrow Fascism." Most of them had only a very hazy notion of Spain, something about sun and long-haired women. The global aspect of the war seemed disquieting to Julio. "A lot of this is an opium dream," he diagnosed. But it is a law of nature that a beautiful unquenchable light lies hidden in the eyes of a man who goes forth voluntarily to fight. And those men, like the ones who had gathered in the Dehesa under Future's command, or with their red berets in Pamplona, or wearing blue shirts in Castile, were prepared to leave everything to go and fight. Many of them signed a document that read: "*I am here in the capacity of volunteer and I am ready to give the last drop of my blood if necessary to save the freedom of Spain, the freedom of the entire world.*"

Fanny sent off six emotional dispatches to her chain of newspapers, stating that the majority of the volunteers were forty or forty-five years old and that the active Communists among them were in the minority. Most of the men were simply displaced persons. Laborers out of work from the ports of Le Havre, Marseille, and Singapore; exiled Italians, soldiers of the French Foreign Legion, fugitives from justice, and of course true idealists who had lost their love for the country that had given them birth, their feeling of dependence on it, and were finding a substitute and a stimulant in a cause they deemed worthy of defending and beneficial to the whole human race.

That sort of classification failed to satisfy Julio García in the end. Sometimes if he was awake at midnight and if Fanny was awake, too—she left the door of her room unlocked for him off and on—he would shake her by the arm and start to philosophize. "What do we know about it?" he would say. "Man is very complex. Every volunteer must have enlisted to escape from some intimate, personal problem. Don't you think, darling Fanny, that everything we do is to avenge ourselves for something intimate, something personal?"

Fanny would smile. "Will you please enlighten me, Mr. García, on why you dare to speak to me intimately and what personal thing you're avenging yourself for every time you kiss me so passionately?"

The couple managed to hold daily chats with the volunteers standing in line. Fanny's knowledge of languages and Julio's liberal invitations made it easy to break the ice. Once in awhile the journalist would nudge Julio and say to him under her breath: "Bring me another one. This one is a dud." Their screening did enable them, however, to meet and talk with a variety of most interesting men. They felt particularly drawn to two of them: an idealistic Swede nicknamed North Pole, and a German Jew called the Negus because his beard was exactly like the Ethiopian emperor's.

The Swede was a man of forty-two, in a state of perpetual indignation because the first question he was asked was always whether he liked to ski. They nicknamed him North Pole partly because of the geographic setting of his country, partly because he had pure white hair. He was a taciturn, observant man whose personality suggested winter. He had been attracted to Spain because he imagined it was a country with formidable mountains, therefore interestingly varied. "People from flat country like mine are all of a piece," he used to say.

Julio countered him: "Blessed be the uniformity of Sweden, Denmark, and Holland... That means everyone must live well."

North Pole gazed at Julio with compassion. "Don't you believe it. Money will satisfy many people, but not all of them. We have all known very unhappy millionaires."

"Then why do you want to fight for Spain? Capitalism, poverty, what will you be fighting for?" Julio asked him.

"I'm an idealist," North Pole answered. "I'm going to Spain to learn. I have nothing more I can tell you for the time being."

The Negus was another breed of man. He was forty-five. He had fought in the 1914 war. He used to show everyone a photograph of himself as a child with an expression both peaceful and stupid. His Jewish origin had kept him constantly on the fringe of drama, until he had begun to feel resentful and had moved to the United States. There he discovered that his vocation was stealing, and consequently he had served time. Now he had come back from America with a little automatic razor, a lighter, and a watch given him by the North American Party, which gave watches to all their people who enlisted for the Spanish war. He was sincere. "I'll go all out against the Fascists. Of course I will. But I hope that the Spaniards will be grateful, too." The Negus used to stare covetously at Fanny, not at her body but at the ring finger on which she wore the three wedding bands.

"Well, my friend, I'll see you in Spain," Julio told him. "But for now we have nothing more to say."

Investigation was fascinating. What about the French colonel, Vincent? And Pauline, André Marty's wife? And Togliatti, who had taken the name Alfredo? Top leaders like those were appointing the officers of lower rank "by finger," according to each man's ambitions and capabilities. North Pole was appointed sergeant; the Negus, lieutenant.

Most of the volunteers were assigned to sections. They entered Spain by rail through Toulouse, Perpignan, or Cerbère. Train 70, which left Paris at night, soon became known as "the volunteer train." Julio García and Fanny decided to take it back to Gerona as soon as the mission of the Purchasing Delegation had been completed. "I want to see them drunk. Plastered! Don't you, Fanny? That will be wild!"

Every day the quota was different but basically the same. The lines were long and as they moved up, friendships were formed, information exchanged. This one would be talking about Turkey, the next about China, the third about Brazil between drinking and singing songs. The Frenchmen sang "La Carmagnole" and "The Young Guardsman." The English sang "It's a Long Way to Tipperary" in time to the train wheels. The Italians sang "Bandiera rossa," and as a rule wore red silk neckerchiefs. But the unifying hymn was "The Internationale," and their manner of giving the clenched fist salute expressed everything from the will to fight, to fear, to boldness.

At Perpignan they were joined by volunteers already in the little town near the frontier, waiting for orders, or lacking the nerve to cross the border on foot. The enthusiasm of those pioneers when they saw that they had with them all the passengers on Train 70 was contagious and injected them all with new spirit.

It was funny to watch the efforts of the volunteers who had been issued Spanish passports to memorize the new names assigned to them and to pronounce them even passably. Many gave up after awhile and chose some easy nickname that could be pronounced in any language. Nicknames emerged that would have bowled over Rainbow. France suggested women's names appropriate to the occasion: Pompadour, Marie Antoinette, Jeanne d'Arc. Italy the names of artists, writers, and saints: Michelangelo, Machiavelli, Dante. And Spain? Philip II and Torero and Olé were names they fought over.

In the Spanish villages along the railway, the passing of the volunteers created a commotion and attracted crowds. Gerona was on the way, and therefore Cosme Vila dispatched groups of demonstrators with flags and placards in every language to the station at the scheduled time. Some of the demonstrations were touching, like the one composed of forty deaf-and-dumb children who had come to Gerona through France. They had been evacuated from a sanitarium in Santander by the soldiers on the Northern front. The forty children were dressed in proper uniforms and each one was given a little paper flag. They stood in a group on the platform underneath the clock. As soon as the train arrived filled with Germans, Poles, and Ukrainians and the faces of the volunteers appeared at the windows all smiles, the forty deaf-and-dumb children opened their mouths to shout and could not, so they waved their paper flags with redoubled frenzy. The volunteers, ignorant of the cause for the children's silence, began to yell and make all kinds of inviting gestures. Finally Olga went to the rescue of both soldiers and children, and standing at the head of a group of Socialist women, she started to scream loudly and repeatedly: "Long live the Revolution! Death to Fascism! Long live the Volunteers for Freedom!"

Their reception in Barcelona was equally well prepared and demonstrative. The Provincial Government, the Russian consul, Owscensco, and Axelrod the man of promises organized the welcomes jointly. President Company's felt a special emotion every time, for he was a spiritualist and he had heard that a great many of the volunteers were spiritualists too. The volunteers made a very short stop in the capital before continuing southward at Largo Caballero's orders. He had selected the small city of Albacete, strategically situated between the Mediterranean and Madrid, as General Headquarters for the International Brigades. The first contingents arrived there on the 12th of October and were quartered in the bullring and the former Civil Guard barracks. The Civil Guards in the region had been executed in July, inside the walls of the barracks, which seemed to be spattered with blood. André Marty, wearing a beret as large as Warning Voice's, addressed the newcomers standing on a chair. But many of them were staring askance at the bloodstains, and especially the two Communist Swiss girls, named Germaine and Thérèse, both trained nurses. The blood in the barracks signified many things, and perhaps it was an evil omen. The blood was the red silk neckerchief of the barracks.

The descent upon Albacete of such a hodgepodge of humanity caused an indescribable convulsion there. The "Internationalists," as they were called, went in one leap from timidity to ferocity, from giving their rations to some poor old man to shooting a whole family if it refused to turn over its dwelling to them. And they could not get used to the idea that the Spanish sun would not boil their brains. They were drinking even more than Julio had suspected, and some of the Spanish women shared their thirst while others locked themselves in their houses behind bolts and bars. At times all the Internationals looked anonymous, identical, the sons of a common father, the offspring of suffering. Sometimes each man would imply a personal, far-off legend dating back to a birthplace in Prussia or at the foot of the Urals. The mixture of accents, of gesture, the ethnic and spiritual mixture was a gigantic amplification of what had gone on among the athletes who had marched to the Aragón front with Durruti. André Marty and his military advisers took care to create, insofar as possible, an atmosphere of complete equality among the men. The uniforms arrived from France, with helmets copied from those of the Alpine *chasseurs.* One of the principal tasks was to provide Spanish interpreters for combined operations. Many reported for duty, and among them was one of the mathematics students whom Cosme Vila had captured in Gerona during the first days after the uprising.

The publication of a newspaper in various languages, to be called *Freedom Volunteers,* was agreed upon immediately, but that did not prevent some units from publishing daily reports and pamphlets of their own. The traveling press donated to the Provincial Government of Catalonia by the "international writers" had come to rest at Albacete, and it turned out that the wintry North Pole was a linotypist. Who would have thought it?

From the first moment, André Marty and Luigi Longo realized that the only effective way of achieving discipline in that "sack of eels" as Dr. Relken called it, was through fear. Accordingly André Marty went to work, and another trench was dug on the outskirts of Albacete, another of the innumerable common graves pitting the Spanish earth, the land of sun, of the old and the long-haired women.

Immediately after Dr. Relken had learned through the press of the volunteers' arrival, he left the Hotel Majestic and moved to Albacete. He brought with him a letter of introduction signed by Axelrod and addressed to André Marty himself, but for the time being he preferred to watch from the shadows and not to use it. What things he found out! Too bad Julio García couldn't be with him! He learned that André Marty had arrived with orders to stamp out the Trotskyites. "Poor Murillo!" the doctor thought. He could see that the technicians were organized separately: the cartographers, the plane-spotters, and so on. He attended various hasty ceremonies for the appointment of political commissars and was aware of how easy it would be for "Fascist spies" to infiltrate that organization. All they would need was a knowledge of three or four languages, a letter of introduction, and discretion. He saw evidence, too, that the best organized service was Health, under the direction of Dr. Oscar Telge. He made a trip to Almansa, where the artillery was encamped, and another to La Roda, where the cavalry was installed under the command of a veteran revolutionary named Alocca, recently a tailor in Lyon.

Horses, men, rifles, machine guns, fieldpieces—Dr. Relken was especially fond of those last because they had come from Czechoslovakia—Alpine helmets and fantastic desert *képis.* What a hodgepodge! And meanwhile, the Nationalist troops were advancing along the road from Toledo to Madrid, and Jorge, at the Sevillian airfield, was concentrating all his five senses on his classes for pilots. Julio was getting ready to return from Paris with Fanny, for the Delegation had completed its work, and the policeman had already pocketed the commission that had been discreetly offered him by a relative of the Krupps. And Stalin wanted everything done by stealth, as usual. Antonio Casal was cursing the English, because according to the papers they were mixing shoddy with goods billed as first class. And all over Europe and America meetings and collections were being organized on behalf of the "Spanish people" and the workmen of Kiev, of Stalingrad, of Leningrad, of Rostov and Odessa still were contributing a day's pay. Madrid was filling up with Russians—air force in the Bristol and Gran Vía hotels, journalists and technicians at Gaylord's. The forty refugee deaf-and-dumb children in the province of Gerona were sent back without their little flags to their idyllic home in the village of Arbucias, where they could stare at one another beneath the trees. And Teo on the Huesca front was still muttering his resentment against Durruti and his sorrow over La Valenciana: "I'll get even."

The influx of volunteers was so great that Albacete overflowed and the men had to be billeted in nearby places. The spiritualists communicated from one place to another by thought transference, and at nightfall, amid the wine fumes and tobacco smoke, everyone was asking questions.

Ah, the war would be everyone's answer to everything! It would be glory, conquest, enrichment, and regeneration. And, in many cases, the sweet ticket to eternity.

TWENTY

THIS time the alarm came from the sea. From the calm blue sea, and specifically from the Bay of Roses, where once upon a time Mosén Alberto had been directing excavations that uncovered a necropolis. The event occurred beneath an autumn moon shortly after Julio García's return to Gerona. Commissioner Julián Cervera received the telephoned warning that "an enemy ship" was cruising along the Catalan coast. The warning proved true; the vessel was the cruiser *Canarias,* which suddenly turned like a white whale into the Bay of Roses and opened fire. Twenty-two reports of big guns that echoed like the last trumpet. One of the shells hit the school building. People fled in panic, for they had no defense against the monster, and its intention was not known; most probably it was to wipe them off the face of the earth. All Catalonia thought the attack was the prelude to a landing, and that the Legionnaires and the Moors soon would be set ashore. This last rumor, which smelled somewhat fishy, ran from mouth to mouth, awakening fear and anger. An impotent and bitter anger, which drew from the lips of Colonel Muñoz the phrase: "From the military point of view I consider all that stuff about troop landings is a hoax," to which Cosme Vila replied: "What seems to me a hoax is that you're a soldier."

Panic seized the region, and in many places militia patrols climbed into trucks and ran along the roads leading to the coast, while groups of women left their homes going in the opposite direction, toward the interior. Many a "Fascist" failed to hide his satisfaction; his skepticism would filter through in a wink. That wink was as good as a nod. Reprisals were taken, in Gerona, in Barcelona, in Lérida, and Tarragona alike. The officers of the *Canarias* had no suspicion that the presence of their vessel, its loom above the water, would spell death for many.

The Committee of Gerona, not yet dissolved despite Government orders, held an urgent meeting. Various detachments left the city for the Bay of Roses with admirable speed; but the most immediate task was to prevent the people in Gerona and the province from aiding the attackers by means of signals and sabotage. In a little more than three hours, the official prison in the Seminary held double its usual number of prisoners, and so did the clandestine Communist and Anarchist Party jails. An order went out to turn in all electric lamps and flashlights. Through some untraceable order, a house in which eighteen persons were locked was set on fire in the village of Orriols.

A regrettable incident occurred on the road to Figueras. Alfredo, the Andalusian, Murillo's replacement in the POUM headquarters, with two militiamen, had decided to take a property owner from the village of Palafrugell "for a ride." Barely a month before that he had said sarcastically as he was being arrested: "Me today; tomorrow we shall see." They were taking him handcuffed in a small car, but as they met a sentry at a checkpoint near a dark wood, the landowner had a diabolic and lethal idea. He stuck his arm out of the car window and shouted: "We're Falangists! Up, Spain! Long live the *Canarias*!" The militiamen standing at the booth reacted as their duty required them. They halted the car in a second and riddled it with bullets, riddled its occupants. The landowner from Palafrugell and Alfredo the Andalusian were killed instantly; the two militiamen were badly wounded.

The news reached Gerona in many twisted versions. Blasco declared, "The guy had guts; you can't take that away from him." Santi, who, unlike Javier Ichaso, was getting more wall-eyed every day, contorted himself like a dancer. "I don't want to kill the elephant in the park anymore; I want to kill the whale now."

"What do you mean whale?" Blasco asked him. "Why that's the Fascist ship *Canarias* there at the Bay of Roses. Can't you see it doesn't spout?"

Luckily Santi was not aware that a Gerundian was a member of the crew of the cruiser *Canarias.* He was the younger son of Don Santiago Estrada, and he would have given anything to know whether the news of the landing was true. The boy was swaying with the motion of the sea. If only the big guns were opera glasses! It seemed to him that he could smell the land, not the sea. Within a few weeks Estrada had come to the conclusion that the sea was excessively the same everywhere, and to see his native shore, the Ampurdán coast, so near was to him like the torture of Tantalus.

Axelrod, now making frequent trips to Gerona and the frontier on the side of Agullana and La Bajol, escorted by his dog, judged that the theory that the blood of martyrs brought forth abundant fruit was typically abstract and Catholic. He believed only in the living, for he knew man was forgetful by nature, and he cited the Soviet Union as an example. Since 1917 it had been dedicated to the extermination of the enemies of the people, and yet nowhere had the alleged fruits sprung from their blood. Hence he was not at all upset by the news of reprisals, fires, graves, and more graves, except in fleeting moments of depression or when he was bothered by some temporary infirmity. "Forward, Cosme Vila!" On the other hand, Vila's wife said to her father, the crossing guard, as she came out of the candlelighted room where the body of Alfredo the Andalusian lay in state and where she had noticed how death strangely had rejuvenated the militant Trotskyite: "I feel very bad because so many men are dying. And I'm afraid for Cosme. Sometimes when Axelrod is talking to him, he looks at him as if he is wondering why Cosme is still alive."

The Gerundians who were persecuted as a consequence of the shelling from the sea were ignorant of such niceties and they made up their minds to leave, not postpone a minute longer their planned escape. Hardly had the *Canarias* withdrawn—twenty-two shells, a waiting period, and then vanishment—when new caravans took the road to France. Laura had not had enough time to tie up all the loose ends, and several of these caravans were surprised by carabineers in the heart of the mountains. Laura, the head of the White Relief, wept disconsolately. The Rosselló sisters, still wondering where the Falangists Miguel and Octavio Rosselló were, tried in vain to convince her that it was not her fault. "I'll never forgive myself."

Two of the fugitives were lucky: Marta's mother and Mosén Francisco. They were making for Barcelona. Marta's mother, the widow of Major Martínez de Soria, had recovered her energy and she decided to ask for an interview with Colonel Muñoz. A few hours after receiving the message, the colonel went in person to the widow's apartment and kissed her hand.

"In the name of my husband, I should like to ask you to find adequate means so that I may join my daughter, and once this has been done, to enable us both to leave Spain, perhaps by sea, through some consulate."

Colonel Muñoz never batted an eye. "Consider it done," he replied. Marta's mother read sincerity in the colonel's eyes. On the one hand she felt grateful to him; on the other she was thinking, "So the top echelons of the revolution have ways to save the people they want to save."

"I am very grateful to you, Colonel Muñoz."

"I will do everything I can."

He was true to his word, and it all came out as though measured by calipers. Major Martínez de Soria's widow was to be driven to Barcelona in an ambulance from the hospital. Colonel Muñoz said goodbye to her at the door of the vehicle and added: "You're to spend tonight in the Guatemalan Consulate, and tomorrow you and your daughter will be provided with passports in order and will walk up the gangplank of an Italian ship about to weigh anchor for Tangier."

"I thank you again, Colonel..."

"I wish you all the luck."

Strange! The major's widow often had dreamed of living under the protection of a consulate. But invariably she had imagined it as belonging to a powerful country like England or perhaps Canada. Guatemala! That was charming. Weren't there mountains in Guatemala covered with white orchids, the most beautiful orchids on earth?

She had had time to get in touch with Ignacio and to talk to him for a moment. Ignacio was stirred, and it seemed to him that a breath of hope had transformed the woman.

"Goodbye, until God wills..."

"Goodbye, and kiss Marta for me. Tell her..." Ignacio made a gesture. "Well, it doesn't matter! Kiss her for me..."

The other fugitive from Gerona was Mosén Francisco. This time Laura herself took care of his business, and most efficiently. Everything went like clockwork. Mosén Francisco was disguised as a mechanic and made the trip in the locomotive of the very train that picked up the International Volunteers at the border. The trainmen, who belonged to the White Relief, hid him in the cab after smudging him from head to foot. During the stops in the stations, Mosén Francisco pretended to be struggling with some cranky part of the machinery, wrench in hand and wearing dark glasses. Between stations, he stared at his beloved countryside through the smoke and soot, and even persuaded his hosts to say a humble Ave Maria when the cupolas of the Church of the Sacred Family came into view in Barcelona, an Ave Maria stronger than the hellish puffing of the train.

Mosén Francisco had arrived before Marta's mother. He anticipated her by forty-eight hours in his flight to Barcelona, enough time for Marta to be able to vouch for the identity of the vicar to Ezequiel.

The priest hardly had set foot in the Barcelona station, hardly had ceased to feel the protection of the trainmen at his side when he had the impression that the entire length of the enormous platform was lined with eyes staring at him inquisitively, beginning with the eye of the clock. He never had dreamed that so many objects could seem like eyes. He tried to keep cool, to dissimulate. All right, he was a priest. And doesn't whatever one is filter through in his gaze, his manner, even though he may be wearing a blue coverall, carrying a UGT card and a box of tools? As he left the station he could hear the train whistles behind him, and for a moment he was afraid that they were police sirens.

His confinement among the mirrors in the Campistol sisters' house had been long. "Whensoever they shall persecute ye in one city, then flee to another."

He hardly knew how to walk any more and he could feel his cheeks turning pale. In front of him he could see nothing but the mountains and the ocherous tones of October, houses, men, the colors of the revolution. The discovery that instincts were running naked and unleashed made an impact on the vicar. He did not know where to turn. He went along the Paseo de Colón, and when he came to the statue of Columbus, he thought, "Why didn't I take the way that passes in front of the Cathedral?" The port was there, gleaming with small searchlights from Odessa, with recently limbered-up coastal batteries. He kept walking up the Paralelo as far as the palaces of the Exposition, which a mob of Aragónese refugees had taken by assault. The palaces that had exhibited the industrial marvels of 1929 now were exhibiting hungry mouths that accented the last syllable in their speech. Refugees! Everyone was displaced by the cyclone of the war.

Mosén Francisco stopped behind a pavilion to urinate and left his box of tools on the ground. He felt freer without it, lighted a cigarette and entered the Rondas. Then, retracing his steps, he turned toward the Barrio Chino, following the advice Ignacio had given him. By the middle of the afternoon he felt exhausted. He sat down in a bar with an inscription on its front that read: "Fewer committees and more bread." Bread! Mosén Francisco was hungry. He ordered a snack and a glass of wine. The wine was wine, but the glass was not a Chalice. He raised it, looked at it, and drank. "In Thee, O Lord, I place my trust; do with me what Thou wilt."

Soon afterward, a woman sat down on his knee. He was more frightened than he had ever been and he almost cried out: "Be still! Why all this?"

"What are you doing here?"

"I'm here."

"You're just out of the hospital..."

"Yes."

She was a woman of no particular age. When the militiamen went by and stared at them, Mosén Francisco could not help pressing the woman to him a little.

"You're stingy. Why don't you ask me to have something?"

"That's a good idea."

Another snack and wine, wine for Loli, wine that was wine, but a glass that was not a Communion cup.

"Tell me something."

"I?"

"Who else?"

Children and dogs went by, dragging along the sidewalk his own childhood and the vows he had taken on the day he was ordained.

"Well, shall we go?"

"I have something I've got to do."

The minutes seemed hours, but the woman weighed very lightly on Mosén Francisco's knees! The dramatic beauty of temptation...

"*¡Salud,* and many thanks, kid!"

Salud, body of God, soul of God...

Mosén Francisco stood up, confused. He paid and started to walk, gradually shedding his numbness, in the direction of the Via Layetana, toward Ezequiel's photography shop. He felt faint; he had no choice but to go there. The signs still were announcing what they had announced to Julio on his trip: "Syphilis, or why not take all of me." "Adam was a man." As he crossed the Ramblas, he watched with some stupefaction a mass of about thirty thousand people heading toward the port to welcome the Russian ship *Zarinym,* bringing food for Catalonia.

When the tide of people had receded, he started walking again until he came to Ezequiel's establishment. He looked inside it; the booths were whirring and a group of militiamen was waiting its turn. Ezequiel was there, posing heads, and he was as Ignacio had described him—very tall, long-haired, making gestures that suddenly looked comical, with an obvious honesty in his whole person.

Mosén Francisco changed his mind and took a taxi. The militiamen frightened him, and as Ezequiel did not know him, his coming would be cause for alarm. Better to go directly to the Calle de Verdi, where Marta could vouch for him.

A quarter of an hour later he was knocking at the door of Ezequiel's house. Rosita opened the door to him, but they had no time to exchange a word. Marta instantly had recognized the vicar's voice from the dining room. She ran to meet Mosén Francisco, but was at a loss to know whether to embrace him, offer her hand, or hug him to her. The important thing was that the vicar had made a good landfall.

When they were seated in the dining room and Mosén Francisco had taken off his dark glasses, he made his request; he would need to stay there with them in that house. He was a coward and needed protection. "Ignacio told me..."

"Don't worry, Father," Rosita cut in. "You're in your own house."

Mosén Francisco felt as though a bird's wing had rubbed his cheeks, restoring their color. "O Lord, why art Thou so good to me? Why has Thou listened to my prayers? Is it because I am not worthy to suffer?"

Manolín was staring curiously at the vicar. The latter was about to ask the boy a question, but Rosita anticipated him with a wonderful question: "Do you like lentils, Reverend?"

How could he warn Rosita not to call him Father? Why was he so clumsy?

Rosita said: "Eze will be pleased to have a priest in the house..."

"Who is Eze?" asked the vicar dully.

"Ezequiel. Who else? A prophet who can foretell everything and not make a cent from it."

"Ezequiel...a good name."

Marta broke her silence suddenly to burst out laughing.

"What are you laughing at, daughter?"

"At the sideburns you're wearing."

"Don't mention them! They look like rifle butts."

Manolín was not saying a word, but he was thinking of something exciting. If the priest stayed on in the house, he would ask to go to confession in a few days. He was much taken with the idea of making his confession in a place not a church. "In the patio, underneath the pine trees, maybe."

Ezequiel came home at one-fifteen, as usual. This time his movie-title greeting was pat. "Let's eat!" he bawled in the vestibule as he was approaching the dining room. "The Negro Whose Soul Was White!"

No problem. "Even though you're a priest, you don't seem like a bad sort." Ezequiel always trusted in his lucky star. At that very moment, at the height of the tornado, he believed with all his heart that nothing bad was going to happen either to him or to his protégés. "Stay here... Let's see if maybe you can convert me. I'm getting a bit soft." He promised they would be happy with Mosén Francisco, for it seemed to him that the vicar was happy and only on the borderline of prejudice. "Yes, stay. You'll often dine on lentils, but just be patient. The lady of the house is pretty good at disguising them. Besides, we're sort of nice people, which is saying a good deal these days."

Marta, in a yellow apron, had finished setting the table and they all sat down. As soon as the tureen was in the center of the table, with steam rising from it as from Abel's bonfire, Mosén Francisco asked permission to say the blessing. "Of course..." Mosén Francisco bowed his head. Manolín peeked to see whether or not he was tonsured. At the conclusion, Ezequiel said to the priest, "I'm glad you don't pray in Latin. Maybe I can understand a few words now..."

No sooner would it seem that the war had become a bare plateau without an end, the Great Monotony, than suddenly it would begin to move like lightning, changing the course of human lives in a flash. Marta had come to know both aspects. Monotony in David's kitchen, lightning in Ezequiel's house. Forty-eight hours after Mosén Francisco had been installed in the family that revolved around Rosita, indeed at the moment when he was saying to himself, "This is a blessing," the news came that Marta's mother was waiting for her daughter in the back of a car parked in front of the door.

"Take only what you can't do without; just some handkerchiefs and a pair of stockings. There's no time to waste."

The Guatemalan Consulate was awaiting the arrival of the women. The password at the door would be "Orchid." Marta reacted to the news as if it had come through a far-off wall. Her goodbyes to Ezequiel, Rosita, Manolín, Mosén Francisco, and the cat all were muddled and emotional. She had tears in her eyes.

"What happened, Mother?"

"First give me a big hug, darling! Tomorrow we'll be sailing for Tangier on an Italian ship. For once, Colonel Muñoz has behaved like a gentleman."

Marta and her mother continued on their adventure without incident. The change made itself felt in the Calle de Verdi; it took their minds several days to adapt to it.

"You've come out the losers," Mosén Francisco said, half serious, half coy.

Rosita already had noticed that Mosén Francisco sometimes exaggerated his humility. "You're quite a flirt, aren't you, Father?"

"What? Well, maybe... But Rosita, for God's sake, don't call me Father."

The vicar felt at home in the house; he had been reprieved from the Campistol sisters' mirrors. He had agreed to be Marta's replacement in helping Manolín with his studies, and the boy returned the favor by introducing him to the subtle world of shadow figures. Stupid Mosén Francisco... He would twist his fingers every which way but never manage to make even the simplest silhouette, that of a rabbit. Manolín, on the other hand, could throw on the wall every kind of militiaman and every kind of priest with startling realism. Ezequiel's old art, his talent for caricature, had enabled him to teach Manolín to be a master. On the day Marta left, they put on a brilliant show with four hands to help them forget their loss. Ezequiel and Manolín created splendid original figures on the wall by synchronizing their twenty figures. Among them a bishop with miter and crosier and a Christ dragging his cross were outstandingly good.

Ezequiel let himself be won over easily to the priest, especially because they enjoyed arguing. In the course of their dialogue, each of them unconsciously distorted his own personality. Mosén Francisco, actually a realist, pretended to believe that life was a tissue of miracles. "It's all a question of faith. Wasn't Moses able to cross the Red Sea? Well, then..."

Ezequiel, who believed in his heart only what could not be proved, pretended to have a logical, even a petty mind. "Don't talk to me about Moses, my dear friend, forget the miracles. We're dealing now with the study of physics and chemistry. See?"

Ezequiel gratified Mosén Francisco by bringing him newspapers and news from outside. The vicar's interest had been awakened and he knew that Ezequiel with an establishment so near Police Headquarters could easily arrange to keep him abreast of the progress of the war and the events in the city.

Indeed Ezequiel often chanced to meet police agents who were friends of his in the cafés near the Photomaton, and he seldom failed to pump them. Mosén Francisco learned through this channel that the Nationalist advance toward Madrid was going forward inexorably and that an organizing junta had just been formed in Valencia to pay homage to Blasco Ibáñez on the coming anniversary of the writer's death.

Mosén Francisco was pained at his own genuine interest in the progress of the war. Hadn't the essence of war been expressed in the saying that it depended upon loving these and hating those? No, he was not made to rejoice upon hearing: "We've caused the fall of six hundred enemies." The fall! What an offhand way to state matters, with what coldness catastrophes are given names!

His conscience remained sharp, lacerating. Even more lacerating was the information that the Bishop of Gerona, the man who had ordained him, who had conferred on him the powers of a priest, had been shot in the cemetery of his city. To add to that, Rosita came home from the outside one day quite upset. As she was returning from a furniture store she had met a moving line of people in front of the Clinic Hospital and had witnessed how they had searched for some lost relative, hiding their pain and looking at the bodies one by one. "Every day a lot of people go through the hospital. It's awful."

Ezequiel confirmed his wife's statement. He had learned of the lines through two photographers, acquaintances of his, whose task it was to photograph the bodies for identification. "I give you my word," Ezequiel told Mosén Francisco, "that those photographs have revealed something extraordinary, something you can't logically ignore. Almost every day they show certain bodies, male only, with an identical hole in them, always in the same place, the palm of the right hand. The doctors in the hospital noticed it and they finally found out what happened. The bodies are those of priests who raised their right hands to bless the militiamen at the moment they were shot. There's always a bullet hole running transversely as the hand was fully opened."

Mosén Francisco caught his breath. He stared at Ezequiel, then at Rosita, and finally could not help uttering a sort of howl. The remarkable evidence offered by the priests of the Barcelona diocese proved to him that life was a succession of miracles. He wept a long time, to Manolín's puzzlement, and felt overwhelmed by the desire to be a good man.

That night he slept poorly. His bed was soft and comfortable, but it seemed to him a bed of nails. He asked himself again why he had run away from Gerona, why he had not gone out into the street and cried out to all the world: "I'm a priest, too, and I beg you to kill me and put a hole through my right hand."

His shame soon was translated into action. On the following day he told Ezequiel and Rosita that he could not stand to be confined any longer. "Help me to find the way to perform my offices, to hear people's confessions and to give them Communion. I don't know how! I suppose in this section there must be..."

They interrupted him. Ezequiel frowned, but Rosita was positive in her answer. "I understand that there are many priests who hear confessions in peasant dress... On the subway platforms, at the ends of the lines in front of some movie houses. A neighbor told me..."

"Let me get this straight. What did you say, Rosita? Explain to me... How do people know the man on the platform is a priest and that he's hearing confessions?"

"Because they've been tipped off by him. 'I'll be reading the paper.' 'I'll be playing with my lighter.' Something like that..."

Mosén Francisco's face lighted up. "Rosita, for the love of God... Would you find people to come to me? If only I could..."

Ezequiel interrupted him. He would not want the priest to die of nostalgia for the past, and besides Rosita was obviously on his side. "Don't worry about that, Father. You'll have customers."

The rest was easy. All that was needed was to select the right spot and have Rosita pass the word along through the neighborhood.

That night Ezequiel brought home a plan of the city and spread it out on the dining room table. Manolín instantly said, "*El Tibidabo!*"

"That won't do, my friend," Ezequiel replied. "Less smoke."

After a long search, they considered it wise to choose a place as far away from the Calle de Verdi as possible, and as near as possible to the Parque de la Ciudadela, alongside the Estación de Francia.

"I could sit down on a bench and be reading *El Diluvio* with a package of cigarettes beside me, at my left."

"L," said Ezequiel marking a spot with a red pencil. "Near the Sirens' Fountain."

The vicar rubbed his chin. "What about my disguise?"

Rosita intervened. "I think the way you're dressed now, in a blue coverall."

"Perhaps you're right."

Ezequiel flung his arms backward, as if doing exercises. "We're missing something," he muttered. "I know! Some letters on the back, as if you were employed by some business firm, or some trademark for..."

"Uralita, S.A.," Manolín cried triumphantly.

To the boy's astonishment, his suggestion was adopted unanimously.

Uralita, S.A.... *El Diluvio,* a package of cigarettes, the Sirens' Fountain... Rosita made the rounds of her neighbors and was astonished at the great number of them who proved trustworthy. "Since there are so many of us, why do they keep us down like this?"

The good news traveled as fast as bad news, and Mosén Francisco began to enjoy himself and to suffer in the Parque de la Ciudadela, next to the Estación de Francia.

It seemed strange to him to be sitting there, reading and rereading the newspaper a hundred times without taking in any of its contents. The grains of sand grew familiar to him, and perhaps some birds that sometimes looked at him as if wishing to go to confession, too. Each time someone approached him from the avenues around him, his heart gave a leap. "This is it..." In spite of himself, he would stiffen. But no. It would turn out to be some distracted soul unaware, unable to discern that pardon for his sins was concealed under Uralita, S.A., embroidered in red.

Presently things began to pick up and people who trembled even more than he began to come assiduously. People who sat down beside him, careful not to crush the package of cigarettes, carrying a book, or a basket, or breadcrumbs for the birds.

"Bless me, Father, for I have sinned..."

"In the name of the Father, the Son, and the Holy Spirit. Amen."

A rosary of sins. Hatred and lust, slander and envy, and family quarrels. Avarice and forgetfulness of God. "I have sinned, Father. I'm a sinner."

"I, too, am a sinner. Depart in peace! May Christ go with you."

The penitent, whether man or woman, would wait a moment, staring at his *espadrilles*, then suddenly rise and leave with a quick look to right and left, feeling himself accompanied by Christ and that priest in the blue coverall who had stared with curious intentness at the palm of his right hand as he spoke the "*Ego te absolvo.*"

There were fruitful mornings and sterile mornings. One day another priest sat down beside him; one day a man with a brace of big pistols. Mosén Francisco's heart suddenly had stopped at the sight of them. Could it be a trap? "Bless me, Father, for I have sinned." No, it was not a trap. Another day Manolín came to him. The boy found the situation droll, and at the end of his recital of trumped-up sins, he whispered in the priest's ear, "No lentils today."

At the end of the time agreed upon, the vicar generally would rise, fold his newspaper, and walk back to the Calle de Verdi. He would cross the entire city to exercise his muscles. As he passed the bars and the miserable taverns, he would be reminded of a blond woman, of no particular age who had said to him: "You're stingy. Why don't you ask me to have something?"

He would stop along the way and muse and look around him. He always walked through the Rambla de Cataluña where one of the soft-drink stands was acquiring the name of Radio Seville because groups of persons met there daily to comment on Queipo de Llano's broadcasts while pretending to discuss football. "The munitions works in Toledo is going full blast again." "When we get to Madrid and open up Prieto's belly we'll have enough fat from it for several generations." "The vanguard of our troops has reached Carabanchel Alto."

Thanks to his wanderings, Mosén Francisco learned that there were guerrilla fighters in the Montseny and that the prisoners on the *Uruguay* had been transferred to the Cárcel Modelo. He was witness to some lugubrious funerals: a driver in the coachbox, an unpainted wooden chest, no cortège and no attendant. He always carried with him a copper for the Red Relief and a bit of tobacco for the old men he would meet on his way, along the sidewalks or in the subway.

"What are you doing to win the war?"

"The nights are cold on the firing line."

One morning the vicar remembered Ana María. He called her on the telephone and made an appointment for the Parque de la Ciudadela. Ana María appeared on time the following day, wearing some earrings like Pilar's. She sat down beside the vicar, not to make her confession, but to ask about Ignacio. Ah, yes, Ana María's sin was to be in love in spite of the passage of time. In love with a boy who lived in a constant state of unease. Mosén Francisco realized that Ana María did not know of Marta's existence, but he said nothing, not knowing whether he was doing right or wrong. They laughed together a good deal, looking like sweethearts. And sunset overtook them there, and later the closing hour of the park. The custodian ordered them out. It was an immense park, somewhat neglected, and the elephant that Santi had wanted to kill was king of it.

TWENTY-ONE

THE "Battle of Madrid" was about to begin. Both the radio and the newspaper headlines, as well as the people of both zones, judged that it would be decisive. Perhaps the whole future of the war was hanging on its outcome. Everyone was preparing for it in his fashion. In Pamplona, Don Anselmo Ichaso had built a symbolic station for his electric line which said "Madrid," and he planned a celebration in his house for the day when the tiny trains would line up triumphantly before the station. In San Sebastián, Warning Voice was planning to open a can of caviar which he had acquired on his last trip to Biarritz and share it with Javier Ichaso, to whom he was still giving lessons in *savoir faire.* In Madrid, Santiago Alvear, José's father was running from one end of the city to the other, shouting, "They shall not pass!" And the Russian writer Ilya Ehrenburg, who was constantly entering and leaving Red Spain, was declaring to his readers: "In spite of the bustle and the lights in the cafés, weariness can be read in the faces of the Spaniards."

As on the eve of elections in former times, the forces of the opposing sides seemed to pause for breath before renewing the struggle. Every Mateo Santos, every Núñez Maza, every Ichaso, that is to say every Nationalist in both zones, was listening to his heartbeat. Every Durruti, every Gorki and Paz with a clipped head, that is, every Red in both zones, also was taking his pulse. The immense ditch that yawned between the two Spains would soon be filled with heroism, generosity, and dead men.

Confidence reigned among the Nationalist forces. Yagüe's column had been reaping a harvest of uninterrupted successes ever since the conquest of Badajoz. Nothing could stop them, and they reached Toledo and Maqueda along the route once taken by Muza the Moor and the Almoravide sect in the eleventh century. They had bypassed those cities and now were standing at the gates of Madrid. They had Madrid within hand's reach, subjected to constant bombings from the air. General Mola was the leading spokesman for the optimists. From the beginning of the campaign, he had been promising, "I'll soon be drinking coffee in Madrid." Some waiters in the Café Molinero had responded wryly by reserving a table marked "General Mola" which could not be touched and had been waiting for the General since July. In those final days of October, Mola had repeated his challenge over the radio and had announced further that to the four columns converging on the city a "fifth column" could be added, the "fifth column" that was composed of numberless "patriots" who were sabotaging the efforts of the defenders from inside Madrid and lending aid to the "liberating troops." Confidence was so high that the foreign journalists invited there for the event were surprised at it, for from the beginning of the war they had been hearing that prudence was the main characteristic of the Nationalist high command. This time it was not. Everything was ready for a breakthrough into the capital and for the immediate and inevitable *coup de grâce.* Lines of supply trucks approached as near the city as they could and were parked on the highways and roads. Some of the trucks were already proclaiming, "Plaza Tetuán, Madrid," "Glorieta de Bilbao, Madrid." Thousands of Nationalist flags quickly were hung out on the balconies, and thousands of portraits of General Franco were ready to preside over every single building in the capital. Preparations were being made for electric current and water supply. Oh, the lip smears on the glasses! And the bands of the various units were tootling happy notes. That confidence was shared by the troops, of course. The Moors would stare at their own indigenous idol, Colonel Mizzian, with an almost superstitious respect. The Legionnaires were galvanized as they listened to the exhortations of their amputee general, Millán Astray, who always carried with him a small book of meditations entitled *Palabras de aliento,* by the Jesuit father Daniel Considine, as well as his side-tilted cap. In addition to their own anthems, the Falangists were singing:

"I have a pain I don't know where
Born of I don't know what
I'll get over it I don't know when
If I'm treated by I don't know whom."

For their part, the Requetés would turn to face Navarre and sing:

"Don't weep, Mother
Because I'm bearing arms.
The body counts for nothing
Only the soul is of value."

The uniforms were as variegated as in a gigantic opera, and many soldiers of the Regular Army carried something edible inside their helmets, particularly tins of preserves, to hand the people in Madrid. Yes, there was Madrid, visible to the naked eye. The news of a victory was being awaited with satisfaction in Rome, in Berlin, in Lisbon, and in Tokyo.

The state of the morale on the Red side was more varied. The professional soldiers, Rojo and Mangada among them, had confidence in their ability to contain the attackers, for the good reason that the men facing them had been fighting without rest since Extremadura. They were bound to be exhausted! And the effective forces on the other side could not add up to more than five thousand men according to the reports of their own espionage service, which was in fact headed by the so-called Dionisio, and also according to the reports of deserters from the Nationalist zone. Five thousand tired men to occupy a capital city with a million-odd inhabitants!

The defense of the city was organized, and it called upon all the resources of intelligence and instinct. Largo Caballero announced to the citizens and the combatants that, thanks to foreign aid, now beginning to be effective, they had at last mechanized armaments that would be adequate for the battle. "We have airplanes, we have tanks, we have the big guns! We can concentrate fifty thousand volunteers in Madrid! Fight! Stand fast, you heroic people of Madrid! Fascism shall not pass!"

In addition, a junta for the defense of the capital was appointed, presided over by General Miaja. With him were Rojo, Pozas, Asensio, and Masquelet, the last an expert on fortification, plus the Russian Ambassador, Rosenberg. The Parties and the Syndicates had set up recruiting stations in the streets and quarters of the city to issue arms and form units as best they could. Troops in active service from the vicinity, from Somosierra, from Cuenca and other cities, left their posts and headed for the capital. Battalions of all kinds were put together hastily: a battalion of barbers, of store clerks, of the cigarette girls of Madrid! Lister and his men arrived—Lister, the Communist singer trained in Moscow—and El Campesino came with his peasants recruited from the Extremaduran fields. El Campesino was a man of the soil who had nicknamed his machine gun a "donkey belly-buster." The Spartacus unit arrived from Andalusia and sternly fell in with the Fifth Regiment, which represented orthodox Marxism. Anyone with a steady pulse was expected to fight to the death; anyone lacking that was to man the fortifications. This dictum was issued by the CNT, whose leaders, Mora, Cipriano Mera, and Del Val could boast of an admirable feeling for command. From morning to night hands that gripped all kinds of utensils dug trenches, trenches again, all around the city, built parapets of sun-dried brick, of sacks, and even of bundles of unsold newspapers, then emplaced weapons upon them and at every loophole. The work recalled the hammerlike rhythms of the Gerona choral society multiplied to infinity.

To top it all, the propaganda services and the intuitions of the people created and circulated rumors with scintillating efficiency. First the press and radio announced that the "Nationalist officials" had received from France a list of a hundred thousand workers to be shot as prizes of war. Next that Franco was going to use some special projectiles he had available to send over some sort of soporific that would put the people to sleep and leave them defenseless. Mola's phrase concerning the "5th Column" also begot hatred. The moderate leaders cried out against the General. "He must be a villain! What's going to stop the hotheads now?" The hotheads were Lister and El Campesino, the countless Anarchists who had come out of the fields and the mountains, and the people already willing to die. A plan to execute the five thousand prisoners in the Cárcel Modelo was unrealized as yet. People's Tribunals were set up as substitutes for the autonomous committees. They tried and sentenced individuals at the rate of twenty per hour. The frenzy was augmented by air raids dropping bombs that became known as "bonbons." One of them fell on the Atocha subway station and turned it into a slaughterhouse.

The government—the ministries and their subsidiaries—was afraid that if it were to move away from Madrid to Valencia it would weaken the morale of the defenders. But the leaders judged that there was nothing else they could do, and Largo Caballero, between the Devil and the deep sea, ordered the transfer. Howls rose from the militiamen, as was to be expected. "Traitors! Cowards! Running away from the fire! They're yellowbellies." They tried to block the removal. The cars leaving for the rear in a procession had to force their way through brandished fists and insults. On the outskirts of Madrid, in the Venta del Espíritu Santo, a group of Anarchist guards, with José Alvear's father among them, halted five ministers and the mayor of the city, Pedro Rico, determined to "deal out" a deserter's justice to them. Del Val, their leader, managed to prevent that by a telephoned order. But the people would not forgive, and that night of cowardly flight was doubly christened "the night of fear" and the "night of gasoline."

The will to stand fast soon was reinforced by an almost magical apparition: the first units of the International Brigades issuing from Albacete. They were preceded by majestic Russian armored cars that took possession of the Madrid streets like circus wagons from some nameless carnival. The guns on their turrets were fingers, accusing, anathema pointing at Mizzian's Moors and the Legionnaires under Yagüe and Millán Astray. They were defying Queipo de Llano, Mateo, and José Luis Martínez de Soria. A momentary silence fell over the city. What was going on? "International war." Some people felt almost flattered, and a large number of dogs, including Axelrod's, got so excited they sounded like Puppy, the boy from Pina. The silence held until suddenly the marching feet of the "Volunteers for Freedom" began to resound. Most of them were shod in hobnailed boots. They were men like towers; they all looked like towers, and it would have been hard to find North Pole among them, easy to spot the Negus. They were wearing Alpine helmets and there were many white kidskin jackets in their impressive ranks. Martial men, veterans, rifles sloped, they knew how to breathe! Their eyes could not be seen, but their expressions could. How they looked but not what they were thinking. Thinking? "Actually everything is born in the brain, isn't it?" Cosme Vila believed so, Mosén Francisco did not. Dr. Relken and Fanny had not settled the question yet in spite of their restless, ever-changing lives.

"They're Russians! They're Russians!" The people were whispering that all those men were Russians, including the idealistic Swede and a platoon of Brazilians who filed past as though they were on the runway of a variety show. The *madrileños* did not know the first thing about those men, where they came from or why they had come. What were their wives like, if they had wives? And they themselves? Had they been children once? How could it be possible that they had left far-off countries to march now in Madrid, drinking in the applause and the balconies? Did they know that Spain paid hunger wages? How could they show their gratitude? With a gentle kiss on their kidskin jackets? "*¡Salud! ¡Salud!*" "What's your name?" André Marty had sent those first battalions into combat from Albacete. They were nicknamed Garibaldi, Dimitroff, and Paris Commune. Who was Garibaldi? What had happened in the Paris Commune? The Soviet General Kleber, a Hungarian Jew who might have played a part in the murder of the Czar's family, was in command of the battalions. Their political leader was the Italian Nicoletti. Almost as soon as he reached the trenches, he stared toward Toledo, turned to look at Madrid, and declared: "To take this city they would need sixty thousand men, unless they can raze it from the air."

The Air Force… In fulfillment of Largo Caballero's promise of the 1st of November, bright new government aircraft materialized in the sky over Madrid. Their makes were unfamiliar: the S-B2 bomber, called "Katushka," the so-called "Chatos," the "Moscas," the "Rasante" and "Natasha" biplanes, and so on. And in particular the very swift "Ratas" fighters with scarlet wings, tracing messages of hope in the blue. "They're ours! They're ours!" The aircraft were accusing fingers, too, pointing at the mere three thousand, five hundred tired men who had arrived before Madrid along the route of the Moor Muza and the Almoravides.

The defensive fervor that spread like blue over the sea fostered the illusion that the garrison was unconquerable. "If I'm giving it all I've got, if I abstain even from eating, if I've gone three days without sleeping and almost without seeing my children, if I'm a poor devil, born a wage slave, or a plumber, or a night watchman, if I'm one of thousands and thousands all like me, and if we have all earned our bread by the sweat of our brow, and are fortifying Madrid now, how can Fascism win? How can we all be wiped out?"

"Fascism can't hurt you, stupid," someone replied. "Fascism is a name. It's got no trigger, no finger to fire with. The ones who'll wipe us out, if we waste our time talking, will be Franco and his followers. They'll be Hitler and Mussolini combined and the grand whore who bore them."

During those critical hours, the leaders of the CNT were like tempered steel, with a mettle that led José Antonio to exclaim one day: "Oh, what a pity those men don't understand us!" How proud of them El Responsable would have been! They ran their eyes over the belt of defenses and said: "It's not enough. There are still breaches in it. We need still heavier forces."

Rosenberg, the Russian Ambassador, on the other hand, said to General Miaja, "I'm pleased with it at last. Madrid is in the same situation as Petrograd in 1918. They'll stand fast if there's discipline."

But the Anarchists knew Rosenberg only through seeing his photographs in the press. Consequently, their three commanding officers, Mora, Cipriano Mera, and Del Val, had made up their minds not to yield the preponderant ascendency the CNT again had deservedly won by offering more volunteers for certain death than any other group. "Miaja, Kleber, Lister, El Campesino! All well and good! But we need our own leader here, the one man who will never betray us. We need Durruti."

"We want Durruti! We want Durruti!" They acclaimed their chief with a single voice that rang hoarsely in the ears of the Russians in the Bristol Hotel who bore in mind Lenin's words: "Many things are still left in the world that must be destroyed by steel and fire if we want the working classes to be free."

Federica Montseny, the Anarchist deputy from Catalonia who had recently been appointed Minister of Health—"Madame Minister" as the page boys called her, was the messenger sent flying to the Aragón front to persuade Durruti. "Durruti... Madrid needs you."

The man who hated homosexuals and diseased prostitutes and who longed to invade Portugal, straightened himself and muttered: "The past doesn't count!" He touched his cap with the patent-leather visor and gave the order to move to Madrid, in the opposite direction to the move made by the government cars.

He brought four thousand men in trucks that went like bullets or else limped like El Cojo. They hurtled toward Madrid along the highway that the French troops had christened the "Boulevard of Catalonia."

"They shall not pass!"

With Durruti went Rainbow, Captain Culebra with his little wooden box covered with a linen cloth, José Alvear with his derby hat, many other well-known Anarchists, and of course Dr. Rosselló and his assistants. The surgeon had been promised the Ritz Hotel by Federica Montseny, to be equipped as an emergency hospital, together with a permit that would enable him to set up his installations to the number needed in stores and other establishments in Madrid.

With Durruti's entry into Madrid, the enthusiasm of the defenders overflowed. For a moment the Internationals seemed to shrink before that human gorilla, whose name, Buenaventura, seemed to presage the best.

"Where is there the most danger?" Durruti asked.

General Miaja replied, "In University City."

"That's what I want," Durruti declared.

How curious that Durruti should want to fight in University City! Would the textbooks laugh at him? Would he be felled by a volume of the encyclopedia? "On to University City!" The Anarchist leader thrust his cap into that sector, near Lister, El Campesino, General Lucasz, and General Kleber, who had sent him a greeting signed with the single initial K from his headquarters in the College of Philosophy and Liberal Arts.

Every chessman was in his place now. Everyone had been assigned to his post, on both sides of the ditch. The Red fighters were short of tobacco, and the Nationalist soldiers were short of cigarette papers. On the one side there were priests and emblems that said: "Stop, bullet!" On the other was Cerillita carrying around a Chalice as a shaving mug. What about General Mola? General Mola considered General Miaja a mediocre commander and placed his trust in his "5th Column." General Miaja considered Franco a first-class strategist and trusted in the numerical superiority of his forces. Fifty thousand militiamen. Obviously the Nationalists lacked the sixty thousand Nicoletti had mentioned and, despite the advice of the Germans, they were not yet ready to raze the city.

What would actually happen was the unknown factor. War went by plan, but it moved mysteriously, too. José Alvear burst into the Café Molinero and undertook to have his coffee at the table reserved for General Mola. His father, disgusted because he had not killed the five cabinet ministers, or at least the mayor, Pedro Rico, had left the Venta del Espiritu Santo and gone home to sleep. A question was hovering in the air over Tokyo, Moscow, London, Prague… Anyone who looked carefully at the map of Europe, particularly at the partitioning and location of its moral and intellectual provinces, would understand that every battle in that war was certain to have wide repercussions in the future.

Yes, war was a kind of alchemy… Soon there would be ample proof of that. At the very moment that a bullet passed through both Durruti's lungs, the Republic of El Salvador was announcing the first official recognition of the Franco government. And Manolín in the Calle de Verdi was asking Mosén Francisco, "Well, how many customers did you have today?"

In the hours preceding the battle, a host of eyes was raised to Heaven, beseeching help. Among them were the round black eyes of Carmen Elgazu. "Protect ours," she prayed, unable to forget that Matías Alvear had been born in that city where so many men were about to die. Ezequiel, in Barcelona, was noticing the progressive tremor of the militiamen's heads as they sat on the stools of the Photomaton. He made one of his lapidary divinations to Rosita: "Call me a cheap prophet if you will, but I promise you that within a week Franco will be dancing a schottische in the Puerta del Sol."

General Varela was to execute the orders issued by Franco's general staff. As usual, he was dressed in a chamois hunting jacket and wearing white gloves, but a shadow of worry was darkening his brow. Everything was ready. Combat vehicles, armored trucks, mortars, superb cavalry squadrons under General Monasterio, aircraft, and high morale. Certainly that! The lofty buildings in Madrid—the Telephone Building, the Post Office, the Royal Palace—attracted the eyes of the soldiers, particularly the *madrileños* in the ranks and those who had some beloved person or object in Madrid. Many others not acquainted with the capital of Spain were on pins and needles with curiosity. Accordingly it was a privilege, though a risky one, to stand guard on a hilltop overlooking the city, a still greater privilege to be equipped with binoculars. After some aerial acrobatics, the Red air force had released some leaflets as a reminder that that particular day marked the nineteenth anniversary of the Russian Revolution.

Conversation was spasmodic. "How far is it from here to the Puerta del Sol?"

"As the crow flies?"

"Yes."

"Well, say half an hour."

"What?"

Breathing would quicken and the mind would spring the question, "When are we going to attack, General?"

Immediately. At dawn of the 6th of November. During the days just before that, the Nationalists had been hunting feverishly for strategically located lookout posts, and the usual involved maneuvers were carried out, maneuvers so alike and so often repeated that they came to be called "blisters," "The Nationalist High Command's blisters." During one of those blisters, near Torreldones, the Red leader Domingo wrapped himself in the tricolor flag and put a bullet through his brain.

Captain Culebra had noticed that his domesticated creature would grow inexplicably excited in the hours immediately before a battle. "I honestly don't get it." That day was an exception, however. The creature was lethargic. It did not want to drink its milk or eat its cheese, and its master and José Alvear, eternally together, stared at each other, puzzled by the anomaly.

"Fire!"

General Varela shouted the order and the spigots of flak and lead were turned on. Aerial bombs and thousands of projectiles fell upon Madrid, sowing death. The slaughter was mindless. Buildings were destroyed—"Be careful, that's where my sweetheart lives!" Monuments were decapitated, pipes burst, and the intimate cables carrying light to homes hung down shattered like the remnants of spiderwebs. Every siren on earth was proclaiming the calamity and no human voice could be heard amid the clamor. The men shot and kept shooting and were shattered like the electric cables. And the parapets, and the trenches, and the hundreds of machine guns? What about General Kleber?

"Be careful, that's the Prado Museum over there!"

"Watch out, that's where I got my high school diploma!"

"Be careful, artillery, I used to love those trees..."

A mortar shell set fire to the monastery of the Trinity fathers. Two mules struck in the belly ran a short distance, dragging their entrails. The *madrileños* took shelter in the subway stations, especially the Cuatro Caminos, Tribunal, Progreso, Antón Martín, and Atocha. The underground platforms became waiting rooms for whatever fate might ordain. The *madrileños* who had not made the shelters in time were picked up by the garbage trucks and hauled off to the morgue.

"We will stand fast!"

Luis Companys, president of the Provincial Government of Cataluña, seemed to hear this shout, for he ordered a pilot sent from Barcelona to drop a symbolic crown of laurel on the besieged city.

When the Nationalist observers judged that the preliminary barrage had done its work, General Varela ordered: "Forward!"

Then the unforeseen played its role. The reply of the defenders was so spirited and punishing that the attackers were stopped in their tracks. "They shall not pass!" The spigots of shell and lead now pouring in the opposite direction, spilled over the Nationalists. The artillery was firing from the immediate vicinity of the Royal Palace; some big guns had been mounted on the top floors of buildings. A chain of machine-gun mouths gleamed on rooftops. The planes of "The Glorious" were crisscrossing the sky, determined to be its master. "They shall not pass!" The entire belt surrounding Madrid spoke with a single voice. The attackers kept shouting: "Forward, it's already ours!" It was not true. Behind every tree, every window, every sandbag, a man with a will was hiding. The moment a position was left unmanned, fresh replacements seemed to sprout from the earth. In certain sectors, militiamen with useless weapons were waiting eagerly for a comrade to fall and leave them a rifle. Women from all the Syndicates were helping as porters, bringing up ammunition and canteens, doing liaison work, and spurring on the men, who seemed incandescent as they offered up their exposed chests and their lives, while at their backs distant records were playing "To the Barricades" and the "Internationale."

General Varela realized immediately that a change in the enemy had taken place. Reports arriving at his command post acknowledged that the defenders had put together an expert army, commanded by intrepid leaders who had at their disposal matériel of excellent quality. General Monasterio, who was using his cavalry squadrons to reconnoiter in search of an opening breach, was concise: "Largo Caballero was not lying. A large portion of the matériel they're using is first-class, and the International Brigades have turned the tide of battle. The enemy we're having to deal with right now bears little resemblance to the guerrilla gang we've known until today."

International Brigades! They provided grounds for worry. Those men whom Fanny and Julio had watched standing in line at the recruiting stations in Paris. General Lucasz, with his political commissar Vittorio, General Kleber with his commissar, Luigi Longo, the Garibaldi, Dimitroff, and Paris Commune Battalions, and many other battalions. "Volunteers for Freedom." A poetic aura still surrounded their intervention. As in Aragón, each man's way of handling himself was a lesson to raw militiamen. They knew how to dodge the enemy fire, their gun-butts fitted onto their shoulders like vacuum cups. They were fighting for so many different things! North Pole was fighting there. And no one was asking him about Sweden or why he had come. His hair was white, his shots were deadly. A linotypist by trade, he was now defending the School of Philosophy and Liberal Arts. The Negus was there, too. He was not thinking about his Jewish race or of Germany, the country of his origin. He was shooting. He was defending Spain, the world; and according to Julio's theory, he was avenging himself for some intimate, personal wrong; he was avenging himself like José Alvear, for the many bourgeois women he had loved in vain, owing to his ugliness and his scanty education. The Spanish Communist leaders were there, too—Jesús Hernández, Díaz, Mije, Uribe...

The Nationalist forces were unable to rally after their surprise. Again and again the high command urged General Varela to charge, to advance, but the infantry hesitated. Especially the Moors. The Moors, excellent at open-field maneuvering on a broad terrain, were crying brokenheartedly over that kind of suburban warfare, hand-to-hand fighting, step-by-step fighting. In addition, they were terrified of both air forces, for "if the body is left maimed and dirty at death, it won't be admitted into the Kingdom of Allah." The Legionnaires were not acting with their customary skill either. They were incomparable in bayonet attack and throwing hand grenades, but when they saw the armored trucks, they checked and stared wildly at their officers. "Forward! Advance!" But the Reds were shouting, "They shall not pass!" And the Falangists and the Requetés were taken aback.

Those were November days, frosty days. Madrid had become a cemetery, a junk pile. The sun came up with the dawn. An irresolute eye that hardly dared to look at the worm-eaten belly of the city. The sun followed its course, loving the children, the children hidden in the Cuatro Caminos, Tribunal, and Atocha subway stations. At dusk it said a livid farewell. An eye bloodshot from weeping for the deaths of the day. When the dead were many, it would stay hidden next day in its unknown lair, and send an icy wind or gray clouds that muffled sound. Clouds that wept for it, a weeping like the *sirimiri* of the Cantabrian coast which Carmen Elgazu recalled with so much nostalgia.

In Madrid changes were occurring like volcanic eruptions. Humble people in the shadow of General Miaja turned heroes and wore stars in their crowns. A bellboy from the Palace Hotel proved so adept at maneuvering the recon cars so as to confront the enemy that he was promoted to lieutenant. The wife of a migrant worker could drive a car with armor plate so skillfully that she was made a sergeant. Four guerrilla fighters under El Campesino, nicknamed Pancho Villa, Sopaenvino, Salsipuedes, and Trimotor, were named captains. There could be no doubt that they were putting up a stubborn resistance. In the rear of the fighting men, in the Talavera sector, the Red pilots sent up long-burning parachute flares that remained aloft to light up their objectives.

General Mola came down from the Northern front and arrived at the theater of war. He came down with no firsthand experience of the potency of the International Brigades. A few hours after his arrival, he ordered a renewed all-out attack with two immediate objectives: first, the occupation of the Casa de Campo; second, the crossing of the Manzanares River.

General Mola's orders were carried out. A part of the wall of the Casa de Campo was destroyed at the cost of much bloodshed, and the Legionnaires and the Spanish Regulars began to fan out among the oak trees around that muddy spot, a spot which, from the air, lent a singular effect of antiquity to the landscape. The Manzanares was crossed, and the Parque de la Moncloa was entered, and University City, too, where two hundred Red machine guns kept firing without a pause. The Palacete de la Moncloa, the French Artists' Residence, the Rubio Hospital, María Cristina's Retreat, and the Clinic Hospital were all occupied. Five thousand prisoners in the Cárcel Modelo were suffering tortures as they watched "their own" force their way to a point near the prison, then fail to reach them.

Mola's work was all in vain. The attacking forces were weak, and there was no possibility of relieving them as long as André Marty kept sending in more and more battalions of Freedom Volunteers from Albacete. They kept bottling up the vulnerable flanks with a precision that was not without beauty.

"The attack must go forward."

Aleramo Berti, the Italian Fascist delegate, was watching the development of operations, and without ceasing to stuff his mouth with fruit drops that had Queipo de Llano's picture on their wrappings, he gave it as his opinion that a stalemate had been reached and that the sensible thing to do would be to withdraw and entrench. Schubert, the German Nazi, nearsighted and shrunken, held that war was war and Madrid must be razed. On the Red side, General Kleber and General Lucasz were at a loss to explain the suicidal stubbornness of the enemy. Their inferiority was manifest. And Lister kept muttering rapidly: "We'll crack them wide open here."

THE chips were down. Nicoletti had estimated correctly that sixty thousand men would be needed to smash the defense of the city. Ezequiel, on the other hand, had been a poor prophet. Carmen Elgazu's prayers got lost on their way to Heaven. For the first time since the 18th of July, the Nationalists had failed, a failure their commanding officers could feel in their very flesh, for Castejón had been wounded, as had the Moorish commandant, Mizzian, and even General Varela had suffered a long, deep graze from three shell fragments.

"Our forces have carried out an encircling movement and have entrenched on the conquered lines."

Don Anselmo Ichaso reacted violently. He canceled his celebration at once, took down the sign on the "Madrid" station he had prepared, and wrote to Warning Voice: "The Information Service has been remiss." Warning Voice, for his part, relinquished his caviar, and his servant Jesusha spent her afternoons sniveling in the Good Shepherd. The disenchantment of the Nationalist home front was so excessive that the foreign journalists waylaid Núñez Maza and asked him: "Does it make sense for you people to get discouraged so easily, to go to pieces this way?" "Do you think this zone could hold out under adversity the way the Red zone has held out?"

The Red zone… In the Red zone, the crowds thronged the streets, hailing General Miaja, Moscow, the CNT, anything revolutionary, as in a sense it behooved them to…

"Madrid, the tomb of Fascism! Invincible Madrid! They shall not pass! Victory is at hand!"

El Cojo believed that victory was in sight, and so did Teo. Congratulations and promotions galore. "*¡Viva Largo Caballero!* Hurray for the men from Hungary, from Czechoslovakia and Paraguay!" Congratulations to the battalion of "The Non-Runners" made up of old and crippled men. Congratulations to the two Swiss nurses, Germaine and Thérèse, whose skill and unselfishness had saved the lives of many wounded men, an to the porters who climbed up on the rooftops to harry the sharpshooters. Congratulations to Dr. Rosselló! Dr. Rosselló had taken over the Ritz Hotel, installed an operating room in the basement, and converted the building into a model hospital. Congratulations to La Pasionaria and Margarita Nelken, who had gone through the lines again and again making speeches, spurring on the militiamen. A state of cordiality was achieved that seemed to promise mutual understanding. El Campesino, communist Hercules, impervious to bullets, said of the Anarchists: "They're not as stupid as I thought they were." Not to be outdone, the Anarchists called General Kleber "a gutty character." José Alvear was busily painting the initials of the FAI on the sidewalks in enormous letters even as his father was dying, riddled with bullets and being congratulated posthumously by the two waiters who threw him into a common grave.

Indeed the only man not prodigal with his praise was the Russian Ambassador, Rosenberg. After seeing how operations had developed, Rosenberg realized that the attack had been launched so poorly that no great hazard had been involved in containing it. "It was like a game, never understand the Spaniards."

He made a trip to Valencia, where he burst into the office of the resident of the government with an imposing escort of military technicians. As he was talking to Largo Caballero, he said: "Russia will help… Russia will give increasing aid. But the Army must be unified quickly and trustworthy political commissars must be appointed. Furthermore, the Anarchists and the POUM must be done away with little by little."

Largo Caballero eyed the ambassador firmly and answered: "Don't forget that we're not in Russia, we're in Spain. Spain is a small country, but a proud one, and her first need is to have confidence in her ambassadors."

THE front was stabilized. Madrid was not conquered. General Mola was not going to have coffee in the Molinero, and all the statues in Madrid were wearing amusing paper helmets. On both sides, from north to south, from east to west, everyone was certain that the war was going to be a long one.

TWENTY-TWO

THE frost and cold of November had turned into rain. God made the rain, and the rain was falling gently over Bilbao, gray over Gerona, yellow over the open country of Castile and the untilled fields of Teruel. It was raining even over the sea. Why should it be raining over the sea? Countless Carmen Elgazus were dreading the approach of winter. The men were immersed in the war. In summer the war had been like the unfolding of a fan, the triumph of the little clear creeks; but not so in winter... The daughter of the proprietor of the Crocodile was the only person who could keep on waving the sign that said "Thanks" there in the madhouse where she was shut up.

A long war... No crashing collapse, no miracles. The two sides would keep on swelling to giant size until one of them would burst and drown the adversary in its juice. A long war...

Carmen Elgazu liked rain because it reminded her of Bilbao. When it rained, she would begin immediately to sprinkle sawdust on the landings of the stairway, and Ignacio, seeing it, was reminded in turn of the Arús Bank and of Don Jorge. When it rained, Carmen Elgazu placed an umbrella stand at the entrance to the apartment to catch the drip, and she would say to Pilar: "Go and put on your rubbers and be careful you don't fall down."

Every time Carmen Elgazu looked at the calendar she saw the date of December 25th printed in red. Would the 25th of December bring with it an explanation of what was happening? Carmen Elgazu would listen to the raindrops hissing into the river. Ah, that white Christmas in Gerona when snowflakes from Heaven had blanched the earth and when the whole family, with Mateo, had climbed to the bell tower of the Cathedral! That was freedom, beauty, and life. That was a thing of beauty, and one felt that the cold was good because it lingered on the skin. What would happen if it should snow now? In war time the cold must cut like a knife. In war time snow must turn into filthy slush. "Lord, protect us. Protect this family that loves Thee."

In the Telegraph Office, Matías Alvear was saying to Jaime: "I won't be able to be in touch with my brother in Burgos on Christmas this year." Then he added. "I feel sure my brother is dead." Matías Alvear was afraid of Queipo de Llano. "He's a brute." He felt that Queipo de Llano was a representative of those on the other side who would be responsible if his brother had died in Burgos.

Jaime told him: "They killed García Lorca. What can you expect?"

Ignacio was also watching the approach of winter with an uneasy mind. Julio had said to him, "The war will be a long one. I'm afraid they're going to call up your quota any minute." It was true. And the boy did not know what to do. France, Nationalist Spain? ... How could he leave those three creatures in the apartment on the Rambla? Yet if he were to be called up, he would have to leave them anyway. He would have liked to escape, as Marta had escaped... But he could not see how it could be done. Laura had suspended the expeditions to France *sine die,* and it seemed that trained dogs were scouring the Pyrenees. What about Julio? Matías Alvear had said to Ignacio: "That's all right, son. He'll wind up seeming like our nursemaid. We'll think for ourselves, and something is bound to turn up..."

Something will turn up... Ignacio's own fellow workers in the Arús Bank were on pins and needles because one of them, Padrosa, already had been called up. Padrosa had had to exchange his pen for a rifle—the opposite of what David and Olga had counseled in the past when they had hoped that Military Service would be abolished—and Padrosa's vacant chair served as a constant warning. The cashier said to Ignacio: "Don't be so foolish as to volunteer. You could get yourself in a mess. If you wait for them to draft you, they'll hand you a machete and you'll eat plenty of trench earth." A machete! How quickly strange words can acquire meaning. The word "machete" became as fixed in Ignacio's mind as if Sidlo, the javelin champion, had thrown it there.

And to make matters worse, Marta had gone. War was a dispersion. Everything had happened as though in a dream. From the kitchen of the school, Marta had gone to Barcelona, to the Calle de Verdi, and from the Calle de Verdi to the Guatemalan Consulate. Guatemala! Another word that suddenly had acquired meaning.

Through the courtesy of Colonel Muñoz, Marta had managed to send a letter to Ignacio, written in a hasty and joyous hand.

> Dear Ignacio:
>
> Everything is turning out fine. For once, Colonel Muñoz has acted like a gentleman. My mother has just come to the Calle de Verdi for

me and we're both going now to the Consulate of Guatemala. I'll write you from there. Sometime tomorrow we'll be sailing for Tangier on an Italian ship.

I shall be thinking of you always. Dearest Ignacio! I had dreamed that we'd be together always, always, but the war has come between us. But I love you. I'll keep on loving you wherever I go, more every day.

As you may imagine, we intend to come back to Nationalist Spain as soon as possible. Perhaps I can be of use to Spain, to the Falange. I'll try to find my brother José Luis, and Mateo there...

I can promise you one thing, Ignacio: I'll do everything possible to join you. Promise me you'll do the same! Will you try? I haven't given up hope. Gerona frightens me... Try to do it. I say it a thousand times over: try to do it...

Always your
Marta

Ignacio was jealous. He was jealous of his country, of "Face to the Sun," of Mateo, and of Marta's brother. "To be of use to Spain, to the Falange..." He was afraid that in Nationalist Spain, Marta would forget everything, that she would forget even how to love and would nourish herself exclusively on yokes and arrows.

"Tomorrow we'll be sailing for Tangier on an Italian ship!" How strangely everything was turning out! "Marta, I dreamed, too, of being with you always, always! I love you, too, and I'll keep on loving you more every day wherever you are! Gerona frightens me, too... And I'm afraid of the coming winter. May God take care of you, Marta!"

FROM the middle of November until the end of the year, many things happened. Guatemala, Italy, and Germany recognized the Government of Franco in Burgos, as the Republic of El Salvador had done earlier. That was an international diplomatic triumph which, though notable, failed to compensate for the military reverses at Madrid. By some strange fate, José Antonio Primo de Rivera and Buenaventura Durruti died within twenty-four hours of each other. José Antonio died on the 20th, executed in Alicante; Durruti died on the 21st, in University City, of a shot fired by an unknown hand from the Clinic Hospital, perhaps by a Communist or a personal enemy.

According to Núñez Maza, José Antonio Primo de Rivera was what he was primarily through natural ability and secondarily because he had drunk in the teachings of Ortega y Gasset. But he was shot to death. The repeated attempts to free him mentioned by José Luis Martínez de Soria to Mateo on the day when the latter arrived on the Alto del León all had failed. The first attempt failed because it depended on a proposal for an exchange of prisoners—the founder of the Falange for one of Largo Caballero's sons who had been arrested in Seville. Despite Prieto's acquiescence in the proposal, the Republican Government would not agree to the exchange, and Largo Caballero himself, convinced that his son had been shot by Queipo de Llano, ignored the proposal. The second attempt failed because it depended on the dispatch of a Falangist emissary, an old guard, to Alicante. The emissary landed in the port of the city on the 24th of September from the German torpedo boat *Graff von Spee* anchored in nearby territorial waters. He had been commissioned to bribe some of the leaders of the FAI, but he failed. Mediation by the Duke of Alva, Sánchez Román, Indalecio Prieto, and several English and French diplomats also failed. And the last attempt had failed, too, for reasons unknown. Lieutenant Salazar took part in that effort, which aimed to make another landing in Alicante and storm the prison. José Antonio, the prisoner, was to be carried off by force.

In the Alto del León this final attempt had aroused everyone's hopes. Lieutenant Salazar's departure had been highly emotional. Seemingly he was to meet six other comrades in Seville, but the lieutenant felt uneasy, and the whole company lined up in front of him singing "Face to the Sun." Salazar said, "I wouldn't mind giving my life to save José Antonio's." They all watched him leave, wishing him luck. "Up, Spain! Spain forever! Mateo was saying to himself, "I'd give my life, too, to save José Antonio's."

The following week was one of torture for the Falangists on the Alto del León. They hardly spoke to one another, and during the hours they had to stand watch, they stared at the stars. "We propose," José Antonio had said, "to give Spain back to the Spaniards, with their pride in being Spanish." God, if only the attempt would succeed! José Luis Martínez de Soria recalled the visit José Antonio had paid the Duce in 1933 and that near the close of it Mussolini had said that the Spanish Falangist was "one of the most beautiful spirits he had ever known."

But fate willed otherwise. Núñez Maza was the one chosen to climb the Alto del León and pass on the bad news to his comrades. He knew none of the details, but the landing never even had been made. In some remarkable fashion, a broadcast from an African radio had alerted the Reds to the plot.

"How could that be?"

"I don't know. Salazar hasn't come back yet. That's all I know."

The next day, one of the drivers who came up with the supply trucks declared in an exalted tone that a most unpleasant rumor was going around

Valladolid. "It seems," he said, "that two of our comrades got drunk when they arrived in Seville and let their tongues run loose to some trollops in a café. That's the reason for the giveaway on the African broadcast from Tangier."

No one would credit such folly. "When Salazar gets back, we'll find out the truth."

For the time being, the only reality was that José Antonio had been tried in Alicante and condemned to death at the instance of several government ministers and the Communist Party.

A fugitive from the Red zone submitted the whole story to the hierarchy of the Falange, to Hedilla and his National Council. During his trial, José Antonio had defended himself with a first-class piece of oratory. As they listened, the members of the court, everyone present in the courtroom—chiefly militiawomen and men who had filled the benches, avid for a close look at the "señorito"—lost the capacity to hate for the time being. José Antonio made clear in the course of his speech his anguish over the river of blood staining Spain and offered himself as a mediator to go into the Rebel zone and try to bring about a cease-fire, an armistice. He pledged his word to return to Alicante and proposed to leave his various imprisoned relatives as hostages.

Unfortunately, his offer failed to bring about the desired effect. And on the 20th of November, José Antonio was led at dawn to the prison courtyard, with two Falangists and two Requetés from the village of Novelda who had been tried and sentenced earlier. The firing squad already was in position.

The five men were lined up, and José Antonio said to the militiamen in the firing squad, "Aim well; you're going to need all your ammunition." He then tossed aside his overcoat, crossed his arms, and moved his left foot onward a little. A volley was fired, and José Antonio fell. He was the first; his four comrades, the two Falangists and the two Requetés from Novelda fell in their turn.

José Antonio's body was taken to the cemetery, and as it was being lowered from the truck a little crucifix he had worn tied to a red ribbon fell off. Tomás Santoja, the custodian of the place, recognized the crucifix and replaced it on his dead chest. Shortly after that the founder of the Falange was listed in Book IV of the Cemetery Register with the number 22,450, grave 5, 9th row, 12th quarter.

The Falangists on the Alto del León were heartsick when they learned those details. Mateo repeated the number 22,450 under his breath and promised to try to remember it; several of his comrades did likewise.

"Salazar hasn't got back yet..."

They swore to one another that they would find out immediately exactly what had happened in Seville.

"No matter how many lives it cost."

"Shall we take a vow?"

"Up, Spain!"

"Arise, forever!"

The news of José Antonio's death spread rapidly through both zones. On the Red side it was reported cautiously, with no encomia. In Barcelona it had come over Radio Seville, originally from the soft-drink stand on the Rambla de Cataluña, and had radiated widely, with a version for every taste. In certain towns, the Fascist girls tied little black ribbons in their hair as a form of mourning. Pilar was one, but Matías Alvear yanked it off her when he discovered it as he had once pulled off César's penitent's belt.

In the Nationalist zone, many of the Falangists, Mateo among them, decided to call José Antonio "the Absent One." Mosén Alberto commented, "That is idolatry." But the expression was apt. José Antonio was indeed the irreplaceable Absent One. In moments of discouragement like those following the failure to conquer Madrid, he had been their guiding star, with his integrity and his warm words. Salazar said, "With him, we'd have been drawn together more closely still..." Drawn closer and tighter. With him, unity had been assured. "José Antonio always took the right, noble, and effective attitude for every circumstance." Now the substitute national leader, Hedilla, a self-educated man from Santander, would feel crushed by his responsibility.

The repercussions from José Antonio's death were wide. Pilar's aunt and her daughter Paz in Burgos could testify to that. The blood spilled in Alicante spattered them. Three Falangists broke into their house, dosed them with castor oil, and then said goodbye with affectionate pats on the cheek.

BUENAVENTURA Durruti was shot in University City in Madrid. The Anarchist god had been striving to take the Clinic Hospital by assault. A bullet pierced him as he was stepping out of his car. Durruti fell, and a harsh cry arose. The leader's staff carried him to the Ritz Hotel, made over into an emergency hospital, where a crowd of doctors in Dr. Rosselló's command tried to save him. Hours of anxiety went by, for Durruti's comrades considered his life the people's patrimony. Even the International Brigades sent messages to the hospital, and General Miaja himself asked to be kept informed constantly. All in vain. Durruti died almost without regaining consciousness. He had just managed to gasp, "Keep on fighting," and when he died the marble halls of the Ritz Hotel witnessed with wonder how hard men who had spent a lifetime defying a great many things could throw themselves to the floor like infants, with yells of outrage.

The body was taken to Barcelona, where Fanny the newspaperwoman estimated that three hundred thousand people had been present at the funeral. Durruti had died among his own men. If he had fallen on enemy soil, he would have been dropped into a humble grave in silence. Or he would have been stripped of his flesh by the ever-neutral crows.

His death was like an electric shock through Gerona, and this time it was Merche's turn to put a black mourning ribbon in her hair. Would she meet Pilar on the street? If so, their mourning would meet beneath the rains of November. Some mourning was permitted; some not. Santi, the mad Santi, was wandering around saying, "I don't want to kill the sea now. I want to kill the Madrid front."

José Alvear was one of those who were beside themselves at this apocalypse. He had come to feel a genuine veneration for Durruti, though he often used to say, "He sure is ugly..." José Alvear called at the Ritz with Captain Culebra, and when he saw the face of the dead Durruti, shrunken on the pillow, he became terribly overwrought. Besides, he was drunk. He started to run up and down the stairs, going in and out of rooms and turning on faucets. Canela, now a nurse just in from the Teruel front, ran after the boy and tried to calm him. "Do be quiet, please!" José Alvear could not contain his fury, and Canela was afraid that he might do something insane.

Suddenly Captain Alvear remembered Dr. Rosselló. He was the surgeon who had made the incision in Durruti, and he had a Falangist son! El Cojo had told José that, and had added: "No one can understand that lot."

José made a grimace and said to Captain Culebra, "Come with me to the operating room."

"What's the matter with you?"

"I just want to ask that quack one question!" José said, and added: "Come with me, I'll behave myself."

His friend yielded and went down to the basements of the Ritz with him. They found the doctor there, washing up in a basin in the hallway, surrounded by his colleagues.

José Alvear planted himself in front of the doctor, and throwing his head back, spat very near him. "Durruti is dead. But I'll bet your Falangist son is still alive."

Quite unperturbed, the doctor picked up a towel and began to dry himself. "What's this all about? What are you doing here?"

José Alvear looked around him. "Did you hear that, comrades? A Falangist son, and here he is laying open Durruti's belly!"

Dr. Rosselló felt several pairs of eyes turn to him. "Listen, you fool," he said with sudden energy as he hung up the towel. "What if one does have a crooked son? My son is nineteen years old. When I found out that he was singing 'Face to the Sun,' I threw him out of the house. What more do you want? Do you expect me to go after him and kill him?"

José Alvear belched, and it looked as though his hand was going for his pistol. Just then the little green light in the corridor went on, meaning that Dr. Rosselló was expected in the operating room. "Come on, make up your mind," the surgeon challenged. "I'm being called into the operating room. Kill me or let me get back to work."

José belched again and stared at Captain Culebra as if asking for advice.

"I warn you," Dr. Rosselló went on, "that the only reason I don't knock you down is because you're drunk."

Having spoken, he began to make his way through his colleagues with dignity. Everyone followed him and Captain Culebra and José Alvear were left alone. Captain Culebra grinned. "That's what's known as the brush-off."

José Alvear staggered. He was keeping to his feet only with difficulty. Where had he left his derby hat? His back kept sliding down the wall until he was sitting on the floor of the corridor, where he stayed. "Durruti is dead," he said. "Durruti is dead. What a dirty mean trick on me."

At that very moment, Salazar was getting drunk in a bar in Valladolid, in utter solitude. He had pushed back his cap and was saying to the woman owner: "Do I look like an idiot? No? Well, I am one."

EVERYONE noticed with surprise that Christmas was near. The first Christmas of the war. Everyone felt both outwardly and inwardly the words Someone had spoken nearly two thousand years ago: "Peace on earth to men of good will." Some man who had looked like any other man. Fairly tall, more than five and a half feet, with the right shoulder probably a little bent from his work as a carpenter. Doubtless a man with an ascetic face. No photograph ever was made of him, but no doubt his face was ascetic. A man with a deep voice. No recording ever was made of his voice, but no doubt it was deep. A man who drove out devils and the Pharisees, who healed the sick and returned the dead to life. If that Man were in Gerona, in Madrid, in Burgos now, how much less blood would be shed!

But the Man actually was here, newborn, with the godlike gift of ubiquity, transformed into a tiny fetus in a woman's body. On his brow he wore a star, not a military decoration, just a star, a light shaped that way. He was to come at the moment when still-births were increasing in Barcelona at a frightening rate, and when the wife of Einstein in the United States was dying, the wife of the man who had made a study of light. He was to come at the moment when Warning Voice was handing his superiors in SIFNE the plans of enemy cities, with objectives for bombers marked. A timely coming. "Peace on earth to men of good will."

The Man was to bring consolation and despair. "Verily my Heavenly Father will deal with ye thus unless ye shall each forgive your brothers in your heart." "Verily I say unto you that all these things shall come to pass upon this generation."

He would be astonished to hear the newsboys crying: "Extra! Extra! Letters of Pope Pius to his sweetheart!" And equally astonished to hear the tireless Núñez Maza addressing the enemy: "Reds! God is on our side!" What was the meaning of such words? Everyone knew that Christmas was coming. And everyone, man and woman alike, would discreetly put in her hair or on his chest a small token of tenderness and sentiment. Yet no one had forgiven his brothers in his heart.

The Provincial Government of Catalonia wanted to abolish the age-old celebration of Christmas and Twelfth Night, replacing those holidays with the "Week of the Child." An abstract child, for the Child-God was concrete. Sheltering love and gifts for the child. David and Olga went to Arbucias, the idyllic village, and as in former years, the CEDA loaded the forty deaf-and-dumb children evacuated from Santander with sweets and toys. Cosme Vila took his little boy, his militant son, for a walk and showed him Gerona with the stamp of revolution on it. The boy no longer chewed his big toe. Instead, he laughingly chewed his father's ear. Doña Amparo mourned with Julio that they had no children, no one to carry on their name. "Have you seen the signs? The Week of the Child! Sometimes it makes me so mad..." Antonio Casal led his three children by the hand to a circus that had just arrived, where the clowns cavorted at government cost and said "pwetty" instead of "pretty." Children were everywhere and Manolín was not excluded, though he occasionally would take a walk to the Consulate of Guatemala. Children who were still children, children who were growing boys and even men, children who raised their clenched fists, children who prayed in secret. "Peace on earth..."

A strange ending to December, a strange Christmas, that of 1936... The Ovid Lodge of Gerona celebrated it as usual with a meeting in the Calle del Pavo. The brothers in the Jakim and Boaz Columns embraced one another with joy over the triumph of Madrid. Colonel Muñoz made a prophecy: "Nineteen hundred and thirty-seven will be the decisive year." In honor of the holidays, the architects Ribas and Massana would have liked to ring all the little bells in their collection. Commissioner Julián Cervera dedicated a memorial to

Unamuno, who just had died in Salamanca, the details as yet unknown, and another to García Lorca. Julio García gave an encomium to Dr. Rosselló, who, in the midst of his titanic labors, had thought to send him a belt of Durruti's for his private museum. Antonio Casal, whose face looked more like a cipher every day according to Professor Morales, took a slip of paper out of his pocket and said that if his figures were correct the "Fascists" had about a hundred aircraft at that moment to the more than three hundred at the disposal of the Republican Government. Casal had imagined that he would be given an ovation, but he was disappointed. The manager of the Arús Bank rose and wished everyone "Happy holidays."

At the front, the chill of eternity was running along the trenches. Many of those in active combat almost could believe that they would not be killed on Christmas Day. On the Alto del León, extra rations were issued. No harvest was being reaped from the sea, certainly, nor from the air, nor from the land. On the contrary, thousands of bullets still were taking their impersonal course amply, and some harbors, in their quietude, looked like the Sea of Galilee.

And the fighting men were singing. To them it was no "Week of the Child." It was Christmas. Some were singing to themselves, others to the whole world.

THE Alvears were celebrating Christmas, too, in their fashion. Several days earlier, Carmen Elgazu had suggested, "We ought to make a crèche."

Matías stared at her and answered, "Don't you even think of it."

"Why not?" Carmen Elgazu had an inspiration. "We can make it inside this little box." She took out of her sewing case a little cork rectangle in which she kept buttons and showed it to Matías. He stared into the little box a moment and sighed: "All right, we'll have a crèche."

On Christmas morning, Ignacio and Pilar made three tiny paper figures on the dining room table: Saint Joseph, the Virgin, and the Child. Matías had the job of making the donkey and the ox, but he could not manage to turn out anything with the least resemblance to either of the animals. "To hell with the pair of them!"

Carmen Elgazu, half joking, half serious said, "It's your own fault. How long has it been since you went to confession?"

Pilar went to her father's rescue and the little cork box soon was transformed into the stable in Bethlehem. They set it on top of the radio and tried to tune in a broadcast of recorded carols. Ignacio was lucky; he found Radio Jaca and they all sat silent and listened devoutly in turn. When it was over, they cautiously lighted wax candles.

During dinner they joked, trying to forget César. Carmen Elgazu set some chicken and some fruit and spice tarts in the center of the table and Matías stuck his ration card in the dish like a flag.

"Don't joke," said Pilar.

"I'm not joking," Matías replied. "I'm laughing, and that's worse."

Ignacio had bought a little Alicante nougat. They all insisted that Carmen Elgazu must eat it, must crunch it with her own teeth.

"But I can't! I can't!"

"Try it... Go on, break it..."

She lifted a piece to her mouth and they all watched her closely, imitating with their own jaws the efforts she was making to chew it.

"Bite hard, chew hard!"

Carmen Elgazu finally burst out laughing and scattered the nougat.

Matías picked the crumbs off the table and ate them one at a time. "This is awfully good," he said.

When dinner was over, they did not know what to do, until Ignacio suggested a game of cards. He knew that his parents enjoyed that, though Matías preferred dominoes. The four of them had never played cards together, and while César had been alive, five had been too many. They played partners, parents against children, in an unequal contest. Matías knew all the games, Pilar none of them. Matías kept winking at his wife, and finally she asked him in astonishment, "What's the matter with you?"

"I'm telling you I have the ace."

"Well, say so!"

The parents won all the games. And many kisses with them. And affectionate glances from Ignacio and Pilar. It was months since Ignacio had enjoyed his family so much. It seemed to him that he was not entirely alone and that there was something in men besides a mind. The game went on until the middle of the afternoon, until shadows began to fall over the river.

They had a peaceful supper, like a picnic near the river, near the fishing pole, near the radio which kept saying to them: "Love ye one another." No one wanted to admit that one of the shadows falling might be César's. In the room there was light, a discreet light in their hearts, and on the dials of the radio. It was Christmas. The thoughts of the four of them were something more than thoughts.

TWENTY-THREE

IN the port of Genoa an oddly impassive man, dressed in the uniform of the Italian Fascist Party, was making a strident speech to four thousand Black Shirts who were embarking to fight in Spain.

"Comrades: This is an important moment. You are going to Spain, a sister nation, to stop Communism from taking over that portion of Europe and sinking its claws into Morocco, that is, into Africa. More than half of Spain's territory is subjected to the vile tyranny of the Red hordes who have launched a destructive action on her soil which can be compared only to that of Genghis Khan or Attila. Patrols armed to the teeth are masters of lives and family fortunes. Cities and towns are being set afire and churches and cultural buildings destroyed. The forces of order, under the command of a number of prestigious professional military men, aided by the Spanish monarchist youth, or those already won to the Fascist way, have risen up against the Popular Front, and for several months now they have been committed to the fight against Moscow and its minions in a cruel, primitive civil war. The Duce has decided to go to their aid, and in so doing he has been motivated only by affection for Spain and the need to answer Communism blow for blow. Anyone who dares to say that any other purpose motivated the Duce is a liar. Italy desires the peace of Europe and the maintenance of good relations with the Western democracies, though still convinced that their political credo is mistaken. What we are doing is nothing compared with the shameful sending of International Brigades organized in France at Moscow's orders, with no few Italian traitors to be found among them. We are doing nothing more than to show the world that the time has passed when Italy could hold back. Wherever we are needed, we shall go. Wherever they provoke us, the Duce will reply. Abyssinia is a living example of that, and your presence here at this time is another. Black Shirts! Italian Volunteers! Go to Spain and respect your Spanish brothers, your brothers in culture and religion, brothers even in the color of their skin. Raise high the flag of Italy forever. Respect the Moroccan forces who are fighting under Franco's command. And never forget that the Spanish man is a noble and jealous man. *Bon voyage,* beloved comrades. This has nothing to do with conquest, it is an embrace. That's it! Go to Spain with open arms, with generosity. Respect their customs. Italy, I repeat, asks nothing in return. Only the pride of having again served the salvation of Europe. Black Shirts, long live Italy! Long live Spain! Long live Fascism! Long live the Duce!"

Four thousand Black Shirts put out to sea, a cold and turbulent January sea. They were men from all over Italy, but mainly from the South, gesticulating and apparently quite happy. They had with them many small musical instruments, especially harmonicas. Prolonged silence threw them into a peculiar depression. Many of them were actually volunteers who had fought in Ethiopia, but a great many more were draftees in the regular service. Their commanding officer, the very young General Roatta, was an energetic sort who believed that the tactics employed by the Nationalists until then should be revised. "Motorization," he said. He had learned this word in the desert, where miles were a formidable obstacle. Armored cars to open a breach, motorized troops, and low-flying aircraft. "It was a serious mistake to attack Madrid head on in successive waves of Infantry." General Roatta looked at his men, more than four thousand of them, and saw that they had had their baptism of fire and that their morale was high. But he placed his trust in machines, in the superiority of steel and wheel. The orders he carried forbade him to meddle in domestic Spanish policy, however. That was being taken care of by the astute Aleramo Berti.

The majority of the men on shipboard had a concept of Spain and its people almost as embryonic as that of the "Freedom Volunteers." Brothers in culture, in religion, in skin color? What did that mean? What about the bullfights? And Arab domination? And those spasmodic dances, sad and twisted, which seemed to letter the word death? What did Avila and Naples have in common, Goya's monuments and Rafael's Virgins? Nothing but the Mediterranean and the concept of God... And a common language root. Oh, no, that was not enough to make them feel a bond in their daily life! Yet the Black Shirts felt kindly disposed toward Spain. In their knapsacks they all carried a tiny red dictionary in which they could look up the translation of *ragazza, barbiere,* and *ciaò*... Each of them would stare at the sea suddenly and ask himself how he had got mixed up in this venture. To fight Moscow? Could it be for the fine uniform? Someone had said: "Dress the idealistic Italian in a good-looking uniform and he'll go off and fight to insure the Greenlanders a supply of dried codfish."

The four thousand men reached the harbor of Cádiz early in January. Aleramo Berti of the Fascist Party was there, along with the recently named

Italian Ambassador and a cadre of military technicians. Their reception was an apotheosis. Queipo de Llano, master of the South, had organized the act to perfection. Cádiz lent itself to such a celebration, for it was a clear, brilliant city, with brush strokes of ocher and pink similar to the tints of many Roman façades. The word "tie" was stressed in the speeches. The anthems drowned out the harmonicas. Flowers seemed to sprout from nowhere, and the *ragazze* buried the Italians under cascades of paper serpentines in the colors of their flag.

The Italians were hungry and thirsty, and Cádiz gave them food and drink. They wanted to parade, and Cádiz let them. General Roatta joined the Spanish military men at once, and the name of Málaga echoed insistently among them. Everything already had been decided. This was only the first detachment. On the fourteenth, another six thousand Black Shirts landed; by the end of the month, an additional four thousand. So many things were needed. It was suicidal to talk about a long war, for to do so revealed an inadmissible feeling of inferiority. Guerrilla warfare was at an end. Italy, the land of motors, of drivers, naturally symbolized everything modern. Meanwhile, certain services for the accommodation of the Black Shirts had to be provided in the region. Signs saying: *Comandamento, Corpo di guardia, Estafeta Legionaria,* and *Posta* were posted. Good hotels had to be found for the officers, and a friendly and pleasant atmosphere established for the men.

Marta and her mother were in the crowd that had gone to the waterfront to welcome the Italians and later to acclaim them through the streets. It was a happy coincidence. After an enforced stay in Tangier which had resulted from the mother's untimely illness, the two women had disembarked only a few hours before the Black Shirts. At the port their emotion was indescribable as they kissed the bicolor flag for which the major had given his life. Their eyes roamed everywhere as Mateo's had when he first had set foot in Valladolid. And when they learned that the Italians were to arrive just after they had docked, they took rooms in the nearest hotel so that they could see what was going on from the balcony and shout themselves hoarse with "*¡Viva Italia! ¡Viva España! ¡Viva el Duce! ¡Viva Franco!*"

They were never to forget their emotion at meeting those men from their "sister nation" who had come to defend Spain. The Black Shirts looked more vigorous and authoritative than they had pictured them. They even looked handsome to Marta, and more exciting than the Spanish soldiers, of course. Some of them looked like Ciano, some like Mussolini. As Marta's mother applauded them fervently, she was remembering the trip the major had made to Rome in 1933, for an interview with Il Duce...

When the parade was over, the Italians were free to spread out over the city, thronging the narrow streets and the cafés and taverns. Like the people of Cádiz, Marta and her mother went out of the hotel to mingle with them, to shake hands with them, to pin medallions on their chests, and to say "Thank you" to them. Marta's mother soon tired and went back to the hotel, but the girl, chagrined to the soul because she was not wearing a blue blouse, kept on walking. Her enthusiasm was deep and quiet. She thought it was symbolic that ancient Italy should come to the aid of Spain through Cádiz, the oldest city in Europe, the three-thousand-year-old Gades.

Not knowing quite how it happened, Marta found herself at the counter of a bar surrounded by dark-faced men who kept calling her *ragazza* and *signorina* and offering her tobacco. She felt confused until one of the faces stood out from the others. It was the face of a boy a little older than Ignacio. A boy who said "*Ciaó…*" to his comrades and, once alone with Marta, invited her to sit in a quiet corner of the place, helping her off with her coat and artfully caressing her scarf.

"My name is Marta."

"I, Salvatore."

"Salvatore! What a pretty name!"

"Bah!"

"Where are you from?"

"From Rome."

"I, from Valladolid."

The waiter served them coffee. Raising their cups, they toasted each other. They toasted Rome and Valladolid, Spain and Italy. They drank to Salvatore's black shirt and those of his comrades. Then they finished the coffee. And Marta smoked! She smoked an Italian cigarette, a Fascist cigarette, scented with the harbor of Genoa and the "*Corpo di guardia.*" Marta told Salvatore that she had escaped from the Red zone with her mother. Salvatore already knew that "the Spanish girls go everywhere with their mother…"

"In Genoa they told us to—*respect,*" and the boy put his hand over Marta's with a laugh. She withdrew hers.

Salvatore then told her that he wanted to be a good person, but Moscow kept interfering with his plans; wars kept interfering. "First Abyssinia… Now Spain… But I like it."

"What?"

"All this."

Marta thought of Ignacio at intervals. If only he could see her now! In a café in Cádiz, smoking and drinking with a man beside her who, after eating her up with his eyes, looked around him and asked, "Why do these people live so poorly?"

The encounter had been pleasant. Marta would go off to Valladolid, but they would write to each other.

"Do you want to be my godmother? In Ita..."

"I'd be delighted!"

Marta told Salvatore that wherever he might be she would be his godmother in Valladolid, in the name of a first-aid kit marked CAFÉ that she had grown fond of; in the name of the Falange and Spain, in the name of the terrible sights; in the gratitude she felt for anyone who loved his country yet left it to defend a just cause far away. "I'll write to you and send you tobacco."

"I'm very fond of chocolate, too..."

A few days later, an oddly excited man in the port of Hamburg, wearing the uniform of the German Nazi Party, was delivering a strident speech to three hundred volunteers, technicians in the Air Force auxiliary services, who were about to embark for Spain.

"Comrades: In the name of our Führer, you are about to leave German soil. You will be dressed as civilians for the voyage, but once you have reached your destination you will be given back your insignia plus the swastika you all wear. You are volunteers for the Führer in the struggle against Communism and against the Popular Fronts under the protection of the democracies. This time it's your turn to fight in a country with a glorious past, Spain. To fight in the ranks of the Condor Legion. The condor, the biggest bird that flies. May the Führer protect you! May Germany protect you! Spain is of primary strategic importance, and it must not be abandoned to the enemy. You must have blind confidence in your commanders, as always, and you will receive from them whatever assignments are necessary. There are two things sacred to the Spaniards: first, their religious feeling; second, the honor of their women. Spain is a Catholic country; you must respect the ideas and the superstitions of her people. Spain is a country of family traditions; you must respect their women, comport yourselves with the utmost correctness. You will be representing the German people there, who are not lending aid with any plans for conquest, but merely in order to make an adequate reply to the International Brigades that Communism had sent to Spain. General Francisco Franco is now the leader of the Spaniards who have risen up against Moscow. As soon as you reach your destination, he will become your leader. Obey him through your own commanding officers. His orders will be law, the same as the orders of your own General von Sperrle. Bear in mind that officially you are going on maneuvers in the Baltic. It is the Führer's will that for the time being no one, not even your families, are to know that you'll be in Spain. Therefore you are to avoid any reference in your letters that would reveal that you are in a southern country. To that end you will be given appropriately stamped postcards. You will likewise be given the regulations of the Condor Legion, a dictionary, and a grammar. Make an effort to learn the Spanish language and try not to make mistakes. You will be fighting beside Italian volunteers, and it is also requisite that you avoid the slightest friction with them. Bear in mind the affection the Führer feels for Il Duce. Not even a gesture that might imply a feeling of superiority. Also great tact in your relations with the Moorish troops. They have even more superstitions than the Catholics; respect them. Keep a clean uniform, give bouquets of flowers, be especially kind to the amputees from the war, the old, the children. That is all for today, and good luck. I am sure you will be worthy soldiers of the Condor Legion and that you will do your duty as Germans. That is all. *Heil, Hitler!*"

Three hundred men dressed as peasants and wearing strange helmets put out to sea. The ship was flying the Panamanian flag, but as it neared the French coast, the Liberian flag was hoisted. They were sailing for Vigo, the Galician port, a city of beautiful river mouths channeled through the earth. They were Nazis, hence endowed with a common idea, a common will. They liked the fact that the condor was the largest bird in existence. They were accustomed to gigantism, to valuing things for their size. Even their matchboxes were outsized, and they liked the sea for being immense. Because they liked big things, the flags of Panama and Liberia struck them as caricatures. They, too, played the harmonica, but more often than not they sang. They spent the voyage singing, drinking beer, studying Spanish grammar, a specially edited military grammar containing all the military terminology, especially pertaining to the branch they served, to cooking, to neatness, and to religion. It seemed strange to them to say "Vatican" and "God" in Spanish. God to them was fat and somewhat choleric. Major Plabb was their commandant, and he told them over and over again until they were tired of it that they were not to meddle in Spanish domestic politics, for the delegates of the Party were directly in charge of that. Of the three hundred volunteers, more than half had a very exact notion of the geography of Spain, as well as of the discovery of America and the reign of Charles V, but they fancied that almost all the Spanish women were dark and that in the South there were entire regions peopled by gypsies. They were affectionately predisposed, for without knowing why, they were fond of Spain. General von Sperrl was not aware of this detail, but Schubert, suspensefully awaiting the arrival of the Condor Legion, knew that it was true. Why did they have to talk about the Baltic if Spain was as beautiful as they had been taught in school and in the recent briefings? "Orders are orders!" That was a fact of life! As for the Italians, how could anyone help taking them as a joke? Ethiopia had been an easy mouthful but they were a lot of braggarts. Their orders were very clear, however, and the Führer was Il Duce's friend. Amputees, old people, children...but of course! Would they be given permission to fire a shot some day? The ship was following its course. Among the three hundred volunteers there were Germans from everywhere, from Prussia, from the Black Forest. As long as they refrained from drinking, punctilio would be the order of the day. They cracked their naïve jokes and stared toward the coasts of the Atlantic, where an eye winked at them from a beacon. They admired Franco, as Dr. Relken did, because he had had the idea of bringing troops from Morocco by air. They argued over the Russian and the French fliers who would be their immediate enemy. According to Major Plabb, the Russians did not know how to fly in limited visibility, and the French were good, but excessively cautious. The Spaniards ought to make excellent fighter pilots; somewhat less excellent bomber pilots... Well, they would see all that when they landed, when they had fitted into their slots, with swastikas on their chests.

The three hundred men arrived in Vigo incognito and were rushed off to Salamanca on a night train. In Salamanca, the Ambassador, Von Faupel, General von Sperrle, and the Party delegate Schubert all were waiting for them. On the following day a great military parade was held in collaboration with the troops. The people's demonstrations were as enthusiastic as those in Cádiz when the Italians marched by. "*¡Viva Alemania! ¡Viva Hitler! ¡Viva España!*" Salamanca was beautiful, its stonework the color of aged human skin... Had Unamuno died? ... How did he die? What did he say? ... Don't ask questions... Goose step, one, two. Perfect. Respect the Vatican and superstitions. Roving girls pinned ribbons and Spanish flags in their lapels. What was the significance of those red berets? Monarchy, backwardness, reactionism... The only important thing was the Falange, its blue shirts speaking of service and empire.

Other satisfied German faces could be seen on the balconies alongside the ambassador and his colleagues. They were the beaming faces of merchants, come to negotiate the exchange of raw materials and to seek payment in shares for the matériel furnished by Germany. Cannon had their price, but what about human lives? How much would a life be worth, a German life cut short in the air or on the earth? Who could tell? The "rebel" peseta of Salamanca was coming to be worth more in London than the "red" peseta. The Reds had opened the strongboxes in the Bank of Spain with acid, and as Julio García had predicted, this had come to the attention of the International Bourse. Furthermore,

Germany could print on her own account a limited number of "red" pesetas and put them into circulation in Barcelona or Madrid. Or drop them from an airplane, or leave them in waterproof cases in the bed of a river...

The people acclaimed those disciplined men equipped with Baltic postcards, with song, and with grammars. The tireless Comrade Núñez Maza was naturally one of the most enthusiastic of the people shouting "*Heil Hitler!*" Comrade Núñez Maza had come to Salamanca on the previous evening for the opening of the National Broadcasting System, a marvel built in Essen, which had been used during the Olympic Games in Berlin. The studios were located in the San Bernardo Building. Franco had spoken into the microphone for the first time at the inaugural broadcast, and later Celia Gámez had sung. The enthusiasm of Núñez Maza, the propagandist from Soria, bubbled over when he learned of the arrival of three hundred technicians from the country that had built that broadcasting device. Núñez Maza admired Germany as much as Salazar did. And he also admired the basic tenets of the Nazi credo: "Racial discrimination, obedience, common labor, and a plan for wiping out the influence of the Jews."

Núñez Maza had said to Mateo in Valladolid, "Anyone who does not follow those people will be left two hundred years behind."

Naturally he would applaud the parade like a child and stare at the volunteers from Hamburg with an expression very like Cosme Vila's on the day Axelrod arrived in Gerona.

After the parade, Comrade Núñez Maza managed to arrange an appointment in the broadcasting studio with the expedition's commandant, Major Plabb, through the good offices of Schubert, who always had been friendly to him. Núñez Maza stood at attention when the major arrived, and greeted him with the Nazi salute. Portraits of Franco and José Antonio, pictures of yokes and arrows, and a map of operations surrounded them.

Núñez Maza would have liked the major to give the people a radio message, but the commandant declined. No boasting. Núñez Maza had to content himself with a chat in bad French, with Schubert having to lend a hand occasionally.

Major Plabb was a sanguine and vigorous man of about forty, an anti-aircraft expert. He spoke as though violently ejaculating his phrases. He was from Bonn, "a very beautiful place where the Rhine flows past, on the way to Cologne," and where, it would seem, the Führer was building huge rest camps for the Air Force on top of a mountain.

Núñez Maza told him he was very grateful for his presence in Spain.

"It's my duty," the major answered.

Núñez Maza took out his tobacco pouch and his cigarette papers and offered the major a smoke. The latter accepted, and to the wide-eyed astonishment of Schubert, he rolled a cigarette, licked it, and placed it between his lips, then brushed off his hands.

"Well, how's that?"

"Magnificent."

The major explained. "There's no secret about it. Before we came to Spain, we learned to familiarize ourselves with a good many things."

Núñez Maza held out his lighter, and no one spoke. Finally the Falangist remarked, for the sake of saying something, "Anti-aircraft must be nice."

"Don't you believe it," the major answered quickly, sending out a mouthful of smoke.

"No? ... Why not?"

The major shrugged roguishly. "I don't like to 'bring down' anything." Schubert smiled. Clearly he liked his fellow countryman. He was about to say, "But sometimes there's nothing else to do. You've got to bring them down," when Major Plabb asked, addressing him instead of Núñez Maza, "Is General Franco a Falangist?"

Schubert took his usual pinch of snuff. "I think not," he said finally.

Núñez Maza particularized, "He thinks we're too far left."

Major Plabb's cigarette was about to come apart in the middle, and he moistened the gummed edge again. Then turning to Núñez Maza he asked, "How many Falangists have you at the front?"

Taken by surprise, Núñez Maza tried to concentrate, but Schubert made his figuring unnecessary by saying, "About eighty thousand..."

"And how many Requetés?"

Schubert took out his handkerchief to polish his glasses. "Fewer. About forty thousand..."

Núñez Maza was staring in astonishment at the two Germans. It seemed to him that the major had pronounced the word "Requetés" with some special significance. Turning to Schubert, he remarked, "You know it all by heart..."

Schubert coughed discreetly. "That's part of my job." Looking at Major Plabb, he quickly added, "Don't you like kings, Major?"

"Not one bit," Plabb replied.

At those words, Núñez Maza's face lit up with an almost infantile joy. The major noticed it and added that Nazism rated the idea of monarchy as decadent, a dead weight. "In Italy, the King is opposed to the Duce's support of Spain. The Duce has had to override him."

He himself was the son of a cooper. He had often watched his father in Bonn struggling to bend wood, and perhaps that was why he was an advocate of action. "I don't get this," he concluded, "I simply don't get it. Spain needs a strong, independent hand. A new hand. I don't understand how marching men can sing 'For God, for Country, and for King.'"

Núñez Maza said mendaciously, "I never sing that."

Instantly he repented of his words. What was wrong with him? He had a quick, brilliant intellect, and yet he felt uncomfortably timid before that cooper's son. And of course it was the fault of the French language that he was expressing himself so stupidly. He pulled himself together and tried to find out whether Major Plabb was abreast of the march of events. He alluded to the failure of the Madrid offensive.

"When there's a war on," the major replied, measuring his words, "no one can be sentimental." Abruptly he pointed his cigarette at Núñez Maza. "One must destroy, if it's necessary..."

"One must destroy." Schubert, still polishing his glasses, was of the same mind. Major Plabb had spoken as if Núñez Maza himself was the person responsible for the salvation of Madrid. "But of course," the Falangist was thinking, "it's one thing to play that theme song if you were born in Bonn and another if you come from Soria."

But would the major change his tune if the city to be destroyed were Bonn? The major was staring long and hard at the portrait of José Antonio. Núñez Maza said to himself, "I get the feeling that Schubert might be a sentimental man like me, but not so Major Plabb." Annoyed with himself, he went on, thinking, "What right have these two men to judge? After all, they're here to defend Spain."

Major Plabb turned back to Núñez Maza. "May I ask a question? Don't answer if you don't want to."

With his characteristically rapid reflexes, Núñez Maza regained control of himself. "Why not? You're my guest."

Major Plabb looked down at the swastika he wore on his chest. "It's about Franco... About Franco again."

"Go ahead."

"You said Franco thinks you're too far left. And what do you people think of him?"

Núñez Maza weighed his words. "Are you referring to the Falange?"

"No, no. I'm referring to the Falangists!"

Núñez Maza scratched an eyebrow. "We think he's a good general, that he's honorable and capable of winning the war."

Major Plabb nodded. "So, then, you're satisfied with the way the war has been conducted up to now..."

Núñez Maza stiffened. "Except for the attack on Madrid, yes."

Major Plabb seemed not quite satisfied. Schubert looked at his watch and said, "Major, it's time to go. They're waiting for us."

"Ah, yes. I'm glad you told me." He got up slowly. "The boy is so intelligent!"

Núñez Maza rose in his turn and did not reply.

"Ah!" exclaimed Major Plabb, taking a few steps and pointing to the street. "The parade, very beautiful."

"Thank you, Major."

"I enjoyed it very much."

"Up, Spain!"

Schubert, intentionally lagging behind, whispered to Núñez Maza, "We can talk later."

The two Germans left. Núñez Maza, the Propaganda delegate, stood quietly for a time, his hands behind his back, rocking up and down on his toes. He was thinking what a tragic thing a civil war was, and that several civil wars were going on in Spain just then. For there were Germans and Italians in the Red zone, too, and Frenchmen on both sides, though in smaller numbers. Three, four, five civil wars in Spain. The Falangist from Soria fished a few coffee grounds from his pocket and put them in his mouth.

On the whole, the war held an allure for him. He could admit to himself that if it were not for the victims, such a fantastic collision of forces would arouse intense jubilation in him; it gave him the measure of his own worth. "Before the war, what was I? A boy from the provinces, with a certain facility for selecting unusual adjectives." Now he was pursuing a grand, an enormous objective that would absorb him at his age of twenty-eight, or any other age, for that matter.

Núñez Maza would have liked to remain alone for awhile to think about the strong hand needed for Spain. But he heard an automobile horn honking below. It was a car crowned with loudspeakers. He decided that he must leave. He drew himself up in front of the portrait of José Antonio, said "Present!" and then turned and left the studio.

But it was his lot to be stopped by other people that day. He met Salazar and Aleramo Berti on the stairway. Both their faces were serious.

"What's the matter?"

"Nothing. We'd like to speak to you a minute."

TWENTY-FOUR

THE stove in the office was cold. The ventilator idle in a corner. A great silence over the city, as if everyone had died. Cosme Vila was sitting in front of his desk, unaware that he was shivering. He had lost weight since the beginning of the war; his spirit was consuming his flesh. Sometimes his worried wife would bring him a lunch. But the Party headquarters so intimidated her that Cosme Vila would say: "Go on home, let me work."

He had to write to Gorki, but he could not concentrate. He was upset. Barcelona had been bombarded from the sea, a baptism of blood that had come on the 13th of January, and had upset Cosme Vila. Sitting next to the cold stove, the Communist leader was staring at everything on the vertical in his office, as though hypnotized. He was not doing it for any particular reason, and he realized that it was useless; but he went on counting. The stovepipe, one. The pencil in his hand, two. The legs of the furniture, three. The lamp hanging from the ceiling, four.... Four, ten, twenty vertical objects in his office. The world is marked off with lines, like the palm of his hand. There must be vertical lines in the heart, too. But that afternoon his heart felt as round as a drum. And the projectiles sent upon Barcelona from the sea must have described a parabola, a curved line, like those that fell upon the Bay of Roses, before falling upon the horizontal earth.

> Dear Comrade Gorki: I'm writing you privately. How are you? My Party always says nothing "nothing new" but I know they wouldn't change that text even if you or some other comrade were to die. Well, what do you think, you rascally perfumer? We'll win the war! We'll win! "Madrid, the tomb of Fascism!" I've hung that phrase up in my office and I never tire of reading it. The Brigades are the wonder of the world! It's too bad you're not here. Yesterday a train came through full of Canadians and North Americans (many Negroes among them) and even Japanese

and Chinese. I can't help it, this solidarity makes a sentimental man of me...a glad man!

Can you imagine me in a good humor? Well, I am. Yes, Comrade Gorki. Remember our first meeting when we formed the Committee... You were a man of little faith, but now you can see for yourself. Aside from that, I'm doing all I can here, always struggling against the FAI and indifference and sabotage. The factories are not producing, there are secret agents and a few technicians. Axelrod has sent two, but the lack of a common language slows things down.

But in any case, the reason for this letter is to talk about you and your work... I'd like to congratulate you on your latest story about the traitor Chamberlain—the English are defending Gibraltar—and on the good progress of your Culture Corner on the Huesca front. It's a strange thing that a war and trenches were needed to enable the Party to teach hundreds of men whom capitalism had abandoned to read the facts and the laws. We have to do it all, to teach it all—a truck will bring you books and pamphlets one of these days—from the alphabet for the men to "painless childbirth" for a woman, a new technique that Professor Lyrie had initiated in Russia. But it's all coming out according to plan. I'm content, though it bothers me to have the stove going when I know you're cold at the front. Ah, Comrade Gorki! When shall we all be together here again to celebrate victory? Well, not all...that can't be... La Valenciana will be missing. And who knows how many more? I'm left without my two students now. I sent them to Albacete as interpreters, and they were enchanted. Alfredo died (I've already told you that) and I thought that would take the steam out of the POUM. But it turns out that Murillo was wounded in Madrid and is on the way to becoming a hero. We'll see that he's treated and sent back quickly. If it were not for the FAI and the POUM! But, as you know, Largo Caballero is a match for them.

Nothing more, Comrade Gorki, you old slacker, you former mayor! Let me know if you've lost weight and whether you're perfuming the place there. I'm in a joking mood, as you see. I am! My father-in-law said to me yesterday: "Any day now you'll be telling us a joke." I don't know that I'd go so far as that, but anything can happen.

Cosme Vila was making up tales... He was pretending to be in a good humor, as he was inventing the fire in the stove. He was doing it for Gorki's sake. Actually he was in a mood of great sadness those days. He was trying to combat it by going to the station to greet the International Volunteers with shouts of joy, repeating again and again, "They shall not pass!" But all in vain. Even Axelrod had noticed it and had stared at him in a manner that signified, "You're not going to fail us now, are you?" To be sure, Cosme Vila was worried by the hordes of children who had come to Gerona after being evacuated from Madrid. And by the conviction that the enemy had planted several spies in Gerona. His conjectures made a mountain out of a molehill, but he would have liked to come up against their ringleader. Added to that, things were not going well in his private life. His mother-in-law was ill, perhaps with tuberculosis, and his wife had put up a sign saying "Week of the Child," thinking to please him, but also had announced that she was pregnant again. That had frightened Cosme Vila, and he had forced her to have an abortion. For the first time she had rebelled, though in very soft words. Cosme Vila had to put her in a car and take her to the hospital where everything went wrong, so that when he saw her later she was lying in a constantly spreading pool of blood. Cosme Vila had not known that the blood of someone near to him could be redder than the Communist flag. He found out that day! And he felt that he loved his wife! He did not believe love could be a kind of weakness *per se,* but it did predispose him to a sort of disorbited happiness. And later when he went back home, he felt lonely. Loneliness, the wound in him which never had formed any scar tissue. He always had been thinking of all the world, he always was writing "hundreds, thousands"—like those who pile up the shards of war—and he felt alone in his house, alone in the office, mesmerized by vertical lines. Yes, the letter he had written to Gorki that afternoon was all invention when he mentioned gaiety... Cosme Vila was sad, and he was not going to tell any jokes to his father-in-law just then. Besides, he was feeling the cold. "I'm not surprised," he thought, "that many wars and revolutions break out in the summer." The cold was paralyzing him. "In spite of all my efforts, I'm probably still a southerner." And he felt guilty that, because he was afraid of infection, he had never once gone in to ask his mother-in-law how she was.

In the office of El Responsable the stove was glowing. CNT-FAI had left the gymnasium and moved to the apartment of one of the Costa deputies. The fan stood idle in a corner. The map of operations, a large photograph of Bakunin, another of Durruti, another of Elisée Réclus, and in a frame a small one of Future.

El Responsable was seated, with his cap on. He was a little Napoleon. He had a small electric burner beside him to heat his coffee. The coffee was boiling over just then and the electrical filaments were trembling and turning livid as if in their death agony. El Responsable often was visited by his daughter Merche, who was trying to make a sweet tooth of him. "Why do I love you so much, Papa?"

"Because I'm just an old crock."

El Responsable was getting set to write a letter to José Alvear, because *La Soli* of Barcelona had published a story on his exploits at the Madrid front and his friendship for Durruti. But what a great effort it was for the man to write anything! His handwriting was childish, h's omitted willy-nilly and, for lack of Gorki's teachings, he could not find the words to express what he was feeling. So he was vacillating, trying to make up his mind to ask Merche for help, and studying the horizontal lines of the room as though hypnotized: the desk, the ceiling, the mosaic of the floor, the sheets of paper, the blotter, his fingers. So many things! How many things spend their time lying down, always lying flat, as if sleepy. The universal sleep...the sleep of inanimate objects. El Responsable, the short man, never had thought of doing that, for he always had wanted to stand tall.

> Comrade Alvear: In case you haven't seen it, I'm sending you *La Soli* where your name appears. You look so good in your picture it's a pleasure, but I'd rather have seen your name for something else besides Durruti's death. I can't get used to the idea yet. And two lines in *El Proletario*! They're scum. I'm out of sorts and very anxious to leave the home front and go with you. So much CNT blood, and it's Hitler's fault and that fop of a Mussolini's that the war is still going on. They bombarded Barcelona from the sea on the 13th. You probably know that already. A good beginning for the year! Every day more and more children from Madrid, evacuated to here are arriving, and it smells to me like Cosme Vila is plotting something for them. When he says he has a headache, hold on tight, curves ahead. Now he's proud as a peacock over those Brigades, when you and I know that if Madrid is saved, it'll be by our men. Of course Morales is a liar, and some day I'm going to let that fellow know that he's not getting away with it. And when I do, I'll jerk off his glasses. And speaking of fellows, I suppose my young nephew El Cojo is behaving himself, considering what a brute he is. Say hello to him, and to Ideal, too, who's gone and got himself married, they tell me. She must be a bird! The sick one here is Santi. He wanted to kill the sea on the night of the Bay of Roses. And the one that's lining his pockets is Julio. I can smell it. Every day he's off to Paris to buy powder and aspirin tablets. I tell you I'm pretty sick about so much exaggerating and so much

> "I was just going to do it." They're sending us leggings from La Soler that fall to pieces as soon as the air hits them, like those bishops in the catacombs. There must be Fascists there, of course there are. I'm sorry I couldn't see you masquerading as a captain. Sometimes I think you and Merche... Well, I'm not saying a word. You've seen how the Fascists have kept mum since Madrid. And they've granted a Laureate to the Virgin del Pilar! Just to clean themselves. We're sending you a truckload of magazines and postal cards. Let's see if those girly postcards won't inspire you. Of course you...
>
> Is it true that you're dancing the schottische for the Communists to the tune of the "Internationale"? And all the time I thought you were sitting in a corner! Well, Comrade Alvear, write some time, and I congratulate you on the piece in *La Soli.*

El Responsable was not being sincere, he did not know why... He was telling a story about his sadness while the truth was that he was passing his days very happily. Good news canceled out bad in his mind. Four CNT Ministers in the Government! Six rebel Fiats shot down over Madrid. The Fascists mum! And to top it all, two new smiles at home, two children from Madrid. El Responsable had taken them in out of nostalgia for the ones Merche might have had by Future. One of them was named Pepe, the other Antolín, and they spent their time running around the arches of the Rambla and cutting out little flags. They were a consolation to Merche, too, and without telling her vegetarian "Pappy" she fed them good beefsteak. El Responsable felt like a grandfather to them when he came home. He also felt like a child. He was glad, too, that Murillo had been "squashed." And glad because he had made a trip to the border and had seen the French gendarmes' képis. El Responsable always had believed them to be a joke. When he saw that they were not, it put him in a good humor that had lasted to the present. Now his immediate aspiration was to find out what the devil Axelrod was up to, for twice in one week he had climbed into a mysterious truck and gone with his dog to a village in the Pyrenees named La Bajol, where there were some famous talc mines. "What would a man and a dog want with talc?" El Responsable felt so happy that he would have gone to the movies except that the only films there were always showed Stalin's mustache. And he was even beginning to laugh at things he used to take very seriously in the early days of the revolution, for example bonds for "support" and the collectivization of the barbershops. Yes, only to think of it made him laugh, and also to think of the bad time "his" prisoners were having there in his private jail. At Blasco's inspiration they had been deprived of any kind of paper, which made them come out of the latrine in distress and walking peculiarly. El Responsable whistled a good deal, especially the songs from *zarzuelas* which were picked up by Pepe and Antolín, the two children from Madrid. Unlike Cosme Vila, he felt stimulated by the cold. The Dehesa, for example, springlike and leafy, seemed to smother him, as if it had too many arms. The Dehesa, stark in January, delighted him, gave him a feeling of freedom. "That's why you love me so much, Merche, because there's nowhere you can take hold of me, I'm just an old crock."

Two men and a woman in what had been the Church of San Félix, in the sacristy, a church now turned into a grocery store, a gigantic cooperative. Bags were piled up, not high enough to reach the ceiling, but to the pulpits. They formed labyrinths for the children of the quarter, who ran around puncturing the bags and filling their pockets if they liked what ran out. The church was redolent of grain, of scorched wood, of hemp. Smoked tongues hung from the columns and even from the vaulted ceiling. Organ tones still were hiding in the interstices of the stone. Footsteps gave forth strange echoes in the silence. On the main altar a pile of dried codfish was lying, looking like a mortuary stand with a coffin. The baptismal font had become a basin for the olive oil that was poured out to be tested for quality. One day Casal's wife had gone in, and not knowing what it held, had used it as if it were holy water.

Antonio Casal, David, and Olga in the sacristy overflowing with wheat from Bulgaria and dried chickpeas. It was six o'clock in the afternoon. The sun had shot itself behind the Rocacorba Mountains. "It looked like an airplane falling into the sea." They did not know whether they felt happy or sad. More likely sad. The three of them would crush any hull they found on the floor with the tips of their shoes. They were talking idly, sitting where the albs and chasubles used to be kept. Antonio Casal still was wearing cotton in his ear and David was smoking. He had taken up smoking "not for the sake of the tobacco, but for the smoke." Olga was wearing a curious patent-leather desert cap that had been thrown from the window of a train by an International Volunteer. She wore it respectfully, as she would wear a soul. No sound could be heard in the church turned grocery store. All three of them were cold. Why were churches always so cold? They were talking at random. David was saying, "The Russians are very fond of chess."

David and Olga were happy that their school was functioning again. The refugee children from Madrid had brought it back to life, and they had found assistant teachers among the boys of Claridad who had studied with Ignacio. Antonio Casal felt sad because his wife had asked him, "What will become of those little ones if Cosme Vila sends them to Russia? You don't suppose they'd send ours there?" She said that because such a rumor was going around the city, and *El Proletario* had not denied it.

Casal's wife was forever asking "Why." Why were there so many trains, so many airplanes, so much death? She never had understood why the sun set. They had three children whom she kept wanting to take to the circus, as at Christmas. She preferred the clowns and even the elephants to the military and the militia. She would have been most pleased if there had been more circuses and fewer Masons.

Antonio Casal and David and Olga were sad because the war was lengthening. They could not delude themselves. If six Fiats were shot down, another six would come. Sometimes when photographs arrived they felt encouraged; but sometimes they were afraid that the war would be lost. Like Cosme Vila, they blessed the militia and sabotage, and by virtue of their work in the Post Office as censors, they were able to read much of the foreign press. They had learned from it that there were militiamen who would throw off their blankets at sunrise to fight without pause until sunset, that an epidemic of malaria had been declared in the country around Madrid, that in the province of Gerona pine trees were being cut down at a great rate, and that *El Demócrata* was protesting it in vain: "Every pine cut down is a battle lost." The three Socialists could foresee the progressive growth of the phantom of hunger, and they were sad about that. Lines were being formed for everything. And not only did the men in the front lines have to be provided for, but also the people of the two cities of Madrid and Barcelona, each with more than a million inhabitants, plus innumerable villages. And the peasants, especially those on the irrigated lands of the East were refusing to plant because patrols had robbed them of everything the year before. "We shall need thousands of churches stocked like this one," David said, "to keep us from having to eat our patent-leather desert hats pretty soon."

All three were happy because Pablo Casals, "the greatest violon-cellist ever born" according to Dr. Rosselló, not only was giving concerts to raise funds for the International Volunteers, but also just had refused to play in Nazi Germany and had publicly declared his loyalty to the cause of the heroic Spanish people. They were sad because the most brilliant of the Spanish gypsies in Granada were dancing nightly for the soldiers, whether beardless corporals or bearded colonels.

Sadness and gladness, what a strange mixture! David had tossed away the stub of his cigarette and Olga had stamped on it. Casal was saying, "Julio is a lynx." And as David's eyes roamed around the place, he suddenly saw a plaster hand in one corner of the sacristy, doubtless from a figure of Christ. He frowned, turned his back, and asked Casal, "Where will the dead find rest?"

Casal and Olga blinked. What a question to come from David's lips! He already knew the answer. The mouths of the dead would be filled with ants or fishes. They would come to rest on land or sea.

"If they're going to rest on land or sea, why are we fighting?"

An unheard-of question. They were fighting for the present, and to insure that generations unborn would have a home and be masters of their thoughts and not have to flee from Madrid or throw off their blankets at sunrise.

"But life lasts such a short while. I don't know whether it's worth all the trouble..."

What was happening to David? Olga went to him. He was having a moment of weakness. Asking questions that, according to El Responsable's father, rose from the viscera. Olga caressed the angular face of her man and Casal turned his back on the couple. The rose windows were black spheres now. Sounds were heard beneath the vault of San Félix. Whether they came from the organ that used to be there and that Teo had destroyed, or whether they were made by the children in the quarter as they went around puncturing bags to pick up grain from Bulgaria, there was no knowing.

ROOM eighteen in the Hotel Majestic, a clean, impersonal room. Axelrod was slowly smoking a Russian cigarette with a long mouthpiece as he lay on his bed. He was recalling his country childhood in Tiflis. The bed-pad had been straw then, or thorns. His childhood had been full of thorns that pierced his skin, and of unsatisfied wants. His parents could buy him nothing, they could not even teach him to read.

He felt happy for a number of reasons. Happy over Madrid, for he had been informed that he would soon be appointed consul in Barcelona, replacing Owscensco, who was being called back to Moscow; happy because the military report on the performance of the Russian aircraft sent to Spain for their baptism of fire had been favorable. Besides, he liked the Hotel Majestic. What could have happened to Dr. Relken? He liked the hotel because its clientele was transient, because friendships were not made there, a fact basic to him, for, like Stalin in his first revolutionary phases, he was afraid that human affections might become a drag on his activities. He was therefore pleased to have sent the following report to Moscow: "In the opinion of the undersigned, the Spanish people are *per se* proud, undisciplined, religious, and susceptible to friendship, which makes it impossible for them to be Communists in the official sense of the word." Within a month of his arrival Axelrod had said to Goriev, "Actually, the only Communist I've met here is Cosme Vila."

Axelrod was happy, and even the black patch over his eye might have been said to smile. He had lost his eye through stupidity during a shooting match in Warsaw. Why did he keep thinking of Cosme Vila, even in the Hotel Majestic? Because, in his opinion, Cosme Vila resembled Lenin, not only physically, as was obvious, but even in some of his mannerisms—for example, resting his hands in his lap with his fingers interlaced—and even in such particular oddities as sitting down on the stairs to write. Yes, Lenin had liked to do that, the same as Cosme Vila: to sit sidewise on a stairstep and write on the tread above. And their austerity... Both men had slept many a night of their lives on the ground or on a pallet without a mattress, and both had known hunger often. The one thing that had bothered Axelrod was the rejection of Lenin's simplicity in one of the most spectacular burials in one of the most spectacular mausoleums that humanity could devise, while Cosme Vila's burial most surely would be as anonymous as his present private life.

Another cause for satisfaction in those early days of 1937 was that Stalin, whose fear of death was known in the Kremlin, had just called in Professor Alexander Borgomolets, a specialist in techniques for prolonging life. Borgomolets and Stalin's head doctor, Nicholas Sparawski, had gone to the Abkhzai region in the Caucasus, where, it seemed, nearly four thousand centenarians still were alive. Stalin had said he was ready to submit to any treatment as long as it would prolong his life. Axelrod accepted all such news as credible, and it did not surprise him, as it had Goriev, that neither *Pravda* nor *Izvestia,* the two leading Russian newspapers, had mentioned it. Axelrod recalled the play on words involving those newspapers that had been popular in Russia. The pun was based on their names—*Pravda,* which means "truth" and *Izvestia,* which means "news." "In Russia we have a *Truth* that carries no news, and a *News* that never tells the truth."

Axelrod was happy. He had told no one the end he was pursuing on his trips to the village of La Bajol in the Gerundian Pyrenees, and the only thing that discommoded him was the forthcoming arrival of one of the heads of the GPU.

A room above the river, above the Oñar. A bed with a bright blue eiderdown quilt. A small night table, chairs, and a dresser. Pilar's face was reflected in the mirror. She had just come home from standing in line for some soap. Having had supper, she sat down in her room, preparing to write in her diary. She never had skipped a day, though she no longer dared to commit herself to paper. She had kept her diary in the secret chamber of her mind. "A mental diary," Ignacio called it, and the phrase seemed appropriate to Pilar, for, as they say, she felt nothing of all that was happening to her or that she dreamed about in her heart... She noted it all in her mind, behind her eyes, beneath her hair. "Does this happen to you, too, Ignacio?" Mateo was her diary. Mateo and her misgivings because she had failed to accept the proposal of the Rosselló sisters. On that night in January when the transmontane wind blew freezing out of France, Pilar was filled with deep sadness. She had to do her own thinking now; Mateo could not do it for her. Pilar scarcely recognized herself. She grasped subtleties that she never had imagined and associated ideas, something that had been forbidden in the Campistol sisters' shop. Ignacio had come to the conclusion that his sister's intelligence had been awakened by responsibility. Pilar was less happy than she had been, however, and as much of the world as seemed possible and thinkable to her also frightened her. She even asked herself what a mirror was and how she could be sure she was not simply a reflected image of someone else!

Ignacio found her writing in her mental diary and toying with her earrings. He kissed her hair. Why should he do that? He used to say to her, "You never think at all." Now he said, "You think too much." Ignacio was wearing an odd beret this winter. It gave him a kind of foreign air. He took it off and exchanged comments with Pilar on the disappearance of Don Emilio Santos, concerning whom they never had been able to learn anything. Pilar felt even sadder, remembering Don Emilio as a silent soul who had passed by with a word of greeting. Ignacio, too, had grown sadder and he sat down on the bed with his hand open as if holding a cup of milk. The brother and sister were alone and they loved each other, near the Oñar, the river unheard and unseen, but there, like life. Ignacio suddenly said, "I know what I'll do. I'll get into the Health Service. Tomorrow I'll start studying anatomy."

Pilar was not paying attention. She was thinking of the Cárcel Modelo and of Don Emilio and Mateo. "In Health?"

"Yes. You know I've tried every way to get to France and there's no way. The guides are scared, and even Julio wouldn't dare go with me to the frontier. I'll enlist in Health, and I bet you that in a couple of weeks I'll go over to Nationalist Spain."

"Why Health?"

"It's human."

"Human... Everything's human," Pilar thought. "Loving and sinning and having green eyes."

"What will we do without you?" she asked him listlessly. She was tired. She did everything and spoke without moving out of her chair.

"And what will I do without you three?"

Loving and doubting. They were all Ignacio could do. He was wearing the stigmata. He was leading too personal a life. He walked around like the rest, but in another way. He put on his beret, and on him it had a fey look. He waited on the clients in the bank and many of them asked him, "What's your name?" They were beginning to address him formally, despite the revolution.

His obsession, the obsession of thousands of boys, was going into the ranks, being drafted. Barracks! Some were walling themselves in to avoid having to report. Some had a pneumothorax, or feigned insanity or horrible illnesses. And soldiers swore shocking oaths when they were inducted, thinking it was expected of them... Ignacio would not mutilate himself or swear. He would study anatomy, particularly everything having to do with the brain, and he would enlist in Health...if he could.

"What can Marta be doing?"

"What can Mateo be doing?"

They felt happier then. They sensed the presence of Marta and Mateo, and of the river, too. There they both were, beside the mirror, in the monastery of the blood.

Carmen Elgazu came in with a gray woolen shawl around her shoulders. She was carrying a shaky tray with two large cups of coffee.

"What's the matter with you two? It's time for bed."

Ignacio paid no heed and went on, "You, Pilar, ought to be doing something. You ought to get some sort of job."

"Where?"

"I don't know. In some office."

"Office?"

"You could be earning something. And keeping your mind occupied."

Carmen Elgazu set one of the cups down on the dresser near Pilar and dissolved the sugar with a spoon. "In an office!" she exclaimed. "With that trash!"

"Why not?"

Suddenly Matías's voice came from the dining room. He just had turned off the radio. "It would be better if Julio could get her a job in food supply."

Carmen Elgazu handed the other cup to Ignacio, and as she stirred in the sugar, she looked soberly toward the dining room. "None of that! With that trash..."

Another silence. A heavy sadness. The four of them were sure that "there's something to be done besides loving one another."

TWENTY-FIVE

THE humorous weekly *La Ametralladora* still was making its way on the Nationalist battle and home fronts. Its humor was based on the absurd, on a frontal attack on a subject and the ready phrase, on stylization of the macabre.

"How old are you?"

"Pepe."

This Pepe signified everything. That the spirit must laugh, that age is nothing, that one must not inquire into his neighbor's business. He was a Pepe born in Madrid, who had seen many things that had seemed changeless disrupted by the war.

"My name is Purita."

"Mine isn't."

The "isn't" was dry and crackling as a rifle shot. *La Ametralladora! La Ametralladora!* ... The weekly was fresh air to the mind, and it soon had a noticeable influence on the lexicon of thousands of fighters. Its modern cartoons were a challenge, and perhaps they would not have pleased Ezequiel at all.

The detractors of *La Ametralladora* were many. Many professional soldiers, many learned professors... The young people were categorizing a person with the words, "He doesn't get *La Ametralladora!*" That was enough. Everyone knew where he stood.

Mosén Alberto was one of the people who detested the weekly. He was not sad in the manner of Cosme Vila; rather he felt out of step, a sadness of the soul that no *La Ametralladora* could heal. Mosén Alberto was still in Pamplona, in the nunnery. He was editing a new catechism that he had picked up in Perpignan, but that did not suffice him. He missed his office in Gerona, the Diocesan Museum, Catalonia... Increasingly, he felt that Navarre was a primal land, a land of instinct. Don Anselmo, with whom the priest had established relations, once said to him, "Father, everything not Catalonia seems primitive to you, including Oxford, Montecasino, and the lamaseries of Tibet." Perhaps it was true. Mosén Alberto felt more Catalonian than ever, and during the lengthy visits he used to pay to Sister Teresa, Carmen Elgazu's sister, he would begin with the same refrain: "Ah, Sister Teresa! When this is all over I shall invite you to become acquainted with my country."

Out of step. He considered the suggestion to enlist in the Catalan Infantry Regiment of Our Lady of Montserrat as a field chaplain, but he did not want to do it. Mosén Alberto was anti-militaristic by nature, and he declined. But that only increased his bad humor. His escape valves were the movies he used to stand in line for occasionally, and especially his sermons to the small group of nuns, who treated him like an archangel.

To be sure, Mosén Alberto was the first to be surprised at the tone of his sermons. He had turned tragic, more so than in 1934 when he had addressed the leftist prisoners in the Gerona prison. He terrorized the nuns with dreadful visions. And when he discovered that those brains under the white coifs offered him no shred of intellectual resistance, he made the chapel ring with echoes. At times the nuns were made to feel totally responsible for the war that was devastating the nation. On the day that Mosén Alberto learned of the death of the Bishop of Gerona, he chose as his text: "The lack of prayer is an indirect means of crucifying." Moreover, the priest was aware of the executions carried out by the Requetés in Navarre. Don Anselmo had summed it up: "For a train to run, the tracks have to be clear," and he never tired of repeating: "It cries out to Heaven."

ANOTHER man impervious to the humor of *La Ametralladora* was Warning Voice. The dentist would leaf through it once a week, and when he read about a cow that had gone into a music shop and asked to have her bell tuned, he exclaimed "What idiocy!" and refused to touch the magazine again. Javier Ichaso, his assistant in SIFNE, was not amused by the publication either, not even by the ineffable dialogues of Don Venerando.

Warning Voice, however, had more reasons for satisfaction than Mosén Alberto. The SIFNE, which had started in an embryonic office, immediately began to take on a formidable growth, thanks to what Warning Voice called "the patriotism of the refugees from the Red zone." Indeed, for one reason or another, the majority of the fugitives, particularly those from the province of Gerona, kept squeezing into that apartment on the Calle de Alsasua, kept clean and shining by the maid Jesusha. People headed for it seeking directions, and Warning Voice, always on the lookout for new Service agents, handled everyone with such solicitude that he began to be known as "the nice Consul." "I, nice! What I'm doing is looking for a good decoder and someone who understands Danish."

The key to Warning Voice's success lay in a shrewd combination of obedience and intuition. His own intuition and his obedience to Don Anselmo Ichaso served to establish a daily mail service between San Sebastián and Pamplona.

Don Anselmo was enchanted with the results. The preparatory base, the network of agents, had been established with extreme care. The initial link-up, now known, that ran from San Juan de Luz through Perpignan and Gerona, reaching to Barcelona and Madrid, had been enriched with unexpected auxiliaries. Notary Noguer, in Perpignan, with the previous consent of Mateo, could count for weeks on the aid of the Falangists Octavio and Rosselló, who had obtained the desired *droit d'asile* after a hard struggle with the French authorities. The notary assigned the two boys to snooping around the merchandise sent to the Reds from the ports of Marseille and Port-Vendres, and the boys gave full satisfaction. In Gerona, Laura won the collaboration of the gravedigger and his wife. In Barcelona, several groups of Falangists led by a young lawyer named Roldan, on the fringe of the autonomous cells whose lack of experience had often provoked Neronic reprisals, gave positive aid to SIFNE. Thanks to the agents in Madrid, captained by a paid spy nicknamed Difícil, General Mola had at his disposal, at last, an up-to-date military cartography, a replica of the file in the War Ministry. The agents in Valencia, directed by Father Estanislao, who had adopted the pseudonym of Marisol, were performing with such brilliance that not a single ship in their sector was able to approach the east coast without its cargo being known and without previous contact with the engineer who had started to build a defensive ring around Bilbao.

As the services gained solidity and cohesion, the work in SIFNE became more and more stimulating. Newspapers from twenty countries were scrupulously read by the staff of Dr. Mouro, the multilingual Portuguese, and attentive listeners caught the radio broadcasts from Europe, Africa, and America. The advice of the "mysterious German" had been taken, so that many keyed messages were sent to the Red zone on the backs of stamps or on ordinary folded newspapers with marked margins, such media being preferred to the use of invisible inks no longer a secret to anyone. The contents of top secret Red papers were delivered to San Sebastián, as well as a large number of used carbon papers, easily read in reverse. In the customs at Hendaye and La Linea, all travelers who could not supply the names of guarantors in Spain were stripped, at times in searches so exhaustive that many of the women reacted with kicks and screams. The agents installed in the enemy zone chose the most unsuspected places to exchange documents: public urinals, doctors' waiting rooms, jai-alai courts. Very often they used lockers in the railroad stations to deposit packages and suitcases.

Of course the tricks were various and the failures many. Captains of merchant vessels, for example, would offer the SIFNE agents in France to let themselves be taken prisoner on the high seas with all their cargo and be escorted to some Nationalist port. But how could anyone know whether the captain would keep his word? Don Anselmo Ichaso decided on principle "to pay after the event, not before." He suspected those who introduced themselves to Warning Voice with a minuscule map of some Red city or zone on which all the military objectives were marked, for they were likely to be pure invention. Likewise he suspected the fantasies of those who boasted of many spontaneous confidants, usually fugitives from the Reds who, when interrogated, would inflate facts and figures at will. And, of course, the vacillations of many Frenchmen who were sincere "*franquistas,*" but who drew back as soon as they scented the possibility that the service to which they had committed themselves might do harm to the interests of their own country.

On the other hand, the service of enemy espionage was proving a most elusive wraith... No doubt about it. Time was proving that it must be taken seriously, in defiance of Don Anselmo Ichaso's theory that the Reds were not capable of putting together a solid organization. Time after time they hit their air-raid targets, and they carried on widespread sabotage, particularly on the railroads and along the Portuguese frontier, through which a good deal of German matériel was entering. The latest effective demonstration of enemy espionage had been made during the battle of Madrid, in the offensive at the Jarama. General Miaja had been forewarned of the operation in full detail. His response and the emplacement of his foot soldiers man by man gave irrefutable proof of that.

Warning Voice had a theory about that. He was building it on logic and had begun to base his labor of counter-espionage accordingly. The main source of enemy spies was the working people. And next, the women. Perhaps he was obsessed by the precedent set by Laura and her group, but he was certain that the widows and children of the men who had been shot would work with fanatical tenacity. Then there were the shepherds...masters of the movements of their flocks and constantly on the move from one pasture to another through the open lands of Huesca, Cuenca, and Granada. Don Anselmo Ichaso hit the ceiling at the idea, but Warning Voice would not give ground. "What do you want me to do? Disguise myself as a carabineer and stand over them with a rifle?" Diplomatic dispatch cases and the reports of foreign press correspondents enjoyed complete impunity… "I take all I can," said Warning Voice, "but they burn me up!" Finally, there was the support of all the leftists on earth. And perhaps, yes perhaps, of some young Moor or other, acting as aide to some officer on the General Staff.

It struck Warning Voice to the heart to think that on the Madrid or Granada front, this important plank in their platform might break down. He could never forget that though most of the Moroccan tribesmen had answered Franco's call to arms unconditionally, many an old chief would whisper to his sons about to leave for the Peninsula the final message: "Go, and kill Spaniards…"

Warning Voice went every day to the Church of the Buen Pastor to take communion before starting his work. This added luster to the reputation he had won among the aristocratic ladies in the cities, that of an unexceptionable gentleman. On Twelfth Night he won a signal triumph: he succeeded in arresting the famous Dionisio, whom Don Anselmo Ichaso had mentioned during their first meeting in Pamplona, and whom the "mysterious German" had pronounced the dragon's head of enemy espionage.

Dionisio! His arrest was incredibly easy. Two agents who were refugees in Vitoria soon noticed as they were tailing an insignificant-looking blond girl, the presence of a man wearing a corduroy cap within fifty yards of where they had picked her up. The man, trying to appear natural, was busy placing a strange artifact at the foot of a very handsome electric power station. "Halt there!" It was all too easy. The man and the girl were taken to the office of Warning Voice. The man refused to speak a word, but that did not help him, for within ten minutes of the start of the interrogation, the blond girl confessed: "His name is Dionisio."

Warning Voice almost wept with joy, and so did Javier Ichaso. The dragon's head! Don Anselmo Ichaso congratulated the dentist, saying, "You're like a fish in water with SIFNE." Warning Voice felt confident that patience and the use of scientific methods eventually would force Dionisio to tell all he knew and to inform on his colleagues. But God willed otherwise. Unlike his fellow townsman, Julio García, Warning Voice never could think of suicide. But Dionisio could. Dionisio killed himself on a morning like any other. While on his way from one of the interrogations in the office of Warning Voice, Dionisio, handcuffed and accompanied by a guard, suddenly pretended to stumble, turned, and threw himself through a window in the hallway.

Warning Voice was terribly upset. He had never imagined such "heroism" in that man with the corduroy cap and the restless eyes. "The rascal!" he muttered. Jesusha, the servant of the dentist and Javier Ichaso, wept when she heard of the incident, as though Dionisio had been one of her own.

THE second activity of Warning Voice, the one that had earned him the name of "Consul" to the fugitives from the Red zone, from Gerona and the province, also brought him a great number of surprises. Many of the newcomers underwent a radical change in a matter of days. They had arrived in San Sebastián as though purified, ready to give their all. But they soon accustomed themselves to thier new circumstances, forgot their recent perils, and found their old selfishness again.

Among the visitors whom Warning Voice received in his office during that month of January were the two Falangists Miguel Rosselló and Octavio. And among the interviews with him requested from France, the one of his brothers-in-law, the Costas, was noteworthy. The brothers made an appointment to meet him in a hotel in Biarritz. Warning Voice received Rosselló and Octavio effusively, even though he disliked the Falange and wanted nothing to do with it. But the adventures of the two boys in the French ports merited seeing them. Notary Noguer had written him: "Octavio crawled along the wharves like a lizard and Rosselló was like a police dog smelling out munitions in crates labeled 'Perfumes' or 'Champagne.'"

After drinking a toast with the boys in the presence of Javier Ichaso, he suggested to them that they should continue collaborating with SIFNE, with Mateo's continued assent taken for granted. The boys made no difficulties; they had grown accustomed to the work.

"For my part, done."

"For mine, too."

Warning Voice smiled, pleased. "You, Rosselló, will be assigned to the Josué group on the Madrid front. You'll leave day after tomorrow with a letter to Colonel Maroto of the Sixth Infantry Legion. He'll give you your instructions. I assume you'll be sent to Red Madrid... Don't worry about that. To visit and come back. Of course, you'll need a cool head; but perhaps you'll be all the sharper for knowing that your two sisters in Gerona are working for the White Relief under my wife's direction, and that your father is in the Ritz Hotel in Madrid, now an Emergency Hospital, saving the lives of dozens of militiamen. All I need is for you to swear to two things: that you won't try to see your father in Madrid, even though we've told you where he can be reached, and that you'll prefer to die rather than fall into enemy hands with documents."

Rosselló thought a moment. "As to my father, I swear... I will not try to reach him. As to the other, I can't guarantee it."

Warning Voice smiled again. "That's the way I like it. You're not a braggart, and I congratulate you on that."

Octavio was assigned to the group called Noé, active on the Granada front. He was to report to Captain Aguirre of the Third Moorish Tabor. When he heard this, Octavio said jokingly, "I'd rather go back to Marseille." His mission was to peep and pry, trace and trail in that sector.

"Keep an eye on the Moors, and especially the young Moors. Never mind, Captain Aguirre will explain it to you…"

The two Falangists were interested in the whereabouts of the other fugitives from Gerona. "A show case," Warning Voice told them. "Jorge, pilot; Mateo you know about; José Luis Estrada, Navy. And now Mosén Alberto, in Pamplona… And here I am, as you see, a bachelor and being invited to all the social doings of San Sebastián society."

Rosselló, son of the Dr. Rosselló who was a brother in the Ovid Lodge, asked the dentist, "In case of my death would you help my father?"

Warning Voice reflected before mimicking the boy's earlier reply. "I can't guarantee it."

Octavio addressed Javier Ichaso, saying, "Have you been told about all the trial balloons in France concerning a possible armistice?"

"You can imagine," Javier replied. "We spend the whole day listening to the radio and reading newspapers."

Warning Voice waxed indignant over such ignorance, such frivolity abroad. Brilliant English parliamentarians, Frenchmen, and Belgians were declaring daily: "The leaders of the two zones ought to meet in a neutral country and agree upon an armistice. And then permit the Spanish people to elect an equable system of government to suit everyone." By the nails of Christ! What did they mean by such a mishmash? Hadn't anyone told them what it was all about? How could justice be married to barbarity, God to La Pasionaria? He, Warning Voice, would never limp along with that. He would carry on the fight to the bitter end, even into eternity. And thousands and thousands of men and women in both zones with him. Biarritz and the democratic governments must be living on the moon.

Biarritz… In that city the Costa brothers were quoting Warning Voice. Once the Costas were safe and sound in France with their wives beside them, they settled themselves in Paris, where they called in the capital they had dispersed in Swiss and English banks, and with their minds easy on that score, and with the value of the jewelry their wives had brought with them at their disposal, they decided to pay a visit to Warning Voice, for they felt disoriented. Warning Voice went to a prearranged meeting in Biarritz. His air of a conqueror was so antipathetic and offensive to the Costas from the first moment, however, that in their annoyance they cut off the interview as quickly as possible. Naturally...the presence there of the two deputies signified a petty victory for the dentist!

"Well? What about benefits for the workers now? What about your contributions for the swimming pool and the democratic football?"

The Costas, once more smoking their Havana cigars, shrugged. Philosophizing was out of place. "What can we do about it? We've all made mistakes."

The dentist shook his head. "Not all. You were mistaken, not I. And your wives, too, I suppose. I have only to see them to know I'm proved right." He paused. "Well, what are you thinking of doing? What do you want of me?"

The Costas felt humiliated. "Nothing. Nothing just now... We'll wait..."

"Wait for what? Certainly, what everyone... Wait for the Navarrese Requetés to free Gerona and give you back the quarries?"

One of the wives spoke up. "It does you no good to have eyes in your head. You're all puffed up with pride, and in the end you're going to be worse off than we are. Let's go now."

The Costas stared at him long and hard. "Go on, go back to San Sebastián and hang a pair of scapulars around your neck."

Warning Voice rose. "So long!" He got into his car, a Citroën that the Service had turned over to him. It had belonged to a Socialist deputy before the war.

Quite unperturbed, he took the road to San Sebastián, whistling as he drove. On his right the sea appeared and disappeared like the feeling of youth in a man. He lowered his window at the checkpoints along the highway and, after saluting, tossed the soldiers a handful of French cigarettes.

Back at his office in the Calle de Alsasua, he found all his aides—his inferiors, he called them—hard at work. As usual, he had an affectionate phrase for his servant Jesusha, who asked him, "Would the gentleman like anything else?" for it was Thursday and she had the afternoon off. Then he took a bath—the room was so clean it looked like a dental clinic—and finally installed himself in his office and called for Javier Ichaso. His euphoria cried out for an audience, and no one could fill that role better than Javier. "What did you think of those Falangists from my home town?"

"I liked them very much. Especially the taller one."

"Ah, yes, Rosselló..." Warning Voice concurred. "His father is a Mason, crazy about music, and a louse. The son is crazy about cars. Any news?"

Javier Ichaso, sitting near the window, slapped one of the crutches he was holding between his legs. "Nothing much. The polyglot Professor Mouro has caught a slight cold..."

"The Portuguese are always catching cold. I wonder why?"

Javier Ichaso was staring at his chief with what seemed like a sneer. That was unusual, for the boy's admiration for the dentist had never lessened. "I heard a picturesque item over the radio: the highest tree in England has just died. A giant conifer about a hundred and fifty feet high. Are you fond of trees, chief?"

"I don't care about them one way or the other. What else?"

At this point, Javier Ichaso decided to drop his unusual attitude. "Nothing important," he said, pointing with an ambiguous expression at an envelope lying on the desk. "This letter from Pamplona... The envelope had been opened... It's from my father."

Warning Voice picked it up and began to read, wondering a little, for the letter had not come by regular mail. As he read, he began to frown with an anger and humiliation similar to that of the Costas a few hours earlier. Meanwhile, Javier Ichaso had lighted a cigarette and was caressing his crutches with an expression almost of amusement.

The contents of the short, brusque letter were undoubtedly meant as a lesson. The Dionisio whom the dentist had succeeded in arresting in Vitoria, the silent, austere man who had tried to run away from that power station, and who on an ordinary kind of day had put a heroic end to his life as he was leaving that very office, was not the real Dionisio, but a double of his. A double who had knowingly sacrificed himself, who had "let himself be arrested" on purpose, and who had killed himself to avoid informing on anyone and so that the real Dionisio could carry on his work with impunity.

Don Anselmo Ichaso left no possible doubt in the matter and offered to supply details. Even the blond girl who had been arrested at the same time knew about the substitution. The suicide was a laborer employed in a Zamora cement works, whereas the real Dionisio, much younger, was a mountaineer and somewhat taller.

Warning Voice could not raise his eyes to meet those of Javier Ichaso, still smoking with ostensible enjoyment... The dentist was as if turned to stone but for a thin white line around his lips.

MARTA Martínez de Soria—Mar-Mar as the Italian, Salvatore, called her in his first letter—understood perfectly the humorous cast of *La Ametralladora,* considered it intelligent and original, but could not laugh at it. Marta was serious, too serious, and with time and its manifestations, her seriousness was taking increasing possession of her face. She could not laugh with *La Ametralladora,* even though the weekly was the only thing that could lighten for awhile the expression of her mother, the major's widow.

Both women had left Cádiz and were living in their own place in Valladolid. They had been given back their apartment and even their old servant, Basilisa by name, who told them that José Luis and Mateo were on the Alto del León in the Onésimo Redondo Company. They sent a telegram to the boys at once, telling them of their arrival. Then, as Ignacio had predicted, Marta dressed herself in blue and wrote her sweetheart a postcard, signed with a pseudonym, which she handed that same day to a friend in the police who was on his way to France. "Post it in France, please..."

Before long, a constant stream of old friends of Marta's mother were calling at the house, most of them soldiers' wives. They had come to welcome her and condole with her on her widowhood. Marta's mother sniffed disconsolately, thinking that if the uprising had surprised them in Valladolid instead of in Gerona, her husband would have been fighting like a madman on some front at that very moment. The injustices of fate and geography were an old story, but no less painful for that to one whose very flesh was wounded. They felt sorry for Marta, perhaps most of all because of her reticence when some question would allude to the manner of the surrender in Gerona.

When Marta learned that the moving spirit of the Woman's Section, almost the Section itself, was María Victoria, the sweetheart of José Luis, she introduced herself at the Headquarters, and in a matter of fifteen minutes was appointed Provincial Delegate for Social Aid, assigned to doing whatever was needed on the home front during the period of quiet on the Northern front, and later in the front lines, to which she would be shifted as soon as the seemingly imminent offensive against Bilbao should begin. María Victoria said to her, "You don't know how wrought up you'll feel as you keep entering the liberated villages. It's an unforgettable sight...even to me, who forgets everything."

María Victoria's ebullience was to prove refreshing to Marta. Her "future sister-in-law" undertook to smooth out her brow within a month. "In less time than it takes to train a second lieutenant." To begin with, she dressed Marta's hair in a new style, clasped a couple of bracelets on her, hung a tiny, very pretty autograph book around her neck next to the embroidered arrows and said, "We have a reputation for being ugly in the Woman's Section, as I know. But that's sabotage, a canard Stalin is sending around. From now on, it's up to you to prove it's a canard, and you can begin by putting on lipstick. Use this one that's straight from Paris."

María Victoria had green eyes. They were constantly changing, but she swore that they were green. Marta, too, had to pay tribute: María Victoria stuck on the back of her hand the gum that she had been chewing. María Victoria's father was a professional soldier, a lieutenant colonel of artillery. He was traveling through Oviedo. He was an imperturbable man who clung to the traditional. If Ezequiel kept citing the future, María Victoria's father did the opposite, constantly citing the past. One time the girl said to him, "Papa, you contradict yourself so often it's harder to divine the past with you than it is the future."

María Victoria was very much in love with Marta's brother, José Luis. When Salazar and his other comrades would laugh at him and call him Kant because he was always studying, María Victoria would join in the chorus, but privately she was convinced that the boy carried within him one of those moving forces which only death can destroy. She loved him so much that she was glad to use Marta as an excuse to say, "Come on, let's go up to the Alto del León. The truck will be leaving here in a quarter of an hour. But...fix yourself up a little, please! Let's see your fingernails. Clean, naturally. But what would you think of putting on a little polish, only a little? Come on, do as I tell you, because I'm the boss!"

They wanted to go to the front rather than wait for Mateo and José Luis to be given a leave. Marta's mother said to them, "Bring back José Luis, at least. He's the only man I have now..."

The truck left. The Castilian route. "Enlist in the Falange!" "Domecq Cognac!" Gray stone, distant sky, and the front not far away. Aloft at the height of bird-flight an icy wind was whistling, and it made the truck driver exclaim, "Say something to me, kids! Something high-toned! I'm freezing to death..." María Victoria liked to ride in the cab of a truck: it made her feel like a man.

The arrival of the two girls on the Alto del León was like an apotheosis. To a man the company had been there for several weeks without a glimpse of a woman. The truck was surrounded in a second by a gang of disreputable, stinking, and bearded gadflies. Marta was afraid that she and her friend would be tossed in a blanket.

"Pinch me, I'm seeing visions!"

"Listen, ragamuffin! What day is it?"

"Shall we draw lots for them, or what?"

"Beautiful..."

"Dazzling..."

"Hi, María Victoria! ... Say, I know you! ..."

"Who's the other girl?"

The other girl was Marta, happy because at the last moment she had put on a little fingernail polish. Happy because those men, authentic in everything from the grease-spots on their tunics to the scent of burned straw and sardine oil, were paying so much attention to them. Happy because soon a flabby giant planted himself in front of them and standing at attention, said: "Nothing new, Generals." That was Salazar who had already been back at his post for a week without letting out a word about the abortive plan to free José Antonio. His comrades had pressed him in every imaginable way, and the lieutenant's reply had been invariable: "No luck." Mateo had said, "If I can ever find out the truth about that story of the drunk in Seville, and if it's so, I wouldn't mind shooting him."

Salazar was about to invite the two girls to have coffee in his domain, but he was forestalled. The Falangists fell in as if for dress parade in front of Marta and María Victoria. A supply sergeant led the march with a bugle. The troop formed up in threes, then began to mark time and sing:

"If you want to marry a girl from here, Go look for the capital in Madrid."

"To the right…march!"

When the parade was over, they were escorted to the advanced post occupied by José Luis and Mateo. The two men and the two women stood trembling, then embraced with ardor. Words failed them. But their eyes spoke.

José Luis finally managed to say, "Where's Mama?"

"Mama stayed home," Marta told him. "We were thinking they might give you leave to go down with us…"

"Yes, I guess they might."

Questions flew back and forth. How was Pilar? How was Ignacio? And Gerona, and the Pyrenees, and the world? What about an Italian ship? Guatemala? Tangier? But what the devil had they been up to?

"It was hardly worth your while to come so far…only to find us looking like ragamuffins."

"And how! … I met an Italian! Besides, he's handsome and his name is Salvatore…"

"You're kidding!"

José Luis had his arms around his sweetheart, the beautiful María Victoria, and was holding her close. Mateo longed to hold Marta, but did not dare to.

"Don't call yourselves ragamuffins," Marta said after a pause. "You're not! Just the opposite! You look to us like the most wonderful men in the world, and I'm going to ask you for your autograph to go into a little book that was given me. You look to us like… I don't know what!"

They tried not to grow too emotional. The two boys tried to give them in a few minutes a living synthesis of the active phase of the front. They provided each of the girls with a helmet. Marta's head was so small that the helmet covered it down to the neck. Then they gave them each a rifle and led them to the loopholes for one symbolic shot. "The Reds are over there behind that knoll. Can you see their smoke?"

María Victoria could not fit the rifle-butt to her shoulder, but Marta did it well at the first try. "My father taught me." Then they told the girls about the bare, closed-in life they were leading. "Cards, lanterns, the gasoline lamp, the cold, the mail, the truck..." Marta added: "The arguments, the jealousies, the home sickness, the godmothers!" And José Luis added the final touch: "And our thoughts!"

The two girls felt as if protected; they were experiencing to the full the feeling that someone was watching over them and over Spain. That those men there on a mountain top were sacrificing themselves for an ideal that would one day be grand, enlightening. "A weapon in hand and the stars above."

"Want a cigarette?"

"Yes, indeed!"

María Victoria took a minuscule pipe out of her pocket. "Don't be alarmed. A German girl gave it to me. It's terrific."

Salazar arrived and, seeing María Victoria's pipe, felt that his mammoth bowl looked ridiculous and hid it.

The shadows were falling over the Alto del León, over all the fatherland. Where they came from no one knew, nor where they reached an end. They were darkening hearts as well as affording man his needed rest. Aloft the wind was whistling more and more strongly as more and more shadows kept coming from nowhere.

Falangists were coming in, more Falangists, arousing a commotion. But they were no longer saying "beautiful" or offering to draw lots for María Victoria and Marta. Mateo had lighted a bonfire, and in its glow each individual's life blazed with the desire to be useful. The two girls threw dry branches on the fire, which flamed with immense suffering. And that was the moment chosen by Salazar to begin singing "Face to the Sun." Everyone joined him. Why, Lord, will the blind not see? Something was dancing in front of their eyes. It was hard to tell if it was sparks from the fire, flakes of snow, or Salazar's remorse ground to pieces.

ANOTHER individual who could not laugh at *La Ametralladora* was Paz Alvear, domiciled at number 12 Calle de la Piedra, in Burgos. Her shaved head now was covered with down. Her sweetheart was from Logroño. Like her father, he was a telegraph employee. Before the 18th of July, when all on earth still had been happy, the boy used to send her a telegram whenever he burned with the desire to be in touch with Paz. Her father would transmit it with a smile, and the messenger boy would go whizzing off on his bicycle to carry it to her at her home.

Paz Alvear was a member of the espionage system in the Nationalist zone, which Warning Voice longed to smash. So was her mother. Apart from working for the Red Relief and distributing food among her father's friends in the UGT who were in hiding, they had not been able to accomplish much, until suddenly their superior in Burgos, a harness maker named Venancio said to them, "Now's your chance." He assigned a job to each of them. Paz was to go out with a little box hung around her neck to sell tobacco, chewing gum, matches, lighters, and flints. She was to go particularly to the cafés frequented by soldiers and *listen.* Her mother was to try to get work as a cleaning woman in some official center or in the home of some official and carry away the papers from the wastebaskets!

"The Fascists will be attacking Málaga now and I'm afraid we won't be able to hold the garrison. But the South is secondary. What matters is to break them when they try to take Bilbao. So keep your ears wide open to anything that has to do with the Northern front." The harness maker spoke directly to Paz. "Don't forget we're asking this of you in memory of your father."

Venancio had been informed of the sacrifice of the agent from Zamora, Dionisio's double. But he did not know the real man either. He knew only that Dionisio was young, that he detested all political parties, and that he loved the syndicates. As for the two women, they had heard Dionisio mentioned only once.

Paz's mother reconnoitered her terrain, but for the moment found nothing. Cleaning women must be known and trusted... On the other hand, Paz began her work at once. Her preparations for it excited her as much as if the future of the world depended upon the acuteness of her hearing. "Kiss my ears, Mother." She covered her head with a bright scarf, and as she stood in front of the mirror she was undecided about making herself out an idiot girl or a frivolous one. She chose the latter. "The soldiers like long penciled eyebrows and lots of mascara." So on with it! Paz gazed at herself. She knew that she was attractive, but she hated the means. The washroom where she was making up was as poor as a finger without a fingernail.

Her little filled tray hung around her neck by a long leather strap that would not rub against her chest. "Do I look all right like this?" She almost laughed. Her mother shook her head. "How awful, child. You look like something..."

That did not matter. Paz was doing it for her father, for her sweetheart, for the Red Relief and the UGT, and to help win the war. She went down the stairs with care. "Of course we'll win! When the Germans and Italians attack Bilbao, they'll get the scare of their lives."

As Paz was nearing the main cafés, words began to run through her mind.

"I don't know whether I'll be any good at this... Soldiers! And Falangists and Moors. They smell like..."

"Tobacco, matches... Yes, sir. They're ten for forty..." What if anyone should recognize me... Machine guns! What are they saying! Nothing, I can't hear... "Tobacco, get your tobacco!" Nothing doing, sergeant? ... You think you're good-looking. If you could see yourself as I see you... Let's see if I can pick up something. My father wants me to find out something. "Any tobacco? Chewing gum, gentlemen! ..." Bah, what a lot of tittle-tattle! That if the major—that if the colonel... Of course we'll win! Not in Málaga, but in Bilbao... "Tobacco!" Well, there's no one here. I'm going to... "What? Yes, I have matches." Pictures of Franco, pictures, pictures. The pictures they had got ready for the occupation of Madrid, of course. It's starting to turn cool. Or maybe it's because I haven't had any hot food... I'd like to sell you castor oil.

At the end of two hours, Paz was exhausted and chilled to the bone. She went into the Café Colón. She entered the washroom and alone there, surrounded by white tiles, she began to cry. Her teardrops fell on the packages of cigarettes. She felt upset and sadder still because she did not know why she was crying. Her father had been a steady customer of that café. During his last few months especially, he had often played cards there. Paz left the washroom and read on the adjoining twin door: GENTLEMEN. Undoubtedly her father had often pushed that door open, for he would grow very nervous when playing cards or arguing. Paz skirted the chairs and, leaving the café, turned toward home. She had a piece of the gum she had been selling in her mouth and she imagined that the first taste of it would make her sick.

She could see her house from a distance, the humble balcony, the Venetian blinds. That was her street, where she had run about as a child, and all her troubles had come along it as well as an occasional butterfly of happiness. As a child she had bounced her ball against every wall and every housefront. "Do it right, no moving, no laughing, first one hand then the other..." Why would they always say "no laughing" when they were little girls? Did the "Fascists'" little girls say the same thing?

Paz went up the stairs and into her house. She was exhausted. Her mother had gone out. Lifting the strap over her head she freed herself of the box and left it on a chair. Before a small mirror that her father had used for shaving, Paz removed the black from her eyebrows and the mascara from her lashes. If only she could remove the blackness from her soul!

Her breasts were sore.

TWENTY-SIX

DURING the early days of February, the awaited Italian contingents had arrived in Spain, where they were formed into the "Black Arrow" and "Blue Arrow" Brigades. Spanish interpreters, the tenor Miguel Fleta among them, acted as liaison agents. The exuberant temperament of the officers and men had won the liking and respect of many people. Yet an obscure national prejudice had given rise to some doubts of the fighting efficiency of the Italians, especially lingering doubts concerning those operating without an admixture of Spanish troops, in spite of the name for valor the flying Legionnaires had earned in active combat. The situation offered a challenge to the Italians: "We demand of you that you know how to die." Salvatore, who was writing to Marta almost every day, mentioned those doubts. "Why such a lack of confidence?" Salvatore believed that being a good soldier did not necessarily entail goose-stepping like the Germans, or covering shirt fronts with skulls like the volunteers in the Foreign Legion.

The Italians landed in Cádiz were to be put to the test in the Málaga operation as soon as Queipo de Llano and General Roatta had reached an accord over the details. Like the offensive that took place during the Reconquest from the Moors, this was to start from the towering bastions in the mountains of Ronda, held by the Nationalists. Soon the word came that the Reds under the command of General Villalba were ready to stand up to it and that they had concentrated a large number of their effective troops in the zone in preparation for it, although they were poorly organized and short of artillery.

The combined Spanish and Italian operation was a success. On the 8th of February the Italians had occupied the city and the port. Queipo de Llano had not misled his radio audience, and the cultivated General Roatta, youngest of the Italian generals who had come to Spain, had displayed superb skill. From the first moment the troops had maneuvered with elegance, rolling back the adversary. The astute use of light artillery, the "motorization" that Roatta had acclaimed, had taken the enemy by surprise. And the flame-throwers! The flame-throwers were making their debut, and their spouts of flame looked like death rays. The Nationalist air force, based at the airfield in Tablada, won mastery of the air. And Jorge, the orphaned Jorge, also made his debut! Jorge had completed his training at that base and released his first bombs, which seemed to drop from his brain. The cruisers *Canarias* and *Baleares* also performed efficiently, bombarding the coast. The dispersion of the Reds was such that for a moment Count Ciano's idea of pursuing the enemy army to Almería and thence to Valencia seemed feasible. But on the height of Motril, prudence or the scarcity of reserves suddenly advised calling a halt to the operation.

The English press correspondent Arthur Koestler was taken prisoner in Málaga, and a mysterious suitcase, the property of General Villalba, was found. Seemingly it contained a rare relic, the hand of Saint Teresa of Avila. Word that it was an authentic relic flew from mouth to mouth, and it was said to have been offered to General Franco so that he could carry it with him throughout the campaign.

The people of Málaga recited the inevitable catalogue of honors. Salvatore, whose lively eyes seemed to penetrate whatever was in front of them, found a number of cadavers in a ravine with grotesque little tails in their mouths. Núñez Maza, who had entered the city with his propaganda equipment, showed Aleramo Berti, Schubert, and the press a newspaper clipping, which itself testified to the killings earned out by the Anarchists. This conveyed congratulations to "the comrades of a burial detail" in the cemetery of San Rafael for their unceasing labors day after day since the outbreak of the revolution. A hospital had been completely destroyed, except for a crucifix, at the foot of which a note written in an untutored hand said: "*We respect you as an innocent.*" A number of the detainees in the prisons had been evacuated by the militiamen and led on foot toward Almería.

The victory of Málaga aroused great jubilation through Nationalist Spain and covered over for several weeks the disenchantment at the failure of the attack on Madrid. Everyone was saying: "Málaga the beautiful." It was as important to conquer the beautiful as the useful. Don Anselmo inaugurated the "Málaga" station. Mateo, recalling that Pilar had been born in Málaga, was beside himself. He was still on the Alto del León, snowed in. "If you don't mind, I'm going to do something outlandish," he said to José Luis Martínez de Soria, and then drank a canteenful of cognac and got drunk, an incredible performance for him. The Andalusian hurrahs swelled, and in the Red zone, Matías himself rose on hearing the news, put his arm around Carmen Elgazu, and forced her to whirl around the hallway a couple of times. Carmen

Elgazu smiled, "Fellow, on the day Madrid falls, you dance my legs off." Soon afterward, the Alvear family watched with emotion as two trainloads of refugees from Málaga arrived in Gerona. They were remembering their stay in that Mediterranean city.

A moral victory with considerable plunder. In the port, two ships, the *Satrústegui* and the *Africa,* besides ten thousand tons of petroleum, railroad trains, and machine guns. The blue sea! The Red command was angry. The Russian military men, spurred on by Orlov, the ardent chief of the GPU recently arrived in Spain, demanded the men who were responsible, and several generals, among them Asensio, Martínez Monge, and Martínez Cabrera, were arrested and imprisoned.

The victory of Málaga (in which Portuguese volunteers called "*viriatos*" had participated) fired the Nationalists. With renewed self-assurance, they hastened to launch a large-scale offensive in the Madrid sector, almost without resting. The plan was not to try to enter Madrid, but to close more tightly the circle around it. The attack would not be frontal, but an encircling maneuver instead, aimed at cutting off with one stroke the highway to Valencia.

The Italian troops were assigned to combat in this operation also. They were rapidly transferred from Málaga with the objective of seizing Guadalajara as soon as the Spanish troops should cross the Tajuña and Jarama Rivers. Roatta had received a bullet wound in Málaga, but it was so slight that the Italian general had recovered and was prepared to repeat his saga of the Southern front.

But the fortunes of war had decreed otherwise... The attack ended with terrible loss of life on both the Spanish and Italian sides. The Tajuña and Jarama Rivers were filled with the corpses of Legionnaires, of Moors, and of "brevet second lieutenants." Bodies formed a pyramid to the height of the banks of the Pingarrón. At the same time in the Brihuega sector, in Guadalajara, the Corps of Italian Volunteer Troops suffered frightful losses. After making a bold and skilled advance, the infantry suddenly found itself immobilized in mud—it had started to rain with extraordinary violence—while the armored cars and other motorized vehicles, mired in the pools in the roads and highways, were not able even to move back.

General Roatta had not foreseen the possibility that the elements would oppose him. Soon the Italians were under fire from various angles, and the Legionnaires were forced to bunch together. "Forward!" Impossible. The motors would not run: they were stalled, and their powerlessness threw the infantry into despair. Added to that, the enemy was glorying in an admirable tenacity and their air force was gaining control of the air because their airfields to the south of Madrid were dry and permitted the take-off of their machines, whereas the airfields that Roatta was depending upon were lakes.

Unexpected vulnerability. The Italian commentators attributed the defeat to weather, and some of them insinuated that certain Spanish troops who should have been distracting the adversary had been idle. However that might be, the Red commanding officers would not be punished this time, quite the contrary. The 13th, 14th, and 15th International Brigades and Lister's and El Campesino's guerrilla fighters covered themselves with glory. Especially El Campesino, who seemed like a force of nature with his jet-black beard and his "donkey belly-buster." "Hey, you Italian macaronis, suck on that!" "Sons of bitches, faggots, sons of the Pope, beat it!" Someone had taught him to say gigolo, and he shouted gigolo at General Roatta. El Campesino even had forgotten Moscow—Lister never said Moscow, only "Home"—and, supported by two dynamiters, he kept throwing hand bombs with a sling in the name of Spain. If the victorious battle had lasted a little longer, he might even have been fighting in the name of The Cid.

The supreme command in Madrid set the bells to pealing, and Fanny cried her eyes out because she had missed it. The caricaturists in the zone, whom Ezequiel admired so much, covered the walls with sketches of Italians with their tails between their legs. The press agencies all over the world broadcast lists of the enormous amount of spoils which had been captured from the mud, with accompanying photographs. Among the articles seized were Italian letters stained with blood, forms for sending money orders, maps, and images of a fiery Mussolini haranguing the crowds from a balcony.

Guadalajara! The word became a symbol joined to the Madrid symbol. The table reserved for General Mola in the Café Molinero still would be vacant a long while... For the second time it had been proved that the Rebel Supreme Command could make a mistake like anyone else. The flame-thrower surprise had been exchanged for streams of water. A local of the UGT in Gerona arranged a dance where David and Olga kept whirling "in honor of the coward, Italy."

THE coward Italy... That was the refrain beating through Nationalist Spain. The Italians were being called openly "*Corriere de la Sera*" (afternoon runners) and the CVT on their license plates came to mean "*¿Cuando te vas?*" (When are you going?). Guadalajara became a dishonor and a joke. "It's one thing to sing opera and another to get your fingers burned." "They ran like Nuvolari!" They ran, they ran. Salvatore kept shouting: "How were we going to run when the mud was up to our knees?" Twelve hundred dead Italians, thirty-five hundred wounded

Italians, turned into a joke. Aleramo Berti wept with rage, while his colleague Schubert, the myopic Nazi, sent an exhaustive report to Berlin characterizing all Mediterraneans without exception as "instinctual beings" and "primitives."

If only Professor Civil could have defended his principles! Furthermore, a great many Spaniards seemed to be glad, or almost glad, of the Italian failure, and among those was Javier Ichaso. He had taken a trip to Biarritz at the behest of Warning Voice, and loudly joined in the diplomats' chorus of ironic laughter, without understanding why. The Italian Ambassador wrote to his Government: "Italian aid arouses torrents of gratitude among the Spaniards toward France and England." Naturally, the nurses in the hospitals had to be excepted, for many romances were born between them and the Italian volunteers, some of them to last until death. Salvatore, wounded in the left hand, was one of those volunteers. Without forgetting Marta, he said to the girl in the Provincial Hospital of Valladolid as she was bandaging his wound, "One word from you, and tomorrow I'll occupy Guadalajara all by myself."

THE consequences of the failure to accomplish the encirclement of Madrid were painful. The Nationalists were obliged to call up more men and to increase austerity on the home front by the establishment of the "one-course dinner." Warning Voice remarked: "All right! That just means serving several courses in one." But the Portuguese *viriatos* and some recently arrived Irish detachments found that the word "sadness" as used by Cosme Vila and El Responsable was accurate. A great sadness took possession of anyone who paused to meditate a little, and only the frivolous and the soldiers temperamentally suited to the enjoyment of camaraderie were free of it. Prayer was intensified, longer candles were burned, and more copies of *La Ametralladora* were sold. Suddenly eyes would catch and hold, saying to each other, "A civil war is a terrible thing."

Just at that moment all sorts of rumors relating to General Franco began to circulate. The word among the Falangists was that the general "was vigorously on the side of a long war, of carrying on the war at a slow pace." Seemingly he had said flatly to the Italian Ambassador, "The war I'm directing is not one of conquest: it is one of liberation. I will occupy region after region, village after village, railroad after railroad. But wherever my troops enter, I must be sure of being able to set up a political regime, and meanwhile I must keep my back protected, and that is still premature. No massive destruction, but rather a previous clinching of our credo on the home front, where I cannot impose excessive sacrifices either. I must concern myself even with the spiritual salvation of the enemy. If I do not act in this manner, I might win the war but lead my country to ruin."

Núñez Maza was the man who alerted his comrades in the Falange to the "gravity of General Franco's attitude." He had had the first warning of it in Salamanca on the day when he met the aggressive Berti, the Fascist delegate, and Salazar on the stairway of the party local. "Come on up with us, we want to talk to you a minute." The interview was brief. When they reached the top of the stairs, Berti snorted as usual and unbosomed himself: "We just want you to know this: Franco is going his own way. He doesn't think the Falange is a leftist outcry any more, but he thinks it's a juvenile and poetic adventure that he'll have to get rid of little by little."

Schubert, the myopic Nazi delegate, gave the second warning, and Núñez Maza felt still more alarmed, for whatever originated in Germany was an article of faith to him.

"Friend Núñez Maza," Schubert said to him, taking his customary pinch of snuff, "I think I can state that Franco has decided to lean progressively toward the side of the Church and capitalism. If the Falange does not react like a thunderbolt...and without a pause for deliberation, you'll find yourself sweeping the stairs in the Carlist clubs in no time."

The third warning came from the Falange itself. Indeed, two days after his interview with Schubert, on the day that a German airplane had sunk the Russian ship *Kommsomol,* Comrade Hedilla, the pro tem substitute for José Antonio, sent for him and said: "Comrade Núñez Maza, it seems that Franco is inclined to unite the Falange and the Requeté, with himself as Supreme Head. This must be considered an abrogation of the doctrine of José Antonio. Go up to the Alto del León and pass on this communiqué to the comrades in the Onésimo Redondo Company."

Núñez Maza shot along the road from Madrid like a ball of fire, and the Falangist slogans written on the walls seemed to him additional warnings. He reached the Alto del León, still snow-covered, and ten minutes later twelve Falangists had gathered in Salazar's hut. Among them were Mateo and José Luis Martínez de Soria. Hedilla's report confirmed the verbal statement made to Núñez Maza, verified all that Berti and Schubert had said, and ended by soliciting the opinion of "the comrades at the front." "Tell me what, in your opinion, is to be done, the course the Falangists must follow."

The meeting by the light of the gasoline lantern was dramatic, presided over by the calendar depicting a blond woman in a bathtub. The men's tunics smelled of the mess, and Salazar was puffing smoke through the bowl of his huge pipe. Since his still unclarified investigation in Seville, he was talking less and reflecting more.

A boy named Montesinos opened fire, after caressing his canteen with both hands. "My opinion is very simple. It is the opinion of Clemenceau: 'War is too serious a matter to be left in the hands of the military.'"

A murmur arose. They were not there to exchange clever phrases, but to make a decision in good conscience, to try to divine the position José Antonio would have adopted had he been present.

Several Falangists wanted to make clear that they were by no means overcome with surprise at it all. For some time they had suspected that the supreme command had gone to General Franco's head, and in support of that they cited the systematic adulation of the press and the arrogance and profusion with which he was having himself photographed. Someone confirmed, with a smile, that the Reds called him General Kodak, but Comrade Montesinos gave the lie to that, declaring that the nickname had been applied to Lieutenant Colonel Dumont of the 14th International Brigade.

Mendizábal, from Administration, intervened. "I don't think there's any mystery," he commented. "It is for that very reason that Franco is interested in a long war—in order to have time to make a myth of himself and thus eliminate all elements that might be able to dispute his power tomorrow. You know how it is with a lightning war: the crown of laurels, a couple of monuments, then back to the barracks."

Mateo and José Luis were indignant. They could not stand to listen to such light talk about a man who since the 1st of July had led the rescue movement with perfect honesty and efficiency, and they believed that if Franco was permitting or cultivating adulation, he was doing so in order to prevent the growth of splinter movements. Mateo concluded: "All leaders have operated in this way, from Abraham and Napoleon to the kings of England and Macía, the former president of the Provincial Government of Catalonia. Furthermore, it has been demonstrated and is obvious to everyone that if Franco did take over the leadership of the nation, it was because the other generals voted it to him."

Salazar, who had belonged to the JONS, went to Mateo's aid. He declared that for the time being nothing could keep him from believing that Franco was an admirable man. "Like all the rest of you, I want the Falange to triumph, and the power to go to the Falange. But it's stupid and untimely to raise the question of that alternative now. Perhaps the fusion of the Falange and the Requetés is inevitable. Anyway, I am not at all sure that we can count on even the minimum number of Falangists who are ready to take over the head offices of the forty-nine Spanish provinces."

That angered Núñez Maza. He talked about defeatism, and pretended to know much more than Comrade Hedilla had said in his report. "It's ridiculous to compare Franco with Abraham and Napoleon. It's not a question here of avoiding 'splinter movements' or any such trifles. Franco has told the governments of Italy and Germany that all he needs from them is simply to be supplied with armament, that he has 'men to spare.' And he has warned them that from the ideological point of view, he will not let himself be moved one inch when it comes to the organization of future Spain. Don't forget that Pétain was his teacher and that the Pope has blessed his flag." Núñez Maza summed up. "I will never submit to the fusion of the Falange with the Requetés."

Montesinos echoed his words, and so did the majority of those present. Salazar's pipe looked like the smokestack of a ship in contrast to the tiny pipe José Luis Martínez de Soria was smoking. One of the Falangists pounded his right hand into his left fist and then showed his comrades a plaque stolen from a train which said: "Do not lean out." Faces were congested. José Luis Martínez de Soria and Mateo would not let their arms be twisted with regard to Franco, however, and they held that his declaration of "ideological independence" was praiseworthy, worthy of a good Spaniard and a man who never would cringe. "I wouldn't think it was a bit funny," Mateo argued, "if I had a swastika tattooed on my head in exchange for a few airplanes."

Salazar rose then, a giant who made the canvas of the hut look like a paper cone, and he stated his opinion that they must confine the discussion to the theme of the alleged Unification.

"That's right," Mendizábal agreed, somewhat overwrought. "I move we vote. That we vote yes or no."

"It's not a question of voting yes or no, since those who must finally decide are Comrade Hedilla and the National Council. We can vote to grant or deny him full power to do what he thinks best, requiring him by all means to consult all the Falangists at the front. Although I suppose he will have done that already."

Silence.

"What do you mean 'do as he thinks best'?" Mendizábal asked.

"Everything," Montesinos answered, stressing his words. "From a simple manifesto by the Falange, published simultaneously in all our newspapers, to direct action if he considers it necessary."

"I vote against Unification."

"Against."

"Against."

Nine Falangists voted against. Mateo and José Luis for. Salazar abstained.

Núñez Maza spoke to the dissidents. "Give us your word that you will keep this secret."

Mateo said, "I think we're of age..."

Montesinos interrupted. "It's that... Let's see if we understand one another. This whole thing may amount to nothing, but, according to the way things are slanting, it may force us to... I don't know what?"

"Why don't you make yourself clear?"

"Nothing."

Another silence fell, pregnant with antagonism, and the meeting was adjourned. Everyone rose and went outdoors to breathe in fresh air. Núñez Maza and Quartermaster Mendizábal got into their car and started downhill toward Valladolid.

They had both understood perfectly what Montesinos had meant to imply: the quietus of Franco... Montesinos was an excitable, irresponsible man. Decidedly, the thing was beginning to take on an ugly aspect. After all, who was Franco? What was he like? How was his personality? Those who knew him gave disparate versions and if Núñez Maza himself, whom the Generalissimo had granted three audiences, had been forced to describe him, he would not have known where to begin. Schubert had said of him: "He's a little colonial general..." Cantaluppo, the Italian Ambassador, on the other hand, held him in high esteem, especially for his self-possession. Mateo was inclined, rather, to consider General Franco a self-assured man, in love with his military profession, with all the combined shrewdness and capability of the Galician. "One thing is beyond dispute: his instinct for command. The other generals had their reasons for choosing him. So then, he was enrolled in the Academy when he was fourteen, if I'm not mistaken. This means his training is strictly military and therefore that his sense of duty, of justice, of discipline, and so on, is different from that of the rest of us, from that of a doctor say, or a lawyer, or the administrative board of a metallurgical enterprise." José Luis Martínez de Soria had recalled that his father had told him of Franco's impressive deeds in the African war. "Not for nothing was he promoted to general when he was thirty-four. What I'm not so sure of is whether he has always been as devoted to the Sacred Heart as he is now."

How was anyone to know? Actually, the majority of the people in the entire Nationalist territory had seen Franco only on the balconies and speakers' stands, in his photographs, certainly innumerable, and they had heard his voice only over the radio. Yes, he was of low stature, but so were Napoleon and Lenin, and so was Mussolini. His voice was much weaker than Salazar's; but after all Salazar could be heard in Tangier at certain moments. María Victoria, the daughter of a long line of professional soldiers, believed that Franco was a man who would elude a schematic definition, more complex than Schubert, than General Roatta, and even than Largo Cabellera. He was said to speak French,

German, and a little English. Surprisingly enough, he had attended courses on tactics at Versailles some time before. At the age of twenty-four, his military duties had forced him to postpone his matrimonial plans again and again, and for that reason the Legionnaires in his command used to sing to the tune of "La Madelon":

> A doughty soldier is our Major Franco
> He puts off his bride to go campaigning.

His coolness, the impression he gave that time was of no matter to him, also were interpreted variously. According to many foreigners, these were virtues that would lead to a triumph in a country like Spain, full of hair-trigger men and hysterical reactions. On the other hand, many Spaniards considered Franco not cool, but marmoreal and incapable of normal reactions. Núñez Maza seriously maintained that intellectuals failed to amuse him, while Marta's mother thought she knew that Franco could recite entire chapters of *Don Quixote* from memory, particularly those in which Sancho Panza was the star.

THE aggrandizement of the figure of Franco as the immediate consequence of the development of the war did not occur in Nationalist Spain alone. Something similar was happening in the Red zone. The Valencian newspapers referred to him as Von Franko, indicating that the rebel general had become "Germanized" and *El Diluvio* began to call him the "international shoeshine boy" referring to "the way he humbles himself before the Fascist powers." The Catalan radio claimed that he was of Jewish origin; the Madrid radios declared that since the time of the conquest of Málaga, before making any decision he would open General Villalba's suitcase and spend two or three hours praying before the relic of Saint Teresa of Avila's hand. The bulletin-board dailies, which made the trench life of André Marty's brigades more agreeable, advised against minimizing the military ability of "the Fascist leader," and Dr. Relken in Albacete never ceased repeating: "Look out for Don Francisco; he knows all about everything."

Gerona was no exception, and throughout the month of March, in the course of which the battle of Guadalajara had taken place, decisions were being made in the Alvears' city which were the equivalent of the one-course dinner in Nationalist Spain. And dialogues were bursting forth similar to that carried on in Salazar's hut. The dialogues, aimed toward endowing the People's Army with incontrovertibly solid bases, already had taken into account the prolongation of the war. "All military career men, including those already retired, or those who have been serving prison sentences, will be inducted into their respective branches, and all men between the ages of twenty and forty-five inclusive must take military training." Meetings, whether held in the party locals or in the cafés, generally ended like the one held on the Alto del León.

"Induction of professional officers." That meant that the men being held in the Seminary, Captains Arias and Sandoval among them, were to exchange prison for barracks; that is, they were to be taken back to their point of departure, now with the slightly superstitious respect of the militiamen. "Obligatory training for men between twenty and forty-five years of age." That meant that the civilians, usually grouped according to their trade or business, were to gather in the Dehesa every day before work, at seven o'clock in the morning, and there, equipped with wooden rifles, mark time and watch their breath rise in the icy air. They did so, with Tower of Babel standing out above all the rest, while the architects Massana and Ribas, forgoing any special privileges, also fell into line. Matías was overage and therefore exempted, but not so Jaime, who cried: "A poet taking military training!" As for Ignacio, he felt the full force of the order, but refused to report and hastily decided on plans for his escape from Gerona.

"Meetings and gatherings in the party locals and the cafés." One of them might serve as an example: the gathering regularly held in the Café Neutral. Again the protagonist was Julio García, whose predicament was worse than ever owing to his trips abroad in the company of important persons. The habitués of the café were again the cashier of the Arús Bank, Tower of Babel, Blasco, David and Olga, Casal, and Colonel Muñoz. And other members of the cast multiplied in the depths of the mirrors. Julio recently had collected another pawn: Murillo, the head of the local POUM, who had returned from the Madrid front with one arm in a sling and wearing the halo of a hero. The nostalgic memory of Ramón, the waiter, was hovering above the tables, too. He had been taken prisoner in Mallorca during the course of the Bayo expedition.

On the day when German aircraft sank the *Kommsomol,* the Russian ship, thus alerting public opinion, Julio put on a memorable "turn" in the Neutral—as Doña Amparo was now describing her husband's interpositions. Of course the policeman's state of mind was suited to his dazzling gifts, for on the preceding evening a hundred and fifty refugee children had left Gerona for Russia. Prodded by Axelrod, Cosme Vila had had his way. And it was expected that before long a like contingent would be sent to Mexico, this time under Murillo's sponsorship, in view of the fact that Mexico had offered asylum to Trotsky, the egregious supreme leader of Murillo and of the POUM. Julio García, who had witnessed the farewell ceremony at the station, had been horrified. The children's expression had been one of bewilderment. Axelrod and Cosme Vila were exhorting them in vain, declaring that Moscow would receive them with open arms, that the Soviet fatherland already was waiting to adopt them and give them every advantage. The children, orphans for the most part, stood shivering in the station. They were cold, they understood nothing of politics, and they felt in their tiny bones that they would not find their respective parents in Russia either, and that was their dearest wish.

That day, Julio García, who had made his appearance in the Neutral showing off a French lighter of wood in the shape of a champagne cork, spared them nothing. Half joking, half serious, addressing whoever was listening to him, he was knocking down with implacable ruthlessness all the reasons for optimism which had lent animation to his hearers after the victory at Guadalajara.

He began by referring to the drafting of new quotas and claimed that the measure would swell the quantity but not the quality of the fighting men. In his opinion so many "Fascists" would be inducted, not to mention *bon vivants* and malcontents, that the already widespread sabotage would be increased a hundredfold. "Can you imagine Don Jorge de Batlle's nephews being given a rifle? Or the four sons of the Treasury delegate who was taken for a ride on the 18th of July? I'd rather not think about it, for the blood of the brave militiamen who would be fighting alongside those gentlemen gives me the creeps..."

As he caressed a huge empty cognac snifter, Julio added, "And the same thing might be said of the induction of the retired soldiers or the ones who were in jail! With the permission of whoever signed that decree and the permission of Colonel Muñoz, right here, I say that would be the living end, to use an expression that enchants Fanny, my beloved tigress, Fanny. It's just as easy to send a bullet through one boar's hide as through another's, to turn your own artillery in the wrong direction, to forget to order ammunition! Some of the said officers will be sent into the war plants, the arms works, agreed. I think I can see them. One will file the heads of the percussion caps so they'll misfire, another will set the sights wrong, another... I don't know what! Supplies will be slow to reach the front and they'll arrive damaged; and when our dear Gorki, Teo, or Major Campos even tries to make use of them, either they won't work, or they'll explode on the spot, or else they'll turn into grasshoppers. Anything at all except to inflict a scratch on the enemy whom *El Proletario* is still calling 'traitor' and 'rebel.'"

Colonel Muñoz, on whom glances were converging, felt obliged to tell Julio that he was exaggerating. In the first place, it was impossible to conduct a war without commanding officers. In the second place, by no means all the officers called up were Fascists. In the third place, an army—assuming a minimum of discipline, of course—was a ratchet that was automatically geared to obey, geared even to force many individuals whose consciences bade them to resist it.

"I don't consider it necessary to offer examples or to give the names of officers and soldiers who found themselves enrolled in the Army of the Republic owing to X circumstances, and who, despite their opposing ideas have done their duty with the best of them." Colonel Muñoz paused, then added, "And of course my theory is valid for the enemy Army. Men whose hearts are with us are fighting for the rebels, pardon the word, and being awarded military medals!"

Julio García carefully set the empty cognac snifter down on the table. "Does this minimum of discipline that my dear Colonel Muñoz has judged indispensable exist in our Army?"

The colonel hesitated. "I like to think so," he said. "Otherwise I think we could not have saved Madrid, nor would we have stood fast at the Jarama and Guadalajara."

The architects Massana and Ribas were a little surprised. The colonel's language here was not the same as that he used in the Ovid Lodge. They guessed that he did not care to make himself unpopular, and they respected his attitude. In any case, they chose to change the subject and, addressing Julio, they asked about the repercussions of the Spanish war abroad: in France, Belgium, and England... "Julio, seeing you're just back from those countries, what can you tell us? What are those people saying?"

Julio felt more at home with this question. "I can't speak for Belgium," he admitted modestly, "I was merely there in passing. But I can speak of England and France...and even Holland. Well, we must face facts. Our war is almost as interesting to those countries as to Spain, and in a certain sense, even more so. I mean, it would be easy to find French and English people much better informed on what is going on here than any of us are... I'm not exaggerating, gentlemen! What do we people in Gerona know, for example? That we shall have to eat a lot of lentils, that José Antonio Primo de Rivera is resting in peace, and that the Internationals get so drunk in Madrid that it's a pleasure. In Paris and London they even know that the Communists want to get rid of Prieto and that the head of the GPU in Spain is named Orlov. But to me the greatest eye-opener came in Holland. How shall I put it? ... It's hard to explain. They don't understand us. The concierge in the hotel, a Hollander without a bicycle, asked me: 'Pardon me. What is a rifle?' They asked Fanny, who was kind enough to go everywhere with me, 'Why are the Spaniards so hot-blooded?' Well, Fanny had to laugh! In short, the truth is this—they consider us monsters. *Voilà.* The Hollanders not only do not commune—forgive the word—with proletarian theories, but the few proletarians left in their country aspire to become the bourgeoisie."

A murmur arose. Antonio Casal, the man most interested in that aspect of the question, interrupted, objecting that perhaps the concierges of the hotels in Holland might have such common aspirations, but that no doubt it was uncommon among the British city people. The Socialist leader was still mesmerized by whatever had to do with England.

Julio García pulled a face of commiseration. "I'm sorry, my dear friend Casal, to have to disillusion you. It's worse in England."

"How is it worse?"

"I'm not exaggerating now, I'm positively not exaggerating. More and more, England hopes that Franco will win... I beg your pardon, gentlemen! England wants Franco to win because if we win, that is, if Stalin wins—Gibraltar will be endangered."

Casal waxed indignant, and so did David and Olga. But Julio burst out laughing, and no one could decide whether he was serious or joking.

Then the policeman revived the subject of decisive weaponry. "You already know my opinion. It's very pretty to see those graybeards—I'm not talking about you, Barber Raimundo—taking training in the Dehesa at seven o'clock in the morning. But that won't halt the unceasing entry of German tanks into the Franco zone, tanks smaller than the Russians'! But more maneuverable, and how! The Russians' are like cathedrals. Neither will it neutralize the effect of the poison gases that will be leaving Naples any minute bound for Cádiz."

Julio was indulging his mania. He was frightening his listeners with his prophecies of terrifying weapons, as Mosén Alberto had frightened the nuns of Pamplona with his unearthly visions.

"In Paris, I had an interview with Professor Risler, a wise Frenchman who offered to open an anti-gas works in Barcelona for us, along with a colleague of his who claims to have discovered a new poison gas. I think that's something positive, not like sending poor babies to Moscow to play the balalaika. Brains are needed. Someone who can discover synthetic gasoline or a formula for making artificial cloud cover. If only one of you could offer such a formula! You, Colonel Muñoz? ... Too bad... What about you, my dear architects? You can't either? What a shame! I'm authorized to offer good pay for it! What are we to do, then? Obviously, there are no brains in Gerona. Waiter, a cup of good coffee! Oh, I keep forgetting, there's no good coffee either!"

After two hours of conversation, everyone felt stimulated. Murillo was listening to Julio, caressing his walrus mustache with his one good hand. Colonel Muñoz was unconsciously examining his fingernails, for he realized that Julio was right on target. As for the cashier of the Arús Bank, he was thinking that the policeman ought to keep his back well protected after daring to use such careless language in public.

David spoke up. "What would you do, then, to win the war?"

Julio rolled his champagne-cork lighter over the tabletop and rubbed his thighs. Finally he replied. "It's quite simple... I'd go looking for someone, or a couple of people, who were willing to lay down their lives."

Everyone was puzzled, and Casal cried, "There are thousands of people willing to lay down their lives!"

Julio nodded. "I know that... But I'm talking about suicide, which is something more unpleasant. Listen to me! We would need someone...how shall I say it? Someone ready to slip across into the other zone and kill Franco and Mola. That, gentlemen, would constitute a serious blow! I'm telling you. A suicide, but a real blow. A perfectly feasible one... That, gentlemen, would paralyze the enemy's motors by long distance."

Everyone felt a moment's stupefaction. Everyone admitted that it was Gospel. Indeed, if some men could commit suicide so as to stall a tank, why shouldn't some one do it to...? By a curious coincidence, Julio was talking that way barely a week after Montesinos had hinted at something similar by the light of the gasoline lantern on the Alto del León.

David eyed Casal fixedly, then spoke to the policeman. "Why don't you take this upon yourself personally, Julio?"

Julio's expression did not change. He shook his head with a smile. "No, no! Unfortunately, I'm not the stuff heroes are made of... Besides, what would my wife say? No, not by any means. I'm not that rash. And after all... Franco and Mola are people, aren't they? They're military men, but still people. Ah, if only Teo were something more than a mere brute force!" Julio turned to Casal. "Of course the ideal person ought to combine a number of qualities: intelligence, zeal, personal attractiveness..." As he said that, he turned toward Olga as though struck by a sudden idea. "Olga, what would you think? ... Couldn't you take this upon yourself, Olga?"

Olga stiffened, realizing this was a joke in bad taste. She did not know whether to get up and leave the café or to slap Julio. Finally she stammered: "You're an insolent man."

Julio was multiplied in the mirrors. "I don't know why you should say that, Olga. After all, what we're talking about is service, isn't it? And we have heroic women as examples..."

David sat as if turned to stone. He was about to say something, surely something forceful to judge by the trembling of his chin, but just then Murillo struck into the conversation from his chair in the corner. "All right, Sir Wise," he said to Julio in a sly tone, "do you think I might combine the qualities needed for this job?"

Everyone stared at Trotsky's disciple. Murillo appeared to be speaking in earnest. He was the head of the POUM, and had been tried on the Teruel and Madrid fronts.

Julio made a gesture. Then he put the French lighter back into his pocket and finally said: "I'm sorry, friend Murillo, but I have to say no to you, for I do not think that you combine such qualities."

"Why not?"

"Because it would take a brave man to set foot in Salamanca, and you're not one. Oh, never mind the fulminations! A brave man—forgive me for mentioning it—does not shoot himself through the hand, as you did in Madrid, so as to be able to come back to the Neutral and have a few drinks with his friends."

TWENTY-SEVEN

THE long war was having its effect on the Alvears, too, on the Gerona and Burgos branches alike, as well as on the only remaining member of the Madrid branch, José. José Alvear had learned of his father's death, but try as he would he could not locate Santiago's body, which was buried with many others in a trench on the Madrid front. The boy was outraged. He glared furiously at the sky—then asked himself who it was up there that was responsible for his orphanhood, and in the end made up his mind to become a dynamiter. He and Captain Culebra had seen some husky men in Madrid wearing a heavy yellow cord across their chests, and when he asked about them he was told they were "dynamiters," a new type of combatant that had emerged as a result of the stalemate on the Madrid front. José thought it would be a fine thing to be a dynamiter, inasmuch as he was yearning to avenge himself on the world. To bore into the earth, and then *poom!* cause it to tremble. He was accepted, together with Captain Culebra, and no sooner had they wound the yellow fuse, the fuse yellow as corn, around their chests, than they felt important.

Subterranean warfare... General Miaja had decided to open underground passages in order to blow up the enemy positions in University City. Asturian and Extremaduran miners were appointed foremen, and the work began. The underground conduits, the electric cables beneath the buildings, and the personnel who were specialists in tunneling, all facilitated the task. Underground warfare! Presently José Alvear and Captain Culebra were burrowing under the earth like moles, as if seeking treasure or veins of ore. The Nationalists would be very slow to duplicate their work, to have available the technique needed to open opposing tunnels. For the time being they could do nothing but post "listening-soldiers" at threatened points. Their mission was to hear...and suddenly to be blown up! Such soldiers were baptized "the sacrifice squads." For the most part they were made up of Legionnaires who were dramatically relieved every quarter of an hour after drawing lots.

A consequence of the drawn-out war... When a mine had exploded, José Alvear would spit on his hands and go up to the surface. There, in the company of his comrades, or of Canela, who paid him a daily visit after a trolley trip from the hospital to the front, he entertained himself by criticizing the Russians lodged in the Bristol Hotel or by writing nicknames on the Madrid monuments, which were covered over to protect them from air raids. They called the one of Demeter "The Modest Girl," and the one of Neptune "Ambushed." Or perhaps they tried to figure out from the bursts where the mortar-shells were coming from. "This one is from Franco. This one is ours."

Canela spelled joy to José Alvear. The girl never forgot to bring him some tidbit. "Phew!" José would exclaim. "What's this, rat or Fascist meat?" Nor to give him a kiss that turned his comrades green with envy. Captain Culebra often said to her, "Leave that sissy and come along with me. Cross over to my line." Canela would decline with a shake of the head. "As long as you're carrying around that box with that loathsome little creature, I wouldn't even dream of it."

In Burgos, the catastrophe at the battle of Guadalajara had inspired new courage in Paz Alvear. That, and the news given her by her immediate superior, Venancio. "Five hundred Russian bombers are just arriving. They're coming by ship, disassembled. That will beef us up!"

Paz Alvear was now a girl with a normal head of hair. She no longer felt like a monster, and she could go out into the street without putting a scarf over her head. She was still selling tobacco in the cafés. But Venancio, who had great plans for her, had entrusted her with a breath-taking mission: to go to Segovia and hold an interview with the widow of the heroic agent who had died at the hands of SIFNE "so that the real Dionisio could move freely."

"Give her this money. And tell her that neither she nor her children will ever want for anything."

Paz Alvear carried out her mission with feeling. The woman cried: "You say I'll never want for anything? I want for everything! My husband is dead."

Paz Alvear returned to Burgos greatly affected. On the way she remembered Mateo for some reason. "What has become of that Fascist sweetheart of Pilar's?" Paz would have liked to meet Pilar and Ignacio. "Fascists, all of them! War is hard..."

Hard and endless...in Burgos and Gerona alike. Indeed, in Ignacio's opinion, "Something's got to be done." In spite of all her resistance and her scruples, Pilar obtained a place in the Department of Food Supplies. Olga's recommendation had been effective. "I understand, I understand," the teacher said when Pilar went to see her. "Don't explain to me." The girl started to work the 1st of April. The offices had been set up in a recently vacated apartment that had belonged to the Costa brothers. While they, in France, were interviewing Notary Noguer because the movements of ships and munitions were beginning to beckon to their business skill, the walls of their apartment in Gerona were covered with graphs and charts on food and with revolutionary portraits. Beneath one of those portraits, the one of Engels to be exact, Pilar was filling out ration cards and more ration cards by hand in Catalan under the supervision of Tower of Babel. He was her immediate superior. "They pass me along from one Alvear to another," the employee of the Arús Bank had said. Tower of Babel had only to begin his military training to discover that his bellicose temper was meager, and that only the Auxiliary services appealed to him. He succeeded in getting a certificate from the Recruiting Station which stated there was a doubtful dark area in his lungs.

Pilar could not put her heart into her work. "Even if it's only filling out cards, it's still collaborating." Besides, several of her co-workers kept glancing at her from the corners of their eyes. Her great comfort was her old friend Asunción, a professional soldier's daughter who was working there, in the same section. "Naturally they need us, because *they* don't know how to write." Asunción kept worrying about Pilar's sudden outbursts. "Be very careful," she warned. "There are only two topics of conversation here—clothes and the movies."

The work of filling out cards demonstrated to Pilar how few Gerundian names she knew. Names and more names that she had never even heard. Sometimes she would try to picture a face or a role behind a certain name. "Florencio Portas? He must be a stonemason. Loreto Rutllán? A fat woman, with three children." "You're wrong," Asunción corrected her. "Look what it says here. Single." Whenever they found the name of a friend, they wrote it zealously. Pilar wanted to handle the S cards so as to be able to write Mateo Santos, but she was left with her wishes. Asunción, on the other hand, was given the letter A. "Here are the Alvears," she said. As she was writing Ignacio's name in a good, round hand, she had an idea that she passed on to Pilar. "What do you think? I don't believe they'd notice it if I put in César's name. You'd have an extra ration."

Pilar turned pale. She was inexpressibly affected and almost burst into tears. "How dare you?"

"I'm sorry, kid. I didn't mean to offend you."

No, she had not been offended. But as it happened, Pilar's nerves were taut. In the street, Murillo, who seemed to wait for her on the corners, would stare at her impudently and even whistle; and in the office, her fellow workers would mutter "Fascist pigs" with crushing frequency. And every week she had to watch when the two Russian technicians who were managing the Soler factory came to see Tower of Babel and were given an official permit that would have done more than satisfy five large families.

Two news items came to Pilar, one good, the other bad. The Rosselló sisters met her on the sidewalk of the Rambla and, pausing for a moment, they slipped her a note. It was in Don Emilio Santos's own handwriting, and was dated Christmas Day. Mateo's father told her that until that date he had been imprisoned in the Cárcel Modelo in Barcelona, but that he was to be transferred any minute to "I don't know where." "Where?" Pilar asked herself, terrified. "And why the long delay in receiving the note?" She went running home more than ever ashamed of not collaborating with Laura and the Rosselló sisters. The family decided to ask Ezequiel to visit Don Emilio and look after him as much as possible.

The good news, better than good, came to Pilar by courtesy of David! He brought her a postcard carrying a French stamp, from Toulouse, with an illegible signature, but in a handwriting that Pilar instantly recognized as Mateo's. It was addressed to her. She stood staring at David, with the postcard trembling in her hand. "But..."

David smiled. "Olga came upon the postcard in the Post Office as she was censoring foreign correspondence. 'Who could be writing to Pilar from France?' she asked me. It wasn't hard to guess, was it?"

Pilar could not summon a word.

"Well... You've got the postcard..."

Pilar offered David her hand. "Many thanks, David."

David bowed, with his usual emotionality, while the girl again went running home, burning up the distance.

THE long war was reaching out for Ignacio too. Two weeks before his quota was to be called up, the boy arrived at a decision because he could foresee that he would be drafted inevitably. He went to Laura, who definitively discouraged him with regard to the possibilities of escaping into France. A month and a half had gone by without the organization of a single expedition: the two latest had cost the lives of seven persons. "You'll have to wait. To wait until the carabineers and the militiamen get back their confidence or grow careless again."

Ignacio then decided to enlist in Health, as a volunteer. Julio received him at home, his glittering built-in bar open. Doña Amparo was at his side, displaying a long necklace of French make. "Where do you want to go?"

"To Madrid."

"Cripes! And you say Madrid, just like that..."

Ignacio hesitated a moment. "All right. If Madrid is out, Barcelona then..."

"All right."

Julio looked serious, more than ordinarily serious. "Tell me one thing, Ignacio. What do you know about Health?"

"As much as you know about buying machine guns."

The reply flashed from the boy like an arrow, and hit the target.

Julio approached him and smiled. His eyes said, "You're a smart kid." "Unless I'm mistaken," the policeman said, "what you need is the Health Service, but doing office work. Isn't that right?"

Ignacio agreed. Then he said, "In any case, I've prepared myself somewhat. Examine me if you want to."

"Let's see." Julio leaned against the built-in bar. "How many bones has my wife?"

"Julio!" Doña Amparo exclaimed.

"Three hundred twenty-seven," Ignacio answered.

"What basic substances are they composed of?"

"Iron, calcium, water, sugar, and blood."

Doña Amparo was staring in turn at the two men with wide eyes. "But what are you talking about? What's the matter with you?"

"Good boy!" said Julio enthusiastically, paying no attention to his wife. "QED. You can count on a job in Barcelona."

Julio wrote a confidential letter to Don Carlos Ayestarán, the former Health Commissioner of the Provincial Government of Catalonia, now the manager of a gigantic drug concern supplying the front and installed in what had been the Church of Pompeya in Barcelona. The supply house was in fact the one that equipped all the hospitals and ambulances on the Aragón front.

Within forty-eight hours, the policeman received an affirmative reply. "Go to Don Carlos Ayestarán with this letter from me... He's a gentleman, remember. Much more decent than I am. He'll put you in contact with a nephew of his with whom it will be very much to your advantage to be on good terms. He shares your own ideas... Yes, that's the way it is. I don't know you very well, but I do know you have your own ideas. His name is Moncho and he works with Don Carlos in the office, though I believe he also works a few hours in the Clinic."

"What did you say his name was?"

"Moncho. He apologized for his name. A smart type."

Ignacio stared at Julio García. He already owed him so many favors! It was impossible not to wish him well.

Ignacio went to Doña Amparo to say goodbye and kissed her hand with natural ease.

"Come off it, kid. Even if I were a London lady..." Doña Amparo added. "Good luck, Ignacio...you know I truly wish you that."

"I know."

Julio was next. "Well..." The boy was at a loss for words.

"Don't say a word. Regards..."

The policeman accompanied the boy to the door. In the hallway, he placed an affectionate hand on his shoulder.

"Julio..."

"Drop it..." Julio paused. "To Barcelona, and take it easy." Then he added unexpectedly, "Take it easy and sabotage whenever you can."

Ignacio stopped dead. "What's in your mind, Julio? Why did you say that?"

Julio's expression did not change. "Just because... Because you will do it." Then he added. "And to me it seems quite natural..."

Once more Ignacio was forced to recognize how astute Julio was. Because from the very beginning it actually had been his intention to commit sabotage. To commit sabotage as often as he could, disregarding the constant threats published in the newspapers with regard to it.

In the apartment on the Rambla, the leave-taking was somewhat pathetic, for they all knew that Ignacio was planning to cross over to "the other side" as soon as possible, which was the reason he would have preferred to be leaving for Madrid.

"What if a chance comes up immediately?" Carmen Elgazu asked, spreading her hands and patting Ignacio's cheeks. "We won't see you again, son!"

"How can a chance come up when I'm going to be in Barcelona?"

"I don't know..."

They avoided a farewell at the station. Embraces were exchanged in the apartment on the Rambla. Carmen Elgazu had packed Ignacio's suitcase with the same loving tremor as when he was getting ready for the Seminary. Matías tried to be strong, but he was constantly clearing his throat and the corners of his eyes looked inflamed. "Go on, son... Write often." Pilar hung around Ignacio's neck and said for the hundredth time: "What will we do without you?"

Ignacio left, dressed as a peasant. He went off to the long war, leaving behind him worlds, loves, and peace. On the train his knees ached so that he could not sit still. The month of April was beginning, announcing itself shyly in the sky and over the fields. Ignacio was smoking unconsciously. He was feeling and dreaming, not thinking. The train was slow and it carried freight, reminding him of the one that had brought them from Málaga to Gerona. Sad people, many people, smoke and soot that got into the eyes and mouth. He was struck by the figure of a dozing porter who had been working the same run for thirty years now, and by the alarm bell. This was a solid little pointing hand that invited him to get up and pull on it. "Stop, stop! A worried boy of twenty is going into the long war against his will! He's ready to commit sabotage..." Under the alarm bell a gilded metal plaque threatened to fine anyone who stopped the train for insufficient reason.

Ignacio arrived in Barcelona at eight o'clock in the morning. Before making his appearance at the office of Health to report to Don Carlos Ayestarán, he wanted to settle the problem of his lodging. He intended to ask Ezequiel to let him live in his house until he could find a pension that would offer him some guarantee of safety. He went up the Calle de Verdi. The photographer, wearing his amusing little string tie around his neck, received him with his unvarying good humor and great cordiality, as did Rosita.

"We'd be delighted, we'd be delighted to solve that problem for you. But the worst of it is we have Mosén Francisco upstairs, you know. The vicar is now occupying the bed that Marta occupied. What do you think, Ignacio? Won't there be too much noise? Won't we all get ourselves in trouble?"

The tone in which Ezequiel spoke and Rosita's expression calmed Ignacio.

"It can be arranged," Rosita declared. "We'll have to find some way..."

Ignacio interrupted. "I'll sleep wherever you want me to. It'll be only for a few days until I can find a pension."

Ezequiel waved his arms like propellers. "What do you think, Rosita?"

"I'm thinking."

"I could sleep with the vicar. It's not ideal at his age, but..."

"I've got it!" Rosita cried. "You can sleep in Mosén Francisco's room on a couch. We'll make up a daybed for you. There's a bedspring in the patio shed and—all right, Ignacio. You can stay here."

"Thank you."

Ezequiel told him about Mosén Francisco. The vicar had obtained the identity card of a militiaman who had died at the front and he was about everywhere all day long wearing a blue coverall and a bandage on his head, as if he had been wounded.

"What's he doing in the streets? Is he still hearing confessions?"

"Oh, everything. He does everything and anything."

Rosita spoke up. "Here's something that even Ezequiel doesn't know, something he told only me. He hides the sacred wafers in the bandage on his head, and every day he distributes them throughout the quarter, among the sick."

"Go on! ... So we've got those, too! So..."

"Don't be angry, Eze... We have to do something, don't we?"

Ignacio went upstairs to speak to Mosén Francisco. He found the vicar still asleep and did not awaken him. He stood looking at that body stretched out on the bed. The bandaged head gave Mosén Francisco a monstrous appearance. Furthermore, the vicar was snoring and breathing heavily. "If only I could guess what he's dreaming about!" The flask of cologne that Marta had used was still on the little table. Birds and flowers on the wallpaper. A ray of light came in through the slats of the blinds and a strong voice outside could be heard crying, "*La Soli! ... El Diluvio!*"

Ignacio went downstairs. Ezequiel was on the point of leaving for his Photomaton. Rosita said to the boy: "We have our meals on time. At one-fifteen. Do you like chickpeas?"

"Yes, very much."

Ezequiel was blowing his nose into a huge handkerchief, for he took inhalations of eucalyptus every morning, holding his nose over a steam kettle.

"Come on, let's go. We can take the same streetcar."

Half an hour later, Ignacio was reporting in the Calle de Paris to Don Carlos Ayestarán. Across the balcony an immense banner with the Red Cross on it, said laconically: "Health." All the personnel wore white coats as in a hospital, and Ignacio recalled Julio's observation: "Don Carlos Ayestarán's obsession is hygiene. If you want to win him over, try to let him find you washing your hands at least three times a day."

Don Carlos Ayestarán received him with exquisite correctness. He did not seem to Ignacio as nervous as Julio had described him. He was wearing a stiff collar and was entirely bald, with a shining pate suitable to a man who gave himself a daily alcohol rub. Ignacio knew that the man had organized an efficient medical network in Catalonia and Aragón that was becoming less efficient, unfortunately, as the stations were being set up closer and closer to the firing lines. As he shook hands with him, Ignacio was thinking: "No one would take him for a Mason." Don Carlos was saying to himself: "No one would say this boy was a seminarian."

"Julio told me that you would introduce yourself to my nephew Moncho. I don't have him here with me these days. He's on leave, but he'll be back on Monday. He'll be your boss. All right, now! Let's get to work...and I hope you'll be careful."

Ignacio was very grateful to Don Carlos for that phrase and for the friendly tone in which it was said. "Don Carlos, if I can be of use to you in any way, now or at any time, I'm at your service."

The Department of Health... Despite the attitude of Don Carlos, the work became a source of uneasiness to Ignacio from the first moment. This was not the Arús Bank, where working meant earning a salary and helping the family. He grew more and more irritated at the thought that "he was collaborating" with the enemy, more so than Pilar in the Office of Food Supply. To have to write "Anti-Fascist Militia," "People's Army," "Karl Marx Column!" An unbearable irritation on which his will might founder and lead him to commit some folly.

He was assigned to work on records in the mornings and in the afternoons to wait on the militiamen in the Health Department who appeared with order sheets, sometimes with simple permits. Ignacio had to handle and validate those orders and have them signed. Then the militiamen would present the requisitions at the Pompeya drug supply company and draw the merchandise.

The correspondence he filed in the mornings threw him into a bad humor. Donations from England, from France, from the United States. For ambulances and disinfectants, serums, and medical kits... What were the great democracies trying to cure? Cosme Vila's stomach ache? Axelrod's blind eye? The militiamen's venereal disease? Ignacio could not rid himself of the thought of all that material passing in front of his eyes while he was helpless to destroy it. He was surprised that the donations sent by the Red Cross were so meager. Don Carlos Ayestarán was indignant. "The Red Cross is failing us. Many lists of people who have disappeared, but of actual aid, nothing." This was as infuriating to Don Carlos as the fact that the Minister of Health was the midwife Federica Montseny of the FAI. "An Anarchist the Minister of Health! And a midwife!"

The afternoon work of waiting upon the militiamen raised a knot in Ignacio's throat. He was always afraid that someone he knew would come in—El Cojo or Ideal. He had believed that any militiaman would repel him on principle, but experience demonstrated otherwise. Some Anarchists turned out even to be likable owing to their ingenuously beaming glance and the logical correlation between their ideals and their attitudes. The Communists, on the other hand... What were they doing with the serums and the adhesive tape? Were they sending it all on to Moscow? Were they infecting the militiamen who were not of their Party? He was similarly repelled by the pseudo-intellectuals of the Estat Català. They talked emphatically, supercharging every word with meaning and emotion, as David and Olga would do whenever they let their guard down. Sometimes Ignacio was stopped in his tracks, as when the "militiaman" was a beautiful girl who came in giving the clenched-fist salute. Ignacio could not help it: his hackles rose at the thought of a beautiful girl brandishing her fist. He never raised his. Neither would he say, "*¡Salud!*" He always found some way to avoid it by pretending that he had to cough or sneeze, or that he was being called to somewhere else.

As for the personnel, his colleagues in the office, they varied greatly. There were at least a dozen typists scattered through the flat, which had belonged to a prominent member of the Lliga Catalana. Within forty-eight hours, Ignacio could define their affiliation beyond a possibility of error. All he had to do was to take note of the jargon they used, the tone of voice in which they replied to greetings, the way they took their first look at the newspapers or the flags, or how they talked on the telephone. At least four of the typists were "Fascists" beyond a doubt. They seldom spoke. The others exchanged news ceaselessly and made jokes about Madrid and Guadalajara.

One girl had attracted Ignacio's attention instantly—the girl at the switchboard. Delicate-looking, self-absorbed, pale as snow. She lived in a state of perpetual fear, seeming to expect a personal catastrophe at any moment. Several times the girl's glance crossed Ignacio's and both sensed a clandestine complicity.

The concierge made more of an impression on Ignacio than the other men, for opposite reasons. An aging militiaman of the FAI without legs, he would drag himself through the office on a little wheeled platform. Sometimes he looked like a toad, yet he was cheerful. His head was larger than normal. His name was Gascon. When the telephone rang, he had to give a mighty leap to reach it. He always wore a wide Sam Browne belt and two pistols. Every morning after reading the newspaper, he would say the same thing: that the ideal place for him would be in the turret of a tank. "Without my legs and with a machine gun up there, I could be up and at 'em!" From the beginning, he eyed Ignacio askance. "So you're from Gerona? ... Why all the ants in the pants?"

Whenever Ignacio wanted to disappear for a few minutes, he would walk through the immense apartment and lock himself in the bathroom. A black-tiled bathroom that rasped his nerves, with two cornucopias lying in the dry tub. Instead of toilet paper there was a stack of pharmaceutical leaflets strung on a wire. The language of the leaflets was precise and optimistic. They promised to cure everything, even the innermost human aches. Ignacio trusted that one day they would cure him of his anguish at having to write "Anti-Fascist Militia" every morning.

On his first Saturday morning they told him: "It's your turn to stand guard at the Pompeya." Good God! He went to the converted church at eight in the morning and entered it as if to hear Mass. He had never been there before. The church was stocked like San Félix in Gerona, but instead of bags of chickpeas and Bulgarian cereals, there were pyramids of wooden boxes here, and mountains of packages pleasant to the touch, with labels in every language. Bandages and gauze enough to cover every wound in the world were stacked on the main altar, strychnine and aspirin in the baptismal font. A labyrinth. And he was alone in it! What if he went into the sacristy and turned on the faucets? Water would start to spread until it reached the door to the street. But the gauze was not to be used as fuses. Gauze and medicaments were to be used for healing, and human pain demanded respect. To hell with such scruples! What about a fire? He could not make up his mind. Then a strange sound came to his ears. The creak of a board and then something being dragged. He went out of the sacristy and saw Gascon, the amputee, approaching on his little platform along an endless aisle between the piles of boxes.

"*¡Salud!* Comrade..."

Ignacio stared at him. He had a pencil behind his ear and this detail made him feel safe. "Hello!"

Gascon said: "I was passing by and I said to myself, 'I'm going in for a minute to see the little priest who's standing guard.'"

"Little priest?" Ignacio blinked.

"So all right! That's just a manner of speaking." Gascon began to roll a cigarette, taking the package of tobacco and the papers from under his thighs. "Anyhow, I made up my mind to believe you're one of us, and I just couldn't do it. Upon my word, I couldn't do it."

"I don't get it."

"Shucks, you don't have to get it. Would you like a smoke?"

IGNACIO kept his fear to himself, but his desire to render those piles of medicaments useless somehow made him so restless that after dining with Ezequiel and Mosén Francisco that night he called the vicar aside before going to bed on the pallet that had been made up for him and told him what had happened. Mosén Francisco answered him sternly. "That would be a base deed. In wartime, medicaments are sacred, even though they belong to the enemy."

"Nonsense! This is a civil war."

"Ignacio...get hold of yourself. Do you hear me? Don't be rash."

Ignacio made a gesture of dissent. Then he smiled. The vicar was talking like that while he was using his head as a ciborium, wearing a bandage that he never took off for fear of a sudden search of the house! "Don't be rash!" Wasn't he, Mosén Francisco, being rash? Perhaps it wasn't rash to keep hearing confessions in the parks and the cinemas, ministering to the dying in the quarter, hanging around the Cárcel Modelo and the barracks in case someone might need his services!

"That's quite another thing, Ignacio. You must recognize that what I'm doing is something else again."

"Yes, I agree. But I can't hear confessions or give Communion. I've got to do something."

"Then go over to Nationalist Spain as soon as you can."

Mosén Francisco! The integrity of the priest sometimes alarmed the boy. He was fully aware that he ought to make the most of their companionship these days. For they would not last long ... He had a presentiment, as Major Campos had had, that he would be drafted and would leave for the Teruel front, that he would be killed in the war.

Mosén Francisco was performing the most daring deeds with a gaiety and nonchalance that were disconcerting. Ezequiel kept saying, "Yes, yes, I know. He'll drag us all to the firing wall, and to top it all, we'll be bound to be grateful to him."

Mosén Francisco and Ignacio had made it a habit to talk for awhile before going to bed. Ignacio was awaiting the arrival of Moncho, the nephew of Don Carlos Ayestarán, but Moncho had not yet come. Hence the vicar and Ezequiel were his only friends. Ezequiel was all man. Despite the outlandish length of his arms, he knew his limitations. When he noticed that the conversation would soar if he was not there, he would vanish at once, pretending to be sleepy, or on some other pretext. Sometimes Manolín stayed with the cat in his arms, absorbed, trying to retain the words that were dancing above the table. And he kept thinking: "Marta would have said this or that now... Marta would have sprung like a tiger here." Manolín was jealous of Ignacio, though he could not understand how one could be jealous of someone and still like him as he liked Ignacio.

One exceptionally fine night, the vicar and Ignacio decided to go up on the roof. The moon was calling them, the moon and the brilliant sky. Each of them carried a chair. Mosén Francisco wrapped himself in the cloak they had given him in the "Karl Marx" barracks. Ignacio had begged a blanket of Rosita. They made themselves comfortable in their chairs. A deep silence lay over Barcelona. In the distance the harbor could be seen, and beyond the harbor, the open sea. Occasionally they could hear the thud of a pick; an air-raid shelter must be under construction in the quarter. Intermittently, powerful beams of light searched the sky from the peak of Montjuich or from the Tibidabo, doubtless on the watch for aircraft.

After commenting on the news of the day—there was a rumor that the Nationalists were about to begin the attack on Bilbao—Mosén Francisco buried himself in his cloak as though it was a chasuble and asked Ignacio: "I bet you don't know what day tomorrow is?"

"Tomorrow?" Ignacio blinked. "Thursday..."

"Just so..." The vicar paused, then added, "Holy Thursday."

Ignacio's heart gave a leap. How could he have forgotten it? "The fact is..."

"Never mind." Mosén Francisco changed his tone. "Do you remember what these days were like in Gerona? The procession...going up to Calvary..."

Ignacio was touched. He huddled into his blanket. "Of course I do... I remember it all." Another pause. "I remember my mother..."

"Just so. Your mother." The vicar went on. "Carmen Elgazu, climbing up Calvary."

Ignacio was slow to reply. "Climbing...and singing..."

"Just so. Singing..."

A long silence fell, stretching seaward.

The vicar then gave Ignacio an incredible piece of news: he had decided to hold the Good Friday procession with a group of friends in spite of circumstances. He had found the solution on the principle that "sometimes the Holy Spirit remembers I exist." The penitents would meet clandestinely on Good Friday afternoon at the door of some church, each dressed in his fashion, as a peasant, a soldier, a militiawoman, or a nurse, and without recognizing one another, they would start to walk at the same hour as in years gone by, more or less as a group, following some traditional route.

"Do you understand, Ignacio? We have to assert ourselves. There will be a couple of dozen of us. I'll go ahead with my head bandaged. That is, I'll be carrying Christ on my forehead. And Ezequiel and Rosita and Manolín and other friends from the quarter will follow in my footsteps, straggling a little and mingling with the passersby along the way. Many nuns would have liked to join us but I forbade it—even for those who would have been able to get a wig. Do you understand, Ignacio? I am truly gratified by this. Do you think anyone will suspect? I think not. Who would ever imagine that a wounded militiaman with a pistol in his belt could be heading a religious procession?"

Ignacio was holding his breath. He was on the point of sobbing; he wanted to shout, "Count me in." But he held back. "No one will suspect," he said, to please Mosén Francisco. But he was afraid, perhaps because it was a big undertaking. And what if Axelrod should come along? Mightn't he have trained his dog to smell out clandestine processions? And what if Gascon should pass, or if Mosén Francisco should suddenly burst out singing, "Forgive us, O Lord!"

Ignacio held his tongue, beneath the stars. Then Mosén Francisco talked to him about the spirit and the will. "The spirit is a noble thing. It can submit to anything. I know a blind man who can tell when there's a rainbow, but not how he knows. Suddenly he'll point his finger and say: 'There's a rainbow over there.' And yesterday I was ministering to a dying boy who handed me all his money to be turned over to the militiaman who arrested him and who's ill now himself."

Ignacio straightened himself in his chair. The first example interested him; the second made him feel uncomfortable for some reason. "What does that have to do with the spirit? Let me think about the procession."

"Yes, it does have to do with the spirit. Love thine enemy."

"Love him? Do you love Cosme Vila?"

"No. But that's only because I'm a poor devil."

"Ought I to give my money to El Responsable?"

"Why shouldn't you, if he were ill?"

Ignacio had grown strangely excited. This always happened to him when he was faced with what seemed to him excessive virtue. "Please, I beg of you. Don't go on. Let me think about the procession..."

Another silence ensued, longer than the preceding ones. Ignacio lighted a cigarette and continued to feel nervous. After several minutes, he said abruptly: "Do you know sometimes I think I can't take it? I want to put my arms around a woman."

Mosén Francisco was not scandalized, though Ignacio had wanted him to be. "You're not going to believe it," he said, "but the day I came to Barcelona I had my arms around a woman for more than half an hour."

"I don't know what you mean."

"Bah!" interjected the vicar, with a gesture. Then he went on. "There's one thing I must ask of you. If you fall into temptation, rise above it immediately. And, of course, conceal it from Ana María."

A few days later Moncho arrived. He had come from Madrid after first visiting his parents in Lérida—his father was a veterinarian—and later going on to Madrid, at his uncle's behest to visit the latest Emergency Hospital that had been established for the troops of the International Brigades. The hospital was an enormous one under the direction of a Canadian physician named Simsley. It had been named Pasteur Hospital. Don Carlos Ayestarán, who felt deeply grateful for the presence of the international troops in Spain, assured Dr. Simsley through Moncho that he would guarantee pharmaceutical supplies, always with the agreement of Dr. Rosselló in the Hotel Ritz. Moncho carried out his mission punctiliously. The boy had reached an intelligent accord with his uncle: they would both lay their cards on the table. Moncho was a Fascist and would be one to the end. Don Carlos protected him out of family loyalty. In return for this protection, Moncho would collaborate with his uncle without ever betraying him, without shirking any order, and without sabotaging his work. If he should decide some day to break this agreement to go into hiding or to pass over to the enemy, he would tell his uncle so frankly and all would be well.

Their mutual faithfulness to their pledged word greatly facilitated matters for Ignacio. Don Carlos was the first to speak of it after scanning Julio's comments. "In the office there's a new boy from Gerona with whom you can plot. Tell him I'm pleased with him, but that he must never play me false. And if the question comes up, let him know that I'm horrified if any of my men has dirty fingernails."

The meeting between Ignacio and Moncho was even more auspicious than the one on the Alto del León between Mateo and José Luis Martínez de Soria. Moncho was twenty-three, somewhat older than Ignacio, and taller. He had studied Medicine, meanwhile practicing as an anesthetist in the Clinic Hospital. His expression was so composed as to be almost forbidding. He was in love with mountains, with excursions, and with snow; his hair was golden blond, bleached by the sun off the peaks. He always wore a white necktie and black shoes, not seeking to contrast so much as to compensate.

"I've been told we'd be friends."

"I hope so."

"I warn you that I listen to Queipo de Llano."

"So do I."

Moncho was the solution even to Igancio's lodging problem. Indeed, things had grown complicated in Ezequiel's house. Twice Ignacio had surprised Gascon lurking in the Calle de Verdi in a light truck from the Debray cafés, and Mosén Francisco had been asked for his identity papers with ill-concealed suspicion as he was leaving the house. Ezequiel told them, "Either we live apart or we die together. Take your choice."

Moncho made a suggestion to Ignacio. "Don't worry. Come to my pension. The landlady is understanding…and beautiful."

It worked like a charm. The pension on the Calle de Tallers was cheap but clean. Formerly it had catered to traveling salesmen, but now it was kept going by drivers of heavy trucks. The landlady accepted Ignacio and gave him the room adjoining Moncho's, an airy room containing a large wardrobe with a mirror. Good God! It had been weeks since Ignacio had seen himself full length… It seemed to him that he had changed a great deal. He looked "impersonal" to himself. "I could as easily be a Health soldier as an employee in a bank."

From the first moment Moncho had divined that Ignacio was an emotional man and that he could not stand loneliness. He needed to have things of his own around him to buttress him. Accordingly, Moncho said to him, "As soon as you've settled yourself, come to my room. We'll have coffee."

Ignacio took only ten minutes. He cleaned his fingernails. Then, going out into the hallway, he called to Moncho with a whistle. The latter opened his door immediately and Ignacio felt cosseted. He went in and sat on his friend's bed. While the coffee was being prepared, Ignacio watched Moncho. He was big-boned and forceful; his gestures were short and precise. "Don't tell me you're left-handed!"

"Go on! I couldn't hide it…"

For some reason, even this detail pleased Ignacio.

"Sugar?"

"Yes. I have a sweet tooth."

Ignacio looked around the room. It reflected Moncho. Six anatomical engravings hung at eye level assailed him, and between them several photographs of the highest mountains in the world caught the eye. The engravings fitted in with his fondness for Medicine, the mountains with his "school for endurance," as he called mountain climbing. On the little table stood the hourglass that Julio had seen in the provincial headquarters when he visited Don Carlos Ayestarán. Then some cards for bridge and a stamp album. Everything had the look of having been measured and laid out by compass.

"Do you know many people in Barcelona?"

"Five or six."

"That's enough for a start."

Moncho loved nature, everything natural. His father, the veterinarian, always had told him that he felt the pain of the animals he treated more than he did his own. "What does your father do?"

"He's a telegrapher."

"So." Moncho reflected and then added: "Don't you think the profession of one's father has a strong influence?"

"I suppose it does."

Ignacio offered him the makings for a smoke, but Moncho declined.

"Why did you choose Health?"

"I'm never very sure why I do things."

Suddenly they felt withdrawn from each other, but soon they came back together. Moncho was talking slowly and glancing often at the hourglass. There was no photograph of a woman in the room.

"I hate the war. Do you?"

Ignacio replied, "Hate is hardly the word for it."

"Some day you must come to the hospital."

The landlady tapped on the door and Moncho went to open it. He talked with her a moment and when he came back he said to Ignacio, "The *señora* wants you to know that the guests are not allowed to have radios."

As soon as the landlady had gone, Moncho lifted a little curtain in one corner and showed him a radio whispering in a corner, concealed among books.

Ignacio smiled. Moncho was in no way like Mosén Francisco or Mateo. He had the self-control of the priest, not for spiritual reasons, but because it was natural to him.

"More coffee?"

"Why not?"

"I can drink all I want and still sleep like a baby."

"Do you like living in a pension?"

"I've got used to it."

The coffee was good. Ignacio enjoyed it. He felt sure that making coffee was another of the things the mountains had taught Moncho. "What peak is that?"

Moncho glanced up at one of the pictures in the row. "Everest." After a pause he added, "There's no civil war on there."

Ignacio felt his imagination running away with him and he found it enjoyable. Why was Moncho so methodical, with "a place for everything and everything in its place"?

"Have you a girlfriend?"

Moncho shook his head, a head like wood with nerves and hair, and looking antique. "I haven't got one, but it's the same as if I had. I go out with a girl older than I am and we get along very well."

"What's her name?"

"I call her Bisturí, my Little Scalpel."

Ignacio could not remember meeting anyone so easy for him to interrogate. "Bisturí?"

"Yes. She likes action, see?"

"No, I don't see... I don't know what action you're referring to. Where shall I put my cup?"

"Right here, on the table."

"Really, wouldn't you like to smoke?"

"Now, yes. Thank you." Moncho lighted a cigarette. "Yes... Bisturí shares my ideas and she helps me."

"To do what?"

"She helps me live...and also to ruin tires. Yes, don't make such a face! Tires on the trucks going to the front. I supply potassic acid, and she and a boy in the motor pool inject it into tire rubber and then the trucks start and pretty soon they're stalled on the road."

Moncho spoke without emphasis. He had a definite goal and he went to it.

Ignacio asked him, "Do you know whether you...let's say Bisturí could find out whether a very good friend of mine is in the Cárcel Modelo?"

"I couldn't say, but we can ask her. What's the name of this person?"

"Emilio Santos. No, please don't make a note of it. Nothing on paper."

"You're right," Moncho admitted. "Emilio Santos. I'll remember it."

They talked awhile longer. Moncho had come back from Madrid much impressed with the things Dr. Simsley, the Canadian physician in the Pasteur Hospital, had told him about the international soldiers. The number of drug addicts among them was high, and in general they comported themselves like mercenaries on foreign soil. But suddenly they would seem to want to right the balance or to reconcile themselves with life, and they would become heroes. "It's not true that all of them are veterans. Some of them had never fired a shot in their lives. What most impressed Dr. Simsley is their stoicism in the hospital. They're fatalists and they're a little childish. A kind word, even a piece of candy, and they'll take any kind of treatment with a smile. Except, of course, for the ones who say, 'Doctor, if you don't fix me up, I'll kill you.'"

Ignacio noticed that Moncho touched on the most diverse subjects with scarcely a change of tone. Probably he had been trained to that. Moncho explained, "Not trained at all... You know what my work in the hospital is—anesthetist. Catch? One whiff of ether...and all men are equal."

Ignacio stared at Moncho's craggy face, then at his white tie and black shoes. "If you're such a skeptic, why are you taking part in the war?"

"For my own peace of mind... I want to be a doctor, see? As a rule the military guarantees public order; so if they win I shall be able to study in peace."

"I don't know whether you're serious or joking."

"Come, come... I'm a simple man."

"What do you attribute that to?"

"To having lived a good share of my life in villages."

"I've always lived in the city."

"That's too bad."

Ignacio's glance took in the room again. The anatomical engravings hurt his eyes, especially the red ones. One of them showed the brain divided into sections, and he recalled his father's remark: "The brain's enclosed, isn't it? That's not for nothing..."

Moncho told him that, depending upon his plans, it might suit Ignacio to have some practice in the Clinic on bandages, injections, tourniquets, and so on.

Ignacio replied, "Of course it would suit me. I'm thinking of going over to the Nationalists."

"So..."

Moncho suddenly turned serious. His hair was as if gilded and his look was cool. He took out his handkerchief, using his left hand, for he was left-handed, and blew his nose.

Ignacio said abruptly, "Another thing, if you don't mind. Do you think man is a free agent?"

Moncho stared at him. "Don't ask an anesthetist that." He paused, then added, "We're surrounded by secret forces. Do you know what I mean?"

Ignacio reflected. "So you think life is worth all the effort?"

Moncho folded his handkerchief and held it in his hand. Then he answered, "Protestantism thinks so."

ANA María... When Ana María heard Ignacio's voice on the telephone in the home of her protectors, Gaspar and Charo, she knew that life was worth the effort. She held the receiver to her ear long after Ignacio had hung up; then, black though it was, she pressed it to her heart.

Soon afterward they were going out together as before, as during that summer at San Feliu de Guixols. They went out that very afternoon indeed, as the clock in the Health office struck seven and as Gascon, the doorman, was saying "*¡Salud*, priestling!" to the departing Ignacio. Ignacio still refused to answer "*¡Salud!*" Usually he said "Good luck" or gave an ambiguous wave of the hand.

He waited for Ana María at the appointed place near the girl's house. He waited for her among the book kiosks on the Rambla, still glutted with the faces of leaders of the Revolution. Ana María appeared on the dot, dressed like a little seamstress. "Did you bring your eyes with you?"

"What a question... Can't you see them?"

They went out together on many other afternoons, and the moment of their meeting was always the same: glances that probed each other, shyness, and a groping for words.

Ignacio, tired of the monotony of the office and of the effort it cost him to write "Anti-Fascist Militia," always suggested some picturesque spot where they could hold hands, gaze at each other, and enjoy themselves. Billiard halls, for example, where no one would call him "priestling," or the Ciudadela Park, where Mosén Francisco was holding his "confessionals," or, still more frequently, the subway platforms. Indeed, they went down to the platform of any subway station that was not crowded and sat down there, watching leisurely as train after train went by. The arrival of a train with its headlight was so inevitable and exact that for a few moments it lent a curious feeling of security to their relationship. Yes, nothing was surer, more foreseeable, than the return of the subway trains. "The subway is like you," Ana María told Ignacio, playing with his fingers. "It goes, but it comes back."

Once or twice they went to the Chiqui Court and bet and lost! "Well, I thought you had some influence here." Always there were lone watchers at the court who glanced frequently at the entrance as though fearing someone would show himself. They often visited Ezequiel, too, in his Photomaton. Ezequiel always was cordial; he would hail them with film titles and take their pictures for nothing. He even made a droll caricature of the girl. But each time as he said goodbye to them, he slipped a paper into Ignacio's hand, a note that invariably said: "Two-timer! What about Marta?"

Ana María felt ashamed because she was almost happy. What about the war? What about her father in the Cárcel Modelo? And her mother, who disliked animals, living in the country? And the prisoners on the *Uruguay,* and the defeat at Guadalajara?

In her fashion, the girl had her own ideas, and often she could deflate Ignacio when he set out to dazzle her with some outlandish theme by giving her opinion. For example, she thought he had a perfect right to set fire to the stores in the Pompeya church. And she agreed with Moncho on the subject of free will. "Free? Ha, ha! I try hard not to love you, and look at me. Here I am in chains." She did not consider love selfish. "I'd give you all I've got." But neither did she believe that love as such merited a return. "Why a return? Love comes, and bang! What do I merit? Nothing. You tickled my feet under the water, and that was it! I was crazy about you, and still am."

Whenever she saw that Ignacio was in the right mood, she coaxed forth his answers. "Would you still like to glide over the water?"

"You're the water."

"Do you remember the sun shining off the sand?"

"You're the sea."

"And that guitar concert in the Colony at San Feliu de Guixols?"

"You're every lovely sound."

What bothered Ignacio was that Ana María mentioned Gaspar Ley to him so often, the man in whose house she was living, and with such vehemence. "What's so exceptional about that gentleman? He manages a jai-alai court to be sure. What else? Why do you say he's an exceptional fellow?"

"Because he is. Come to the house and you'll find out."

"To the house? I? Come, come."

He was jealous. That was because he liked Ana María more and more. She was courageous and efficient. Her father, in the Modelo, could count on her. And so could Gaspar Ley and his wife. She did everything with sprightliness and gaiety. Often she would walk along the Calle de Paris to look up at the Health offices. And Ignacio seldom came home to his pension without finding a note from Ana María in his pigeonhole. Sometimes it was nothing but the name Ana María, the wrapping from a lump of sugar that he had used in a café, or a subway ticket. She often sent him postcards showing a landscape or a monument in Gerona, and particularly the Dehesa, the staircase to the Seminary, or the arcades of the Rambla.

One day the girl stared long at him and said threateningly, "You must promise me that you won't go over to the other zone... Promise me."

Ignacio held her glance. "Are you serious?"

Ana María shyly folded her hands in her lap, then replied, "Yes and no." They were both quiet then. They had met on the platform of the Liceo station. The trains reached the end of their run there and turned around, while above them the city was enveloped in a rosy haze composed of light, smoke from the war plants, sudden passions, and the great round April sun that just had set.

Another time Ana María asked him, "Why don't you give me Pilar's telephone number at Food Supply? I'd like to call her from home. Wouldn't that surprise her?"

GLOSSARY OF PERSONS

1. *Fictional Characters*

The Alvear Family

Alvear, Matías: Telegraph operator in Gerona.
Alvear, Carmen Elgazu de Alvear: Wife of Matías.
Ignacio, Pilar, and César: Children of Matías and Carmen.

Priests

Iturralde, Reverend Germán: Chaplain of a Basque battalion.
Mosén Alberto: Director of the Diocesan Museum in Gerona.
Mosén Francisco: Vicar of San Félix parish.
Padre Marcos: Field chaplain.

Monarchists

Ichaso, Don Anselmo: President of the Carlist Club of Pamplona. An engineer.
Ichaso, Germán: Son of Don Anselmo. Requeté, killed in action.
Ichaso, Javier: Son of Don Anselmo. Requeté, wounded in action.
Oliva, Luis: Requeté in Our Lady of Montserrat Regiment.
Oriol, Pedro: Head of the Traditionalist Communion in Gerona. Shot in the cemetery.
Warning Voice: Gerona dentist. Editor of *El Tradicionalista*. Head of the SIFNE.

Falangists

Batlle, Jorge de: Falangist in Gerona.
Haro, Conrado: Falangist in Gerona.
María Victoria: Delegate from the Social Auxiliary of Valladolid.
Martínez de Soria, Fernando: Falangist from Valladolid. Son of Major Martínez de Soria. Killed in 1935.

Martínez de Soria, José Luis: Falangist from Valladolid. Son of Major Martínez de Soria. Volunteer in the Alto del León contingent.
Martínez de Soria, Marta: Daughter of Major Martínez de Soria. Ignacio Alvear's fiancée. Head of the Woman's Section of Gerona.
Mendizábal: Falangist from Valladolid.
Montesinos: Falangist from Valladolid.
Núñez Maza: Falangist from Soria. National Propaganda Delegate.
Padilla: Falangist from Gerona. Civil Guard.
Roberto: Falangist from Gerona. Civil Guard.
Rodríguez: Falangist from Gerona. Civil Guard.
Rosselló, Miguel: Falangist from Gerona. Son of Dr. Rosselló.
Salazar: Falangist from Salamanca. Syndicate Delegate. Second Lieutenant in the Militia.
Sánchez, Octavio: Falangist from Gerona. Employee in the Department of Works.
Santos, Mateo: Head of the Party in Gerona. Pilar's sweetheart.
Susana: From the Woman's Section of Valladolid.

Communists

Axelrod: Russian. Party Delegate in Catalonia.
Crespo: Former taxi driver. Cosme Vila's chauffeur.
Eroles: Head of the Cheka in the Calle de Vallmajor in Barcelona.
Goriev: Russian. Axelrod's aide.
Gorki: Mayor of Gerona. Political Commissar on the Aragón front. A perfumer.
Morales, Professor: Prosecutor to Cosme Vila. President of the Special Court for Counter-espionage.
Pedro: A patrolman.
Teo: A soldier from Gerona. Volunteer on the Huesca front.
Valenciana, La: Soldier in Gerona. Militiawoman on the Huesca front.
Vasiliev: Russian. Former delegate in Catalonia.
Vita, Cosme: Party chief in Gerona. Former bank employee.

Socialists

Alvear, Arturo: Telegraph operator in Burgos. Brother of Matías.
Alvear, Paz: Daughter of Francisco Alvear. Spy in Burgos.
Casal, Antonio: Head of the UGT in Gerona.
David and Olga: Schoolteachers in Gerona.
Dionisio: Spy.
Tower of Babel: Employee in the Arús Bank.
Venancio: Spy in Burgos.

Trotskyites

Alfredo, the Andalusian: Murillo's aide in Gerona.
Murillo: Head of the Party in Gerona.
Salvio: Marble-worker in Gerona.
Orencia: Salvio's sweetheart.

CEDA

Estrada, Alfonso (*Fiddler*): Son of Don Santiago Estrada. A student.
Estrada, Sebastián: Son of Don Santiago Estrada. A student.

Izquierda Republicana

Ayestarán, Don Carlos: Pharmacist. Health Delegate in Barcelona.
Costa brothers: Businessmen. Deputies from Gerona.
García, Julio: Policeman in Gerona.

The Catalan League

Noguer, Notary: Head in Gerona. Former mayor of the city.
His wife

Anarchists

Alvear, José: Cousin of Ignacio. Militia captain.
Alvear, Santiago: Brother of Matías, in Madrid. Militiaman.
Blasco: Bootblack in Gerona.
Cojo, El: Nephew of El Responsable, in Gerona.
Dimas: Head of the Committee of Salt (Gerona).
Future: Militia captain on the Aragón front.
Ideal: Militiaman on the Aragón front, from Gerona.
Merche: El Responsable's daughter. Future's sweetheart.
Responsable, El: Head of the FAI in Gerona.
Santi: Soldier in Gerona. The Benjamin of the organization.

Masons

Ayestarán, Don Carlos: Pharmacist. Health Delegate in Barcelona. A friend of Julio García.
Campos, Major: Of the Gerona garrison. Artilleryman.
Casal, Antonio: Head of the Gerona UGT. Printer.
Cervera, Julián; Police Commissioner in Gerona.
García, Julio: Policeman in Gerona.
Manager of the Arús Bank: Member of the Gerona chapter.
Massana, Architect: Of the Estat Català in Gerona.

Muñoz, Colonel: Of the Gerona garrison. Infantryman.
Ribas, Architect: Of the Estat Català in Gerona.
Rosselló, Dr.: Director of the Provincial Hospital in Gerona.

Militiamaen

Agustín: Of the Salt Committee (Gerona).
Almendro, El: On the Madrid front.
Batet: Aviator from Gerona. Trained in Russia.
Castillo, Miguel: Of the Lister Division. Killed in the Battle of Jarama.
Corbata, El: Prison guard from Gerona.
Culebra, Captain: Of the Durruti Column. Friend of José Alvear.
Dynamite: On the Madrid front.
Gascón: Janitor in the Health Delegation in Barcelona. Amputee.
Gil: Companion of Durruti. Shot in Zaragoza.
Hoyos: Of the Ortiz Column. A Murcian.
Landrú: Of the Durruti Column. A French volunteer in Communications.
Milagros: Of the Durruti Column. From Gerona.
Pancho Villa: Scout for El Campesino.
Puppy: Of the Durruti Column. A boy from the village of Pina.
Rainbow: Of the Durruti Column.
Royo: Companion of Durruti. Shot in Zaragoza.
Salsipuedes: Bodyguard of El Campesino.
Sidonio: On the Aragón front. Volunteer from Almeria.
Siberia: Weaver from Tarrasa. On the Aragón front.
Sopaenvino: Rural guard of El Campesino.
Trimotor: Rural guard of El Campesino.

International Volunteers

Gerardi: An Italian.
Negus: A Hungarian. Lieutenant.
North Pole: A Swede. Sergeant. Linotypist.
Pistolas, Papa: A Bulgarian. Ascaso Column.
Polvorín: A Bulgarian. Of the Ascaso Column.
Redondo: A Venezuelan.
Sidlo: A Pole. Champion javelin thrower.

Others

Alvear, Manuel: Nephew of Matías Alvear, in Burgos.
Ana María: Former sweetheart of Ignacio. From Barcelona.

Andaluza, La: Prostitute in Gerona.

Benzin: German woman in the Nazi Party.

Bermúdez: Police Inspector in Barcelona.

Bernard: Marble-worker in Gerona. Former employer of César.

Berti, Aleramo: Italian Fascist delegate.

Bisturí: Moncho's sweetheart.

Bolen, Raymond: Belgian journalist.

Campo, Amparo: Julio García's wife.

Campoy: Fakir.

Campistol sisters: Dressmakers in Gerona.

Canela: Gerona prostitute.

Civil, Professor: Ignacio's and Mateo's teacher.

Corbera: El Responsable's former employer.

Charo: Don Gaspar Ley's wife, in Barcelona.

Difícil: Espionage agent in Madrid.

Durao, Dr.: Medical aide to Dr. Rosselló.

Elgazu, Jaime, Josefa, Mirentxu, and Lorenzo: Brothers and sisters of Carmen Elgazu de Alvear.

Eloy: Basque boy, refugee in Gerona.

Estanislao, Padre: A Franciscan. Fifth Column agent, nicknamed Marisol.

Ezequiel: Photographer in Barcelona. Friend of Julio García.

Germaine: Swiss nurse.

Fanny: English journalist.

Ibarra: A prizefighter, in the Calle de Vallmajor Cheka.

Jaime, the Poet: Telegrapher in Gerona. Friend of Matías Alvear.

Jesusha: Warning Voice's maid, in Pamplona.

Laura: Warning Voice's wife.

Ley, Gaspar: Of the Chiqui Jai-Alai Court in Barcelona.

Loli: Barcelona prostitute.

Manolín: Ezequiel's son, in Barcelona.

Mati, Grandmother: Carmen Elgazu de Alvear's mother. In Bilbao.

Moncho: Anesthetist. Friend of Ignacio Alvear.

Mouro, Professor: A Portuguese. Agent for the SIFNE in San Sebastián.

Parapet: Legionnaire on the Madrid front.

Padrosa: Employee of the Arús Bank.

Plabb, Major: German. In the Condor Legion, anti-aircraft.

Proprietor of the Crocodile Bar: In Gerona.

Raimundo: Barber in Gerona.

Ramón: Waiter in the Neutral Café, Gerona.

Relken, Dr.: Archeologist. Jewish, expelled by the Nazis.
Roldán: Lawyer. With the 5th Column in Barcelona.
Rosita: Ezequiel's wife.
Rubio, El: Former aide to Major Martínez de Soria. Musician.
Salvatore: Marta's pen pal. Italian volunteer in The Blue Arrows.
Schubert: German. Delegate of the Nazi Party in Burgos.
Sigfrido: Nurse in the Pasteur Hospital in Madrid.
Simsley, Dr.: Nurse in the Pasteur Hospital in Madrid.
Thérèse: Swiss nurse.
Tocino, Manuel: Pardoned by Gorki.
Vega, Dr.: Medical aide to Dr. Rosselló.
Zamorano: Dr. Rosselló's chauffeur.

Professional Soldiers

Aguirre: Captain in the Regular Army.
Arias: Captain in Gerona.
Astier: Lieutenant of the Ski Company.
Ayuso: Corporal of a Falangist Company on the Aragón front.
Benítez, Brigadier: On the Teruel front.
Cajal, "Kiddo": Corporal of the Ski Company. Watchmaker.
Campos, Major: From Gerona. On the Teruel front.
Casserole: Ski Company soldier. Cook.
Colomer: Lieutenant in the Ski Company. On the Huesca front.
Cuevas: Commander in Chief of the Ski Company.
Delgado: Lieutenant in Gerona.
Guillen: Ski trooper. Fanner from Valle de Tena.
Herráiz: Major.
Laguna: Sergeant on the Teruel front.
Maroto: Colonel.
Martínez de Soria, Major: Commander of the uprising in Gerona.
Martín: Lieutenant in Gerona.
Muñoz, Colonel: On the Teruel front. From Gerona.
Palacios: Captain of the Ski Company.
Pascual, Dámaso: Ski trooper. Weigher from Jaca.
Romá, Second Lieutenant: Of the Gerona garrison.
Royo: Ski trooper. Farmer from Valle de Tena.
Sandoval: Captain, in Gerona.

2. *Historical Characters*

Spanish Falange

Hedilla: Provisional National commander.
Primo de Rivera, José Antonio: Founder of the Party.
Primo de Rivera, Pilar: Sister of José Antonio.
Ledesma Ramos, Ramiro: A founder of the JONS.
Redondo, Onésimo: A founder of the JONS.
Serrano Súñer, Ramón: "Old Shirt." Generalissimo Franco's brother-in-law.

Political Leaders of "Red" Spain

Aguirre, José Antonio: President of the Basque Government.
Alvarez del Vayo, Julio: Foreign Minister.
Azaña, Manuel: President of the Republic.
Barcia, Augusto: Prime Minister of the Azaña government.
Besteiro, Julián: President of the Cortés.
Companys, Luis: Head of the Catalan Generalidad.
Giral, José: President of the Government.
Irujo, Manuel: Minister of the Basque Government.
Kent, Victoria: Deputy of the Republican Left.
Largo Cabellera, Francisco: President of the Government.
Maciá, Francisco: Former President of the Provincial Government of Catalonia.
Martínez Barrios, Diego: President of the Council.
Montseny, Federica: Minister of Health.
Negrín, Juan: President of the Government.
Nelken, Margarita: Deputy.
Prieto, Indalecio: Minister of War.
Rico, Pedro: Mayor of Madrid.
Sánchez Román, Felipe: Member of the Hague Court.

Officers of the Spanish National Army

Franco Bahamonde, Francisco: Generalissimo of Land, Sea, and Air Armies.
Alonso Vega, Camilo: Infantry Major, raised to General.
Aranda Marta, Antonio: Colonel on the General Staff. Raised to General.
Asensio Cabanilles, Carlos: Lieutenant Colonel of Infantry. Raised to Brigadier General.
Cabanellas Torres, Miguel: Infantry General.
Castejón: Major of Infantry. Raised to Colonel.
Cortés: Captain in the Civil Guard. Defender of the Sanctuary of Nuestra Señora de la Cabeza.

Dávila Arrondo, Fidel: Infantry General.
García Valiño, Rafael: Infantry Major. Raised to General.
Goded Llopis, Manuel: Infantry General. Shot in Barcelona.
Kindelán Duany, Alfredo: Air Force General.
Martínez de Campos, Carlos: Artillery Major. Raised to Lieutenant General.
Millán Astray, José: General. Founder of the Spanish Foreign Legion.
Mola Vidal, Emilio: Infantry General. Killed in air accident.
Monasterio, José: Cavalry Colonel. Raised to Lieutenant General.
Moscardó, José: Colonel. Defender of the Alcázar in Toledo. Raised to General.
Muñoz Castellanos: Artillery Colonel. Raised to General.
Muñoz Grandes, Agustín: Infantry Colonel. Raised to Division General.
Ortiz de Zarate, Joaquín: Lieutenant Colonel of Infantry.
Queipo de Llano, Gonzalo: Cavalry General. Raised to Lieutenant General.
Rey d'Harcourt: Infantry Colonel. Defender of Teruel.
Sanjurjo Sacando, José: Infantry General. Killed in air accident.
Solchaga, José Enrique: Lieutenant Colonel of Infantry. Raised to General.
Varela, José Enrique: Infantry General.
Vigón, Juan: On the General Staff.
Yagüe Blanco, Juan: Lieutenant Colonel of Infantry. Raised to Lieutenant General.

Officers of the Spanish "Red" Army

Asensio Terrado, José: Colonel on the General Staff. Raised to General.
Bayo: Captain. In charge of the troop landing in Mallorca.
Casado López, Segismundo: Cavalry Major. Raised to Colonel.
Díaz Sandino, Felipe: Infantry Major. Raised to Colonel.
Mangada Rosemar, Julio: Lieutenant Colonel of Infantry. Raised to General.
Martínez Cabrera, Toribio: Colonel on the General Staff. Raised to General.
Martínez Monje, Fernando: Colonel on the General Staff. Raised to General.
Mascalet Lacaci, Carlos: General in the Engineer Corps.
Miaja Menan, José: Infantry General.
Pérez Farrás, Enrique: Artillery Colonel.
Pozas Perea, Gabriel: Infantry General.
Riquelme, José: Infantry General.
Rojo, Vicente: Lieutenant Colonel of Infantry, Raised to General.
Ullibarri, Mariano G.: Infantry General.
Villalba, José: Artillery General.

"Nationalist" Air Force

García Morato, Joaquín: Captain.

Haya, Carlos: Captain.
Satanás: In the García Morato Esquadrille.

"Red" Air Force

Bourjois: French volunteer.
Gilles: French volunteer.
Griffith: English volunteer.
Martin, Drew: English volunteer.
Rexach: Spanish volunteer.

Officers of the International Brigades

Alocca: Former tailor from Lyon. Commander of Cavalry in the 15th Brigade.
Dumont: Former Colonel in the French Army. Commanding Officer of the 14th Brigade.
Kleber (Lazar Fakete): Of Austro-Hungarian origin. Soviet General, in command of the 11th Brigade.
Kopic: Bulgarian. Commanding Officer of the 14th Brigade.
Krieger: Italian, former Communist Deputy from Trieste. Chief of Staff of the 12th Brigade.
Malraux, André: French writer. Organizer of the Air Arm.
Montage: Former officer of the British Army. Major in the 13th Brigade.
Lucasz (Matei Zalka): Of Hungarian origin. Commanding Officer of the 12th Mixed Brigade.
Renn, Ludwig: German novelist. Chief of Staff of the 11th Brigade.
Vincent: Officer in the French Army. Colonel of the Brigade General Staff.
Walter: Of Polish origin. Soviet General. Professor at the Military Academy of Moscow.

Political Leaders of the International Brigades

Bineto: Political Commissar. Active in the Reeducation Camp in Júcar.
Broz, Josip (Tito): Yugoslav.
Debruchère: Belgian. President of the Second International.
Ford, James: Leader of Negro workers in the United States.
Fox, Ralph: English writer. Political Commissar of the 14th Brigade.
Godwald, Clement: Czech.
Herz, Paul: German Socialist leader.
Karanov: Bulgarian.
Maleter, Pal: Hungarian.
Marcucci: Leader of Italian Communist Youth.
Marty, André: French. Chief Organizer of the Brigades.
Menov: Bulgarian.

Nicoletti, Mario: Italian. Political Commissar of the 13th Brigade.
Longo, Luigi: Italian.
Smirna: Hungarian writer.
Telge, Oscar: Doctor.
Thorez, Maurice: Secretary General of the French Communist Party.
Togliatti, Palmiro (Alfredo): Italian. Of the Communist Party.
Vittorio: Italian. Political Commissar of the 11th Brigade.

Guerrilla Commanders

Ascaso, Joaquin: In Command of the Ascaso Column.
Beltrán, Antonio (El Esquinazao): Former mechanic. Leader of 43rd Division.
González, Valentin (El Campesino): Division Commander.
Lister, Enrique: Former stonemason. Division Commander.
Modesto, Juan: Former carpenter. Commander of an Army Corps.
Ortiz: Former carpenter. Commander of the Ortiz Column.
Tagüeña: Commander on the Sierra and Madrid fronts.

Spanish Communists

Díaz, José: Secretary General of the Party.
Hernández, Jesús: Member of the Central Committee. Minister of Public Instruction.
Ibarruri, Dolores (La Pasionaria): Member of the Central Committee.
Mije, Antonio: Member of the Central Committee.
Uribe, Vicente: Member of the Central Committee.

Russian Communists

Gaiskis: Ambassador to Spain.
Ledarsum, Leo: Chekist in Valencia.
Orlov: Commander of the GPU, in Spain.
Owscensco, Vladimir Antonoff: Consul General in Barcelona.
Rosenberg: Ambassador to Spain.
Stepanov: Adviser.

Trotskyite

Nin, Andrés: Head of the Party in Spain.

Iberian Anarchist Federation (FAI)

Ascaso, Joaquin: Commander of the Ascaso Column, Huesca sector.
Del Val, Eduardo: On the Madrid front.
Durruti, Buenaventura: Commander of the Durruti Column, Zaragoza sector.

Fernández, Aurelio: Head of the Commission of Investigation, in Barcelona.
García Oliver, Juan: Minister of Justice.
Mera, Cipriano: On the Madrid front.
Montseny, Federica: Minister of Health.
Mora, Teodoro: On the Madrid front.
Ortiz: Commander of the Ortiz Column, Teruel sector.
Tomás, Belarmino: Chief in Asturias.

Germans in Nationalist Spain

Von Faupel: Ambassador.
Von Sperrl: General.

Italians in Nationalist Spain

Bostico: General.
Cantaluppo, Roberto: Ambassador.
Gambara: General.
Roatta: General.
Rossi, Aldo: Fascist Delegate, in Mallorca.

Correspondents of the Foreign Powers

Ehrenburg, Ilya: Russian.
Hemingway, Ernest: American.
Koestler, Arthur: English.

Spanish Nationalist Correspondents

Sevillano
Spectator
Tebib Arrumi

3. *Personages Mentioned*

Abraham: Biblical character.
Alba, Duke of: Spanish aristocrat.
Alberti, Rafael: Spanish poet.
Alfonso XIII: Last Spanish monarch. Dethroned 1931.
D'Annunzio, Gabriel: Italian writer.
Aragón: French poet.
Armengaud: French war commentator.
Atholl, Duchess of: English aristocrat.
Attila: King of the Huns.

Attlee, Clement: English political leader.

Bakunin, Mikhail: Russian founder of international Anarchism.

Baroja, Pío: Spanish novelist.

Baudelaire, Charles: French poet.

Benavente, Jacinto: Spanish dramatic writer.

Benlliure, Mariano: Spanish sculptor.

Bienvenida: Spanish bullfighter.

Blasco Ibáñez, Vicente: Spanish writer.

Blum, Léon: French politician.

Bogomolets, Alexander: Russian scientist.

Casals, Pablo: Spanish violon-cellist.

Cervantes Saavedra, Miguel de: Spanish writer.

Chamberlain, Arthur Neville: English politician.

Chaplin, Charles (Charlie): Motion picture actor.

Chesterton, Gilbert K.: English writer.

Chevalier, Maurice: French actor.

Chopin: Polish composer.

Churchill, Winston: Prime Minister of Great Britain.

Ciano, Count Galeazzo: Italian politician. Son-in-law of Mussolini. Member of Fascist Grand Council.

Cid, El (Rodrigo Díaz de Vivar): Spanish hero.

Clemenceau, Georges: French politician.

Coloma, Luís de: Spanish novelist. Jesuit.

Comas y Solá, José: Spanish astronomer.

Cortés, Hernán: Conqueror of Mexico.

Cot, Pierre: Minister of Air in the French Government.

Dante Alighieri: Italian poet.

Danton, Georges-Jacques: French revolutionary.

Deledda, Grazia: Italian writer.

Dietrich, Marlene: Motion picture actress.

Dostoevsky, Fyodor: Russian novelist.

Du Guesclin, Bertrand: French adventurer.

Ulianova, María Ilinicha: Sister of Lenin.

Eden, Robert Anthony: English politician.

Fagalde: French general.

Fátima: Daughter of Muhammad, wife of Alí.

Fleta, Miguel B.: Spanish tenor.

Flynn, Errol: Motion picture actor.

Freud, Sigmund: Austrian scientist.

Gable, Clark: Motion picture actor.

Galán, Fermín: Captain in the Spanish Army. Captured in Jaca in 1930. Shot.

Gámez, Celia: Spanish artist.

Gandhi (*Mohandas Karamchand*): Leader of the Hindu Nationalist Movement.

Ganivet, Angel: Spanish essayist. Diplomat.

García Hernández, Angel: Captain in the Spanish Army. Captured in Jaca in 1930. Shot.

García Lorca, Federico: Spanish poet. Shot in Granada in 1936.

Gardel, Carlos: Argentine singer.

Genghis Khan: Mogul emperor.

Glazunov, Alexander: Russian composer.

Goebbels, Paul Joseph: Minister of Propaganda of the Third Reich.

Goering, Hermann: Air Marshal of the Third Reich.

Gomá, Isidoro Cardinal: Spanish Archbishop of Toledo. Writer.

Gorki, Maxim: Russian novelist.

Goya, Francisco de: Spanish painter.

Hepburn, Katharine: Motion picture actress.

Hitler, Adolf: Founder of the Third Reich.

Huxley, Aldous: English writer.

Iparaguirre, José María: Basque troubadour.

Kant, Immanuel: German philosopher.

Keats, John: English poet.

Keyserling, Count Hermann: German philosopher.

Kipling, Rudyard: English novelist.

Larra, Mariano de: Spanish writer.

La Serna: Spanish bullfighter.

Lenin, Vladimir Ilyich: Leader of Russian communism.

Leonardo da Vinci: Italian scientist and painter.

López Ochoa, Eduardo: Spanish general. Shot in Madrid.

Loyola, Ignatius: Saint. Founder of the Society of Jesus.

Luther, Martin: Founder of Protestantism

Lyrie: Russian scientist.

Machado, Antonio: Spanish poet.

Maeztú, Ramiro de: Spanish essayist.

Muhammad: Founder of Islam.

Malatesta, Enrico: Italian anarchist.

March, Juan: Spanish financier.

Marx, Karl: German philosopher. Founder of Marxism.

Mata, Pedro: Spanish novelist.

Mateu, Miguel: Spanish industrialist.

Moro, Muza: Arab general.
Morral, Mateo: Spanish royalist.
Murillo, Bartolomé Estaban: Spanish painter.
Mussolini, Benito: Founder of Italian Fascism.
Neruda, Pablo: Chilean poet.
Nietzsche, Friedrich: German philosopher.
Oliveira Salazar, Antonio: Portuguese statesman.
Ortega y Gasset, José: Spanish philosopher.
Paulina: Wife of André Marty.
Pemán, José María: Spanish writer.
Petrarch, Francesco: Italian poet.
Pirandello, Luigi: Italian writer.
Pitigrilli, Dino Segre: Italian humorist.
Pius XI: Pope.
Ramón y Cajal, Santiago: Spanish scientist.
Rasputin, Gregory: Russian monk.
Ravel, Maurice: French composer.
Reclus, Elisée: French writer and geographer.
Rieu, Vernet: French war commentator.
Risler: French scientist.
Romanones, Count of: Spanish politician.
Roosevelt, Franklin Delano: President of the United States.
Rosales, Luis: Spanish poet.
Rousseau, Jean-Jacques: Swiss philosopher.
Sanzio, Rafael (Raphael): Italian painter.
Shaw, George Bernard: Irish writer and dramatist.
Socrates: Greek philosopher.
Sparaywski, Nicholas: Stalin's doctor.
Spengler, Oswald: German historical philosopher.
Stalin, Joseph: Leader of the Soviet Union.
Thiers, Adolphe: French historian.
Tirso de Molina: Spanish writer of comedies.
Tono: Spanish humorist.
Torerito de Triana: Spanish bullfighter.
Torras y Bages, José: Spanish bullfighter.
Trotsky, Leon: Russian politician. Founder of Trotskyism.
Unamuno, Miguel de: Spanish philosopher.
Vázquez de Mella, Juan: Spanish politician.
Velazquez (Diego Rodríguez de Silva): Spanish painter.

Zamora, Ricardo: Spanish football player.
Zumalacárregui, Tomás de: Carlist general.

CLUNY MEDIA

Designed by Fiona Cecile Clarke, the Cluny Media *logo depicts a monk at work in the scriptorium, with a cat sitting at his feet.*

The monk represents our mission to emulate the invaluable contributions of the monks of Cluny in preserving the libraries of the West, our strivings to know and love the truth.

The cat at the monk's feet is Pangur Bán, from the eponymous Irish poem of the 9th century. The anonymous poet compares his scholarly pursuit of truth with the cat's happy hunting of mice. The depiction of Pangur Bán is an homage to the work of the monks of Irish monasteries and a sign of the joy we at Cluny take in our trade.

"Messe ocus Pangur Bán,
cechtar nathar fria saindan:
bíth a menmasam fri seilgg,
mu memna céin im saincheirdd."

Made in the USA
Las Vegas, NV
08 April 2022

47068648R00226